MURDER IN BARCELONA

By Christina Koning

a&b

MURDER IN BARCELONA

CHRISTINA KONING

Allison & Busby Limited
11 Wardour Mews
London W1F 8AN
allisonandbusby.com

First published as *Twist of Fate* in 2021 under the name A. C. Koning
This edition published by Allison & Busby in 2023.

10 9 8 7 6 5 4 3 2 1

ISBN 978-0-7490-2949-4

Typeset in 11/16 pt Sabon LT Pro by Allison and Busby Ltd.

By choosing this product, you help take care of the world's forests.
Learn more: www.fsc.org

FSC
www.fsc.org
MIX
Paper | Supporting
responsible forestry
FSC® C171272

Printed and bound by
CPI Group (UK) Ltd, Croydon, CR0 4YY

For James and Marina

Chapter One

'I must say I'm terrified,' said Cecily Nicholls. 'I mean – what do you think film stars eat?'

'Not very much, from what I can gather,' was her brother's reply. 'Aren't they always banting?'

'Worse and worse,' said Mrs Nicholls. 'What am I going to feed them?'

'I should give them just what you give everyone else,' said Frederick Rowlands, from his seat in the big bay window with its panoramic view of the sea. Not that he could see the view, of course, but he could hear the soft swishing of the waves as they fell against the shore, and smell the faint tang of salt and ozone. 'Delicious home-cooked food, made with fresh produce from local farms and fishermen. They'll eat it up – quite literally!'

'I hope you're right,' said his hostess. 'Honestly, I'm beginning to wish I'd never accepted this booking.'

'I can't think why you did,' said Jack Ashenhurst mildly. 'Since it's giving you such a headache.'

'Bookings are down this year,' his sister reminded him. 'And we've had several cancellations. People just don't have the money to spare.'

'I realise that. But surely, the regulars . . .'

'The Pollards have cried off. Her mother's ill. And Colonel and Mrs Rutherford have booked for two weeks, instead of their usual three.'

'All right, all right, I get it,' said Ashenhurst, with a groan of comic despair. 'So these film people are really our saviours, in a way?'

'I suppose so.' Mrs Nicholls didn't sound convinced. Ashenhurst did his best to rally her, 'Come on, old thing! We've had large bookings before. Remember that time they held the regatta off Lizard Point? We were booked solid for ten days.'

'It isn't the numbers as such,' said his sister. 'It's . . . Here, I'll read you what Miss Brierley's letter says.'

'Who's Miss Brierley when she's at home?'

'She's secretary to Miss La Mar. Dolores La Mar,' she added, as if this ought to mean something to him. 'The sultry temptress with the dark brown voice.'

'Never heard of her.'

'Jack! Surely even you . . .'

'She was in *Spurned Lovers*, opposite Marcus Mandeville,' put in Edith, who had been sewing name tags on her youngest daughter's gym kit. 'I thought she was rather good, actually. Fred enjoyed it, too – didn't you?'

'Leave me out of it,' laughed her husband. 'I'm not a good judge of actresses, these days.'

'Well, this one sounds like a prima donna,' said Mrs Nicholls. 'Listen to this: "*On days when she is filming, Miss La Mar will require breakfast at six a.m., consisting of two soft-boiled eggs, one slice of thinly buttered toast, which must be hot, and a cup of very weak tea without milk (lemon is preferred). Her bath should be drawn at half past six, and a fire (laid the previous night) lit in time for her to dress (her maid will assist her with dressing, and must therefore be allocated a room next to Miss La Mar's). She will require a cup of hot, strong coffee without milk or sugar while she is waiting for the car to arrive at seven a.m. When she returns from a day's filming, she will require the water to be hot for her bath, and a fire to be lit in her room, as per instructions. On days when she is not called until later, she will rest in her room, or on the terrace set aside for her exclusive use, until such time as shooting is set to begin. She must on no account be disturbed during these hours as she will need peace and quiet in order to learn her lines and to get into the right frame of mind for the day's filming schedule . . .*" There's more,' she added gloomily. 'But you get the general idea.'

'I'll say! She sounds like a perfect tyrant,' said Dorothy Ashenhurst, coming in at this moment. Her brother begged to differ.

'I should have said it was all fairly routine stuff myself,' he said. 'Most actresses need to prepare, and as for the stipulations about breakfast, I have to say I

9

agree with her. Nothing worse than cold toast and weak coffee.'

'Oh, we all know that you're familiar with the film star type,' laughed Jack Ashenhurst. 'What was the name of that glamorous femme fatale you got so pally with in Berlin?'

'I suppose you mean Magdalena Brandt,' was the reply. 'And I was hardly pally with her. We met a few times, that's all.' Which wasn't quite the whole truth, but Rowlands had found it expedient to say as little as possible on the subject of his relations with the lovely star of the German cinema.

'Even so, it's given you an insight into how these film types behave,' said his friend. 'I vote we assign special duties as regards Miss Dolores La Mar – or whatever her name is – to Fred.'

'Thank you very much,' said Rowlands. 'But I'll have you know that I'm here on holiday. I'm going to do nothing for the next two weeks but eat, sleep and go for an occasional gentle stroll with my wife along the clifftops, if it's all the same to you.'

But in that fervently expressed wish he was, as it turned out, to be disappointed.

Rowlands was two days into his annual holiday, having joined his wife and daughters at the Cornish hotel run by his friend and brother-in-law, Jack Ashenhurst. The holiday had become something of a fixture in the Rowlands' family calendar – a welcome break from

London and the pressures of working life, as well as a chance to escape, if only for a time, from greater worries. The news from Germany was as disturbing as ever, but it was Spain which had been most in the news, these past few weeks – displacing even the coverage of the coronation, which had taken place in May, and which had itself dislodged the abdication scandal from the front pages.

As he had been packing his suitcase for the holiday, Rowlands had heard the news on the wireless about the bombing of Madrid by Falangist artillery. Given that the Nationalists were being openly supported by Hitler, who'd authorised the bombing of Guernica by the Luftwaffe a few months before, things were starting to look very nasty indeed, he thought. 'A penny for them,' said his wife, who had left her seat on the far side of the hotel lounge and now stood beside him. For a moment, she rested her hand on his shoulder.

'You wouldn't want to know,' he replied, keeping his voice light. But Edith knew him too well to be fobbed off.

'I thought we'd agreed that you'd put work out of your mind for the next few weeks,' she said. 'Leave worrying about finances to Sir Ian.'

In his capacity as Secretary to St Dunstan's, the institute for the war-blinded, of which he had been a member since being invalided out of the army in 1917, Rowlands was all too familiar with the claims being made on the organisation's resources – at present stretched to the limit because of building the new centre at Ovingdean. 'I wasn't thinking about work – or not only that,' he said. Because of course the question of whether – or rather, when – there would be another war was one in which he and his fellow St Dunstaners took a passionate interest. For men of their generation, who had been through one war, the prospect of another was intolerable. Some of them had sons who'd be of an age to fight, if it came to that. Not for the first time, Rowlands thanked his stars that he had daughters.

'Well, whatever it is, try and forget about it while you're here,' said Edith. 'You'll do no good to anyone, fretting about what you can't change.'

'Just as well not everybody thinks like that,' muttered Rowlands' sister, who never could let an opportunity pass for making a political point. 'Otherwise the Republicans would have been crushed by those Fascist bullies a long time ago.' Rowlands groaned to himself. Dorothy had never outgrown the revolutionary zeal to which she'd adhered as a girl. Not that she was alone in idealising the Republican cause, or in hero-worshipping those who'd gone to fight for the International Brigades. Edith could be no less stubborn when it came to defending her own point of view.

'You surely can't believe that a few hotheads playing at soldiers can make that much of difference?'

'Hotheads! These are men – and women, too – who are prepared to make the ultimate sacrifice for what they think is right.'

'And what of their families?' said Edith. 'Do they have to make the ultimate sacrifice, too? Some of your brave soldiers are little more than children. How would you feel if Billy decided to run off to Spain?'

'Happily, that's an academic question,' put in Jack quickly. Six years of being married to Dorothy had made him adept at heading off contentious topics. 'If we're expecting these film people the day after tomorrow, hadn't we better make sure everything's ready for them? Dottie, you're in charge of allocating rooms. Ciss,' – this was to his sister – 'you'd better run through the week's menus again with Mrs Jago. I'll handle the drinks side of things. I gather these people like their cocktails, so I'd better check that there's plenty of gin. Come on. We've no time to sit around jawing about the problems of the world. We've a hotel to run.'

They were just sitting down in the hotel lounge for a preprandial glass of sherry on the day in question when a powerful motor car – a Rolls-Royce from the sound of it, thought Rowlands – drew up in the courtyard outside. A moment later, Danny, the Ashenhursts' adopted son, rushed into the room, followed by his brothers, Billy and Victor. 'Dad . . .' he said excitedly.

'I know, old man,' said Jack, getting to his feet. 'This will be the new lot of guests. And do try not to run,' he added as the three boys clattered out into the hall to inspect the arrivals, or rather, the vehicle in which they had arrived, thought Rowlands, smiling to himself. Walter Metzner, who at sixteen perhaps considered himself too grown-up to get excited about a car, joined the adults in the room at that moment, with the Rowlandses' three girls.

Voices were heard in the hall, Jack's amongst them, as he welcomed the arrivals to Cliff House. 'But this is charming!' cried a woman – the famous Dolores La Mar, Rowlands assumed. 'Quite remote and rustic, don't you think, Horace?' A moment later, the lady made her entrance in a cloud of *Joy*, followed by some of the other members of her party. 'Why, you didn't tell me there'd be *young* people!' she exclaimed from the doorway ('Where she stood looking like Theda Bara, draped from top to toe in mink,' said Edith afterwards). Miss La Mar's remark was evidently addressed to her secretary – Miss Brierley, of the letter – since it was she who replied, with some embarrassment, 'Oh! I didn't know . . . That is . . . I didn't think to enquire.'

'I'm sure the young people will keep to their own part of the hotel,' said Cecily Nicholls quickly. 'And we've agreed that the tennis court nearest your windows should be out of bounds.'

'But this is too bad!' cried the actress. Rowlands wondered whether her accent was American or something more exotic. 'For the young people to be kept from their amusements on my account. Come, introduce me,' she added, with the faintly peremptory note that showed she was used to having her commands obeyed.

'Well, I'm Cecily Nicholls, and this is my brother Jack Ashenhurst, whom you've met, of course . . .'

'I meant the children,' interrupted Miss La Mar, with the mixture of playfulness and steely determination to have her way which Rowlands guessed was her *modus operandi.* 'It's the children I want to meet.' Then, with a cooing laugh, to mitigate her rudeness, 'There'll be time enough for the rest of us to get acquainted. Horace – my husband – will tell me who you all are, won't you, my sweet?'

'Rather,' said the man Rowlands assumed must be the film star's husband, stepping forward to shake hands with Ashenhurst, and then with Rowlands. 'Name's Cunningham,' he said. 'How d'you do?' From this brief contact, Rowlands received the impression of a man no longer young, but still upright and vigorous. A force to be reckoned with in spite of his seeming reticence. Although anyone would seem subdued beside the ebullient Miss La Mar. This must be the Horace Cunningham whose name appeared with some regularity in the financial columns of the newspaper, thought Rowlands, not that he himself took much of an interest in those, but Edith had inherited some shares from her father, and so her daily reading aloud of the paper sometimes took in what was happening in the City and on Wall Street. *Cunningham was in steel, wasn't he – or was it railways?* Probably both, thought Rowlands, his attention momentarily diverted from the comedy that was being played out in the hotel lounge.

'Such charming girls!' Dolores La Mar was exclaiming as Rowlands' daughters were presented to her. 'What are your names, dears?' When she was told, she gave another little cry. 'Margaret! How perfectly sweet! Now, let me guess . . . you're the clever one. And you,' – this was to Anne, the Rowlands middle child – 'you must be the pretty one. Which leaves you' – this was ten-year-old Joan – 'as the pet of the family. Am I right?' She gave a gurgling laugh. 'Of course I am.'

What a performance, thought Rowlands, not without a certain grudging admiration at the way the prima donna was getting them all to eat out of her hand. Although he and Edith had never encouraged such labels – the 'pretty one', forsooth! All his daughters were beautiful, to his mind, and clever, too. He didn't need some superannuated starlet to tell him so. Having disposed of the Rowlands girls, Dolores La Mar had moved onto the Ashenhursts' three sons and their cousin. 'Now, don't tell me . . . you must be the eldest, to judge from your height.' She must be addressing Billy, who had put on a growth spurt recently, Rowlands knew. 'What a tall young man! You must be six foot.'

'As a matter of fact,' said Walter Metzner, in his clear, almost unaccented English, 'I am the eldest. My cousin is one year younger.' Miss La Mar paid no attention to him, however, but turned her attention to the youngest member of the group.

'I'd say you were related – this tall chap and yourself. You have a look of one another.'

'He's my brother,' said Victor Ashenhurst. 'I'm nine,' he added proudly. 'But I'm tall for my age.'

'I can see that,' said the actress, with her throaty laugh. 'Well, perhaps you two tall fellows . . . and you,' she added off-handedly to Danny, 'will be terribly kind and bring in my luggage? There's rather a mountain of it, I'm afraid.

But I'm sure such big, strong boys will be up to it.'

'My dear, Carlos will manage perfectly well,' put in Cunningham. 'Young Quayle can give him a hand,' he added drily. But the boys were already out of the door, with their cousins in hot pursuit.

'It's a wizard car,' Danny Ashenhurst could be heard enthusing. 'A Phantom III with Mulliner coachwork – latest model. I saw one just like it in *Practical Motorist* – only midnight blue, not silver-grey.'

A brief silence fell. 'Well,' said Mrs Nicholls. 'You'll want to see your rooms, I expect. We've put you in the Blue Room – that's the one with the best view of the sea,' she added. 'Your maid is in the dressing room next door, and Miss Brierley . . .' But Dolores La Mar wasn't interested in these arrangements.

'Oh, Brierley will see to all that, won't you, Brierley?' she said to this factotum. 'What I'd really like at this minute is a very dry martini. Travelling always gives one such a terrible thirst, don't you find?'

'I . . . ah . . . I'll just fetch some ice,' said Jack Ashenhurst, disappearing from the room. Another slightly awkward pause ensued before Miss La Mar went on, 'I must say, this is all perfectly delightful. When Hilly – that's my wonderful director, Hilary Carmody – told me the location shots for *Forbidden Desires* were to be filmed in Cornwall, I pictured something wild and dangerous. But this . . .' She must have made some gesture to encompass the view from the window, 'Is so peaceful.'

'It does get quite wild during the winter months,' said her hostess. 'And I think the scenery along this coast is generally considered quite rugged.'

'Oh, I leave all that sort of detail to Hilly,' said the other with a laugh. 'My job is just to turn up and deliver my lines.'

'Which you do marvellously well, darling,' said a voice from the doorway. 'I say – I don't suppose there's one of those for me?' Because Ashenhurst had by now returned with the ice and was busy measuring gin into a cocktail shaker before adding a dash of vermouth.

'I hope a twist of lemon will do?' he said to Miss La Mar once this operation was complete. 'The local shop doesn't stock olives.'

'That'll do fine.' She took the drink from him without further ceremony and turned her attention to the newcomer. 'I was wondering where you'd got to, Larry. You've been an age.'

'I was helping to bring in the suitcases,' was the affronted reply. 'At least . . . I would have helped, but your chauffeur chappie said he could manage. And then a perfect *horde* of little boys rushed up and insisted on carrying things.'

'I shouldn't have thought you'd object to *that*, darling.'

While this inane chatter was going on, Ashenhurst was engaged in distributing drinks to the rest of the party. Cunningham refused a cocktail but said he'd have a whisky. Miss Brierley requested a sweet sherry. Only when these two had received their drinks, did he turn to the man to whom Dolores La Mar had been talking. 'A dry martini, I think you said?'

'Ooh, yes please! Laurence Quayle's the name, by the way,' added this ebullient young man. 'But do call me Larry. Everybody else does.'

While these introductions were going on, Rowlands turned his attention to the man standing next to him. 'Did you have a good journey down, Mr Cunningham?'

'Not too bad, thanks,' was the reply. 'Of course, one can't get up much speed after one descends into these Cornish lanes, but I've a competent driver, so . . .' He let the sentence tail off, but the implication was clear. A man of his standing and financial worth needn't trouble himself overmuch with what he paid others to do.

They were joined at that moment by the star, perhaps curious to inspect the man to whom she had not yet had cause to speak. It was possible, thought Rowlands with a certain wry amusement, that she was as yet unaware of how impervious he and Ashenhurst were to her more obvious charms. Of course, other things – not least a woman's voice – could be powerfully seductive. So far, he had not found Dolores La Mar's voice especially so. There was something too studied about her manner – hardly surprising in an actress, he supposed. Although he had known another actress whose voice had enchanted him even as he knew she was using it to get her own way. But then few women – whether actresses or not – could compare with Magdalena Brandt.

It seemed that Miss La Mar had picked up that at

least one of those present had failed to succumb to her charm. 'And you are?' she said, addressing Rowlands in what he described to himself as 'honeyed tones'. He introduced himself.

'This is my wife, Edith,' he added since the latter had now joined them. But the film star showed little interest in Edith.

'You know,' she murmured, still holding Rowlands' hand in hers, 'you look very familiar. Have we met?'

'I don't think so.'

'Strange. I could have sworn . . .'

'You might have seen Fred in pictures,' put in Jack Ashenhurst, with a laugh. Rowlands could have clouted him.

'Really?' Suddenly she was interested. 'You mean you're an actor?'

'No, no. My brother-in-law was joking.'

'But you were in a film,' insisted Ashenhurst. 'You can't deny it, old man.'

'It was a very small, non-speaking role in a German production,' said Rowlands with a shrug. 'I'm not sure the film was ever released.'

But this was evidently enough to establish his credentials with Dolores La Mar. 'I might have known you were an actor, with a face like yours,' she said. 'Rather distinguished. A good profile, too. I must ask Hilly if we can use you.'

'No, please don't . . .' Rowlands started to say, but – as was her wont – she cut across him.

'Only I will give you one tip – you must learn to *look* at the person you are addressing.'

Rowlands smiled. 'I assure you, I would if I could,' he said.

'Well!' was Edith's muttered comment when, a few minutes later, their little party – summoned by the banging of a gong – was making its way towards the dining room. 'Talk about vamping.'

'Shh. She'll hear you.'

'She's too busy listening to the sound of her own voice for that!'

'Even so. Ah, good evening, Colonel . . . Mrs Rutherford.' For he had heard that couple approaching – guests of long-standing at Cliff House Hotel.

'Evening,' was Colonel Rutherford's gruff reply. He was retired Indian Army, with all that that implied about his bearing and manner. 'By Jove! Who is that rather splendid gel?'

'That's Dolores La Mar.' Then when this failed to elicit a response, Rowlands added, 'She's a film actress.'

'Is she, by Gad? Handsome piece, saving your presence Milly.' This was to his wife, whose only comment was a sniff. 'Can't say as I think much of that pansy she's talking to. Actor, too, I shouldn't wonder.'

'I should think you're right,' said Rowlands. He and Edith and the girls took their places at their usual table next to the south-facing window where they were joined by Billy and Walter, while the Colonel and his lady made their way to a table in the bay window, exchanging murmured greetings with the Simkins family: Daphne and John, and their twin sons Jonathan and Rory, who were already seated. The Simkinses, too, had been coming to Cliff House for some years so that the boys had almost become members of the Ashenhurst–Rowlands tribe – a state of affairs made more interesting by the 'understanding' which had grown up between the eighteen-year-old Jonathan Simkins and Rowlands' seventeen-year-old daughter, Margaret. Although in Rowlands' opinion, she was too young for any such engagement, unofficial or otherwise. She still had her exams to do, and there was Cambridge Entrance looming, too.

At the big table along the far wall, the actors and their entourage had taken their seats, with Dolores La Mar at the centre, facing into the room. Her remarks were therefore impossible to ignore since, like all those of her profession, she had developed the art of projection. 'Come and sit by me, Larry,' she was saying. 'Horace, you're on my other side. I like to keep my men close by,' she added, with what Rowlands suspected was her trademark gurgling laugh. 'Brierley, you can sit next to Larry.' It crossed Rowlands' mind that by placing the secretary between Laurence Quayle and Dorothy, who was at the near end of the table, the actress was effectively preventing his good-looking sister from receiving any share of the young man's attentions.

Not that it would bother Dorothy in the slightest: she'd made no secret of her disdain for 'these acting types', as she called them. 'People who make a living out of

pretending to be somebody else – what sort of job is that?'
she'd said when the question of how the film party was to
be accommodated had been discussed a few days before.

'I must say I think that's rather unfair on actors,'
Jack had objected mildly. 'They give pleasure to a lot of
people.'

'To say nothing of the way they – or rather, the films in
which they act – can communicate ideas,' put in Rowlands
slyly. 'I'm sure your friends in the Soviet Union would
agree.'

'They're not my friends, as you call them,' said his
sister. 'And I hardly think the kind of romantic tosh most
of these film companies put out can compare with films
designed to educate the masses.'

'Propaganda, in a word,' said Rowlands cheerfully.
'No, thank goodness Elstree hasn't so far stooped to
that!' To which the erstwhile champion of the Russian
political experiment's only reply was a contemptuous
snort. Of late, Dorothy's enthusiasm for the Communist
regime had been noticeably less strident. Perhaps even
she was beginning to realise that there was a difference
between ideology and reality? Now, as the soup course
was served (fifteen-year-old Jenny Penhaligon having
being trained by her aunt, Mrs Jago, the hotel's cook,
in the niceties of waiting at table), Rowlands could hear
his sister making a determined effort with Miss Brierley.

'I hope you're enjoying the soup? I made it myself, you
know.'

'Oh yes, it's very nice.'

'I always think a chilled soup is best on a summer's evening, don't you?'

'Oh, yes.' Rather a nervous young woman, thought Rowlands, although working for someone like Dolores La Mar would be enough to make anyone self-conscious. Further along the table, the conversation had turned to the whereabouts of the rest of the party.

'I can't think what's happened to Hilly and Eliot,' said Dolores La Mar. 'They set out at the same time as we did.'

'Yes, but in a far less powerful motor car,' said Laurence Quayle. 'You've grown so accustomed to the Rolls, darling, that you've forgotten what it's like to rely on a car whose top speed barely reaches forty miles per hour.'

'I'm glad to say I've never had to set foot in such a rattletrap,' was the reply. 'Why Hilly doesn't get himself a better car, I can't imagine.'

'It isn't Hilary's car. It belongs to Miss Linden, as you well know,' said Quayle, in the same tone of indulgent amusement with which he had received all the prima donna's salvoes. 'And she can't afford anything better – not while she's still earning the pittance Management pays her.'

'She's paid what Management thinks she's worth,' said Miss La Mar, a shade testily. 'When she's worked her way up to having her name at the top of the bill, she can think about trading in that horrible little car for a better one.'

'Oh, we all know you're the Rolls-Royce sort,' said Quayle silkily. 'Lucky for you that Horace here is so "oofy", isn't it, darling?'

'I'll have you know,' said the actress, her voice rising, 'that I was earning top rates long before I married – isn't that so, Horace?'

'Certainly, my dear.'

'So you see it's all nonsense about my relying on Horace's money . . . Yes, yes. Take it away.' This was to Jenny Penhaligon, who – nervous no doubt at her proximity to the star – was making a bit of a performance about collecting up the empty soup plates.

'Won't you have some of this lobster salad?' Dorothy was saying to Miss Brierley. 'It's Mrs Jago's speciality.'

'Thank you, but I never eat fish,' said the secretary, with a nervous little laugh. 'The soup will do for me.'

'But surely you'll need more than that?' said Dorothy. 'I can have Cook make you an omelette, if you like.'

'Oh, Brierley's one of the nuts and beans brigade,' sang out Dolores La Mar from along the table. 'Never eats anything remotely edible, as far as I can tell. It's why she looks so washed-out.' Before she could elaborate on this theme, there came the sound of a car pulling up outside, followed by the slamming of car doors. A moment later, the late arrivals made their entrance.

'Please don't get up,' said one of them – his deep, warm tones identifying him as a leading man, if ever there was one, thought Rowlands. 'We're abominably late, I'm afraid'.

Chapter Two

'It's all my fault,' said another voice – a young woman's – sounding cheerfully unrepentant. 'I took a wrong turning after St Austell, and then my map-reader got us even more lost.'

'I did not,' said the Leading Man, with dignity. 'You managed that perfectly well by yourself.'

'Children, children!' said a third member of the party. 'Cease this unseemly squabbling at once, or our kind hostess will regret that she ever agreed to have us. Hilary Carmody,' he added, to Cecily, who had risen with the others. 'You must be Mrs Ashenhurst.'

'Actually that's me,' said Dorothy. 'This is Mrs Nicholls, my sister-in-law.'

'Delighted to meet you both,' was the affable reply. 'So which of you gentlemen is Mr Ashenhurst? Since I seem fated to get people's names mixed up this evening.'

Introductions were duly performed, and then the newcomers, consisting of Carmody, the leading man (whose name, it transpired, was Eliot Dean) and the young lady who'd been driving – a Miss Lydia Linden – took their seats on the opposite side of the table to Dolores La Mar and her consorts.

'Well, you took your time,' she said, addressing Dean, apparently, for he seized her hand across the table and kissed it.

'Darling,' he said. 'Did you miss me so very much?'

'Oh, we all miss your sparkling wit, don't we, Horace?'

'I couldn't possibly comment,' said Cunningham drily. 'May I give you some wine, Miss Linden?'

'Rather. I say, what scrumptious grub! I'm absolutely starving.'

The conversation was necessarily suspended while those still in need of a first course were hastily served, and those awaiting the *boeuf en daube* which was to follow it had their plates changed.

'At last!' said Dolores La Mar, not quite sotto voce. 'Something hot.' Fortunately the dish, when it came, was of a quality to silence even the most difficult to please, and for the next few minutes an appreciative silence reigned. When at last the talk at the big table resumed, it was of the arrangements for the rest of the film crew – cameramen and lighting technicians – for whom room could not be found at the Cliff House Hotel.

'I always recommend the Paris Hotel if we're full,' said Ashenhurst. 'They should be able to accommodate your people quite satisfactorily.'

'The Paris Hotel?' This was Miss La Mar. 'I must say, I'm surprised that the budget stretches to that! And why wasn't I given the choice? The Paris Hotel sounds rather more my thing than . . . well.' She let the comment hang in the air. Really, thought Rowlands, half-amused and half-annoyed on his friends' behalf. She really doesn't care what she says, or whom she offends. It was explained to the actress that the Paris Hotel was in fact a decidedly rustic inn, named after a ship which had been wrecked on that rocky coastline at the end of the previous century.

'So you see, it wouldn't be at all your thing, darling,' said Laurence Quayle fondly. 'Unless you fancy roughing it with the locals.'

After dinner, the film party and their hosts retired to the lounge for coffee, leaving Jenny Penhaligon and her cousin Sally Trelawny (also drafted in for the summer season) to clear the tables. The Rowlands family followed suit. Even ten-year-old Joan was given permission by her mother to stay up an extra half-hour in order to share in the excitement of having real-life film stars on the premises. Although Joan's taste in films ran more to *Queen of the Jungle* and *King Solomon's Mines* than to the romantic productions in which, Rowlands supposed, Dolores La Mar and her colleagues displayed their talents.

His elder daughters seemed suitably captivated, however. 'I think Miss La Mar's frock is so elegant,' breathed Anne, provoking the tart reply from her mother that she didn't imagine oyster-coloured satin was the most practical wear for scrambling about the cliffs with a sketch pad (Anne's favourite pastime, during these past weeks). Margaret, too, seemed somewhat overawed by the new arrivals, or by one of them in particular.

'I must have seen every one of Eliot Dean's films,' Rowlands heard her say to Jonathan Simkins. 'He was marvellous in *Chance Encounter*. But I think *Strange Destinies* is my favourite.'

'He looks a lot older in the flesh than he does on the screen,' was the disgruntled reply. 'I suppose one's seeing him without all that make-up.' Rowlands suppressed a smile. Poor young Simkins was evidently feeling the pangs of jealousy. On the far side of the lounge, the prima donna was holding court on the chaise longue.

'Come and sit by me, Eliot. Horace can sit over there, next to Brierley. You don't mind do you, Horace? Eliot and I have things to discuss, and it'll only bore you.'

Her co-star accordingly seated himself on her right-hand side. 'Delightful spot, this,' he said, presumably having taken in the view from the windows. 'I shouldn't mind a walk later, along the clifftops. Blow away the cobwebs after that infernal drive. There's going to be a magnificent sunset, from the look of it.' It really was a beautiful voice, thought Rowlands. Mellifluous, and yet indisputably masculine. If this was what star quality sounded like, he supposed Eliot Dean had it. 'Ah, thank you,' said the leading man to Dorothy, who'd just handed him a cup of coffee. 'What do you say, Liddy? Fancy a walk?'

'I don't mind,' was the reply. 'Thanks. Two sugars, please.' At least this one wasn't watching her figure, thought Rowlands. 'Yes, I'll go with you,' went on Miss Linden – for it was she. 'Just as long as you don't expect me to go very far. I'm simply *longing* for my bed.'

'You can't go to bed yet! It's not half past nine. I thought you young people were supposed to be fresh air fiends.'

'I can't think where you got that idea,' said Laurence Quayle, from the floor at Miss La Mar's feet. He gave an affected little shudder. '*This* young person prefers his creature comforts. Catch me striding about on clifftops! No thank you *very* much.'

'It's funny,' said Dean. 'But I never think of you as young, Quayle. Although you can't be more than – what? Twenty-five?'

'I'm twenty-two. Yes, I suppose one must rather lose touch with what it's like to be young once one enters middle age,' said Quayle sweetly.

'Middle age! I'll have you know I'll be thirty-five next birthday.'

'Precisely,' said Laurence Quayle. Rowlands wondered if the animosity implicit in his remark was real or put on for effect. It was hard to tell with actors.

'I wouldn't mind a walk,' said Jonathan Simkins in an undertone to Margaret, who had been helping her aunt hand round the coffee cups, and now joined her family at the near end of the lounge. 'Coming, Megs?'

'No, thanks. Walter'll go with you, won't you, Walter? He was saying he felt like a breather.'

'*Ja*, I will come with you. There will be a fine view of the moon in conjunction with Venus and Jupiter across the sea tonight, I think. The moon will be full tomorrow night and so . . .' But Jonathan evidently didn't care a hang about the moon, or Jupiter – at least, not if he had to see them with Walter Metzner rather than with his preferred companion.

'I suppose,' he said bitterly to Margaret, 'you'd rather stay stuffed up in here?'

'Yes,' she said. Because across the room, Eliot Dean was getting his own back on his adversary.

'If you'd like to give me a game of tennis tomorrow after breakfast, Quayle, I'll show you who's middle-aged and who isn't,' he said with a laugh.

'You forget,' said Hilary Carmody. 'Tomorrow after breakfast we'll be shooting your first scene with Dolores.'

'Yes, but that'll take ages to set up. You know how particular Joe the Sparks is with his lighting. Plenty of time for me to thrash young Quayle here in straight sets, and still be in time for my cue.'

'Speaking of which,' said Dolores La Mar, perhaps feeling that she had been out of the conversation long enough, 'can I *implore* you, Eliot dear, not to come in with your line *quite* so quickly after, "If you want to know, I've come to get away . . . from everything." There should be a pause there before you say, "Have you?"

The line's supposed to *resonate*.'

The pause which followed this remark was worthy of the West End stage-trained actor Eliot Dean had been before he'd turned to making films, thought Rowlands. 'Isn't that,' said the actor at last, 'rather up to Carmody to decide?'

'Oh, leave me out of it,' was the director's cheerful reply. 'But I don't think we ought to be talking shop on our first evening, do you? Very tedious for Mr and Mrs Ashenhurst and their guests.'

'Not at all,' said Ashenhurst courteously. 'As you may have gathered, we lead a rather quiet life here. Any change from that is very welcome, especially for the younger folk. Wouldn't you say so, Danny?'

'Rather,' agreed his adopted son, with some enthusiasm. As well as having a fondness for motor cars, Daniel Ashenhurst was a devoted cineaste, with a predilection for cowboy films and adventure stories. If Eliot Dean was not exactly in the league of Tom Mix, he at least belonged to the same world as the one inhabited by that veteran of a hundred westerns. For that alone, Danny was prepared to give him the benefit of the doubt. But this reminder that the younger members of the party were still present was enough to call forth a summons from Edith to her youngest daughter that it was time to go to bed ('But Mummy . . .') and the same injunction from Dorothy to Victor, who looked half-asleep already, she said.

'You'd better go, too, Danny,' she added, to that gentleman's mortification. 'You know you've got to be up at six to feed the chickens. It's almost ten o'clock.'

'Goodness, what frightfully early hours one keeps in the country,' drawled Laurence Quayle. 'Why, in London one would only just be getting ready to go out.'

'Then thank heaven we're not in London,' said Dean, getting to his feet. 'I'm off for my walk. Coming, Liddy?'

'All right.'

After this, the party began to break up – somewhat to Rowlands' relief. One could have too much of a good thing, he thought, always supposing that the actors were a good thing. As Ashenhurst had said, it made a change from the quiet tenor of their life in Cornwall. The question was: having come here to escape London life, with all its noise and bustle, did he and his family really want such a change?

Next morning, Rowlands rose early, as was his custom during these summer months. Never a heavy sleeper, he usually found himself awake by the time the birds began to call, whether it was in his suburban street at home or, as now, beside the sea. The fact that they were gulls not sparrows made not the smallest bit of difference. Leaving Edith asleep, he made his way from their bedroom, in what was called the 'old wing', along the passage to the bathroom, which they shared with three other rooms. This part of the building – once a farmhouse – was sixteenth century, with the low ceilings and sloping floors common to that delightfully irregular architectural period. He was used to it by this time, but when he'd first started coming here, he'd taken a few headers down the stairs. Even now, he was careful to tread warily in case a loose board might trip him. Not so the young woman – for he guessed it was a woman – who came hurtling around the bend in the corridor, almost ending up in his arms. 'Oh! *Lo siento*!' she cried, revealing herself to be the Spanish maid. 'Sorry . . . so sorry.'

'Don't mention it,' he said. 'I say, I hope you're not hurt?' but she had already turned and fled in the opposite direction. Evidently the sight of a strange Englishman in a dressing gown was too much for her, thought Rowlands wryly. After he'd washed and dressed, he descended the stairs to the hotel kitchen. Here he found Mrs Jago supervising her 'girls': 'Now remember, Sal – she wants 'em soft-boiled . . . Morning, Mr Rowlands.'

He returned the greeting. 'Is there a cup of tea to be had?' he asked, guessing that this would have been the first thing to have been attended to, Mrs Jago sustaining herself throughout the day with cups of this refreshing beverage.

'There is indeed, Mr Rowlands, sir. If you'll sit yourself down, I'll pour you one directly. Not out of *that* pot,' she added darkly, evidently alluding to the smaller vessel, designed for one person, that was even now being placed onto the tray with the other breakfast things for Sally or Jenny to carry upstairs. 'The tea in *that* pot's as weak as water. Not but what it wasn't asked for as such,' said Mrs Jago, still in the same tone of dark foreboding. 'Notions!' she concluded, with a proper scorn for all such faddiness. 'All right, Jenny, you can take'n up now, there's a good girl. She said six o'clock and six o'clock it'll be to the minute. Now then, Mr Rowlands,' went on the cook, turning her attention to the more serious business of pouring out – this time from the large earthenware pot that stood at the centre of the table – 'here's your tea. And a good strong cup it is.'

Rowlands nodded his thanks and took a sip of the powerful brew. 'Anyone else about?'

'Just Master Danny. And didn't he look pasty-faced this morning! Late nights,' said Bessie Jago, in the tone of one who had seen the ruinous effects of these on many others, 'don't do a growing boy any good. I told'n, I said, "Master Danny," I said, "you want to watch yourself, staying up till all hours . . ."'

'Well, at least he got up in time to feed the chickens,' said Rowlands, to stem the flow. Recalling his own days of having to perform the same task, at the same early hour, made him grateful that those days were over. He'd never been cut out to be a chicken farmer.

'There was that foreign woman, too,' said Mrs Jago, setting down her teacup with a meaningful sniff. 'Eye-talian, or some such.'

'Spanish,' said Rowlands. 'You mean Miss La Mar's maid, I suppose?'

'Is that what she is? All I know is she came in here, quarter to six it was, wanting to know was the water really hot for Miss Whatsername's bath.' Another disdainful sniff. 'Told her it wasn't my job to see to the boiler. That's Pengelly's job, that is.'

'I expect,' said Rowlands, doing his best to soothe these ruffled feathers, 'she didn't know who else to ask.'

'No doubt,' was the reply. 'All I can say is, Mr Rowlands, that we never had this kind of thing before. People asking for tea – plain boiled water, more like – and baths to be hot at six in the morning.'

'Everything all right?' said Cecily Nicholls, appearing in the doorway at that moment. 'Ah, good. I can see you've got everything in hand, Mrs Jago.'

'Yes, well . . . As I was saying to Mr Rowlands here . . .'

'There'll be five for early breakfast,' went on Mrs Nicholls, cutting short this threatened outburst. 'That's poached egg on toast for Miss Brierley, and the rest of them bacon and eggs and all the trimmings, except for one lot of kippers – that's for Mr Quayle. But I'm sure you've made a note of all that already, Mrs Jago.'

'Yes'm.'

'Good. Then it's just the coffee at seven for Miss La Mar – and any of the others that want it. I said we could provide flasks, but so far only Mr Dean has taken me up on that.'

'The tall gentleman – yes,' said Mrs Jago, adding with a slight unbending of her manner, 'Saw'n in *Day of Reckoning*. Ever so good, he was.'

'Then that's all settled,' said Mrs Nicholls. 'I knew I could rely on you. Breakfast at eight for everyone else, of course . . . If you can spare a moment, Fred,' she went on when these arrangements had been dealt with, 'there's something on which I'd like your advice.' She took his arm – managing to do this without making him feel he was being dragged along, as was sometimes the case with those well-meaning souls who imagined that being blind meant you'd lost the use of your other faculties – and the two of them went out onto the terrace at the back of the hotel. This was deserted at that hour, the sun having yet to move round to that quarter. 'I thought you looked as if you needed rescuing,' said Rowlands' companion when they were out of earshot. 'Bessie Jago is a treasure – we couldn't manage without her – but she does run on sometimes.'

'She obviously feels that Miss La Mar's crowd have overstepped the mark as regards the behaviour proper to hotel guests,' said Rowlands, with a smile.

'Yes, although I can't imagine why she should be getting so up in arms. We've had people down from London lots of times.'

'But not film people.'

'No, but we had that theatre crowd from the Minack two seasons ago, and she was as nice as pie about them. I really don't know what's got into her.'

Rowlands hesitated a moment. 'Maybe,' he said, 'it's the foreign element she objects to.' He related Mrs Jago's remarks about Dolores La Mar's Spanish maid. 'Some people are suspicious of foreigners, you know.'

'I can't have that,' said Mrs Nicholls firmly. 'It was bad enough just after the war, with some people not wanting to have anything to do with Germans. But at least there were reasons for that.' She herself, she didn't need to say, having had such a reason – the loss of her husband of two weeks to a German bullet. 'I'd better speak to her, I suppose. Although the last thing I want is for her to give notice when we're in the middle of our busiest time.'

'I'd leave it a few days, if I were you,' said Rowlands. 'Things have a habit of settling down. Was there anything you wanted to ask me about?' he added as they reached the end of the terrace and descended the steps that led to the lawn beneath. 'Or were you just offering me an escape route?'

'As a matter of fact, there was something.' Cecily Nicholls was silent a moment as the two of them began to stroll along the path that led around the side of the hotel to the front drive. 'It's actually rather beastly. I haven't said anything yet to Jack. He's got a lot to deal with at the moment, and I didn't want to worry him . . .' Again she paused. Rowlands knew better than to press her. People generally said what was on their minds if you gave them the chance. 'The fact is, there's been a letter. It was addressed to Jack, as it happens, but naturally I open all his correspondence – at least,' she corrected herself, 'all his business correspondence. Anything that looks personal I leave to Dorothy, of course.'

Rowlands nodded his appreciation of this point, and she went on, 'I'd assumed that this was just something of that kind – a business letter, or a circular. It was just a cheap envelope, with a single sheet of paper . . .' She broke off.

'What did it say?' asked Rowlands.

'It said: "Those who harbour traitors will die", I thought it was a joke at first – some silly game the boys were playing. Traitors and death threats.' Mrs Nicholls gave an uncertain laugh. 'It sounds like something out of a bad film, doesn't it?' They had by now come round to the front of the hotel.

'When did this letter arrive?' asked Rowlands.

'Yesterday. By the second post.'

'Have you mentioned it to anyone else?'

'No. That is . . . I asked Danny if he knew anything about it and he said no. He's a truthful chap, as a rule, and so . . .'

'I'm sure he had nothing to do with it,' said Rowlands. 'But I'm glad you told me.'

'Yes, so am I. These things are rather nasty, aren't they?'

'Very. But try not to worry. When the moment's right, I'll have a word with Jack.' Further conversation was cut short by the sound of the Rolls drawing up in front of the main entrance. Presumably this was to take Miss La Mar to the shoot, thought Rowlands. The driver got out, and began to polish the windscreen, to judge from the squeaking of chamois leather on glass.

'Well,' said Mrs Nicholls, 'I'd better get on, I suppose. Are you coming in, Fred?'

'I'll take another turn around the garden before breakfast,' he said. Although his real reason – he could not have said why – was to get acquainted with the only member of the film party he hadn't yet met. 'Fine morning,' he accordingly said to the man, still busy with his polishing. The answer to this was a non-committal grunt. 'You're out and about nice and early,' went on Rowlands, not deterred by this. Again, the reply was terse.

'She wants it so. *L'actriu*.' Rowlands guessed he meant Dolores La Mar, although the word – presumably 'actress' – he'd used was unfamiliar . . . *some kind of dialect, perhaps?*

'Of course,' he said; then, aware it was rather a clumsy change of subject, but not sure otherwise how to engage the attention of this taciturn type, 'You're from Spain, aren't you?'

'Catalunya.'

'Lot of trouble in your part of the world recently.'

'Trouble!' The chauffeur gave a scornful laugh. '*Sí*, there has been much trouble, like you say. They will not rest, *els feixistes*, until they have killed us all.' Again, the unfamiliar word – Rowlands guessed this must be Catalan. *Los fascistas* would have been the Spanish version. He was turning away with a polite murmur of commiseration when the man said, 'Cigarette?' thrusting the pack towards him.

'Thanks.' Although Rowlands would have preferred one of his own brand. But he interpreted this gesture as a sign that he had been accepted, if somewhat conditionally, by the other. As he bent his head to allow the chauffeur to light his gasper, trying not to cough as he inhaled the smoke from the rough-tasting tobacco, he reflected that it was hardly surprising if the fellow's manner was a bit off-putting. Knowing that your country was in the process of being torn apart by fanatics would be enough to sour the temper of any man.

For the next few moments, they smoked their cigarettes in silence, the Catalan evidently being in no mood to enlarge upon his earlier remarks. And no wonder, thought Rowlands, if things were as bad as all that. Even though he tried to keep abreast of things as far as possible – listening to the news on the wireless and getting Edith to read the main stories aloud to him from the newspaper each day – it wasn't easy to stay as up to the minute as he'd have liked. 'When were you last in Catalonia?' he asked.

'Four months ago,' was the reply. 'I left just after Guernica . . . You know what happened there?'

'Yes. Terrible business. One wouldn't have thought even the Germans capable of such an atrocity.'

'As you say, it was terrible. And it was the Francoists who were responsible, murderers that they are, even if it was the Luftwaffe who dropped the bombs.' The chauffeur spat, suddenly, upon the ground. 'After that,' he said, 'we knew it was impossible to stay. But Caterina – that is my sister, you understand – had heard of a job in London, working for *l'actriu*, and so we came here.'

'Ah, that must have been your sister I met just now,' said Rowlands, gesturing vaguely with his cigarette in the direction of the hotel. But the other made no reply, because at that moment the front door opened and Dolores La Mar came out, deep in conversation with someone. It was immediately apparent from the tone of this that all was not well, as far as the actress was concerned.

'But darling,' she was saying in a petulant voice as she descended the short flight of steps to the drive, 'I really don't see what the difficulty is . . . Surely you can make whatever changes to the script you like? You're the director, aren't you?'

'I was, when I last looked,' replied Hilary Carmody, for it was he. 'All right, Casals' – this to the chauffeur – 'you can take us down to the village. The camera crew should have finished setting up by this time.'

'Only I do feel that the sub-plot with the girl weakens the whole film,' went on Miss La Mar as she made her leisurely way towards the Rolls, the passenger door of which was now being held open for her by Casals. 'I mean, the audience isn't going to be interested in the *girl*. She's nothing but a minor character. It's the love affair between Desirée and Edward they'll be interested in.'

'Darling, if we're to get you into make-up, and ready for your first scene with Eliot, in time to take advantage of the morning light – which is what I particularly want for this scene – then we're going to have to get a move on,' said Carmody, good-humouredly. 'I do see your point about Lydia's character, but . . .'

'I don't see why she has to be in the picture at all,'

said the actress, getting into the car. 'As for having Eliot – I mean Edward – fall in love with her, that's patently absurd. Edward's supposed to be in love with *me* – that is, Desirée. The audience won't like it if he comes across as fickle.'

'But darling, he only falls for Laura after Desirée's death.'

'And that's another thing,' said Dolores La Mar. 'I mean, does she really have to die? It seems like such a miserable ending.'

'That's the story we're working with, I'm afraid,' said the director, going round to the other side of the vehicle and getting in beside her.

'And as I said, the story can be changed,' was the retort. Casals shut the door on this remark, and any further conversation was cut off from Rowlands' hearing. Casals got into the driver's seat and a moment later, there came the sound of the Rolls driving away. At once, Rowlands dropped the remnant of his acrid-tasting smoke on the gravel and ground it out with his heel. Time for breakfast, he thought. He'd better go and see if Edith and the girls were down.

Chapter Three

But neither his wife nor his daughters had yet joined the actors in the hotel dining room where the early breakfast was being served. Rowlands, in no particular hurry for his, sat down at his usual table and, feigning interest in the newspaper which had been left next to Edith's place (she was in the habit of reading the headlines to him over their first cup of coffee), let his thoughts wander. That girl – Caterina Casals – had been upset about something. He wondered what it was. Of course, having a mistress like Dolores La Mar would be enough to get on anyone's nerves. A voice broke into these reflections, 'I'm sorry, but she's nothing but a . . . I'm too much of a lady to say it,' said Lydia Linden from the actors' table.

'Rhymes with witch,' muttered Laurence Quayle. The actress stifled a giggle.

'I didn't say that.'

'You didn't have to, darling,' he said. 'Ooh, yes! I'd love some more coffee,' he added, presumably to Mrs Nicholls, whose murmured enquires as to whether everyone had everything they needed interspersed these exchanges.

'The fact is,' went on Miss Linden, biting into a piece of toast, 'she's trying to get me thrown off the picture. I call that low, I really do.'

'Ignore it,' said Eliot Dean. 'She's just letting off steam. She'll have forgotten all about it by tomorrow.'

'Yes, but I won't,' said Miss Linden. 'I don't mind admitting it's shaken my confidence. I mean, when someone practically tells you to your face that you're surplus to requirements.'

'It's only that one scene with you and Dean she objects to,' said Quayle innocently. 'Cut that, and Dolores'll be a perfect lamb.'

'Yes, but it's my big scene,' objected Miss Linden, then realised he was trying to get a rise. 'Oh, you are the limit!' she exclaimed. 'I believe you're on her side.'

'Not I, darling. Totally impartial, as always.'

'In any case, it'll be Carmody's decision, about what does or doesn't go into the picture,' said Eliot Dean. 'What Dolores wants doesn't come into it.'

'Doesn't it?' The young actress sounded so forlorn that Rowlands, who had been listening to this exchange with some interest, felt a momentary rush of sympathy. Poor young thing! Evidently her maid wasn't the only one Dolores La Mar had managed to upset that morning. Nor was Rowlands alone in being moved by the ingénue's plight. 'Look, I'd put it right out of your mind,' said Dean earnestly. 'It's not worth getting upset about.'

'Perhaps not, but . . .'

'Dolores just says these poisonous things for effect,' said the actor. 'Most of it's just hot air.' At which remark, Laurence Quayle was overtaken by a choking fit, perhaps not unconnected with the fact that Horace Cunningham had just walked in.

'Good morning, everybody,' he said. 'I see that I'm a little early. Don't let me delay the rest of you, if you've got to get off.' There was an infinitesimal but perceptible pause before everybody started talking at once.

'I say, is that the time? We'd better get a move on.'

'Yes, don't want to be late on the first day of shooting.'

Within minutes, the dining room had emptied of all but the two latest arrivals. 'Well,' said Cunningham as he took his seat at the table just vacated by the actors, 'it looks as if we have the place to ourselves for the moment . . . Mr Rowlands, isn't it?'

'That's right,' said Rowlands, feeling not a little embarrassed at having been party to the conversation about Dolores La Mar. He wondered how much of it Cunningham had overheard. But the other seemed determined to put him at his ease.

'Fine day again,' he remarked as Mrs Nicholls came in with the coffee.

'Yes, isn't it?' Rowlands replied. The next few minutes

were taken up with the ordering of breakfast, and with the necessary to-ing and fro-ing between kitchen and dining room which ensued. Only when platefuls of bacon and eggs had been placed in front of both of them, and supplies of tea and coffee replenished, did the entrepreneur venture a further remark.

'I expect,' he said affably, 'you must find all this film business rather a change from what you're used to?'

Rowlands, who saw no reason to enlighten the other as to his previous experience of the film business, agreed that it was a change.

'Film people are different, I've found,' went on Cunningham, with the air of a man used to having his opinions deferred to. 'It's taken me a while to realise that. When I first met my wife . . .' He broke off, as if he had said more than he meant to. 'The fact is, they can be volatile,' he continued. 'Forever getting themselves worked up about things you and I would consider to be perfectly trivial. Then, after a great deal of fuss and hot air . . .' So he did overhear what Dean had said, thought Rowlands – 'It's forgotten. One minute they're at daggers drawn, the next everyone's the best of friends.'

'Well, they *are* actors,' said Rowlands, who felt he'd had enough of the older man's sententiousness. 'One might expect them to take a rather dramatic view of things.'

'Quite so.' Cunningham put down his knife and fork. 'I was sure you'd understand, Mr Rowlands.' Which the latter supposed was an oblique way of asking him to dismiss Eliot Dean's acerbic remarks about Dolores La Mar from his mind. Judging that no reply was necessary, he merely smiled, and went on with his toast and marmalade. A moment or two later, Cunningham pushed back his chair. 'Well, must be getting along,' he said. 'The stock market waits for no man, I'm afraid.' Rowlands took this to mean that he was off to read the financial columns of the newspapers. Unless perhaps Jack Ashenhurst had managed to set up a special telephone line to the City, communications in Cornwall being notoriously unreliable. Cunningham going out met Edith coming in: an awkward little exchange followed.

'Goodness!' said Rowlands' wife when they were alone. 'I feel as if I've just been bowed to by the Bank of England.'

Rowlands smiled. 'That's probably not so very far from the truth,' he said. 'Girls not up yet?'

'Oh, they've been up and about for a while. Joan's gone down to the beach with Victor. Something about looking for a smugglers' cave. Anne's gone off sketching.'

'And Margaret?'

'Oh, Margaret . . . Thanks, Cecily, I'll just have toast and marmalade,' said Edith as Mrs Nicholls put her head around the door to ask what she'd like for breakfast. 'And tea, please . . . Yes, Margaret got up at the crack of dawn to walk down to the village. She said she wanted to watch the filming. I said she might, as long as she didn't get in the way of the actors.' Then, seeing her husband's face, 'Oh, come on, Fred! Don't tell me you didn't go through a phase of being interested in film stars?' He couldn't deny it.

'All the same,' he said. 'Don't you feel she's a bit young?'

'Don't be stuffy, Fred. She's seventeen.' She chuckled reminiscently. 'In my day, it was curates. Why, I remember getting up at six every Sunday to go to early service, just because a certain Mr Devereux was preaching.'

'Hm,' said Rowlands. 'You never told me about *him*.'

'There wasn't anything to tell. He was tall and thin, with a long pale face that made one think he must have a secret sorrow. All the girls in the parish were in love with him.' Edith took a bite of her toast. 'Including me. Fortunately, all that came to an end when the All Stars Dance Band came to the Theatre Royal at Poole. There was one young man who played the trumpet . . .'

'All right, I get the picture,' he said. 'Anything in the paper, today?'

She unfolded the newspaper. 'Home news or international?'

'International, please.'

She turned a page. 'There's been more fighting in Madrid. Buildings shelled by the Falangists. Quite a lot of casualties. Do you want me to read the whole report?'

'No, that's all right.'

'And the Japanese have occupied Peking.'

'So it'll be war . . .'

'It certainly looks like it.'

'Lord, what fools these mortals be,' murmured Rowlands. He threw down his napkin and got to his feet. 'I'm going for a walk. Coming?'

'In a minute. I just want to check my shares.' Not that she had many of these – some railway shares she'd inherited from her father, and a few war bonds – but she liked the thought of having a nest egg for when times got worse, which they seemed very likely to do, thought Rowlands grimly. What with civil war in Spain – and now this business in China – it was all looking rather precarious just now. As he descended the steps that led from the terrace to the front drive, he met Margaret coming in the other direction.

'Hello, Daddy!' she called. 'Have I missed breakfast?'

'I should think you're just in time,' he said, pausing to light a cigarette – one of the milder variety he favoured. He could still taste the Caballero. 'Your mother said you'd been down to the village.'

'Yes – to watch the filming. They've roped off one end of the High Street – by the smugglers' cottages . . . I say, Daddy, what do you think it would cost to go to stage school?'

'Too much,' he said. 'Why? Are you thinking of going on the stage?'

'Not really.' She hesitated. 'I was thinking more of films, actually. It looks like an awful lot of fun.'

'Are you any good at acting, do you think?' He kept his tone light, but inwardly he was dismayed. His studious daughter, captivated by the glare of the footlights, or arc lights, in this case. It didn't bear thinking about.

'That's the whole point,' said Margaret airily. 'One doesn't have to be good at acting, in films. One just stands there while they point the camera at one. It looks perfectly simple.' Since this had been very much his own experience of acting in a film – if you could call sitting at a café table and pretending to read a newspaper 'acting' – he felt unable to contradict her. He took refuge in evasion.

'What does your mother think?'

'Oh, Mummy thinks it's quite all right, don't you, Mummy?' For Edith had just that moment come out of the front door of the hotel.

'What's this?' she said. Then, when it had been explained to her, 'Well, I don't see why you shouldn't have some acting lessons.'

'But . . .' said Rowlands. He felt a sharp kick on his ankle.

'We'll talk about it later,' said Edith to her daughter. 'Now I should hurry if you don't want to miss breakfast.'

'What's all this about acting?' said Rowlands when Margaret had gone inside. 'I thought she was going to try for St Gertrude's.'

'You know, for a clever man, you can be awfully stupid sometimes,' remarked his wife. 'Of course she's going to try for St Gertrude's. But do you think she'll be any keener to do Cambridge Entrance if you pour cold water on her acting aspirations?'

'Well . . .'

'Trust me,' said Edith, linking her arm through his. 'I know what I'm talking about when it comes to girls and their fancies. Now, which way do you want to go? The cliff path or the rose garden?' But Rowlands had another idea.

'How do you feel like a walk down to the village?' he said.

When they reached the picturesque street where the filming was taking place, it was to find that nothing very much was going on even though there were a great many people milling about, and several large vans – full of equipment, presumably – drawn up in front of the row of whitewashed, tumbledown cottages which were amongst the village's most attractive features. 'Although everybody looks very busy,' murmured Edith to her husband. 'There are people lugging great cameras about, and moving lamps and other paraphernalia into position. But nobody seems to be doing any acting.'

'I expect they're taking a break,' replied Rowlands, recalling the frequency with which these had occurred during his previous experience of the filming process, four years before, in Berlin. 'I'm sure they'll start again before too long.' And indeed he had not finished speaking before there came a shout – 'Places, please!' – after which Hilary Carmody's measured tones could be heard requesting Miss La Mar's presence on the set. 'Who else is here?' said Rowlands to his wife while this was going on.

'Well,' she said, 'there's that rather vain young fellow, Quayle – he's whispering something to the Linden girl that's making her laugh. Then there's Eliot Dean. He looks rather annoyed about something. Keeps glancing at his watch. My goodness, people do look different with make-up on! They've darkened his eyebrows, which gives him a rather fierce expression . . . Oh, here's Dolores La Mar at last . . . I suppose it's the leading lady's prerogative to keep everybody else waiting.'

'Here I am, Hilly, darling!' sang out this lady with what seemed to Rowlands an artificial sweetness. 'Just got your summons. I thought you'd finished with me for now?'

'Not quite,' was the calm response. 'I want to run through the end of the scene again. From when Edward sees Laura for the first time.'

'I thought we'd talked about that.' A chill had entered the actress's voice.

'So we did, dear heart.' Carmody might have been soothing a fractious child. 'And we'll discuss it later, but not here. We'll take it from the end of Scene One. Outside Seaview Cottage.'

'That's old Mrs Penhaligon's place,' whispered Edith to her husband. 'It's the prettiest one in the row, with the thatched roof. Lovely roses, too.'

'We'll start from your speech, beginning, "I've been so alone . . ." Eliot, are you ready?'

'I've been ready for ages,' was the laconic reply.

'Good. Then – action!'

It was uncanny, Rowlands said to Edith afterwards, the way actors could switch into their roles, just like that. One moment, Dolores La Mar was a petulant fishwife, the next, a sensitive creature who had known love and loss: 'I've been so alone . . . So very much alone. It means so much to me to have someone who'll listen.' There was a pathetic catch in the voice which made all those listening hold their breath.

'You know I'll always listen.' This was Eliot Dean, in the character of Edward – a slightly more exaggerated version of his usual urbane self, Rowlands surmised. It struck him that actors must find it difficult to distinguish between their real selves and those they put on for the purposes of make-believe. 'I'll always be your friend,' Eliot/Edward was saying. Now it was Dolores/Desirée's turn to sound sincere: 'Ah, if only I could *believe* that . . .'

'Cut! Dolores, darling, I thought we'd agreed that the stress should be on the final word: "If only I could believe *that*." You've put it on the penultimate word.'

'Do you want me to do it again?'

'Yes, please. Let's take it from, "I'll always be your friend." And – action!'

'I'll always be your friend.'

'Ah, if only I could believe *that*—.'

'Miss Lefevre . . . Oh! I'm sorry. I didn't realise . . .' This was a new voice: that of Lydia Linden, Rowlands realised. Rather good, too, he thought, waiting to hear how the scene would develop. But his anticipation was not to be rewarded.

'You've done it *again*!' Dolores La Mar's voice rose to an ugly shriek. 'Coming in before my line has had a chance to resonate.'

'Dolores . . .' This was Hilary Carmody. She ignored him, continuing to storm at the girl.

'There's supposed to be a *pause* after I say the line. Then, and only then, do you come in. Or didn't they teach you about dramatic pauses at whatever third-rate drama school you went to?'

'I . . . I . . .' stammered Miss Linden. She sounded on the verge of tears. 'Excuse me.' A moment later she rushed off.

'That was uncalled for,' said Eliot Dean angrily. 'Poor kid! She was doing very well, I thought.'

'She cut me off,' insisted Miss La Mar. 'It ruined the whole scene.'

'Five minutes, everybody,' called Carmody, then, in an undertone to his leading lady, 'All right, Dolores. We'd better have this out. I told Lydia to come in when she did. She's meant to be interrupting. That's the reason she apologises. No, don't shake your head. You know perfectly well I'm right. Now I think you owe her an apology.'

'Over my dead body,' said Dolores La Mar sweetly.

'Really, Dolores . . .'

'Do you know, all this has given me the most ghastly headache?' said the actress. 'I think if you've finished with me for the time being, I might go back to the hotel, and put my feet up for an hour or two. I find this early rising rather wearing.'

'It's not the only thing that's wearing,' murmured Dean, as his co-star swept off. 'She's caused nothing but trouble, ever since she came on set.'

'Let's get on, shall we?' said the director, ignoring this remark. 'I'd like to run through your scene with Lydia – if someone can persuade her to join us.' But Miss Linden – perhaps emboldened by the sound of her rival's motor car starting up – had already returned to the fold.

'Sorry I flounced off,' she said. 'It's just that she gets my goat.'

'You're not the only one who feels like that,' said Eliot Dean. 'The woman's a public menace. Shall we take it from the top, Carmody?'

'If you would. All right, everybody – places. Scene Two, Take One. And – action!'

The little scene that followed was quite different in mood from the one which had preceded it. Instead of the heightened emotion, verging on melodrama, which had characterised the exchanges between Dolores La Mar and her co-star, there was restraint and subtlety. A young girl – played by Miss Linden – walked along the street, carrying an armful of parcels (or so Rowlands gleaned from his wife's whispered commentary). She – Miss Linden – encountered an older man (Mr Dean's character) who addressed her: 'I say – do let me give you a hand with those. They look rather heavy.'

'That's awfully nice of you, but I can manage, thanks.'

'Then at least let me open the gate for you.' The creaking of a gate followed, then a faint cry from Lydia

56

Linden – 'Oh!' – as the parcels slipped from her grasp.

'Didn't I say you should have let me help?' The amused tone in which Eliot Dean spoke did not conceal the interest his character evidently felt for the young woman.

'You're right. It was silly of me.'

'Cut! You need to make that pause longer, Liddy, darling. Look at him before you speak.'

'All right. Sorry.'

'Take it from, "Didn't I tell you . . ." And – action!'

'Didn't I tell you you should have let me help?'

This time there was a brief, but discernible, pause.

'You're right. It was silly of me . . . Oh, thanks ever so much!' – as the parcels were returned to her, presumably.

'Don't mention it. You know, you really shouldn't take things so much to heart.'

'I don't know what you mean.'

'Don't you?' Eliot Dean gave a sceptical laugh. 'Well, have it your own way. But don't think I haven't noticed the way she speaks to you.'

'If you mean Miss Lefevre, she's been awfully kind to me. She took me in when I was desperate.'

'As no doubt she reminds you twenty times a day! No, don't go.'

'I've got work to do, Mr Domville. Thank you for picking up my parcels.' There came the sound of brisk footsteps walking away, followed by that of a door being closed.

'Well, I'm damned,' said Eliot Dean softly.

'And – cut!' said Carmody. 'We'll print that. Thank you, everybody. Nice to see that some of us can do our jobs with the minimum of fuss. Take twenty minutes. Dean – a word, if I may.' The two men walked off, leaving Miss Linden and the rest of the crew to gather around the catering lorry that was dispensing coffee.

'Had enough?' said Rowlands to his wife.

'I think so. Although it is rather fascinating, the way they go about it,' she went on as they threaded their way through the crowd. 'I can see why you got so involved, that time in Berlin.'

Back at the hotel, they found that – rather than having carried out her expressed intention of going up to rest – Miss La Mar was holding court in the lounge. Surrounding her was a chorus of young admirers, among them the Rowlandses' two elder daughters, their cousins (excepting Walter) and the Simkins twins. 'Yes, it takes dedication if you want to make it in pictures,' the actress was saying as the two of them came in. 'I wasn't much older than you are when I got my first role.' It must have been Margaret she was addressing, thought Rowlands, but then he heard Anne say, 'I'm not sure I'd be very good at acting.'

'Nonsense! With looks like yours, you could do very well, child . . . But here are your parents, now,' said Dolores La Mar. 'Ask them. I am certain they will agree with me.' If Rowlands was certain of anything, it was that he would never agree with this woman about anything.

But then he heard Edith say, 'Agree about what?'

'Why, that if one wants something enough, one must be prepared to fight for it,' was the reply. 'I was just saying to your daughter here that if she wants to make something of herself, she should lose no time. Fifteen isn't too young to start in the film world. I had just passed my sixteenth birthday when I got my first walk-on part. Those were the silent days, of course.' She gave a musical laugh. 'It was a short called *Tea for Two*. I played the maid. Very silly I looked, too, in a cap and frilly apron – but it was a start, you see?'

'What makes you think,' said Rowlands, interrupting this fond reminiscence, 'that my daughter would be any good at acting? She's never shown any sign of it up to now, have you, Anne?'

'No, Daddy.' But there was a wistful note in his middle daughter's voice.

'Ah, that is so like a father – to object to his little girl's wanting to make a name for herself! My poor dear papa was the same . . .' A little sob escaped the actress. 'So protective. But you see, nowadays we make sure that our young ladies are well-chaperoned on set. We invite their mamas along, to keep a strict eye on them.'

'That's all very well,' said Edith, for whom this remark had no doubt been intended, 'but Anne's still got her matriculation exams to sit. She doesn't have time for amateur dramatics.'

'But Mummy . . .' This was Margaret. 'Miss La Mar was just explaining that one can do one's lessons on set.

They have special teachers, and . . .'

'It all sounds marvellous,' said her mother smoothly. 'Now, I think you've taken up quite enough of Miss La Mar's valuable time.' Because at that moment, Muriel Brierley – who must have been hovering nearby, Rowlands supposed – came forward.

'M-Miss La Mar . . .'

'Yes, what is it?' said her mistress, with barely concealed impatience.

'J-just the post. It's mostly fan mail. Drake's have forwarded a great pile . . .'

'You can deal with all those, surely? Send a signed photograph, with best wishes et cetera.'

'Yes, b-but . . . There are these others. One from Mr Farnham, I think.'

'Dear Dickie!' said Dolores La Mar, with her throaty laugh. 'Always so attentive. I'll answer it later. Anything else?'

'J-just this. I d-didn't recognise the handwriting, and so I thought . . .'

'Well, don't stand there gawping – open it!'

'Come along, girls,' said Rowlands firmly. 'And you too, Danny and Billy. Let's leave Miss La Mar in peace.'

Shepherding his little flock in front of him, he had reached the door of the lounge when there came an exclamation from the actress. 'What the *hell* . . . ?' Then, her voice rising with her temper, 'If this is your idea of a joke, Brierley, you're going to be very sorry.'

'But . . . but . . .' stammered the secretary.

'Out you go, all of you,' said Rowlands to his youthful charges. Then, turning back towards the two women on the far side of the room, 'I say, is anything wrong?' With Edith at his heels, he crossed the room in a couple of strides. 'What's happened?' he asked since there had been no reply to his first question. Miss Brierley could only sob, 'I d-didn't know . . . I swear I didn't know,' while from the actress there came only a furious muttering.

'I tell you, somebody will pay for this . . . Oh, stop your snivelling, Brierley. I don't really think you wrote it.' It was Edith who took the letter from her hand and read it aloud.

'*All traitors must die, as you will die, you evil bitch*. How perfectly filthy,' she added. 'I wonder who could have sent such a thing?'

Rowlands remembered the letter Cecily Nicholls had told him about earlier that morning. Another death threat, although that had been more of a general warning. 'The police should be informed at once,' he said.

'What's all this about the police?' said a voice from the door. It was Horace Cunningham.

'Your wife has had a rather nasty letter,' replied Rowlands, turning towards him.

'A letter? Let me see it.' The entrepreneur took it from Edith. 'Hmm,' he said when he had glanced at it. 'The usual muck. I don't think we need trouble the police with this, however.'

'But surely . . .'

'Actresses get used to this sort of thing,' said

Cunningham. 'Regrettable, but true – isn't it, my dear? I think the best way to deal with this is to put it in the fire. Dolores, it's time for your rest. You'll be wanted on set at two.'

'All right, Horace,' said the actress in a subdued tone.

'She looked white as a sheet,' said Edith when the couple, followed by Miss Brierley, had left the room. 'Who on earth do you think could have written such a beastly letter?'

'I've no idea,' said Rowlands. 'But I'd like to find out.'

'Fred, is that you?' Jack Ashenhurst put his head around the door.

'Present and correct,' said Rowlands.

'Jolly good. Only I wanted to ask you . . . I say, is it a bad moment?'

'Well . . .'

'You'd better tell him, Fred.'

Briefly, Rowlands summarised what had happened. 'I'm afraid it's not the first such letter, either.' He told his friend what Mrs Nicholls had said to him that morning.

'Do you mean Cecily received one of these things?' The anger in Ashenhurst's voice was obvious. His sister was very dear to him. Rowlands hastened to reassure him.

'I rather think it was meant for you – as the proprietor of the hotel.'

'A sort of warning-off, you think?'

'Something like that.'

'How very unpleasant,' said Ashenhurst. 'I might have known there'd be trouble of some kind with this film lot. I rather wish we hadn't agreed to have them.'

'Do you really think it can be one of them who's responsible?' said Edith.

'Bound to be, I should think.' Ashenhurst lowered his voice, although there was no one apart from themselves in the room. 'I mean, it can't have escaped your notice, either of you, that there's a fair bit of ill feeling towards our prima donna on the part of her fellow thespians.'

'Yes, but – death threats?' said Edith. 'Isn't that going rather far, even for actors?'

Chapter Four

'What was it you were going to ask me?' said Rowlands to his brother-in-law.

'Oh, nothing much. I've some cans of paraffin which need to be taken down to the cottages. I'd ask Pengelly, only he's busy rolling the tennis courts. So if you wouldn't mind lending a hand . . .'

'Glad to,' said Rowlands. Running a hotel, he knew, was a lot of work, much of it consisting of such small but important jobs which helped to keep the place ticking over. It would give him a chance to talk over the matter of the letters with Ashenhurst. The two men had been friends for a long time – since they'd first met at St Dunstan's in 1917, soon after Rowlands had been invalided out of the army. Ashenhurst had been the one who'd shown him the ropes – quite literally – since ropes and wires had been strung about the spacious Regent's

Park mansion which had become their temporary home, in order to guide newly blinded inmates through the unaccustomed darkness.

It had been Ashenhurst – himself blinded only a few months before – who had shown Rowlands that life might, after all, be worth living. The gratitude he had felt for the other's practical support had soon turned into a warm friendship, which had deepened over the years, and been further strengthened when Ashenhurst had married Rowlands' sister. Theirs was an easy comradeship, in which each could follow the other's mental processes, without the need for speech. Now, as they collected the cans of fuel – necessary for the oil lamps, which were the holiday cottages' only source of illumination – Rowlands at once picked up on the direction of Ashenhurst's thoughts when the latter said abruptly, 'So what do you think I should do?'

'I'd call the police. They take such matters seriously.'

'Didn't you say that Cunningham was against the idea?'

'What Cunningham thinks is beside the point. One of the letters was addressed to you, wasn't it?'

'That's true.' The friends trudged on in silence for a few minutes, each holding a heavy can in either hand. The path – a rough track, running between hedges of blackthorn – was a familiar one, with no obstacles to be negotiated beyond an occasional loose stone or tuft of coarse seagrass. It was one of the reasons, apart from the agreeable nature of the company, that Rowlands had come to relish his holidays in Cornwall, which successive visits had made almost as familiar as his own London home. That was the thing about being blind: one relied to a great extent on what one already knew to be there – although of course one could never take anything for granted. The world was full of moving objects and people. Training one's memory wasn't the half of it.

'If I get George Chegwin in on things, he'll only stump around, asking a lot of damn fool questions, and frightening the women,' said Ashenhurst, who had evidently been chewing things over – PC Chegwin, the local constable, being a conscientious, but somewhat unimaginative, character.

'I wasn't suggesting you should involve the local police force,' said Rowlands as they reached the fork in the path that led to the clifftop cottages. 'You'll remember I've got a friend at Scotland Yard?'

'You're surely not suggesting we should bring him into it?' said Ashenhurst. 'I mean, nothing's actually happened yet.'

'Do you really want to wait until it does?' said Rowlands. 'Besides, I was only thinking of telephoning Alasdair Douglas at this stage. His advice might be useful, that's all.'

'I can see that,' said his friend as they reached the first of the cottages and pushed open the garden gate. In the same moment, the door of the cottage flew open.

'Morning!' cried Colonel Rutherford in his cheerful baritone.

'Good morning, Colonel. Here's your paraffin, as ordered.'

'Good show.' The other hastened to relieve Ashenhurst of his burden. 'Not that we've had much need of the lamps, these light evenings,' he said. 'But the Mem sometimes likes to read a page or two of her latest thriller before we turn in – don't you, my dear?' Because at that moment, they were joined by Mrs Rutherford, a quiet little woman, whose taste for this bloodthirsty kind of fiction seemed at odds with her gentle demeanour, Rowlands thought. But perhaps that was to underestimate a woman who, by her husband's account, had 'roughed it' in a variety of remote hill stations across the subcontinent, and had dealt with a range of emergencies from outbreaks of typhus to political insurgencies without ever losing her sangfroid. Now she said, 'Don't talk such rot, Johnny. You know you like a good murder, as much as I do.'

'Maybe so, maybe so,' admitted her husband, somewhat sheepishly. 'Well, mustn't stand here gassing all day. I'll just put these in the woodshed, and then we ought to make tracks if we're to be in time for luncheon' – the couple having elected to take their meals at the hotel; although, as Colonel Rutherford was quick to point out, the 'Mem' was perfectly capable of knocking up a tasty snack out of tins and a dash of curry powder, should the need arise. Rowlands, who had set down his two cans upon the path, now picked them up again.

'Where do you want these?' he asked Ashenhurst.

'They're for next door,' was the reply. 'A new guest

arrives the end of the week. Lady writer, I gather.'

'Company for you, my dear,' said the Colonel, returning from carrying out his errand. 'A literary lady, no less.'

'We had one of those at Poona, as I recall,' said Millicent Rutherford. 'Used to recite reams of her own verse to the subalterns after dinner – most of it dreadful stuff.'

'Well, I hope Miss Barnes won't bore you to death with poetry,' laughed Ashenhurst. 'I gather she writes detective stories. Come on, Rowlands, old man. We'd better drop these off and then get back to the house. As the Colonel says, Mrs Jago'll be wanting to serve lunch.' But Rowlands' attention had been arrested by something else.

'Did you say the lady's name was Barnes?' he asked. 'I know someone of that name; I wonder if it can be the same one? What age is she, do you know?'

'No idea. It was Dorothy who took the call.'

'Did I hear my name?' said Rowlands' sister, coming out of the empty cottage at that moment.

'Ah, there you are, Dottie! I was just saying to Fred here . . .'

'Give me a hand with these, will you?' said Dorothy, piling blankets and sheets into her husband's arms. 'You, too, Fred. I thought these could do with a good airing before our guest arrives.'

'Sometimes I feel I'm nothing but a packhorse,' grumbled Ashenhurst good-humouredly as the three of them started to walk back towards the hotel. 'I say,

Dottie,' he began once more. 'What age would you say our lady writer was?'

'I couldn't say exactly – I only spoke to her on the telephone. About thirty, I'd guess.'

'What's her Christian name?' said Rowlands. His sister thought for a moment.

'Can't remember. Something fanciful. Evadne or Eirene or some such.'

'Might it be Iris?'

'That's it! Why, do you know her?'

'I believe so,' said Rowlands thoughtfully. Now what on earth, he wondered, could Iris Barnes, journalist and sometime SIS operative – last encountered on the night train from Berlin to Paris – be doing in sleepy Cornwall?

He had little opportunity to reflect on this interesting question over the next few days, which were as busy as days ever got in this sleepy backwater. It amused him to compare what passed for being busy here with what it meant in his London life. The former might include a swim before breakfast, followed by a walk down to the village or along the cliffs, with a picnic lunch or a pint of beer to be enjoyed at some point, and so on, throughout the leisurely day. Of course it was different for Jack and Dorothy, with so many guests to cater for, particularly now this film company had arrived. They spent their days ordering supplies, overseeing meals and dealing with the multiplicity of requests – and occasional complaints – from a constant stream of visitors. Even so, you couldn't call the life here busy in the way that London was busy.

A memory of his daily journey to work by train and Underground, with its noise and smells and jostling bodies, briefly interposed itself between Rowlands and the beauty of the Cornish evening.

Of course, he admitted to himself, as he strolled across the lawn to join the others on the terrace for preprandial drinks, you couldn't deny that these actors worked pretty hard. Getting up at the crack of dawn to go down to the village for the shoot, lunching on sandwiches from the catering van before further takes (the jargon was coming back to him) consumed the afternoon. Then returning to the hotel for drinks and dinner before sallying out again, as often as not, so that the director could take advantage of a moonlight effect. Yes, he supposed they worked hard enough.

In honour of their guests, the Ashenhursts were serving champagne cocktails. These went down very well with almost everybody; Rowlands himself would have preferred a beer, and his wife said she'd stick to sherry, thanks, because cocktails gave her a headache. But for the rest of the assembled adults, the heady combination of brandy and champagne seemed to be having the desired effect of breaking down barriers and overcoming natural reserve. Whether this was a good thing or not Rowlands didn't permit himself to wonder. But he noticed that, under the influence of the potent brew, even his normally reserved sister was starting to unbend. She and Muriel Brierley appeared to be getting on like a house on fire. 'It must be an interesting life,' Rowlands heard her say.

'Travelling all over the world, as you do. I spent some time in Argentina once.'

'Oh, travel's all very well,' replied the secretary, sounding a little less meek and self-effacing than on the previous occasions Rowlands had been made aware of her presence. 'I . . . I mean, Buenos Aires is a fascinating city – the Paris of South America they say, don't they? – but it's so hot, and then there's the language problem.'

'Oh?'

'Most of the nicer people speak English, of course,' said Miss Brierley. 'And the hotel staff, for the most part. But it's always so difficult dealing with railway porters and the like.'

'Ah,' said Dorothy. 'I see what you mean.' Because of course that would be her life, poor young woman, thought Rowlands – arguing with porters about lost luggage, and with hotel receptionists about mix-ups over rooms.

'Oh, the people are charming of course,' went on Miss Brierley, perhaps afraid she had given the wrong impression. 'Such lovely, old-fashioned manners. But one gets rather lonely, being so far from home.'

'Yes,' said Dorothy. 'I remember that, too.'

On Rowlands' left, an amicable argument was taking place between the director and his leading man.

'I still don't see,' Eliot Dean was saying, 'why he has to be a drunk. I mean, I can do drunks, of course – nothing easier – but . . .' Here he adopted an exaggerated slurring of the speech which Rowlands guessed was not the result of one cocktail too many but merely a trick of his trade. 'It maksh one look so bally unattractive, 'fyou shee whadda' mean . . .'

Carmody laughed at this performance, as he was meant to, but said firmly, 'It's in the script, I'm afraid. Edward's supposed to be fond of the bottle.'

'But only until he's rescued by the love of a good woman,' put in Lydia Linden, who must have come up at this moment.

'Yes, I was coming to that,' said Dean. 'The scene where Laura walks into the cottage and I'm lying dead drunk on the sofa . . . doesn't it strike you as rather, well, undignified?'

'That's the whole point,' said Carmody. 'We're meant to see Edward at his lowest ebb. As Liddy says, it's when he falls in love with Laura that things take a turn for the better. Now, I really think we should give over talking shop.'

But Dean wasn't finished. 'I mean to say – what sort of a girl would be attracted to a man like that? A . . . a lush. It doesn't seem plausible.'

'He's an artist, isn't he?' said the girl. 'Plenty of women like the artistic type, even if they do hit the sauce from time to time. Why, you should've seen some of the chaps I was at RADA with! Positive dipsomaniacs, some of 'em.'

'What a very colourful life you seem to have led.' It was Dolores La Mar who spoke. It seemed to Rowlands that a certain chill fell across the company as she did so. 'Horace dear,' she went on. 'Do fetch me another of these divine cocktails, will you? I feel I deserve it, after the day I've had.'

'Surely it wasn't as bad as all that, darling?' said Laurence Quayle, sauntering over to join the group. 'I thought our scene together went rather well.'

'It was all right, I suppose,' said the actress grudgingly. 'But . . .' Her voice took on a shriller note. 'Horace, I thought I asked you to get me another drink?'

'Another drink. Certainly, my dear.' It crossed Rowlands' mind that those who knew Cunningham solely in his role as international financier would have been surprised at the meekness with which he complied with his wife's request.

'That's another thing I wanted to talk to you about, Hilly,' went on Miss La Mar, turning her attention to the director. 'That line of Desirée's. I don't like it.'

'Which line, Dolores?'

'That line. When she's talking to Larry – I mean Louis – and she says, "But darling, I'm so much older than you are."'

There was a stifled snort from Lydia Linden.

'And then he says, "You're ageless. You just grow more and more beautiful with every year,"' said Carmody.

'Exactly. I don't see why he has to say that, either. Ah, my drink at last!' she cried as Cunningham returned. She took it from him without thanks and gulped it down. 'It's ridiculous, the way he keeps harping on my . . . on Desirée's age.'

'It's in the script,' said Carmody. A steeliness had entered his voice. But if his leading lady detected this, she took no notice.

'"It's in the script, it's in the script,"' she chanted, in exaggerated mimicry of the director's diffident tones. 'I'm sick of hearing you say this.' She lowered her voice dramatically so that only those standing in her immediate vicinity could hear her. 'Let me tell you something. Scripts can be changed.'

'Dolores, we've been though all this.'

'Yes, and you always give me the same answer! I've got to say these stupid lines because "we can't afford to reshoot the scenes."' Again, the cruelly accurate mimicry of Carmody's voice. 'Well, let me tell you, Mister Director,' she went on. 'We *can* afford to reshoot if I say so! May I remind you that Horace here is a major investor in this rotten picture, and if I'm not happy with it, then he won't be happy either, will you, Horace?'

'No, I won't be happy at all,' agreed Cunningham quietly.

Fortunately, at that moment, Mrs Nicholls announced that dinner was served, and the party began to move towards the dining room, downing drinks as they went. Rowlands, who was waiting for his wife, was one of the last to leave the terrace, and so was privy to another exchange.

'She can't do that, can she?' It was Lydia Linden.

'What – cancel the picture? Certainly she can,' replied Eliot Dean, who had lingered to finish his cigarette. 'Didn't you hear what she said? That hubby of hers owns a controlling share in the production company. If she tells him to withdraw the funds, he'll do it. Easy as winking,' added the actor, with a mirthless laugh.

'But . . . surely that would be cutting off her nose to spite her face?' said Miss Linden, sounding genuinely perplexed.

'You obviously don't know Dolores as well as I do,' said Dean. 'I should say she's entirely capable of doing just that. After all, her career's not likely to suffer because of it. She's got a rich husband to see her through the lean times.'

'Lucky for some,' said the girl, then, as if the thought had just occurred to her, 'I thought you and she were such friends?'

'Not especially. I mean . . .' He gave an embarrassed laugh. 'I suppose we *were* friends, at one time, but . . .'

'I heard rather *more* than friends,' said Miss Linden coolly.

'Who told you that?' The actor's suave manner seemed momentarily to have deserted him. 'And even if it were true – once – it isn't the case now. The fact is, Liddy . . . dear girl . . .' But Miss Linden appeared not to have heard him.

'Come along,' she said briskly. 'We don't want to be late for dinner, do we? I'm starving.'

Dinner passed without incident, or at least without any renewal of the ill-tempered conversation which had marred the cocktail hour. The talk amongst the actors was general, most staying off the subject of whether or not the 'show', as the saying had it, would 'go on'. Only Laurence Quayle saw fit to allude to the contretemps.

'Well!' he said brightly as the first course was cleared, and the second handed around. 'I wonder how much longer we'll all be together like this? If a certain party has her way, our days at the Cliff House Hotel might be numbered.'

'I say, what an unusual ring!' interjected Cecily Nicholls, who was passing the actors' table on her way back from dealing with some minor problem in the kitchen. 'Such an attractive design!'

'Oh, do you like it?' said Dolores La Mar, for it was she to whom Mrs Nicholls had spoken. 'Horace bought it for me in Venice, didn't you, dear?' Her husband murmured his agreement. 'It's got quite a colourful history,' went on the actress. 'I gather it belonged to some sixteenth-century contessa – a present from one of her lovers.'

'It's very pretty,' said Mrs Nicholls, who (Rowlands suspected) had only admired the ring in the first place as a way of changing the subject and thus averting another quarrel.

'Isn't it? I'm very fond of emeralds. And the chased gold design is attractive. But the best thing about my ring is that it contains a secret.' She must have touched a hidden catch to release a spring, for there was a murmur of surprise from those around the table. 'You see?' said Miss La Mar, gratified at once more being the centre of attention. 'The top lifts up, to reveal what's hidden inside.'

'My dear,' said Horace Cunningham in a warning voice. 'I thought I urged you not to . . .'

'Poison,' said the actress triumphantly. 'It's a poison ring, as used by the Medici. So of course it's got some poison inside it.'

'What kind of poison?' Laurence Quayle sounded genuinely fascinated.

'Some South American thing – curare, I suppose. I got it when we were on our Argentina tour. The most *sinister* old Indian sold it to me . . . Oh, don't look like that, Horace!'

'I thought you'd thrown it away,' he said.

'Don't be so stuffy! What would have been the point of that? It's a poison ring, as I said.' She clicked it shut.

'Luckily, it doesn't hold very much,' said Eliot Dean. 'So I think we're all safe from Dolores's murderous wiles.'

'On the contrary,' retorted the prima donna. 'There's quite enough poison in my ring to ensure a very deep sleep – with little chance of waking – for the entire household.'

'I think you should throw it away at once,' said Hilary Carmody, his tone unaccustomedly grave.

'Nonsense! That would spoil the whole effect,' was Miss La Mar's reply. 'I should have thought you, of all people, would understand that, Hilly darling!'

After this brittle exchange of views, conversation lapsed once more, and a listless mood prevailed in the big dining room. This was no doubt a consequence of the heat, which had diminished not a whit. It was almost too hot to eat, thought Rowlands, toying half-heartedly with his cold ham and salad, even though Cecily had evidently gone to some trouble to order the lightest meal possible, with that local speciality Cornish ice cream, finishing up the repast. 'Oof!' said Edith, who disliked the heat. 'I wonder when this weather's going to break? It feels as if we're in for a good storm.'

'Oh, Mummy!' This was Joan. 'We want the nice weather to last until at least the end of the week. It's the tennis tournament on Saturday – remember?'

'In which case, it's time you were in bed,' said her mother. 'Tennis tournament or no tennis tournament, you can't afford to miss out on sleep at your age.'

'But Mummy . . .'

'No buts. It's gone eight o'clock. When I said you could have dinner with the grown-ups, I didn't mean you could stay up until all hours.'

'I've my shell collection to finish cataloguing anyway,' said Joan good-naturedly.

'Well, don't stay up too late doing it,' said Edith. 'And Joanie, you really must take care not to leave that bucket of yours about.' This, Rowlands knew, was Joan's pride and joy, bought with her pocket money at the village shop. 'I almost fell over it last night when I came up to tuck you in. What do you keep in it, anyway? It's made an awful mess on the floor of your room.'

'Shells. Crabs. Sea urchins, sometimes,' said Joan, with the satisfaction of the born collector.

'Make sure you keep them outside in future,' said her

mother. 'I'll be up to turn off your light in ten minutes.'

Joan's two elder sisters had plans of their own for the evening. Anne, Rowlands knew, was engaged in putting the finishing touches to a landscape she was working on, while Margaret announced that she and Jonathan were going for a walk down to the village. 'Don't stay out too late,' said Rowlands. 'If you're not back by half past ten, your mother and I will send out a search party.'

'Really, Daddy,' was the amused reply. 'I'm not a child, you know!' Which, as Edith pointed out when they were alone, was nothing but the truth.

'At her age, you'd already been going out to work for a year,' she said.

'Don't remind me,' said Rowlands. 'If I can spare my children that, I'll feel I've achieved something.'

Coffee was served in the lounge, as on the previous evening, and the company made its way there in fits and starts. Amongst them were some of the younger generation. As he and Edith took their places on their usual sofa nearest the door, Rowlands overheard a snatch of conversation between Walter Metzner, and the other Simkins twin. Its significance didn't strike him at the time. 'I tell you, I would not hesitate,' Walter was saying, with the quiet determination that Rowlands had come to recognise as characteristic. 'There is no question about it. If I decide that this is the right thing to do, then I will do it.'

'Easy for you to say,' said the Simkins twin – Rory was his name, Rowlands recalled. There was a faintly jeering note in his voice. Walter, however, seemed unperturbed by this.

'Yes, it is easy to say – and yes, I would do it if I had made such a decision. Many others have done so. I believe their cause is right.'

'You can't possibly know whether their cause is right or not.'

'After Guernica,' said Walter quietly. 'Everybody knows. Now you will excuse me, please. I have some letters to write.'

So they were talking about Spain, thought Rowlands. Even though he didn't share his sister's enthusiasm for the Republican cause, he had gleaned enough about the political situation to know that young Metzner was right. After the bombing of innocent civilians by the German airforce, everybody should know which side they were on.

Edith was already handing round the coffee cups to their immediate circle, which consisted of themselves, John and Daphne Simkins, and Jack Ashenhurst. Rory Simkins, after hanging disconsolately around the edge of the group of adults for a few moments, muttered something about going for a walk. 'What an energetic lot our children are!' remarked Daphne Simkins, a pleasant, if – to Rowlands' mind – rather insipid woman, who seemed content to sit and marvel at the sporting prowess of her husband and sons (all keen tennis players, hikers, and sailors) without feeling the need herself to engage in anything more active then sitting in a deckchair, complaining of the heat. 'Always dashing about.'

'Yes, it would seem that the allure of the film world has palled,' said Ashenhurst. 'A good thing too, if you ask me. Much healthier for young people to be out in the fresh air, than to be bothering their heads with all that malarky.'

'As it happens,' said Edith drily, 'there's some filming going on tonight, down at the harbour. Mrs Jago told me. It's her niece's pub, the Blue Anchor, they're using, apparently. I imagine that's where Margaret and Jonathan have gone.' As she finished speaking, there came a brief altercation from the far side of the room where the film company was gathered, grouped as usual around its star.

'I thought I'd made it clear,' Hilary Carmody was saying, in his most patient tones, 'that only those involved in the pub scene are being called. That's Dean, of course, and Clarence Fothergill, who's playing the landlord – a nice little cameo part for him, dear old fellow. Apart from those two, there are a few extras – non-speaking parts, of course – and Miss Linden.'

'Of course,' said Dolores La Mar witheringly. 'It seems as if you can't shoot a scene without her.'

'Now, Dolores, there's no need to take that tone. Lydia's a part of the scene and nothing you can say will change that.'

'I wouldn't be too sure of that,' said Miss La Mar, her voice dangerously calm. 'I don't think you can have been listening to what I said earlier.'

'I was listening all right,' said Carmody coldly. 'All I can say is you'd be making a big mistake if you pull out of the picture now.'

'Oh it won't just be me,' she shot back. 'There's the little matter of Horace's money, too.'

'That of course will be Mr Cunningham's decision,' said the director. 'And now if you'll excuse me, we're already running late. Dean, we'll take Lydia's car, I think. Lydia, are you ready?'

'Ready and waiting,' was the reply.

'Good. Then let's get going. Dolores, we'll talk about this later.'

'I'll be asleep later,' said Dolores La Mar sweetly. 'If you want to talk to me, it'll have to be now.'

'I can't spare the time right now. Perhaps,' said Carmody in a voice like ice, 'tomorrow morning first thing would suit you?'

'I suppose it'll have to,' said the prima donna. 'Although I can't promise that you'll like what I have to say any more tomorrow than you do now.'

'That's a risk I'll have to take.' Then Carmody was gone, taking the two actors with him and leaving what seemed to Rowlands to be a definite atmosphere behind.

Chapter Five

Now that the sun had set, the air grew cooler, and the Rowlandses strolled in the garden for half an hour. They talked of this and that – whether the spell of hot weather would hold, and if Edith should break the journey home in two weeks' time by spending a night or two with a friend in Poole. 'It seems silly not to take up Frances's invitation,' she said as they walked slowly across the springy turf. 'It must be three years since she stayed with us in Kingston.'

'You should go,' said Rowlands, pausing to light a cigarette. 'I can manage quite well for a few days. Margaret's getting to be quite a good little cook, and besides, your mother will be back by then, won't she?'

'So she will. Very well, I'll write to Frances tonight.'

From the base of the cliff along whose top they were walking came the murmur of waves breaking on the rocks, a sound which was usually enough to calm jangled nerves and reduce the listener to a pleasantly soporific state. But tonight Rowlands hardly heard it. He felt restless and dissatisfied – a mood he connected with the antagonism he had witnessed earlier between various members of the cast of *Forbidden Desires*. 'D'you know, I think perhaps Jack was right? It was a mistake to have these film people here,' he said. 'They've spoilt the place, with their constant bickering. I'll be glad when they've gone.'

'I don't imagine the girls would agree with you,' said Edith. 'It's been a bit of excitement for them.'

'For Margaret, perhaps.'

'Anne, too.'

'I didn't think she was all that interested.'

Edith laughed. 'Where do you think she is at this moment, if not down at the harbour with the others? And before you say anything, I told her she might go. It'll make a change for her to do something other than messing about with paints.' This talk of their elder daughters reminded her that she still had to look in on Joan. 'Stay close to the house, won't you?' she said when Rowlands expressed a wish to finish his cigarette before turning in. 'We don't want you wandering off and falling over a cliff.'

He assured her that he wouldn't do anything so rash, and that he was only going to take another turn on the terrace. Which was how he came to be standing directly beneath the open French windows that led onto the balcony of the room above, in time to hear what followed.

A woman's voice – it was Dolores La Mar's – sounding

quite near. She must have come out onto the balcony, Rowlands thought. 'I suppose you think you've been very clever, don't you? But if you imagine anything you say will make me change my mind, you've got another thing coming . . .' Then, in answer to something that was said by whoever was in the room behind, 'I tell you, you haven't heard the last of this! If I find you've said anything about this to another living soul, it'll be a matter for my lawyers. Now get out of my sight.'

Not wanting to draw attention to his presence, Rowlands remained frozen for a moment, until the slam of the French windows from above told him that Miss La Mar had gone inside. He wondered who it was she'd been addressing – Carmody, perhaps? Although surely he was down at the harbour by this time? Of course, he might have come back for just this purpose. He pushed open the French doors that led from the terrace into the main lounge, having first thrown away the stub of his cigarette. He half-expected to find the room empty – most of those earlier assembled having already decamped to baths and bed, or in the case of the filming party, to a night's work. But the smell of a fine Havana told him he was mistaken. 'Ah, Rowlands! Taking the night air?' It was Horace Cunningham. So, whoever it was, it hadn't been her husband whom Dolores La Mar had been berating.

'Yes,' he replied. 'I think we might be in for a storm.'

'It's oppressive enough. Some rain would clear the air.' Then, as Rowlands moved towards the door,

Cunningham said, 'Join me for a nightcap? There's quite a decent brandy on the sideboard.'

'I won't, thanks all the same. I'm expecting my daughters and the Simkins boys back at half past ten. Thought I'd walk up the drive and meet them.'

'It's not a quarter past yet,' said Cunningham. 'You've time for a snifter.'

'No, thanks. But I'll sit with you while you have yours.'

Cunningham got up and went over to the sideboard. There was the sound of a decanter being unstoppered, and of a measure being poured out. 'I expect you'll be glad to see the last of us,' said the entrepreneur as he regained his seat. It was so exactly what Rowlands felt that he answered too quickly, 'Not at all. It's been very interesting.' Cunningham gave a short, unamused laugh.

'Interesting! That's one word for it. Well, we'll be out of your hair sooner rather than later, if my wife has her way. And she *does* like her way,' he added drily.

'Forgive me if this sounds impertinent,' said Rowlands. 'But was she serious about stopping work on the picture?' Again, Horace Cunningham laughed.

'Serious?' He had a trick, Rowlands noticed, of echoing his interlocutor's last word. 'Who can say if Dolores is serious, except Dolores herself? All I know is she's asked me to call my lawyers in the morning about withdrawing my investment in the production.'

'That does sound as if she means it,' said Rowlands, wondering how this would affect the film company's agreement with the Ashenhursts' hotel. It was all very well for the likes of Cunningham to talk about cancelling films and withdrawing funds, but other people's livelihoods were involved. As if the other guessed his unspoken comment, he said, 'Oh, don't worry! Whatever happens, Avalon Productions will pay its bills. I'll see to that.' Just then, a small commotion in the hall outside signalled the return of the Rowlands girls and the Simkins twins. A moment later the four of them burst into the lounge, full of the excitements of the evening.

'Oh, Daddy, it was such fun – you should have come with us! cried Anne.

'Daddy, they let me stand behind the bar, polishing glasses,' cut in Margaret breathlessly. 'Miss Linden said I did it very well. I ought to have a screen test, she said.'

'That was very nice of her,' said Rowlands. 'But aren't you a bit young for standing behind bars?'

'Oh Daddy, don't be such a spoilsport! I wasn't actually serving drinks.'

'Glad to hear it,' he said. 'Now, it's time you two were off to bed. Thank you for walking them back,' he added to a Simkins twin – whether Rory or Jonathan he couldn't be sure, since both sounded pretty much the same.

'That's all right, sir,' said Jonathan – or was it Rory? The foursome said their good-nights and sloped off, still chattering excitedly of camera angles and boom shots.

'Well, well,' said Cunningham. 'It appears your daughters have caught the acting bug.'

'So it would seem.'

'It is easily caught,' went on the other in a meditative tone. 'But not so easy to cure oneself of the disease. Fine girls,' he added as Rowlands too made a move to go. 'I should think you're proud of 'em, aren't you?'

'Oh yes,' said Rowlands.

'Good show. Never had any children m'self – first wife was an invalid, y'know, and of course Dolores has had her career. Well, good night to you.'

'Good night.' Climbing the stairs, Rowlands thought over his conversation with Cunningham. What an odd fish he was! A most unlikely consort for the volatile Dolores La Mar. Well, they said that opposites attracted. Yawning, he let himself into the bedroom.

'Fred? Is that you?' his wife mumbled.

'Go back to sleep,' he said. 'The girls are back now.'

'Good.' Soon she was asleep once more. Rowlands undressed and put on his dressing gown, then went along the corridor to the bathroom, which was shared by the other rooms on this floor, the exception being those occupied by Dolores La Mar and her spouse, which were linked by their own bathroom. He ran a bath, hoping that the clanking of the pipes wouldn't disturb his neighbours, then recollected that Dean, who had the room next to the Rowlandses, Miss Linden, whose room was at the end of the hall overlooking the garden, and Carmody, who had the room facing onto the terrace, would still be out filming. As a rule, Rowlands preferred a morning bath, but tonight he felt in need of a good long soak, to ease away the tensions of the day. He was just thinking about getting out when he heard the car pull up on the gravel outside, and the voices of those disembarking from it calling good night to one another. The actors were back, then. He judged it to be about half past eleven.

He towelled himself dry, then, having made sure that he hadn't left the floor slippery for the next person, let himself out of the bathroom and set off in the direction of his room. As he did so, he heard raised voices – one of them a man's – coming from the direction of Dolores La Mar's room; evidently she wasn't yet asleep, either. 'I've told you,' she said shrilly, in answer to whatever the other had said. 'Nothing you can say will make me change my mind.' A moment later, someone came rushing out of the room, and along the corridor, almost colliding with Rowlands. Whoever it was muttered an apology, then hurried past. Carmody, thought Rowlands – unless it was Dean? Well, whoever it was wasn't his concern. Taking care not to wake his sleeping wife, he got into bed and prepared himself for sleep, but it was a while before sleep came. As he lay there, listening to the roaring of the sea, and the wind rattling the branches of the fir tree outside the window, something – not indigestion, but its psychological counterpart – troubled him.

The guns were loud tonight. Each burst of shellfire struck the ear like a physical blow, making one's teeth rattle in one's head like peas on a tin drum. Crack. Boom. Thump. *The noise seemed to come from overhead – yet*

the enemy was at least a quarter of a mile away, surely?
Crash. Boom. Flash.

A white light flooded the sky with unearthly light, penetrating even his closed eyelids. He woke with a start, to the heavy drumming of rain.

Fragments of his dream remained with him. He had been back there again, he knew – to the hellish landscape of the Western Front. He and some of his pals – Tommy Peachum was one, and Reg Driver – were pushing a loaded limber up the mud-encrusted slope of the Salient. The horse had got stuck in the mud – or perhaps there never was a horse at all, just the three, no, four of them: himself, Peachum, Driver and another man whose face he never saw. Because he *could* see, that was the fact of it, just as he always could in dreams. There they all were, shoving the heavy gun up an incline that never seemed to end, slipping and sliding under the weight of the thing, which seemed always about to roll back down on top of them. 'Shoulders to the wheel, eh?' grinned Tommy, revealing a mouthful of bad teeth. Nice chap, old Tommy – *but wasn't he dead? Stepped on a mine, poor bugger.* 'What a game, eh?' he muttered, grinning his death's head grin. 'What a bloody game.'

What was it that had woken him? The thunder, perhaps, or the cry of a night bird? The roaring of the sea had subsided, he noticed, drowned out by the sound of the rain. He felt for his watch. Two o'clock. Yes, it must have been the rain that had woken him. Even so, it took him a while to drop off again. A feeling of unease

– perhaps engendered by his dream – was hard to shake off, so that when he woke again at six, he knew there was little point in trying to sleep any longer. Moving about the room as quietly as possible so as to avoid waking Edith, he washed, shaved and dressed. Then, closing the door softly behind him, he stepped out into the corridor.

As he made his way along it towards the stairs, he became aware of a faint sound – a harsh sobbing, as of someone in distress. 'Who's there?' he called. Rapid footsteps came towards him. Then the woman – for it was a woman – gave a low cry that seemed to mingle anger and fear.

'Let me pass. It is not I who have done this.' It was the maid, Caterina Casals.

'Done what? What are you talking about?' he demanded. But before he could get her to explain herself, she slipped past him, and ran down the stairs.

Before he had time to make sense of this encounter, there came a shout from the far end of the corridor. 'Oh God! Help, somebody! Why doesn't somebody come?' The voice was Horace Cunningham's. Without further thought, Rowlands ran in the direction from which the cry had come, almost colliding with Cunningham outside the latter's door.

'What's the matter?' he cried. 'Is somebody ill?'

'It's my wife,' said Cunningham in a flat voice. 'I can't seem to wake her. I'm rather afraid she may be dead.'

Rowlands gaped at him. 'But . . . are you sure? I mean . . .'

'I'm quite sure,' said Cunningham. 'See for yourself if you don't believe me.' He stood aside, as if to let the other man pass. 'It was the girl who found her,' he went on, meaning Miss Casals, Rowlands assumed. 'She came hammering on my door not three minutes ago, yelling blue murder.' But Rowlands was already inside the room, and in two swift strides had reached the bed. It was apparent from the briefest examination of the still form that lay there, that Cunningham had been right in his assessment. Dolores La Mar was dead, and had been for some time, it appeared, from the coldness and rigidity of her flesh.

As Rowlands bent closer, desperately searching for a pulse in the slender throat, he caught the whiff of a pungent smell. He sniffed again to make sure, but it was unmistakeable: garlic. Which was strange, because there hadn't been a trace of garlic in the meal they'd had last night. The long list of rules submitted by Miss Brierley in advance of the actors' arrival had specified that it must on no account be used in any of the cooking. Miss La Mar wouldn't stand for it, she'd explained – it put her off, during close-ups, if her co-stars stank of the stuff. And yet here was the smell of garlic, reeking from her open mouth.

'What in God's name is going on?' said a voice from the open door. It was Eliot Dean. A moment later, he was inside the room. 'Dolores!' he cried hoarsely, pushing Rowlands aside. 'What's the matter with her? Wake up, Dolores!' Then, on a note of rising hysteria, 'Why doesn't she wake up?' He must have made some move towards the inert figure on the bed because Cunningham said sharply, 'Don't touch her!'

'I wasn't going to,' was the reply. 'Or . . . or only to check that she . . . that she . . .' Suddenly he broke down. 'How did it happen?' he cried. 'She was perfectly well last night.'

'We should call a doctor,' said Rowlands, who had reached the conclusion by now that even this expedient could only confirm what was obvious to them all. 'In the meantime, I'll get my wife. She's had medical experience, and so . . .' But just then there came another voice: it was Cecily Nicholls.

'What's happened?' she asked. 'Has there been an accident?'

'It's Miss La Mar,' said Rowlands, stepping aside to let her get closer to the bed and its pathetic cargo. 'Can anything be done for her, do you think?'

She came closer. 'No,' she said after a few moments. 'She's beyond help, poor woman.' Swiftly, she took charge. 'Mr Dean, would you please take Mr Cunningham downstairs? He's had a shock. Ask Mrs Jago – you'll find her in the kitchen – to make you both some tea. Lots of sugar – that's right.' She waited until the two men had gone before saying to Rowlands, 'I don't think there's much Bill – Dr Finch, that is – will be able to do, but he'll have to be called, just the same.'

'Yes,' said Rowlands, thinking that there'd be the matter of the death certificate to sign.

'Could you ask Jack to ring him?' Mrs Nicholls went on. 'I'll wait with her until he gets here.'

'All right. Do you want Edith with you?'

Mrs Nicholls said that she did. 'What a dreadful thing to have happened,' she said. 'If only we'd had some idea that she wasn't well.'

Rowlands paused in the doorway. 'What do you think it was? Heart?'

'I couldn't say,' was the reply. 'But it looks as if she'd taken a sleeping powder. There's an empty paper beside the glass, and some kind of whitish residue in the bottom of it.'

'I shouldn't touch it, if I were you,' said Rowlands quickly. 'Just in case . . .'

'What do you mean, Fred?'

But he wouldn't – or couldn't – say what it was he meant. It was just a feeling he had. 'I'll get Edith,' he said.

His wife was awake when he entered the room. 'What's going on?' she said sleepily. 'I heard shouting.' He explained as succinctly as he could, and then passed on Mrs Nicholls' request for Edith's company, repeating what he'd said about being careful to avoid touching the objects in the dead woman's room as far as possible. 'But why, Fred?' said Edith as she hastened to get dressed. 'You surely can't think there's anything untoward about this, can you?'

'I don't know. We'll have to wait and see what the doctor thinks. But if she'd taken sleeping powders, it

94

raises the possibility that she might have miscalculated the amount.'

'An overdose, you mean?'

'Perhaps.'

Outside the door of the room they parted – Edith to join her friend, and Rowlands to inform Jack Ashenhurst what had happened. He found the latter already up and about, having been roused, like Rowlands himself, by the sound of voices and hurrying footsteps. He said he would telephone Dr Finch. 'With any luck, we should catch him before he goes out on his early morning rounds,' he said as the two men descended the stairs. Leaving Ashenhurst to make his call, Rowlands followed the murmur of voices to the lounge.

'I just can't believe it,' Horace Cunningham was saying. 'Last night she was alive and well, and now she's . . .' He broke off, as if the dreadful word choked him.

'Drink up, old man,' said Eliot Dean, who was presiding over the drinks tray where, to judge by the smell, he had been dispensing brandy to the bereaved man, as well as to himself. Mrs Nicholls' suggestion of sweet tea had obviously been disregarded. 'Ah, Rowlands, there you are! Any news?' Dean seemed to have pulled himself together, at least, thought Rowlands. He replied that nothing more would be known until the doctor arrived.

'Was Miss La Mar in the habit of taking sleeping powders?' he asked Cunningham, who seemed not to understand him at first.

'What's that? Sleeping powders? Yes, we both took

them, from time to time. Why? Is it important?'

'Probably not,' said Rowlands.

'Well, all I can say is that it's a rotten thing to have happened,' said Dean, taking another swig of brandy. 'Woman like Dolores . . . still relatively young . . . height of her career . . . Damned shame.'

A silence followed, during which the three of them reflected on these words. 'I think,' said Cunningham after a moment, 'I'll go and lie down for a while.' Just then, Ashenhurst put his head around the door to say that the doctor was on his way.

'Do please accept my condolences,' he said to Cunningham. 'This must have been the most dreadful shock.'

'The most dreadful shock,' echoed the bereaved man. He went out and they heard him stumping upstairs.

'Poor old fellow, it's really knocked him for six,' said Dean. 'White as a sheet he looked, just after we found her. Thought a little pick-me-up was in order,' he added sheepishly, evidently referring to the brandy. 'Hope that's OK?'

'Oh, quite,' said Ashenhurst. 'Fred, can I talk to you for a minute?'

'Don't mind me,' said the actor. 'Just off for my bath, as it happens.'

The others waited until he had made himself scarce, then Ashenhurst said, 'Come into the kitchen with me, will you? I feel in need of a nice strong cup of tea. Unless you'd prefer a brandy?'

'Not I,' said Rowlands. 'I'd rather keep my head clear.'

'I know it's wrong of me to think like this, with one of my guests lying dead,' said Ashenhurst as they went out into the hall, 'but I'm afraid this is going to be very bad for business.'

'People die all the time,' said Rowlands.

'Yes, but it always seems worse when it's somebody famous. I mean there's more fuss made, especially if the press get hold of it.'

'I shouldn't worry about it. Does Dottie know?'

'Do I know what?' said Ashenhurst's wife, choosing this moment to come downstairs. She listened in silence as the state of affairs was explained to her. 'Good God,' she said when Rowlands had finished speaking. 'Do you think somebody did her in?'

'Dottie! That's in very poor taste,' said her husband.

'I don't see why,' she said. 'They've all been fighting like cats and dogs ever since they got here. And Dolores La Mar wasn't exactly the most popular person around. It seems to me entirely likely that one of 'em took things to their logical conclusion.'

'As far as we know, she died in her sleep,' said Rowlands. 'It appears she may have taken a sleeping powder. Anything else is just speculation . . . as you should know, Dottie.'

'All right, all right. I'm as horrified by what's happened as you are. Just because the woman was a monster, doesn't mean she deserved to die.'

'No,' said Rowlands. 'We should all bear that in mind.'

In the kitchen, Mrs Jago was in the process of comforting Jenny Penhaligon, who was in floods of tears. 'Never known anything like it,' she said truculently. 'People dying.' She seemed to take it as a personal affront. 'Tell you one thing, it wasn't nothing to do with the tea.' This provoked a fresh outburst of weeping from Jenny. 'There it sits, waiting to be taken up to the poor creature. And nobody to take it. She . . .' – by this Rowlands guessed she meant Miss La Mar's maid – 'hasn't been seen since she came bursting in here half an hour ago. I says to her, I says, "There's your mistress's tea, ready and waiting for her," and do you know what she says to me? "My mistress, she is dead," is what she says. Straight out, like that. Upset poor little Jenny no end.'

'I'm sure it's very upsetting for all of us,' said Dorothy, in a placatory tone. 'But somebody's got to carry on, and make sure people get their breakfasts. We're relying on you, Mrs J.'

'Of course, madam.' The cook sounded not displeased by this appeal to her managing skills. 'Jenny, stop that bawling at once, d'you hear, and get them trays ready.'

'You'd better make sure there's plenty of strong coffee,' said Dorothy as she poured tea for herself and the two men. 'I've a feeling people are going to need it.'

A short flight of wooden steps led to the chauffeur's rooms, which were above the garage. His tone, when he answered Rowlands' knock, was unfriendly. '*Si*?'

'I'd like to speak to Miss Casals, please.'

'She don't want to speak to you. Or anybody,' added the chauffeur. He was about to close the door when Rowlands interposed his foot.

'I understand if she's upset,' he said pleasantly. 'But it's most important that I speak to her.'

'I tell you, she will not speak to anybody.' The man's voice held a threatening note. But then, from behind him in the room, came another voice.

'Who is it, Carlos?' Her brother muttered something in what Rowlands guessed was Catalan. 'I will speak with him,' said the girl.

'Thank you,' said Rowlands. 'Then may I come in?'

At a word from his sister, Casals stepped aside, muttering under his breath, and Rowlands entered the sitting room of the small flat. This – part of a former stable block, now converted to staff accommodation – still retained an olfactory reminder of its former use: faint smells of leather harnesses and straw mingling with the more recent odour of petrol. 'What is it you want?' said Caterina Casals. She did not ask Rowlands to sit down.

'You were the one to find Miss La Mar's body, were you not?' If she could be blunt, then so could he.

'I did not kill her,' she retorted.

'Nobody's suggesting that you did. Can you describe to me exactly what you found, I mean, what you noticed when you first came into the room?'

'Why? Why do you want to know this?' interrupted Casals. 'You are trying to say she is to blame because *l'actriu* is dead?'

'Of course not. I merely want to find out the truth,' said Rowlands.

'But why?' demanded the chauffeur. 'You are not a policeman, I think.'

'No, but . . .'

'Leave us, Carlos.'

'I will not leave. How do you know that this man – *el cec* – is not trying to trick you into saying something you should not?'

'I said, leave us.' The girl's tone left both men in no doubt that she would brook no further argument.

'As you wish . . . sister.' The last word was delivered with a sneer, but Casals did as he was told, shutting the door behind him none too gently. When the sound of his footsteps descending the steps had faded away, Caterina Casals said, 'I will tell you what I found. There is not much to tell. I went in as usual, to wake my mistress, and to run her bath. I spoke to her, but she did not reply. When I drew open the curtains, I saw that she was dead.'

'What time was this?'

'I do not know exactly. A little before six, perhaps.' Rowlands nodded. It had been just on six when he had left his room, a few moments before encountering the maid in the corridor.

'Did you make any attempt to revive Miss La Mar before you gave the alarm?' She took a moment to consider this.

'I did not touch her, if that is what you mean. I could

see she was dead. I have seen dead persons before.' She emitted a harsh bark of laughter. 'There were many dead in the streets of my city before I came here. Once you have seen one such, you know the look of them.' Rowlands knew from his own experience what it was she meant.

'Was there anything else you noticed? Anything that was different about the room?' Again, she took her time about replying.

'Nothing.'

He knew he ought not to put an idea in her mind that wasn't already there, but he couldn't resist saying, 'Are you sure? Was everything just as usual?'

'I have told you. There were her clothes on the floor where she had dropped them, for me to pick up in the morning. This was as usual.' He detected a faint edge of sarcasm to the words. 'Her copy of the script was upon the floor. She liked to read over her lines for the shooting next day before she slept,' she added indifferently. 'Her glass of water was on the small table by her bed, with the sleeping powders.'

'So she had taken these – the sleeping powders – as far as you could tell?'

'I think so. The paper packet was empty . . .' She broke off, as if something had just occurred to her. 'That is strange,' she said. 'I remember now that the box of sleeping powders in the bathroom was empty. I saw it when I was tidying the room yesterday. She must have found another somewhere.'

'Are you sure about this?' said Rowlands. 'I mean, that the box was empty?'

'Oh yes, I am sure. It is my job to pay attention to such matters. But I have a question for you, Señor. Why do you want to know these things?' A suspicious note entered her voice. 'Are you sure you are not from the police?' Rowlands smiled.

'I wouldn't be of much use to them, now would I? You must have realised that I am blind.'

'In my country, police informers are to be found everywhere,' was the reply. 'And now, Señor, if you have no more questions, I have work to do.' Although what that work could be now that her mistress was no more, was hard to guess, thought Rowlands.

Chapter Six

A car was pulling up in front of the hotel as Rowlands reached the steps leading to the terrace; a moment later, a man got out, shutting the door of the vehicle behind him. Footsteps crossed the gravel. 'Hello,' said a voice with an agreeably dry intonation. 'I believe we've met, haven't we?'

'That's right, Dr Finch,' said Rowlands, turning to face the newcomer and holding out his hand. 'I'm Frederick Rowlands. You attended my youngest daughter when she had a touch of the sun two summers ago.'

'Mr Rowlands, of course. How nice.' The two men shook hands. Bill Finch had been in the RAMC during the war, having joined up straight from his studies at Guy's. It had been another of his generation of medical students who had administered first aid to Rowlands at the dressing station where he'd been taken after the explosion which had taken away his sight. He remembered how nervous the young man had seemed – he must have been no more than nineteen or twenty – his fingers trembling as he'd probed and swabbed. It had been a heavy day for casualties, Rowlands recalled. As he'd sat there, numb with pain and shock, surrendering himself to the young surgeon's tentative ministrations, he could hear the screams and sobbing of those more gravely wounded than himself coming through the canvas walls of the hospital tent. What a start to a career in medicine, he thought. After that, the prospect of routine hospital work must have seemed like a blessed relief.

As the two men mounted the steps towards the hotel entrance, the door opened. 'That you, Bill?' said Jack Ashenhurst. 'I thought I heard the car.'

'I came as soon as I could,' said the doctor as the three of them went inside. A brief, rather awkward silence followed. 'Well,' said Finch. 'You'd better show me where I'm to go.'

'I'll take you.' Ashenhurst, followed by the doctor, began to climb the stairs. 'You'd better come too, Fred,' he said. 'Seeing as you were the first to find the body.'

'Actually I wasn't the first.'

'I know. But Cunningham's no use. He's all to pieces.'

Rowlands said nothing more and the three men walked in silence up the stairs and along the corridor that led to Dolores La Mar's suite. As they reached the door, there came a shout from behind them. 'Mr Rowlands! Is it true what they've been saying about Miss La Mar?' It was Muriel Brierley. She sounded out of breath, as if she had been running. Rowlands turned to face her.

'I'm afraid so,' he said gently.

'But I talked to her only last night,' she gasped. 'She was quite well then. What could have happened?'

'That's what Dr Finch is going to find out,' said Rowlands. 'I think it best if we let him get on with it, don't you?' He went to take her arm, to guide her back to the stairs, but she dodged past him, just as Ashenhurst opened the door of the room where the dead woman lay. Muriel Brierley gave a low cry of horror.

'My God! It *is* true!' What confronted her, Rowlands could well imagine, even though he couldn't see it for himself. Death is seldom pretty, except in films. And although the sight of the dead woman was (mercifully) denied him, the pervasive smell in the room – that peculiar odour of stale garlic he'd noticed earlier – made his gorge rise.

Fortunately, Edith was on hand to take charge. 'Come along, Miss Brierley,' she said. 'You can't do any good by staying here.'

'But she's dead! cried the secretary, in tones of rising hysteria. 'Can't you see she's dead?'

'I'm afraid she's right,' murmured Cecily Nicholls to Dr Finch as Edith led the sobbing woman away. 'Mr Rowlands and I checked for vital signs about twenty minutes ago and found none. We haven't touched the body apart from that,' she added.

'You did exactly the right thing,' said the doctor,

fumbling in his bag for his stethoscope and other instruments. 'As indeed I would have expected.' He was silent a moment as he prepared to make his examination. 'Perhaps you gentlemen would wait outside? Mrs Nicholls can assist me – that's if you don't mind?' he added to the latter.

'I don't mind.'

'Excellent. Then if you'll let us get on . . .'

The two men at once withdrew, Ashenhurst closing the door behind them. 'Awful business, this,' he said with a shudder. 'I suppose it must have been some ghastly accident.'

'Has it occurred to you that it might not have been an accident?'

'What – suicide, you mean?'

'I wasn't thinking of that. I told you about that letter.'

'Good Lord, yes – I'd forgotten that. But you surely can't imagine . . .'

The door opened and the doctor put his head out. 'I think somebody ought to call the police,' he said. 'There are some features of this death that suggest it might not have been from natural causes. It wasn't,' he added grimly, 'a peaceful death.' It was what Rowlands had feared.

'Perhaps you'd better ring the police, Jack.'

'All right.'

'And take Mrs Nicholls with you,' said Dr Finch. 'She's been stuck in this beastly room for quite long enough.'

'I didn't mind,' said Cecily. 'Edith was with me.'

'Even so,' said Bill Finch. 'You need a change of air. A strong cup of coffee wouldn't do you any harm, either.'

'I'll see to it,' said Ashenhurst. 'Come along, Ciss.' A thought appeared to strike him. 'What shall I tell the others – Cunningham and the rest? They'll want to know the latest.'

'Just say that Mrs . . . Miss La Mar, is it? Say that she died from unknown causes. The police will put them in the picture soon enough.'

'Right you are,' said Ashenhurst. When he and his sister had gone, Rowlands turned again to the doctor.

'So you think there was foul play?' he said.

'Can't say for certain until after the PM,' was the reply. 'But the signs don't look good. The contorted position of the body, for one thing – suggestive of spasmodic reaction. Tell me,' he went on, 'did you notice anything in particular when you touched the body?'

'It was cold,' said Rowlands. 'No pulse at all. And there was something else . . .'

'Yes?'

'There was an odd smell. I'd almost have said it was garlic.'

'It's an indication that arsenic is present in the body,' Finch replied. 'But again, we'll have to wait for the residue of what's in the glass to be analysed before coming to a conclusion.'

'You suspect, then, that there was something not

right about the sleeping powders?'

'I couldn't possibly say, until we've had the residue tested,' said Finch. 'I say, that's odd!'

'What do you mean?'

'Well, the glass and the carafe of water and the empty paper of sleeping powders are on the little table beside the bed, but there seem to be traces of white powder on the glass top of the dressing table, too. I suppose it's possible that in emptying the contents of the packet into her glass, your Miss La Mar spilt a little on the dressing table, amongst all this clutter of perfume bottles and jewellery, but even so . . .'

'What kind of jewellery?' said Rowlands sharply.

'Oh, just the usual kind of thing that women of her sort like to adorn themselves with,' he replied. 'Earrings. I suppose these must be real diamonds . . . a rather elaborate ring . . .'

'Don't touch it!' said Rowlands.

'I wasn't going to.' The doctor sounded somewhat taken aback at the other's change of tone.

'I didn't mean to shout,' said Rowlands apologetically. 'But it might be important. Could you describe the ring?'

'Certainly. Although why you should think it matters, I fail to see. It's a gold ring with a large green stone . . . probably an emerald.'

'I thought so,' said Rowlands. 'The poison ring. It's the one she was wearing last night.' Briefly, he described the conversation at dinner the previous evening. Finch listened in silence.

'How perfectly beastly,' he said when Rowlands had finished. 'Do you mean to say that there was actually poison in that thing?'

'Curare, she said.'

'Oh, that's all rot, whatever she said. This is as clear a case of arsenic poisoning as I've seen.' Gingerly, he took a step nearer to the dressing table in order, presumably, to examine the ring more closely. 'Yes, I see what you mean,' he said. 'The top of the ring, with the green stone, lifts up. Even without touching it, I can see that it's open now. And I'm willing to lay odds that traces of whatever was inside it – curare or arsenic or some other nasty stuff – will be found at the bottom of that glass.'

In the dining room, the mood was one of subdued shock. As Rowlands walked in, followed by the doctor, all conversation ceased for a moment. Then several people started speaking at once:

'Ashenhurst said the police will have to be involved.' This was Eliot Dean.

'Shockin' business.' Colonel Rutherford.

'I can't believe it. Why, only last night, we were talking, in this very room.' A hysterical-sounding Laurence Quayle.

'I'm afraid it is true,' said Rowlands. 'And the police do have to be involved.'

'But why?' Horace Cunningham sounded bewildered. 'Surely there can't be any doubt about how my wife died? It was a terrible accident.'

'I'm sure the police will consider every eventuality,' said Rowlands. This must be hell for poor Cunningham, he thought. Fortunately at that moment Dr Finch took charge.

'Why don't you come into the lounge with me, sir?' he said to the widower. 'It'll be quieter in there, and you can ask me any questions you like, in private.' The older man agreed to this and the two of them went out, resulting in a general lightening of the atmosphere. The babble of questions began again.

'What exactly happened? Is there some suggestion that it was suicide?' demanded Dean. 'Because if that's being suggested, all I can say is, it's poppycock. Dolores wasn't the type.'

'And you knew her so *well*, of course,' said Quayle with scarcely concealed malice. 'Bosom pals, weren't you?'

'Why, you insufferable little swine . . .'

'I think,' said Hilary Carmody, cutting across this outburst from his leading man, 'we should all try and stay calm until the police arrive. Wild speculations won't help matters. Lydia, you're looking awfully pale. Why don't you go and lie down?'

'I'm all right,' said the actress, although she sounded far from all right. 'It's just so dreadful. Poor Dolores. When I think that I . . .' She couldn't go on for a moment. 'I just wish I'd been nicer to her, that's all.'

'Very touching, I'm sure,' said Quayle nastily. 'But weeping crocodile tears won't bring her back.'

'That's enough,' said Carmody. 'We're all upset. No need to take it out on other people.'

'Mrs Jago is making breakfast for anyone who wants it,' said Dorothy, evidently judging that some form of distraction was needed. 'If anyone would prefer to have it in his or her room, it can be arranged.' With the thought of food acting as a restorative, the antagonism which had sprung up like a bitter little wind subsided, and most people took their seats at their usual tables. Rowlands took the opportunity to ask his sister if the children had yet made an appearance. It seemed to him of the utmost importance that they should be kept out of this. So he was relieved when she said, 'Mrs J's giving them all breakfast in the kitchen. I've told them to keep out of the main rooms.'

'Good idea,' said Rowlands. 'We don't want your boys – or my girls, for that matter – getting mixed up in a police investigation, if we can help it.'

It hadn't taken Bob Chegwin, the local policeman, very long to decide that he should call in reinforcements. This sort of thing was outside his experience, he said. 'Last death I had to look into was old Enoch's – breaking his neck tumbling down the cliff steps after he'd taken drink,' he said. 'Accident o'course, but I had to carry out my investigations nonetheless. Dangerous spot, that,' he added. 'You'd know all about that, I reckon, sir.' Ashenhurst said wryly that he did. Four years before, he'd broken his leg slipping over on the same cliff steps in icy weather. 'But this . . .' Chegwin's eloquent silence took in the room in which they stood, whose sickly-sweet odour of death had grown stronger, it seemed to Rowlands, in the few minutes since he'd left it. 'Well, Mr Ashenhurst, sir, I don't mind admitting it's not what I'm used to.'

'No, indeed,' murmured Ashenhurst.

'So you're telling me, Doctor,' Chegwin went on, 'that the lady might have taken poison?'

'Taken or been given,' was the reply. 'I won't know until after the post-mortem. If I'm allowed to do it,' added Finch. 'The police might prefer to bring in their own man.'

'Yes, well, that remains to be seen, Doctor,' said Chegwin, his breathing stertorous as he finished noting down the essentials in his notebook. 'How do you spell the lady's name, sir?' Rowlands told him. 'Thank you, sir. Well, Mr Ashenhurst, I think, under the circumstances, it's certainly a case for Truro. If I might use your telephone . . .'

'Certainly,' said Ashenhurst.

'And we'll have this room closed up, sir, if you don't mind. I take it there's a key?'

'In the door,' was the reply. 'But it wasn't locked when we found her.'

'That's all right, sir,' said the policeman as the four of them exited the room, leaving its still and silent occupant in sole possession. He turned the key, and pocketed it. 'So what's the room next door to this one, Mr Ashenhurst?' he asked as the little party began to walk back towards the stairs.

'That's a bathroom,' replied the other. 'There's a connecting door from the bedroom – that is, Miss La Mar's room.'

'Ah yes, I saw that, sir. But it can be reached from the corridor, too, I take it?'

'Only when the door's unlocked. I think it's locked now, isn't it?'

The policeman rattled the door handle. 'So it would seem, sir. And what's this room?'

'That's another bedroom. Mr Cunningham's, as it happens. Miss La Mar's husband,' he added, for Chegwin's benefit. 'There's a dressing room connecting the two bedrooms, but again, the doors can be locked if one or other of the parties so chooses.'

'Right you are, sir.'

'Mr Cunningham won't be able to answer any questions just now,' put in Finch. 'I've given him a sedative. He's had a bad shock.'

'Very good, Doctor,' said Chegwin. 'But I think we'll keep everybody else away from this part of the hotel, if you follow me? If I'm calling Truro in, I don't want them saying I haven't done my best to leave things as tidy as possible.'

Inspector Frank Trewin of the Cornish Constabulary was a different order of policeman from that of the affable Constable Chegwin: younger, more acerbic in manner and, thought Rowlands, no doubt considerably more ambitious. The suspicious death of a celebrated film actress on his patch might, if carefully handled, be the making of him. Certainly he wasted no time in getting to the hotel. It was just under an hour after Chegwin's telephone call that the police Wolseley, driven by one of Trewin's subordinates, drew up in front of Cliff House, and the inspector, his sergeant, and two others Rowlands guessed must be the photographer and fingerprint expert, got out. They were met by a small reception committee, consisting of Ashenhurst, the doctor and himself. 'Right,' said Trewin briskly. 'Where's the gentleman who found the body?'

When it was explained to him that it had been the husband of the deceased who had found her, and that the said gentleman was presently lying down, recovering from the shock, he seemed unperturbed. 'All right – I'll get to him later. First I'll take a look at the scene. Mr Ashenhurst, perhaps you'd lead the way? Doctor, you'd better come along too.'

Finding himself dismissed for the time being, Rowlands joined the rest of the hotel's guests in the dining room, where Constable Chegwin, left in charge, was under siege. 'I say, Constable, how long is all this going to take? Some of us have better things to do than sit around all morning while the police do whatever it is they do.' This was Laurence Quayle.

'I couldn't say, sir, I'm sure,' replied the imperturbable Chegwin.

'Yes, but surely there's no need for us all to stay cooped up in here?' This was Hilary Carmody. 'I mean,

114

nobody's more shocked by Dolores's death than I am, but it can't do any good for us to hang around all day.' He hesitated a moment before saying what he said next. 'It may seem awfully callous, but . . . well, I've got a picture to finish, although God knows if I ever will finish it after what's happened. But at least I should put the film crew in the picture. They'll be wondering why the actors and I haven't turned up this morning. One can't just take days off in this business, you know. It all costs money, even to keep people standing idle.'

'If you'll just take a seat, sir,' said the officer of the law in a soothing tone. 'I'm sure the inspector will get to you as soon as possible.'

With which bland formula those assembled had to be content. There was some muttering, but most seemed to take it in good part. Rowlands himself took the opportunity to seek out his wife in order to ask her how the children had reacted to the news. 'Oh, they seem to have taken it in their stride,' she said. 'Joan's only comment was. "Well, she *was* rather old, poor lady," which, given that Miss La Mar was almost certainly younger than I am, made me feel thoroughly ancient! Margaret seemed quite upset. I suppose it's the first time she's encountered death, poor lass. Anne was very quiet. I never really know with Anne,' said her mother, 'whether she feels things or not.'

'Oh, she feels things,' said Rowlands. 'You can be sure of that.'

At the table next to the one where he and Edith were

sitting, the Simkins family were finishing their breakfast. 'We missed all the excitement,' Daphne Simkins was saying, in her fluting voice. 'John had gone out for his walk as usual at seven, and I was having a little lie-in. You can imagine how I felt when he told me that the police had arrived.'

'Very distressin' for you,' said Colonel Rutherford, who, with his wife, had joined them. Rowlands thought wryly that the Colonel seemed to have rather a penchant for the helpless, feminine type, although his own wife was anything but helpless. Mrs Simkins took a sip of coffee and immediately put down her cup.

'Darling, this has gone cold,' she said to her husband. 'Do you think you could ask Mrs Nicholls if she'd very sweetly bring us some more?' As John Simkins went to do her bidding, Rowlands reflected that, for some people, even sudden death was of less consequence than their own comfort. A few minutes passed. From time to time, desultory conversations on inconsequential topics broke out, only to dwindle away again as the speakers realised the futility of trying to carry on as usual. For Rowlands, the silence which had fallen upon the room was as expressive as speech would have been. The nervous tapping of a foot indicated that the owner – he guessed it was Laurence Quayle – was far from at ease, as did the restless pacing of another of the room's occupants; he knew it was Eliot Dean even before Quayle's irritable outburst.

'For God's sake, Dean, can't you sit still for a minute?

You're giving me a headache, marching up and down like that.'

As suggestive were the smaller signs – coughs, sniffs, and clearings of throats – by which human beings betray anxiety. Lydia Linden, Rowlands noticed, had a peculiarly persistent cough, which gave the lie to her otherwise calm demeanour. Apart from the sounds within the room, there were those from outside it, indicating that the routines of the hotel were continuing, if not as usual, then at least with some semblance of normality. A thunder of feet descending the stairs – that would be one of the boys; Danny, Rowlands guessed. A murmur of voices from the terrace outside, instantly hushed. He recognised Anne's among them. He was glad if she and the other children had got out of the house for a bit. This oppressive atmosphere wasn't good for them. He'd talk to Edith later about whether she and their daughters oughtn't to get away from here for a day or two. *There was her friend in Poole, wasn't there?* Perhaps they could go there.

As he was turning this possibility over in his mind he heard a car draw up outside. This would be the Police Medical Officer, he thought, recalling a previous occasion when he'd been the witness to an untimely death. That had turned out to be murder. This . . . well, he couldn't be sure. But something about it troubled him, as it had obviously troubled Dr Finch. It was half past ten by Rowlands' watch before the police sergeant who had arrived with Trewin put his head around the door.

'Inspector Trewin'd like to speak to Mr Rowlands.'
At once a chorus of voices assailed him:

'Do we have to stay here much longer?'

'I mean to say, we're all upset, but . . .'

'Can you at least tell us what is going on?'

To which the sergeant replied in the same unflappable tone as the one Constable Chegwin had used. 'All in good time, ladies and gentlemen. Mr Rowlands, if you'd come with me, please.'

Trewin had ensconced himself in the small sitting room next to the front door, which Ashenhurst used as a study. As the sergeant ushered Rowlands into the room, the inspector was just finishing a telephone call. '. . . that's right, sir . . . the MO's taking look at her now . . . Yes, sir . . . Of course, sir . . . We're sending the ring and the glass for analysis . . . Yes, that's right, sir. We won't know until after the PM, but it looks very much like it . . .' A few more remarks were exchanged between the inspector and his interlocutor before Trewin ended the call and said, 'Ah, Mr Rowlands. Sorry to keep you. My Chief Constable's taking an interest. Do take a seat, won't you.'

Rowlands did as he was asked, feeling for the back of the chair that stood in front of the desk – Ashenhurst's desk, usually – before seating himself upon it. Something about the careful manner in which he performed this simple act must have alerted the other to the fact of Rowlands' blindness, for he said, 'I take it that you and

Mr Ashenhurst went through the war together, sir?'

'We met during the last year of the war – at St Dunstan's, the institute for the war-blinded.'

'I see,' said Trewin. 'And Mr Ashenhurst is your brother-in-law, I understand?'

'That's right.' From previous experience, Rowlands was aware of the meticulous checking and cross-checking of evidence that went on in any police investigation, but privately wondered if this wasn't taking things too far. 'My wife and I and our three daughters spend every summer in Cornwall, with my sister and her husband,' he volunteered, thinking that it might help to get the preliminaries over with as quickly as possible.

'Yes, we get a lot of visitors in the summertime,' replied Trewin. 'You needn't write that down, Sergeant,' he added to this factotum, who had been dutifully scribbling. 'So,' went on the inspector. 'Perhaps you'd like to tell me how it was that you came to find Miss La Mar's body?'

'Certainly,' said Rowlands. 'It was just after I heard Mr Cunningham call for help. I went to see what the matter was, and found him outside Miss La Mar's room. He seemed distressed and said he'd been unable to wake her and so . . .'

'One moment,' said Trewin. 'Where exactly were you when you heard Mr Cunningham give the alarm? I'm not entirely clear about the layout of this place.'

'I'd just come out of my room,' said Rowlands. 'My wife and I have the room two doors down from Miss La

Mar's suite, and Mr Cunningham had come out of his room into the corridor, and so . . .'

'I follow you,' said the inspector. 'So you heard the alarm being given and went straight there?'

'Well, yes,' replied Rowlands.

Trewin must have noticed his hesitation for he said sharply, 'Was there something else?'

'Only that I'd already encountered Miss Casals – that's Miss La Mar's maid – in the corridor. She was obviously upset, and so . . .'

'What did she say to give you that impression?'

'I . . . I can't recall exactly. She was upset, as I said. Sobbing. I asked her what the matter was, and she told me to let her pass. I . . . I don't remember if she said anything else.' It was a lie, of course, but he was damned if he'd put a noose around any woman's neck. 'She ran downstairs,' Rowlands went on, glad of the one advantage his blindness gave him: facial imperturbability. 'It was then that I heard Mr Cunningham call out.'

'All right,' said the policeman. 'We'll check the maid's story later. What happened then?'

'I spoke to Mr Cunningham, as I've said, and then I went into Miss La Mar's room to see if there was anything I could do . . .' Again, he hesitated, but this was to give himself time to find the right words to describe what he'd found. 'She . . . she was quite cold, and I couldn't find a pulse, so it seemed to me that she must have been dead for several hours.'

'You touched the body?'

'Yes. But only to make sure she was beyond help.'

'Which proved to be the case, in your estimation?'

'Yes.'

'As it happens, the doctor has confirmed this assessment,' said Trewin, leaving the comment 'Lucky for you' unspoken before carrying on. 'He – Dr Finch – puts the time of death between midnight and five o'clock this morning. Which would tally with the time you say you found her.'

'Yes. It was sometime after six. Say six-thirty,' said Rowlands.

'And yet the doctor tells me he wasn't called until just after seven,' said the inspector. 'Was there a reason for the delay?'

'It took a few minutes before I was able to find Mr Ashenhurst, to tell him what had happened,' said Rowlands. 'Mr Dean, who has the room next door, had heard the commotion and came out of his room at that moment. Then Mrs Nicholls arrived. I suggested that she should examine Miss La Mar, to confirm that she was dead.'

'It sounds as if there were rather a lot of people in the room at that time,' said Trewin. 'Mr Cunningham, yourself, then Mr Dean and Mrs Nicholls. Which won't,' he added, 'make the job of the police any easier.'

'Perhaps not,' said Rowlands. 'Although I don't think any of us were thinking of the police just then.'

'The public never does think of these things,' was the reply. 'Dr Finch tells me,' he went on, as if there had been no change of subject, 'that you were the one who alerted him to the matter of this "poison ring".' He pronounced the words with some distaste.

'That's right,' said Rowlands. 'Miss La Mar herself drew attention to it at dinner last night.'

'Did she indeed? Was there a reason for that, do you think?'

'I don't follow . . .'

'I mean, is it possible she was intending to take her own life, and wanted to make sure everybody knew it?'

'It's certainly possible, but . . .'

'You don't think so.'

'I didn't get the impression from the rest of her conversation that she was suicidal, no.' Briefly, he outlined the substance of what had been said at the dinner table. 'If anything,' he concluded, 'I'd say Dolores La Mar was in a triumphant mood rather than otherwise. Relishing her power over the other people there, if that makes sense?'

'Because, as you've just explained, she had the whip hand when it came to letting the film go ahead, or not going ahead?'

'Exactly.'

'And you're suggesting that this might have caused a bit of resentment.'

'I'm not suggesting anything,' said Rowlands. 'You asked me if I thought Miss La Mar seemed likely to want to kill herself, and I've said no. The rest is mere speculation.'

'Point taken,' said Inspector Trewin. 'Well, I think

that'll be all for now, Mr Rowlands. Unless you've anything more you wanted to add?'

'No, I think that's as much as I can tell you,' said Rowlands, starting to get to his feet. As he did so, there came a knock at the door, and Dr Finch put his head in.

'Just to let you know that I'm off, Inspector,' he said. 'Full list of patients to see, you know . . .'

'Yes, that's all right, Doctor,' replied Trewin. 'If you'll just look in at the station later – about two o'clock – you can sign your statement when the sergeant here has typed it.' Finch said that he would do so.

'Have you a minute?' he said to Rowlands as the two of them went out into the hall. He waited until he had closed the study door before continuing. 'I mentioned what you'd told me to the inspector. About that ring she left on the dressing table.'

'I gathered that,' said Rowlands. He related what Trewin had said in his phone call to the Chief Constable.

'Yes, well, that was my doing,' admitted the doctor. 'And then Haggarty confirmed my suspicions about arsenic poisoning and so . . .' But Rowlands' sharp ears had caught the sound of a door closing softly. It came from the far side of the hall, probably the lounge, he thought.

'Is someone there?' he said.

'I don't think so,' said Finch. 'Ah, here's Dr Haggarty now.' Because that gentleman was even now descending the stairs, his ponderous tread that of a man who evidently enjoyed the good things of life to the full, thought Rowlands. The rolling cadences of the Medical Officer's voice confirmed this impression.

'There you are, Finch!' he boomed. 'I've finished with her now – at least until I get her on the table. I'll be doing the PM after lunch, if you'd care to come along. Say half past two?'

'All right,' said Finch. 'I'll be there.'

At that moment, the door of the study opened. 'Ah, Inspector,' said Haggarty, on catching sight of that official. 'You can get your men to take her away now. Mortuary van's outside, I take it?' Trewin confirmed that this was so, and gave an order to his sergeant, 'Get Chegwin and young Hammett to bring her down – tell them to go carefully, mind! And make sure none of the guests leave the dining room until it's done. The maids, too. We don't want any outbreaks of hysterics.' As he spoke these words, a thought occurred to Rowlands.

'My daughters,' he said. 'They're outside on the terrace. I don't want them to see this.' He made for the front door – the quickest way out. 'I'll go and warn them to keep away from the front of the house.'

'Right you are, sir,' said Trewin. 'We wouldn't want the young ladies upset.'

Chapter Seven

But if the girls and their cousins were about somewhere in the grounds of the hotel, Rowlands couldn't hear them. Most likely, on a glorious day like this, they'd taken themselves down to the beach. Then he heard a shout – 'Coo-ee! Daddy!' It was Anne, coming towards him from the lawn at the front of the house. He remembered, too late, that there was a tree there – a great spreading cedar – up which she liked to climb, and where she would sit, for hours on end, reading and daydreaming.

'What are you doing here?' he said fiercely. 'I thought you were with the others.'

'They've gone down to the cove,' she replied. 'But I wanted to wait. I thought you'd come out eventually. Daddy, what's going on?' Before he could think of an answer, the thing he'd been dreading happened: the front door opened and someone – two men, it became evident – came out, moving with an awkward, shuffling gait. The reason for this was not hard to guess. 'They're carrying somebody out,' said Anne. 'On a stretcher. Is that . . . ?'

'Yes,' he said. 'Don't look.' Because even though he himself was oblivious to the sight, his imagination could supply what it was his daughter was seeing: Dolores La Mar, making her last exit, wrapped not in satin and furs, but in the more utilitarian covering of a hospital blanket. Beside him, Anne gave a little shudder, and hid her face against his jacket. 'It's all right,' said Rowlands, wondering if it ever would be again, for her. 'Come on. Let's go and find your sisters. They've gone down to the beach you said?'

'Yes. They're with Jonty and Rory, I think.' The elaborate casualness with which she brought out the boys' names made him wonder: was there some heartbreak here? But then he thought, she's only fifteen, for heaven's sake. Much too young to be bothering about that sort of thing. Edith would say he was old-fashioned, of course. They crossed the lawn, which descended in a series of broad terraces. 'Boys are rather silly, aren't they?' said Anne as they reached the gate that opened onto the steps, which were cut into the cliff face.

'Are they?' He tried to keep the amusement out of his voice.

'Yes. They're only interested in silly stuff . . . Like drinking beer. And . . . and holding hands.'

'I see.'

'It isn't,' said Anne thoughtfully, 'that I mind. About the holding hands, I mean. It's just that there are so many things I'd rather do.'

'What kind of things?'

'Oh, I don't know. All sorts of things. Like . . . painting pictures, and writing books . . . and flying planes.' So she hadn't forgotten that particular childhood dream, he thought.

'Well, I think you've got lots of time to do everything you want to do,' he said. 'Take my arm, would you, as we go down this bit? I don't want to come a cropper, like poor Uncle Jack.' As they reached the bottom of the steps, he could hear the voices of the others drifting towards him along the beach, with Joan's clear tones rising above the rest.

'We said best of three. So that means I've won.'

'Your second shot was useless.' This was her old sparring partner, Victor.

'They're skimming stones,' said Anne.

'I rather gathered that. Gosh it's hot!' said Rowlands. 'Have you got your hat on, Annie?'

'Yes,' she said. Rowlands rather wished that he'd worn his. This weather must break soon, surely? At the water's edge, Margaret came up and stood beside them, threading her arm through her father's.

'Is it over?' she said in a low voice.

'For the time being,' he said. 'Although the police are still here, of course.'

'It's all so beastly,' she said with a shiver. 'I almost

127

wish . . .' She broke off. 'Oh, I don't know.'

'You wish we'd never come, is that it?'

'S'pose so. But that's stupid. I mean, I love it here, only now it's as if everything's spoilt.'

'I know what you mean.' For a moment, he said nothing more. It was good to be standing here, with his girls beside him, letting the clean salt-smelling air fill his lungs, and listening to the murmur of the waves, and the far-off shrieking of seagulls. 'What do you say about getting right away from Cliff House for the day?' he said. 'We could ask Mrs Jago to pack us up a picnic lunch, and take a nice long walk along the coast.'

'Can the boys come?' said Margaret.

'Of course the boys can come. We'll see if Uncle Jack wants to tag along, too.'

But Ashenhurst, when asked if he would like to join the expedition, declined, with some reluctance. 'I really ought to stick it out here. The police aren't yet finished with interviewing the guests. People are rattled – and no wonder. They're going to need a lot of jollying along. And that's my job, I'm afraid . . .' Dorothy was no less determined to stay and 'man the barricades', as she put it.

'It wouldn't be fair to leave it all to Jack,' she said. 'Although I do wish the police would hurry up and clear off.'

'I'm sure they're working as fast as they can,' said Rowlands.

'They're still not letting us into the room,' his sister

went on, ignoring his remark. 'It needs a thorough clean before we can think of putting anyone else in there.' Rowlands didn't say what was in his mind, which was that if it turned out that Dolores La Mar had been poisoned, then the room would remain closed off as a murder scene.

'I'm sure the inspector'll let you know what's what as soon as he can,' he said.

'Well, I hope so,' said Dorothy. 'We're running a hotel here – or trying to.'

'I'll stay, too,' said Edith when the idea of the picnic was put to her. 'I'm sure Jack and Dorothy could do with an extra pair of hands.' It was Dorothy, surprisingly, who persuaded her.

'We'll manage perfectly well,' she said. 'It's not as if there's actually much we can do until the police let us back into that room. And Cecily can lend a hand if we need one . . . By the way, has anybody seen her?'

'She went out for a breath of air,' said Jack. 'Said she had a bit of a headache.' Which was hardly surprising after being cooped up in an airless room with a dead woman, thought Rowlands.

'Come along,' he said to Edith. 'Get your hat. We're leaving in five minutes.'

They set off along the cliff path towards the Lizard, and beyond it, Lowland Point, a favourite, if not especially taxing, route which would bring them, via St Keverne – a picturesque village a few miles inland – back to their starting point. As was usually the case, the younger members of the party – the Rowlands girls, their cousins and the Simkins twins – strode on ahead, their voices drifting back towards Rowlands like the cries of so many seabirds. He and Edith strolled along at a more sedate pace. It was good to get out of Cliff House and its atmosphere of barely suppressed hysteria, he thought. To be out in the fresh air, feeling the sun on one's face and smelling the delicious scents of wild thyme and gorse, was a relief after the oppressiveness of the past few hours – a relief apparent in the boisterous cries of, 'Race you, slowcoach!' and 'Oh *do* come *on*, you lot!' to be heard from up ahead.

A thought struck him. 'No Walter?' he said to Edith, having failed to detect the soft guttural accents of the young German amongst those of the others.

'No, he wasn't with the others when I told them about the picnic,' said Edith. 'I expect he's sloped off somewhere. You know what boys his age are like.'

'Mm.' Walter, at sixteen, was a rather serious young man. Hardly surprising under the circumstances, thought Rowlands, with his mother and sister living in Berlin – not a comfortable place for Jews just then – and his brother a political refugee in Amsterdam. Rowlands, who had liked the hot-headed Joachim Metzner, hoped he'd managed to stay out of trouble in the four years since the two of them had last met. He was checked in the middle of these sombre thoughts by Edith's pulling on his arm.

'I say, isn't that Cecily in the lane, with Dr Finch?'

Sometimes it seemed to Rowlands that his wife forgot

his disability entirely. 'I suppose it must be, since you say so,' he said mildly.

'Yes, it *is* them,' was the reply. 'Oh Fred, do slow down for a moment! You always stride along so fast.' He did as she asked, wondering why Edith, who was herself quite an energetic walker, should suddenly prefer to dawdle. He had his answer a moment later. Because at this point, the path along which they had been walking ran parallel with the lane that led from the hotel, separated from it only by a hawthorn hedge. It was on the far side of this that the other couple stood, screened from view, but not from being overheard.

'It's no good, Cecily, I won't have it,' he heard Finch say, with a tenderness which surprised him, coming as it did from this rather dry and austere type. 'I won't have you worn out by all this.'

'It's all right, Bill,' said Mrs Nicholls. 'You needn't worry. I'm a lot stronger than I look . . . Oh!' Because at that moment she must have realised they were not alone. 'Hello, Edith . . . Fred. We were just . . . That is, Dr Finch and I met in the lane and—'

'I realised after I'd left the hotel that I'd forgotten my medical bag,' put in Finch hastily. 'Mrs Nicholls kindly brought it to me. Lucky she did so, or I'd have had to come all the way back.'

'Very lucky,' said Edith innocently. 'We're just off for a walk. Do join us, if you'd like, Cecily. I won't ask you, Dr Finch, because I know how busy you are.'

'Thanks,' said Mrs Nicholls. 'But I really ought to be

getting back. Dorothy and Jack will need a hand with the lunches.'

'I'll run you in the car, if you like,' said Dr Finch.

'Oh, there's no need,' was the reply. 'It's only a few steps. Enjoy your walk,' she said to the Rowlandses. 'See you around, Bill.'

'Cecily . . .' But she was already walking back in the direction from which she had come. Then Bill Finch, too, took his leave, sounding rather distracted. A moment later, they heard his car start up in the lane.

'Well, well,' said Edith, in a satisfied tone.

'Well what?' he said. Women could be so obtuse, sometimes.

'Oh nothing.' She took his arm, and they resumed their walk. 'Only I shouldn't be at all surprised if those two don't come to an understanding one of these days.'

It was four o'clock by the time they got back to Cliff House, and Rowlands was looking forward to a cup of tea and one of Mrs Jago's home-made scones. The walk had done them all good, he thought: the children seemed to have regained their usual high spirits, while he and Edith had fallen into a companionable silence, with neither feeling the need to say what he guessed was uppermost in both their minds – the question of what they were to do. For his part, Rowlands was of the opinion that the sooner Edith and the girls left Coverack for Poole, the better. But when he'd put this plan to his wife, she didn't seem keen. 'It's a lot to ask at such short notice. I mean, Frances is an old friend, but to take on the whole family . . .'

'I'll stay, of course,' he put in quickly. 'Jack and Dorothy'll need some help getting things back to normal.'

'Then I should stay, too,' said Edith. 'And the girls won't want to cut short their holiday. Honestly, Fred, you worry too much.'

'I just don't think it's very good for them to be caught up in all this . . .' he began, but she cut across him.

'Fiddlesticks! Children are tougher than you think. Besides which, they've already seen the worst of it. Sending them home isn't going to change that.'

'I suppose not.'

'No, if you ask me, the best thing we can do is to carry on as if everything were just as usual,' she said, as they reached the gate that led from the cliff path to the hotel's garden, having left the girls and their cousins to go down to the beach. 'You'll see. They'll forget all about it in a day or two.' But in this she was wrong, as it turned out.

At the hotel, the Rowlandses found a scene in marked contrast to the one they had left behind. Instead of the inertia and depression of a few hours before, there was bustle and, if not high spirits, then certainly an improved mood. A car – Lydia Linden's, it transpired – had been brought round to the front of the house, and Miss Linden herself, accompanied by Laurence Quayle, was on the point of walking out of the front door as they came in. 'We're off for a spin,' she explained. 'It's such a glorious day. And there's no point in sitting around feeling sorry for ourselves . . . I mean,' she added hastily, 'it's simply awful what's happened to poor Dolores, of course, but nothing we can do will change that. Come on, Larry.'

'Coming, old thing,' said Quayle, then, to the Rowlandses, 'Well, toodle-oo.' But as the two actors descended the steps to where Miss Linden's Morris was parked, another vehicle – the Wolseley, of course – could be heard arriving. A moment later, the car pulled up and doors opened, to allow Inspector Trewin and two of his junior officers to get out. Since the police vehicle was now blocking the drive, Miss Linden, seated next to her companion in the Morris, gave a protesting toot on the horn. When this had no effect, she leant out of the window on the driver's side.

'I say, Inspector, let a chap out, will you? Your great big car's in my way.'

'I'm sorry, miss,' said Trewin, with what seemed to Rowlands a certain grim satisfaction. 'But I'm afraid I shall have to ask you to get out of the car. You too, sir,' he added, evidently addressing Quayle.

'But why, may I ask?' said the girl. 'Don't tell me I've committed a traffic offence already?'

'It's not that, miss. I'll be asking the same of everybody else,' said the inspector. 'That is, to return to the hotel . . . assuming they're not already here.'

'Well, you won't find anybody else, apart from the staff,' said the girl. 'Hilary – that's Mr Carmody, our director,' she added for the inspector's benefit, 'left a couple of hours ago. He's gone down to the village, to let the camera crew and technicians know what's happened.

Eliot – Mr Dean – went with him. There's obviously going to be no filming today, and so Larry and I thought we'd go for a drive. What I don't understand,' she went on, getting out of the car, and slamming the door behind her, 'is why we have to stay. I mean, we've already answered your questions, haven't we?'

'Ah yes, miss – but that was this morning,' was the reply. 'Things are different, now.'

'In what way different?' demanded Quayle. 'You're talking in riddles, man.'

'I can make it as plain as you like, sir, if you'll just come with me . . . You too, Mr Rowlands, sir, and your good lady. The fact is,' went on Inspector Trewin as he climbed the steps towards the front door, 'it turns out that things are a lot more serious than we thought at first.' He rang the bell, and the sound reverberated within the house.

'But . . . but surely it was an accident?' said Lydia Linden. 'An overdose of sleeping powders.'

'It would appear not,' said Trewin curtly. 'Ah, Mr Ashenhurst,' he went on as the door was opened by that gentleman. 'I'm afraid there's been a development.' The five of them, followed by the two junior police officers, trooped into the hall, and stood in a sombre group as the inspector explained why he had come. 'I'll need to talk again to everyone who was here last night,' he said.

'Are you sure that's necessary?' This was Ashenhurst. 'Surely my guests have already told you all they know?'

'You must let me be the judge of that, sir,' was the reply. 'In a case of murder . . .'

'Murder? Who said anything about murder?' said a voice from the top of the stairs. It was Horace Cunningham. A brief but electric silence followed this interruption as all those present considered the implications of what they had just heard.

Then Trewin said, 'I assume you must be the deceased's husband, sir?'

'I'm sorry,' said Ashenhurst. 'I didn't realise that you hadn't already met. This is Mr Cunningham, Inspector. Mr Cunningham, this is Inspector Trewin, of the Cornish Constabulary.'

'Someone said something about the police being called,' said Cunningham vaguely. It occurred to Rowlands that he might still be suffering from shock. 'But what's all this about Dolores being murdered? It can't be true.'

'I'm afraid it's all too true, sir,' said Trewin. 'The postmortem findings were that your wife died from arsenic poisoning. There were traces of it in the glass in which she dissolved her sleeping powders, and in an emerald ring which I gather she was wearing last night.' Lydia Linden gave a small cry.

'It's all right, ducky,' said Quayle. For the first time, Rowlands liked him. 'Come along. Why don't I fix you a nice stiff drink?'

Cunningham, however, seemed unable to take in what had been said to him. 'It's impossible,' he said. 'Don't you see? It's all a dreadful mistake.' He had by now descended the stairs.

'I'm afraid there's no mistake about it,' said Trewin.

'The post-mortem showed that she had enough arsenic in her stomach to have killed her several times over.'

'Is this really necessary, Inspector?' protested Ashenhurst. The Inspector ignored him.

'Perhaps,' he went on, opening the door of the study, 'you'd be so good as to come in here, Mr Cunningham? Then we can discuss things at our leisure.' But Cunningham didn't seem to have heard him.

'Yes, yes, a dreadful mistake,' he went on eagerly. 'You see, I believe that the poison was meant for me.' There was a moment's stunned silence.

'What makes you think that, sir?' said Inspector Trewin, in the level tone of voice Rowlands guessed he must employ when dealing with deranged members of the public.

'Why, man, because this sleeping powder – the one you say poisoned Dolores – came from the box next to my bed. It's a fresh box, only just opened. One packet had been removed from it, however. I noticed it this morning.'

'Why didn't you mention this before, sir?' said the inspector sharply.

'Nobody asked me,' was the reply. 'One thing I can tell you is that there've been attempts on my life before now. Oh, you needn't look surprised, Inspector,' Cunningham went on. 'A man in my position makes many enemies.' He sighed. 'It would appear that on this occasion one of them has done for poor Dolores.'

'And yet that poison pen letter was addressed to Miss

La Mar,' said Rowlands quietly.

'A letter? What letter? Why wasn't I informed of this?' demanded Trewin. 'I think, Mr Cunningham, sir, you'd better come and make a full statement. As for the rest of you, I'd be obliged if you'd wait in the lounge until Sergeant Moon can get around to you. If you'd let all the other guests know that I'll be wanting to speak to them, it would be a help, Mr Ashenhurst,' he added. 'It strikes me that there may be a number of other things I haven't yet been told.' Trewin turned to his subordinate. 'Constable, you'd better get down to the village as soon as you can. Tell Mr Carmody and the rest of his crowd that I want 'em all back here at once. You can take the car,' he added magnanimously.

'Yes, sir. Thank you, sir.' The police constable made a swift exit.

'Carry on then, Sergeant,' the inspector went on, to his remaining officer. 'You know the drill. Names, reasons for being in the hotel, whereabouts between the crucial times . . .'

'Which are?' Rowlands paused on the threshold, to allow Edith to precede him into the hotel lounge.

'From whenever Miss La Mar retired to bed and six o'clock this morning when her body was found,' said Trewin. 'We need to establish who was the last person to see her alive.'

* * *

'So tell me,' said Inspector Trewin after a moment's silence, during which Rowlands assumed the other had been studying him, 'about this letter.'

'Do you mean the one sent to Miss La Mar?'

'Why?' said the policeman. 'Were there others?'

'One, to my knowledge.' Rowlands explained about the letter addressed to Jack Ashenhurst, which Mrs Nicholls had opened and read. He and the inspector were once more seated in Ashenhurst's study, with Police Constable Kitto taking notes.

'Hmph,' said Trewin. 'I should have been told of this before. And this letter – the first one – did that also contain a threat to Miss La Mar's life?'

'Not in so many words,' replied Rowlands. 'I think it said something like "All traitors will die" or "Traitors must die" – or something equally melodramatic. Mrs Nicholls thought it was a schoolboy prank at first.'

'Did she indeed?' Trewin gave a disdainful sniff. 'A pity she didn't think to share the information with the police.'

'I don't suppose it occurred to her to do so,' said Rowlands. 'As far as any of us knew, Miss La Mar's death was a dreadful accident – or suicide.' He didn't add that he had wanted to call the police when the second letter had come, and that he had suggested as much to Ashenhurst. Better not muddy the waters and, with hindsight, it was probably a good thing he hadn't carried out his intention of ringing Alasdair Douglas. This local copper would hardly thank him for having called in Scotland Yard.

'This letter,' the inspector went on. 'The first one, I mean. Did Mrs Nicholls keep it?'

'I'm afraid I can't tell you,' said Rowlands. He ventured a joke. 'Even if she had, it wouldn't have been of much use showing it to me.'

'No.' Inspector Trewin didn't laugh. 'But you were present when the second letter arrived, I understand?'

'When it was opened,' Rowlands corrected him. 'I assume it must have arrived by that morning's post. Miss Brierley would know. My wife was also in the lounge when the letter was read.'

'What exactly did it say?' said Trewin. 'Because we haven't been able to find it amongst the deceased's papers. Seems she must have destroyed it.'

'That was certainly what Cunningham advised her to do.'

'Was it? A pity,' said the inspector. 'No chance then of cracking the case with the aid of fingerprints!' He gave a mirthless laugh, and Rowlands realised that he had just heard what passed for a policeman's joke. 'So can you remember what this one said, Mr Rowlands?'

'I can, as a matter of fact. It said: "All traitors must die, and you will die, you evil bitch." Rather nasty.'

'Indeed. Funny about the "traitors" part – that it was in both letters, I mean. Suggests they were probably written by the same person. I do hope,' said Inspector Trewin, sounding more cheerful than he had at the start of the interrogation, 'that Mrs Nicholls can lay her hand on that letter.'

Aside from the question of the letter and its whereabouts, Trewin seemed most interested in the timing of the whole affair – when Rowlands had last seen the dead woman, or rather, heard her, preoccupied him greatly. 'It must have been just after ten,' said Rowlands. 'Say a quarter past. I was on the terrace having a smoke, after my wife had gone in. I heard Miss La Mar talking to someone in the room overhead. The French windows onto the balcony must have been open.'

'Any idea who it was that she was talking to?'

'I'm afraid not. I didn't stay around long enough to hear more than a few words before I went inside myself. Whoever it was must have been inside the room while Miss La Mar was near the French windows. At any rate, it was only *her* voice I heard clearly.'

'Pity,' said Trewin. He was silent a moment, tapping his fingers on the desk in a nervous staccato. In the chair next to Rowlands, the police constable diligently scratched away in his notebook. 'I don't suppose you could tell if it was a man or a woman – that she was talking to, I mean?

'I'm afraid not.'

'Hmm,' said the inspector. 'But you could hear her all right?'

'Loud and clear. She was an actress, after all.'

'I don't follow.'

'Good at projecting her voice,' said Rowlands.

'Oh, I see. So what was it you heard her say?' Rowlands told him.

'At least, I think that's what she said,' he added. 'I

141

didn't know at the time that I'd be having to give evidence to the police.'

'Well, from what I've been able to gather from our brief conversations, Mr Rowlands, your memory's more accurate than most.'

'It's had to be,' replied Rowlands drily.

'So what do you think she meant by it, sir?' the inspector persisted. 'Saying whoever it was would be sorry for saying what they'd said. That sounds like a threat to me. What was it she was afraid they were going to say, I wonder?'

'I couldn't tell you,' said Rowlands. 'But I think you're right – she was desperate that whatever it was wouldn't become generally known.'

'Hmm,' said Trewin. 'Do you think it might have been a case of blackmail? Something to do with these letters, perhaps?'

'Blackmailers don't usually kill their victims, do they?' said Rowlands. 'Not that I'm an expert in these matters, but . . .'

'Yes, yes,' said the other irritably. 'I take your point. So this gets us precisely nowhere – unless we can identify the person she was talking to in her room last night. Was she on bad terms with anyone, do you know?'

'It's more a question of who she *wasn't* on bad terms with,' said Rowlands. 'To the best of my knowledge, she'd already quarrelled with several people in her entourage that day.'

'Had she, indeed? And when was this exactly?'

Briefly, Rowlands recounted what he'd overheard at the cocktail party.

'So you're telling me she had a falling-out with Mr Carmody?' The inspector sounded quite gratified by this information.

'Not just with Carmody – with Dean, with Miss Linden . . . with just about everybody who was there,' said Rowlands. 'As I mentioned before, she'd threatened to pull the plug on the whole show.'

'So she did.' The inspector sounded even more pleased by this. 'And you've told me her threat was real,' said Trewin. 'She really could have put a stop to the whole business?'

'I imagine so. You'll have to ask Mr Cunningham.'

'Oh, I will,' said the inspector. 'You can be sure of that.' Trewin was silent a moment. 'So whoever was with her in her room at ten-fifteen or just after was, in all probability, the last person to see her alive.'

'Not the last, no,' said Rowlands. Briefly, he recounted what he had heard on his way back from the bathroom that night. 'It must have been around half past eleven. I don't know who it was she was talking to, other than that it was a man, but she was certainly alive then.'

'Hmm,' said the other. 'And you say these film people had returned to the hotel by that time?'

'I believe so, yes.'

'Then that broadens the field, rather than otherwise,' said the inspector, adding, with a grim little laugh, 'Not what we policemen like to hear, as a rule.'

Chapter Eight

With the return of Carmody and his leading man from Coverack, the police interrogations could begin in earnest, with the actors and other guests once more awaiting their turn to be questioned in the hotel lounge. The ennui which had resulted from this was alleviated by the arrival of tea, and the low murmur of conversation was interspersed by the clink of cups and saucers and the handing round of plates of bread and butter and Madeira cake. Foremost amongst the topics being addressed was, unsurprisingly, the dreadful news that Dolores La Mar had been murdered, with her husband's sensational assertion that he was the intended victim coming a close second. 'I don't know how I'm going to be able to sleep tonight,' twittered Daphne Simkins, putting on the little woman act for all she was worth, thought Rowlands. 'I mean . . . with a *murderer* about . . .' She gave an affected little shudder.

'No need to be frightened, m'dear.' This was Colonel Rutherford. 'Plenty of good strong men and true to see the blighter off, should he have the gall to show his face again.'

'Yes, but would we *recognise* his face if we saw it?' said Quayle slyly. 'Since none of us know who he – or she – is. It could be any one of us.' This provoked a little scream from Mrs Simkins, and an angry, 'Well really! That's a bit thick,' from her husband.

'Don't talk rot, Larry,' said Lydia Linden, evidently recovered from her own fit of nerves. 'Of course it isn't any of us. It stands to reason that it must have been an outsider.'

'And why, pray?' said Quayle silkily. 'I should have thought the evidence suggested precisely the opposite.' It seemed to Rowlands that Quayle was enjoying himself. It was almost as if he knew something the others did not.

'Of course it has to be somebody from outside,' put in Eliot Dean, who had been silent up till now. 'Cunningham himself suggested as much, from what you've told us.' So it was Quayle who'd told the others of the entrepreneur's startling allegation, thought Rowlands, guessing that Inspector Trewin would probably have preferred to have kept the matter quiet. Since Cunningham himself was presently closeted with the police, the speculations concerning his statement grew wilder and wilder.

'I don't doubt that it'll turn out to be the work of a gang,' said John Simkins, still bristling after his contretemps with Quayle. 'These East End types'll stop at nothing.'

'I hardly think,' put in Hilary Carmody mildly, 'that an East End gang would have come all the way down to Cornwall to carry out their assassination – if that's what it was.'

'Yes, but the stuff – arsenic or curare or whatever it was – must have been planted beforehand, don't you see?'

'It was planted by Dolores herself,' put in Quayle. 'We all saw that ring, with its interesting contents.'

'Yes, but who put the stuff in her glass?' said Dean.

'I think,' said Carmody, 'that we ought to leave such speculations to the police, don't you? All we know are the bare facts. She was killed. Somebody killed her.' At these words, there came a gasp from the far corner of the room, where (Rowlands now realised) Muriel Brierley had been sitting all this while.

'I . . . I can't bear it!' she cried. 'The way you're all calmly discussing it. It's . . . it's horrible.' She rushed out, letting the door of the lounge slam behind her. A silence followed this abrupt departure. It was broken by Laurence Quayle.

'Well,' he said. 'Who'd have thought that quiet little mouse would have been capable of so much passion?'

'Oh, do shut up, Quayle,' snapped Eliot Dean. 'I'm getting sick of hearing your voice.'

'Entirely mutual, I'm sure,' was the acid reply. But then Carmody intervened once more.

'Muriel's right, you know,' he said. 'It *is* rather

horrible to be sitting here over our tea, talking about what's happened as if . . . well, as if it were merely a matter of academic interest.' He was silent a moment. 'Whereas the fact is that Dolores is dead . . . and I for one am very sorry.'

'Go and see if Miss Brierley's all right, will you, Dottie?' said Ashenhurst in an undertone to his wife.

'I was just about to,' was the reply. 'It seems to me that poor girl has had rather a lot to bear, this past couple of days.'

Feeling that he, too, had had enough of all this speculation and backbiting, Rowlands took himself off, telling Edith that he was going to see where the girls had got to. He guessed they would still be down on the beach – where else, on an evening like this? 'Tell them to come in and wash their hands for supper,' she called after him.

'All right.' He'd have let them forgo the formal meal – it was too hot to eat much – in favour of cooking up one of the messes of sausages and tinned beans they seemed to prefer above all other fare. He wondered if Edith would have been such a stickler for convention if they'd had sons instead of daughters.

Crossing the stable yard towards the cliff path that led down to the beach, he heard rapid footsteps approaching. 'Hello!' he called. 'Who's there?' The footsteps came to a halt.

'It is I, Herr Rowlands,' said Walter Metzner. 'I . . . I was just going for a walk.'

'So was I,' said Rowlands. 'If you've nothing better to

do, you can come with me down to the cove, to fetch the others. You missed a jolly picnic earlier today,' he went on as the two of them fell into step.

'*Ja*. I . . . I had some things to do.'

'Of course.' A boy – or young man, rather – of Walter's age might very well prefer his own company to that of a middle-aged couple and a lot of younger children, thought Rowlands, although Margaret was quite grown-up these days, and those Simkins boys must be all of eighteen. But Walter was a quiet sort, who went his own way. Rowlands liked the young German, who, at sixteen, was growing up to be a more responsible version of his brother, Joachim. A good thing, too, thought Rowlands, recalling that irascible youth and the scrapes he had got himself into during Rowlands' sojourn in Berlin. He wondered if he should ask what news there was of Walter's mother and sister. But before he could frame the question, Walter, who had been striding along in silence, said abruptly, 'I have had a letter from my sister. You will remember her, perhaps?'

'Certainly I remember Clara. How is she? Are she and your mother well?'

Walter said nothing for a moment. When at last he did speak, his words tumbled out in a rush. 'She . . . my mother . . . is *not* well, I fear. She and my sister must leave their home, you see. It is because they are Jews – the only ones in that building – and so they have been told they must go . . .' He seemed unable to continue.

'But that's terrible,' said Rowlands. 'Where are they living now?'

'They are staying with a cousin of my mother's. My . . . my sister does not know how long they will be able to stay. She . . . my sister . . . has been dismissed from her job.' Clara Metzner had been working as a teacher in an elementary school, Rowlands knew. 'Now she and my mother have nothing. No home, no money. I cannot bear to think of it,' said Walter, his voice choked with unshed tears.

'I'm so sorry.' Rowlands patted the boy's shoulder. The gesture, like the words, seemed utterly ineffectual. 'I wish there was something I could do,' he said. 'Perhaps I could send money.'

'They would confiscate it,' was the terse reply. There was no need to ask who 'they' were. 'And besides, I do not know what address to send it to. The letter was posted over a month ago. Clara says they can only remain with Cousin Ida a few days. It is dangerous for her, too, you see. They . . . my mother and sister . . . could be anywhere by this time.' Again, his voice sounded unsteady. 'But it is kind of you to suggest this, Herr Rowlands,' added the young man, who was polite to a fault. 'You have always been kind to our family. Why, without your help, I would not have come to England. For this I will always be grateful.'

'It's only what anyone would have done,' said Rowlands. 'As for your mother and Clara, I'm sure we can think of something . . .' He let the sentence tail off. A feeling of helplessness overcame him. What could he do, after all? Walter Metzner's family were as lost to him as if . . . well, as if they had never existed. He and the younger man had by now reached the little wicket gate that led out onto the cliff steps. Without being asked, Walter gave Rowlands his arm as they began to descend. From below, came the cheerful sound of voices – Rowlands recognised that of his youngest daughter.

'Come on! Who wants a race?' As they reached the bottom of the steps, Joan spotted her father and cousin. 'Daddy! Walter! You'll race me to the breakwater and back, won't you?' Rowlands declined the challenge.

'It's much too hot for running, Joanie.'

'I will race you,' said Walter. 'But you must have a head start, since I am tall and you are small. On your marks. Get set – go!' With a shriek of joy, Joan dashed off along the beach while her cousin counted punctiliously to ten. Then he, too, set off – his long, loping strides soon bringing him level with his young cousin, to judge from the renewed shrieking.

'She'll make herself sick if she carries on like this,' said Anne, coming to stand beside her father.

'She needs to let off steam,' he said. 'I think we all do, after the day we've had.'

Drinks were being served on the terrace at the back of the hotel when Rowlands returned with his little party in tow, the young people disappearing at once to tidy themselves for the evening meal, which, though informal enough as to dress, required something a little less casual than shorts and sandshoes. Rowlands himself felt in need of a wash and a shave, and accordingly went up to his room to perform these ablutions and to change his shirt. When he had done so, he went downstairs again, slipping outside by the front door. He didn't feel like joining the others just yet. Perching himself on the low wall that ran the length of the terrace, he had just lit a cigarette when he heard a car turn into the drive and pull up in front of the hotel. There was the sound of a car door being opened. Someone got out, slamming the door shut. Someone climbed the steps towards where Rowlands sat. 'Good evening,' said a voice. 'I wonder if you can tell me . . .'

But Rowlands had already got to his feet. 'Good evening, Miss Barnes,' he said. He had, of course, been half-prepared for this meeting. She had had no such opportunity to prepare herself.

'Good Lord!' she exclaimed. 'What on earth are *you* doing here?'

'The same as you, I imagine. That is, I'm on holiday.'

'Yes, of course.' She recovered her sangfroid as quickly as he might have expected. 'How very nice to see you again.' She hesitated a moment. 'Listen . . .' she went on, with what might have been mere embarrassment at being placed in an awkward situation, but which Rowlands read as something more. A warning, perhaps.

'It's all right,' he said. 'I won't say anything.' He didn't need to spell out what it was he meant. At his last encounter with Iris Barnes, she'd got him out of a hole, but only because it suited her purpose, and her allegiance to the secret organisation she served. That she would not want any of this mentioned to anyone else went without saying. Rowlands wondered now what had brought her here – that it had to do with her job he was not in doubt. But regardless of this, there was something she should know. 'Before you go any further,' he said. 'I'm afraid I've some rather unpleasant news.'

'Oh?'

'The police are on the premises – or they were, until an hour or so ago. They're investigating a murder.'

'Not Horace Cunningham's?' she demanded sharply. Knowing what he knew of her, Rowlands was less surprised than he might have been at her knowing Cunningham's name, and the fact that he was staying at Cliff House. It merely confirmed his suspicion that she must be here on some kind of official – that is to say, clandestine – business.

'It was his wife who was murdered,' he replied.

'Ah!' It was hard not to interpret this exclamation as one of relief. 'When did it happen?'

'Last night. She was poisoned.' He hesitated a moment before saying what he said next, but she'd find out the state of affairs soon enough, he supposed. 'Cunningham believes that the poison was meant for him.'

'Hmm. What kind of poison was it?' Again, he wasn't surprised by her coolness, which some might have called callousness.

'Arsenic,' he replied. 'Traces were found in the glass in which she dissolved her sleeping powders. There's some uncertainty as to how it got there, but poison was also found in an emerald ring she was wearing.'

'Not quite the method we'd anticipated,' Iris Barnes said drily. Then, evidently deciding she'd heard enough for the time being, she descended the steps to where the car was parked. There was the sound of the boot being opened. 'I don't suppose you'd give me a hand with my bags, would you?'

'Of course.' He threw his cigarette away and went to help her. 'You don't seem very surprised by what I've told you,' he couldn't resist saying, as he relieved her of the two suitcases. 'Were you expecting something of the kind?'

'Oh, we try and anticipate everything, Mr Rowlands,' she said. 'But I can't discuss this now.' Because at that moment the front door opened and Ashenhurst looked out.

'Miss Barnes, isn't it?' he said. 'I thought I heard the car. Welcome to Cliff House! I'll just get someone to help with your luggage.'

'This gentleman is already doing so,' she said. 'Very kind of you, Mr... er...'

'It's no trouble,' said Rowlands.

'I say, how remiss of me!' replied Ashenhurst. 'Rowlands, this is Miss Barnes, who's going to be staying at Sea View Cottage. At least, she was . . .' He seemed momentarily dumbfounded by the thought of what he had to say next. 'I'm afraid something rather awful's happened,' he managed at last. 'The fact is, there's been a . . . a sudden death.'

'Mr Rowlands was just telling me about your murder,' said Miss Barnes.

'Oh! Well, I'd fully understand if you prefer to stay elsewhere. I can recommend a few places.'

'Thank you. But I'll be quite all right here.'

'Oh, good. Well, if you're really sure . . .'

'I am.'

'Splendid. Rowlands, if you'd bring Miss Barnes's bags inside, I'll get Pengelly to take them down to the cottage in the handcart,' he added, then to his guest, 'My wife will show you where to wash your hands. Unless you'd rather I took you down to the cottage straight away?'

'Actually,' said Iris Barnes. 'What I'd really like is a cocktail – a dry martini, if such a thing can be procured. It's been a long drive.'

'Nothing easier,' said Ashenhurst, then as Dorothy came out to greet the new arrival, 'My dear, this is Miss Barnes.'

'Hello,' said Dorothy. 'You're the detective lady.'

'That's right. A rather travel-stained and weary detective, as you see. Your husband has promised me a reviving drink, however.'

'Coming up,' said Ashenhurst. 'We'll be on the terrace – through the lounge and out the glass doors – when you're ready . . . Dottie, can I leave it to you to show our guest where everything is?' When the two women had gone upstairs to perform that feminine ritual known as 'powdering one's nose', Rowlands followed

154

his friend into the lounge, whose French windows stood open, letting in the warm summer air, with its scents of thyme and lavender mingling with that of cigarette smoke, and the low murmur of conversation from those gathered on the terrace outside. Ashenhurst went straight to the cocktail trolley where he began to assemble the wherewithal for a dry martini. 'So that's our lady writer?' he said. 'You seem to have hit if off with her, Rowlands, old man.'

'I suppose I have.'

'I must say, I was glad that she didn't take fright about staying here when she heard about the murder,' added Ashenhurst in a low voice. 'She's obviously not the nervous type.'

'No,' said Rowlands. 'She's certainly not that.'

'So what kind of books do you write?' The question, addressed to the new arrival, came from Daphne Simkins, calling across from the table where she sat with her husband and sons, on one side of the dining room. The object of her enquiry was at the table next to this in the bay window, which was also occupied by Colonel Rutherford and his wife.

'Can't have you sitting all on your lonesome,' said the gallant soldier, always with a mind to the welfare of the ladies (God bless 'em). Iris Barnes had accepted this invitation with evident pleasure; nor could she have chosen a more profitable source of information, thought Rowlands, bearing in mind the Colonel's garrulous tendencies. Now she considered the question before replying. 'Detective stories, mostly. Murder mysteries, I suppose you could say.'

'You've certainly come to the right place, then,' opined Colonel Rutherford.

'Johnny, really!' said his wife. 'That's in rather poor taste.'

'Sorry, m'dear, if I've spoken out of turn. But no sense in pretending it hasn't happened.'

'I suppose you've heard about our little drama?' said Mrs Simkins, apparently well recovered from her *crise de nerfs*.

'Yes,' was Miss Barnes's succinct reply. 'Most unpleasant for you all.'

'Oh it *was*! I thought I'd never get over it, didn't I, dear?' This to her husband, who was engaged in demolishing his pudding. His reply was a muffled assent. 'So,' went on Mrs Simkins, returning to her first topic, 'Would I have read any of your books?'

'I don't know. You might've. *Red-handed in Rome*. That's one of mine. *Slain in Soho*. That's another.'

'Mm. I don't think . . .'

'Are you writing a new novel?' asked Millicent Rutherford, with some interest. Rowlands remembered that she was an aficionado of the thriller genre.

'Yes. That is, just as soon as I've thought of a plot.' Iris Barnes gave a short laugh. 'I was hoping Cornwall might provide me with some inspiration. I don't think I expected quite as much as this, however.'

After this little exchange, conversation lapsed for a

while, as pudding plates were collected up and cheese and biscuits brought out. They were a sadly depleted party that evening, thought Rowlands, with even the usually resilient Miss Linden pleading a sick headache, and Eliot Dean saying he'd rather have a tray in his room so that he could go over his lines for tomorrow. 'Although what the point of that is, since we're not even going to finish the picture, I can't for the life of me see,' said Laurence Quayle.

'Who says we're not going to finish the picture?' This was Carmody. Quayle seemed momentarily taken aback.

'I assumed that since we've lost our leading lady . . .'

'Well, don't assume. As long as we're in Cornwall – and by my reckoning, that'll be for another week – we'll be continuing with the film. We owe it to Dolores, in my view.'

'Admirable sentiments,' said Quayle. 'I'm sure she'd have appreciated that. Especially since,' he added waspishly, 'she was so determined to kill the picture just before she died.'

'That's enough, Quayle.'

'It's true, isn't it? I mean,' the younger man went on, 'it was all rather convenient, don't you think, that she never got the chance to put her threat into practice?'

'What the hell are you implying?' It was the first time that the usually imperturbable Carmody had lost his temper in Rowlands' hearing.

'Nothing, old boy. It was merely an observation.' Once again, Rowlands had the impression that Quayle knew more than he was saying.

'I think,' said Cecily Nicholls, 'that if everyone's finished, we'll move into the drawing room for coffee.'

Following their brief exchange soon after her arrival, Rowlands had assumed that Miss Barnes would keep the fact that they knew one another to herself. So he was startled when, as the coffee cups were being handed around, she did exactly the opposite. 'I don't suppose you remember me, Mr Rowlands, but we have met before. It must be seven or eight years ago.' It was actually only four years since they'd last run into one another in Berlin, under very different circumstances from these, but he wasn't about to correct her. 'Yes,' she went on. 'It was at one of Celia West's parties – she's Celia Swift now, of course.' Was it Rowlands' imagination, or did his wife – who was sitting beside him – give a start at the mention of the society beauty's name?

'I . . . Yes,' he said. 'I remember now.'

'Do you mean *Lady* Celia Swift?' drawled Laurence Quayle. 'Isn't she married to some Irish lord? I saw her picture in *Titbits* the other day. I must say, she looked absolutely stunning, although she must be all of thirty-five.' Impertinent puppy! thought Rowlands. He bit back an angry retort.

'Yes, that's the one,' said Iris Barnes, apparently innocent of the havoc she had caused. 'Of course, I was only a lowly journalist at the time. Writing articles about "What the Modern Girl Wants" for various silly women's magazines.'

'Fancy!' said Daphne Simkins, who was doubtless a devotee of such articles. 'And now you're a famous author . . .' If she'd meant to embarrass the newcomer, she failed in the attempt. Miss Barnes merely laughed.

'I have a certain following,' she said. 'Readers who enjoy a good puzzle – and aren't too squeamish about a few dead bodies. But tell me,' she went on, 'do the police have anyone in mind for Miss La Mar's murder?'

'Oh, any number of us,' said Quayle facetiously. 'I was grilled to within an inch of my life about my movements on Friday night. When had I last seen or spoken to Dolores, and had I seen or heard anything suspicious?' He allowed a pause to elapse. 'If only it had been so!' he sighed. 'Whereas the fact is, I was tucked up in bed by half past eleven, and so missed out on all the fun.'

'That's a rather insensitive way of putting it,' protested Hilary Carmody. 'I'm just glad poor Cunningham can't hear you, that's all. He was looking quite dreadful at dinner this evening, I thought.' From which Rowlands gathered that the entrepreneur was not presently of their company. He hadn't been aware that the man had slipped away, but it didn't surprise him.

'My apologies,' Quayle was saying. 'But, as you've pointed out, the old boy isn't here to be offended. And you did ask, you know,' he added to Miss Barnes.

'So I did,' she replied. 'And you've given me a very clear picture.'

The next day was Sunday, which brought with it a necessary lull in the proceedings surrounding the untimely death of Dolores La Mar. After what Laurence Quayle had described as the 'grilling' of the guests and staff of Cliff House Hotel, the police had not returned to that establishment, although a police constable still kept watch outside the room in which the actress had died. Requested to remain in Coverack until after the inquest – which was to be held the following day – the cast of *Forbidden Desire*s whiled away the time as best they could. When Rowlands and his family returned from church, it was to find a group of the actors occupying the lounge, together with the Simkinses and Iris Barnes. The latter was playing patience. 'I can never get it to come out,' she was complaining. 'I must have wasted hundreds of hours at it.'

'I wonder that you're not busy writing away,' said Mrs Simkins, clicking her needles (she was always knitting something, Rowlands had noticed).

'I did a few hours first thing this morning,' was the reply. 'I find my brain works best before six a.m., as a rule.'

'How frighteningly efficient,' said Quayle. 'Do you know, I believe I have read one of your mysteries, Miss Barnes? The one in which the murderer puts the poisonous snake in his wife's slipper.'

'*Murdered in Marrakesh*,' said the author. 'Yes, that was an enjoyable one to research.'

'You must have visited some awfully interesting places,' said Lydia Linden.

'Oh, I get about,' replied Miss Barnes. 'Although I'm just as likely to find myself in Kensal Green as in Katmandu.' Perhaps only Rowlands understood what it was she meant, everyone else no doubt putting her

160

remark down to authorial vagueness. But to someone in her line of work – a spy, in effect – all places must seem equally fraught with intrigue and danger.

'Well, all I can say is, you must do all right for sales if you can afford a nifty little motor like the one you've got parked outside,' said John Simkins. 'Latest model Jaguar, isn't she?'

'Yes. My little indulgence,' replied Miss Barnes demurely. 'Such a pretty shade of red.' Just then, Cecily Nicholls came in with a tray of glasses of sherry, and the conversation turned to other things.

'I must say – no offence to our kind host and hostess – but I'll be glad to get away from here,' said Miss Linden.

'Well, you'll have to stick it out for a bit longer,' said Quayle. 'You heard what Hilary said.'

'What am I supposed to have said?' Carmody took a glass of sherry from the tray, murmuring his thanks to Mrs Nicholls as he did so.

'That we'd all have to stay another week,' was the reply. 'To finish the film. Although quite honestly, I can't see how we can finish it without Dolores.'

'Then it's a good thing you're not the director,' said Carmody. 'As a matter of fact,' he went on, 'I've got some good news for you all . . . that is, for those of you involved with the film. I've just been talking to our sponsor – Mr Cunningham, I mean – and he's very keen for the picture to go ahead. He believes it's what Dolores herself would have wanted,' added Carmody, ignoring Quayle's snort of incredulity. 'A fitting tribute to her memory. Fortunately, we have enough footage – shot both on location and in the studio – to make finishing the film possible. With a little judicious rewriting of the script . . .'

'Ha!' said Quayle.

'We should be able to finish *Forbidden Desires* to everyone's satisfaction. Including, I hope, that of our audience . . . Ah, there you are, sir,' he said as Cunningham himself came in. 'I was just telling the cast the good news. About the film,' he added when the entrepreneur did not immediately respond.

'Of course,' said the latter stiffly. 'Yes, good news indeed. My late wife would have wished for nothing less than that her memory should be honoured in this way.'

'But the ending,' persisted Quayle. 'How are we going to manage the ending? I mean with Dolores – I mean Desirée – gone, and Edward about to leave for South America . . .'

'As I said – a little rewriting will be necessary,' said Carmody. 'But I'm sure we can make it work. And what's a more popular ending than a wedding? Dolores herself made the point that people like love stories, not sad endings. A match between our leading man and our charming ingénue should prove a popular finale.'

'How perfectly lovely for you, Lydia, darling!' There was a note of acidity in Quayle's voice which was at odds with his congratulatory words. 'You'll get your starring role at last.'

Chapter Nine

Smoking a cigarette in the garden after dinner, Rowlands found himself accosted by Iris Barnes. 'Ah, Mr Rowlands! I've got you to myself at last. Walk with me as far as my cottage, will you?'

'Glad to.' She took his arm. For a few minutes, they strolled along in a silence made vivid by the distant shushing of the waves, and the scent of wildflowers along the hedgerow.

'What a heavenly place this is! I don't wonder that you and your family love it so,' she said. Rowlands made a sound indicative of agreement. 'I like your wife very much,' Miss Barnes went on. 'And your girls are delightful. The middle one – Anne, isn't it? – is very like you. Rather shy, of course, but I get the impression that she doesn't miss much. Talented artist, too.'

'Mm,' agreed Rowlands, wondering where all this

was going. He found out soon enough.

'Then there's the boy,' she went on, in a thoughtful tone. 'The one who was with you that time in Berlin. Oh, he's grown up a lot, of course.'

'I take it you mean my nephew, Billy?'

'That's the chap. He *is* the boy from the train, then?' She was referring to the occasion, four years before, when Rowlands and Billy had had to flee for their lives from Germany. Iris Barnes had helped them escape, but only, Rowlands suspected, because it had suited her ends.

'That's right,' he said. 'What of it?'

'Oh, nothing. I wondered if he'd recognised me, that's all.'

'Have you changed very much?'

She laughed. 'Well, my hair's a different colour – it was fair, and now it's red. I'm wearing spectacles, although of course these are only plain glass, my sight's as good as it ever was. And my clothes are more frumpish . . . that is, more suited to a "lady writer". But that's probably not the sort of thing a boy would notice.'

'Probably not.'

'I suppose what I'm driving at is – can I trust him to be discreet? I don't want people knowing who I really am.' And just who is that? wondered Rowlands.

Aloud he said, 'I'm sure Billy won't say anything – if indeed he's realised that he's met you before.'

'Let's hope so,' she said. 'With luck, I should be away from here within the next few days – that is, if there are no further incidents.' He supposed she was referring to

Dolores La Mar's death. Suddenly he'd had enough of her half-truths and obfuscations.

'Tell me,' he said. 'Why are you really here? I assume it's got something to do with Horace Cunningham?'

'You assume correctly.' They had reached the garden gate of Sea View Cottage. From the open window of Cliff Crest Cottage next door, came the mellifluous voice of Bing Crosby, singing 'Too Marvellous for Words'. Colonel and Mrs Rutherford evidently possessed a wind-up gramophone. In spite of the more than adequate cover provided by the music, Miss Barnes apparently preferred to take no chances of being overheard. 'Come inside a minute, will you?' Rowlands did as she'd asked. 'I've some whisky, if you'd like one.'

'No thanks,' he said. 'I oughtn't to stay long.'

'All right.' She didn't ask him to sit down, and remained standing herself. 'We've been interested in Cunningham for a while,' she said. 'Especially with the political situation in Spain being what it is.'

This was unexpected. 'Spain?' he said. 'I don't follow. Surely he's just a businessman?'

'A businessman with considerable holdings in Spanish railways,' she replied. 'And it's no secret that he's been supplying funds to the Nationalist cause.' So Cunningham, too, wasn't quite what he seemed – his cold, reserved manner concealing something altogether more fanatical.

'But I still don't see . . .'

'Then when he started receiving threatening letters, we decided it ought to be looked into. After all, whatever one might think of the Francoists, one can't have British citizens in fear of their lives.'

'How did you know about the letters?'

She was at once on the alert. 'Do you mean there've been more since Cunningham came here?'

'Two, to my knowledge. But one of them, at least, was addressed to Miss La Mar. And it's she who was killed.'

'Yes, but I can't imagine these Republican revolutionaries – or whoever it is who's been issuing these threats – can have been interested in her. She was just an actress. It's Cunningham who must have been the intended victim.'

'Which is what he said himself,' said Rowlands. He thought for a moment. 'So when did he first approach your . . . your department . . . about these threats to his life?'

'Oh, he didn't approach us directly,' was the swift rejoinder. 'Scotland Yard passed it on to us.' Iris Barnes gave a short, mirthless laugh. 'Our Mr Cunningham pulled strings with the Assistant Commissioner. His kind always believe in taking things to the top.'

'When was this again?' he persisted.

'About a month ago,' was the reply. 'Six weeks, perhaps. Why? Is it significant?'

'Only in that he must have known about the threats before he came here,' said Rowlands. 'Yet he said nothing about them, even when another letter was read in his presence. In fact, he made light of it, passing it off as just the kind of rubbish people send to actresses. If he'd received threatening letters before – addressed to himself – it seems odd that he didn't mention it.'

'Perhaps he didn't want to frighten his wife unnecessarily,' said Miss Barnes.

'Perhaps.' Rowlands wasn't convinced by this, however.

'Even if he had said something,' she went on, 'it wouldn't have prevented the attempt on his life. He was just lucky that he wasn't the one to take those powders.'

'I suppose that's one way of looking at it,' said Rowlands, feeling suddenly that he wanted very much to be outside, breathing the fresh air of the summer night.

The inquest, which had been convened in the village hall, was at two; according to Edith Rowlands, practically the whole population of the place had turned out – the suspicious death of a film star being an event so unusual as to bear comparison with the last time Coverack had made headline news, with the wreck of the SS *Paris* at the end of the previous century. That there were those amongst the older inhabitants who could recall that earlier catastrophe Rowlands was not in doubt. He wondered, as he took his seat in the row reserved for witnesses to be called, whether Dolores La Mar's murder would be remembered for quite as long, or if, like all things belonging to that greater world summed up in the word 'London', it would rapidly fade into obscurity. He rather hoped so: the place deserved better than to be coupled forever after with the uglier word, 'murder'.

Although there were of course those present, he gathered from his wife's description, who had made it their business to keep the events of the past few days in the public mind for as long as possible. 'I suppose those rather disreputable looking fellows at the back of the hall must be journalists,' was Edith's comment. 'Down from London, do you think?'

'I expect you're right,' he replied. He wasn't looking forward to his own part in all this, and hoped it would be over as quickly as possible. Both fell silent as the coroner, preceded by a rather officious type whom Rowlands guessed was his clerk, entered the hall, now transformed by the presence of these officials into a court of law. There was a disconcerting moment after the coroner had taken his seat when those assembled wondered if they had come to the right place. Because it was then that the coroner, in a dry voice like the rustling of dead leaves, announced that they were gathered there to conduct an inquest into the death of a certain Mary-Ann Cunningham, née Plunkett, who seemed to bear no relation to the late actress at all.

'Her real name, I suppose,' whispered Edith, as a general murmur went around the room.

'Quiet please,' said the coroner's clerk severely. Then there was no sound except for the scratching of pencils in notebooks as the row of reporters got down this first surprising fact. Although it surely wasn't that much of a surprise, thought Rowlands, given the propensity of actors for adopting names other than those they were born with.

It was the police medical officer, Dr Haggarty, who was called first, as might have been expected – his orotund tones giving a suitably theatrical flavour to the proceedings. When asked by the coroner to give his opinion as to the cause of death he was succinct. 'Arsenic poisoning, bringing about seizure and death.' At this, the pencils scribbled furiously, only pausing when the doctor went on to give a more detailed account of his findings at the post-mortem. These, not being suitable for sensitive readers of the newspapers to which the wielders of the pencils were contracted, could be safely ignored.

'Dr Haggarty,' said the coroner when this description of stomach contents and lividity of flesh had come to an end. 'You first examined the deceased soon after death, I gather?'

'That is correct. Although,' said the Medical Officer, making no attempt to conceal his irritation at this fact, 'I was not called immediately. By the time I made my first examination several hours had passed, by my calculation, from the estimated time of death.'

'And when was that?' rustled the dry leaves.

'As I said, it can only be an estimated time,' boomed the other as if, thought Rowlands, he were onstage at the Old Vic, instead of giving evidence in a village hall. 'But I would say between midnight and five a.m.' The pencils scribbled once more.

'Thank you, Doctor. That is all for the present.' Next to be sworn in was Constable Chegwin. He, too, appeared to be making the most of this opportunity to perform.

'At oh-seven-hundred hours on the twenty-first August 1937, I was summoned by telephone to the Cliff House Hotel, to investigate a reported fatality. I then proceeded to the aforementioned address on my bicycle.'

'You may leave all that out,' said the coroner. 'Simply tell the court what it was you found at the scene.'

'Yes, sir. Right you are, sir.' Chegwin sounded momentarily as if he'd been put off his stroke. 'I . . . I found the deceased . . . that's to say, Miss La Mar . . . or Plunkett, I should say . . . lying on the bed in the room which I have reason to believe was hers . . .' Stifled laughter from the reporters' bench.

'Silence!' from the usher.

'Go on, Constable,' said the coroner. 'Very well, sir. I . . . I ascertained from Dr Finch . . .'

'You are referring to the local General Practitioner, are you not?'

'Yes, sir. He . . . Dr Finch . . . had arrived about twenty minutes before I did . . .'

'That would have been at around a quarter past seven, I take it?'

'Yes, sir. Dr Finch gave as his opinion that the lady had been dead for several hours. I then took it upon myself to close up the room, and to telephone Police HQ at Truro.'

'Thank you, Constable. You may stand down.'

A brief whispered exchange ensued between the coroner and someone else – Inspector Trewin, guessed Rowlands, although he couldn't be sure. Then the dry leaves rustled once more. 'I should now like to call

Caterina Casals.' At once, a buzz of interest went around the room. 'I really must have quiet while the court is in session,' said that dry, emotionless voice. 'Otherwise I shall have no choice but to clear it.' Silence accordingly fell as the witness made her way to the chair at the front of the room, which had been placed there for that purpose.

'You are Caterina Casals?'

A silence followed; no doubt the girl had merely nodded. 'You must answer yes or no,' said the coroner, not unkindly.

'Yes. That is my name.' The voice, with its distinctive accent, hardly rose above a whisper.

'You are . . . or rather, you were . . . the deceased's personal maid?'

'That is so.'

'Can you tell us in your own words, Miss Casals, exactly what you did on the morning of Saturday, twenty-first August . . . that is, the morning of your mistress's death?'

A long silence ensued, during which even the scratching of pencils in notebooks ceased. 'Miss Casals? You must tell us what you know. Come, come, there is nothing to be frightened of.' Because the young woman must have conveyed, by some look or sign, how very much she disliked being questioned.

'I did not kill her,' she said, raising her voice for the first time.

'No one has suggested any such thing,' said the coroner with an edge of impatience. 'All I want to know is what you did that morning.'

'I did nothing,' said the girl. 'Only what I always did. I went to her room to wake her, as I did every morning. But this time, I could not wake her . . . because she was dead.' The pencils scribbled furiously at this.

'So you attempted to rouse your mistress,' prompted the coroner, 'and having failed to do so, what then?'

'I do not understand.'

'Did you cry out, or raise the alarm in any way?'

'I went to his room,' was the reply. 'He was asleep . . . or so it appeared. I had to call loudly to wake him.'

'By "him", you mean your master?'

'Yes,' said the girl reluctantly. 'That man over there.' She must have pointed to where Cunningham was sitting, for the coroner said, 'All right. You've made that clear. So when you'd woken your master, what then?'

'He – that man – went into my mistress's room. I heard him cry out. That is all.'

'You did not stay to assist him?'

'There was nothing to be done,' said Caterina Casals flatly. 'I went downstairs. He will tell you – the blind man.' This time, her pointing finger must have been directed at Rowlands. 'It was he I met as I went away.'

'Yes, we'll get to the next witness in due course,' said the coroner. 'Now I want to ask you about the night before your mistress's death – that is, the Friday night. When exactly was the last time you saw your mistress alive?'

For a moment, Caterina Casals seemed dumbfounded.

'Why do you want to know this?'

'Just answer the question, please.'

'I . . . I saw her when I went to turn down her bed. It was sometime before ten, I think.'

'Could you be more precise?'

'Perhaps it was earlier. Half past nine. I cannot say.'

'All right. Between half past nine and ten. And how long did you stay in Mrs Cunningham's . . . Miss La Mar's . . . room?'

'I . . . I do not know exactly. Perhaps ten minutes. I had to arrange her things for the morning.'

'You are referring to her clothes, and so forth?'

'Her clothes, yes. The things on her dressing table, too. She liked everything to be ready for her in the morning. If anything was out of place, she would be angry.'

'And these things on the dressing table – of what did they consist?'

'I do not understand.'

'What were they exactly?'

'The usual things a woman has,' said the maid indifferently. 'Powder. Perfume. Lip rouge. I do not wear these myself, but she was an actress.'

'What about jewellery? Was there anything of that sort, too?' asked the coroner, in his dry leaves voice.

'Her ruby necklace, her diamond bracelet, and her pearls were locked in the lacquer box where I always put them after she has taken them off.' Miss Casals gave a haughty sniff. 'I am not careless, if that is what you mean.'

'Nobody's implied anything of the kind,' said the

coroner. 'I merely asked if you remembered seeing any items of jewellery. Small items,' he added helpfully. The maid was silent a moment.

'I suppose you mean her earrings. She had just removed these, and so I had not the chance to put them away with the others. Her ring, too.'

'An emerald ring, was it not?'

'It had a green stone, yes,' said Caterina Casals after a moment. 'I do not know if it is an emerald. An ugly thing, I thought it . . . She called it her poison ring.' There was absolute silence in the courtroom after these words, a silence broken at last by the coroner.

'And were you aware that there was poison in it?'

'I do not understand.'

'I mean – did you ever see the poison?'

'I told you – she spoke of it. It was a kind of joke to her. I did not touch the ring.' She gave a little shudder. 'I thought it unlucky.'

Having exhausted the subject of the poison ring, the coroner moved on to the sleeping powders. 'In your statement to the police, you said that the box of sleeping powders from which your late mistress had been in the habit of extracting the paper packets containing the drug in question was empty – is that not so?'

'I saw that it was empty, yes.'

'And yet she had evidently found a supply of the powders elsewhere, for use that night?'

'She must have taken one from the box in *his* room. The box that belonged to him.'

'You refer to your master, Mr Cunningham, do you not?'

'I have said so.'

'And you have no explanation as to how the poison that was found in the glass of water in which your mistress's sleeping powders were dissolved got into the glass?'

'It was not I who did this.'

'I was not insinuating that you did. I merely asked . . .'

But she had evidently had enough of his questions. 'I have told you I did not do it,' she said, her voice growing shrill. 'Nor did I kill her. You cannot make me say that I did.'

From the back of the hall come another voice: that of Carlos Casals. 'My sister has done nothing, do you hear, old man?' In two strides, he had reached the coroner's bench. The latter sounded unperturbed.

'Sit down, Mr . . . er . . . Or I will have you removed from the court.'

'We are leaving,' retorted the chauffeur. 'Come, sister . . .'

'You're not going anywhere, my lad, until Mr Ffoulkes says you may.' This was Constable Chegwin, exercising his official duty. But Ffoulkes, the coroner, had evidently had enough of the Catalans.

'I have finished with the witness for the present,' he said in his dry-as-dust voice. 'She may step down. And I would remind the gentlemen of the press here assembled,' he went on, 'that recording anything other than the witness's own words will be treated as contempt of court.'

When the Casals siblings had quitted the room, and the furore occasioned by their outburst had died down, Rowlands heard his name called. 'The chair's to your left,' whispered Edith. He knew that already, from the direction that the witnesses' voices had come, but he squeezed her hand by way of acknowledgement.

'You are Frederick Charles Rowlands?' He answered in the affirmative. A few further confirmatory details were solicited before the question Rowlands had been dreading was put. 'You have heard the evidence of the previous witness, Miss Casals?'

He agreed that he had.

'Can you confirm that you saw Miss Casals shortly after she had left the deceased's room?' Rowlands hesitated only a moment. It was a common enough mistake.

'I didn't actually *see* her, sir. But I certainly *met* her, in the corridor leading from Miss La Mar's room, just after six a.m.'

'Yes, yes,' said the coroner, seemingly not at all put out by his blunder. 'And you were sure it was she?'

'Yes, sir. She – Miss Casals – spoke to me.'

'What did she say?'

'She asked me to let her pass,' said Rowlands. 'I did so.'

'That was all? She said nothing more?'

Nothing that she had not already said in court,

thought Rowlands. 'She sounded rather upset,' he replied. 'I asked her what the matter was, but she did not stay long enough to tell me.'

'Very well.' There was a brief pause, presumably while the other made a note. 'You may proceed, Mr Rowlands.' Then when Rowlands did not immediately go on. 'What happened after Miss Casals left you?'

'I heard Mr Cunningham cry out. His room was just along the corridor from mine, next to Miss La Mar's. I went straight there and found him outside Miss La Mar's room. He said he thought his wife was dead, and so I went to see if there was anything to be done. It was apparent – even to me – that there was not.' At these bleak words, a silence fell upon the courtroom, with even the busy pencils pausing for a moment.

'Thank you Mr Rowlands. That is all for the present.'

Several other witnesses were called – Cecily Nicholls, Jack Ashenhurst, Dr Finch – contributing his or her observations of the events of that dreadful morning, but adding nothing that Rowlands hadn't heard before. Then it was the turn of Horace Cunningham. At once, there was a stirring on the press bench as the bereaved man got up from his seat across the aisle from where Rowlands and his wife were sitting. It struck the former that Cunningham's step had become, in those few days, the shuffle of an old man, an impression confirmed by Edith, who murmured, 'Poor soul! He looks quite ill.'

Prompted as before by the coroner, Cunningham confirmed that he was Horace Arthur Cunningham, that he resided in Eaton Square, and that he had been accompanying his late wife, Mary – stage name Dolores La Mar – whilst she was engaged in making a film.

'Thank you, Mr Cunningham, that is very clear,' said the coroner in a respectful tone he had not thought it necessary to adopt with the other witnesses. 'I should like at this juncture to offer my sincere condolences on your sad loss.'

Cunningham thanked him in a low voice.

'It is my melancholy duty to have to ask you some questions about the night of your wife's death, or rather, the morning on which it was discovered. I hope this will not prove too taxing for you, but as you will appreciate, it is unavoidable, in the circumstances.'

'I understand. Ask whatever you must.'

'Very well.' The coroner rustled his notes and cleared his throat, although it made no appreciable difference to the dryness of his voice. 'I should like you to cast your mind back, Mr Cunningham, to the last time you saw or spoke to your wife, the night before her death. Can you tell me what time that was, approximately?'

Cunningham took his time replying. 'I . . . I am afraid I cannot remember the precise time,' he said at last. 'It was certainly after eleven – perhaps half past. I was on my way to bed, and I called good night to her, as I passed the door into her room . . .'

'One moment. When you say 'the door into her room', you are referring to the connecting door between your room and the one occupied by your wife?'

'That is correct,' said the entrepreneur. 'She . . . my wife . . . replied in kind, and then I closed the door . . . the connecting door, as you say.'

'And that was the last time you spoke to her?'

'It was.' Again, there followed a silence. 'If I had known . . .' said Cunningham, in a broken voice. 'If I had only known . . .'

'I am sorry to cause you distress, sir. I have only a few more questions. There was, I believe, a bathroom between your room and your wife's – is that correct?'

'It is. That was the door I meant – the door of the bathroom. Both rooms opened into this.'

'I see. And was it in the bathroom cabinet that Miss La Mar's sleeping powders were kept?'

'I believe so.'

'But we have been told by your wife's maid, Miss Casals, that the box of powders was empty.'

'That may be so. I cannot say.'

'Of course not. You have said in your statement, however, that there was a second box – one full of powders that had been prescribed for your own use?'

'Yes, that is so.'

'But one of the packets from this box had been removed, had it not? The packet which was later found beside Miss La Mar's bed?'

'Yes.'

'It was this packet which may have been adulterated with the poison which later killed your wife, was it not?'

179

'It would appear so.' Cunningham's voice was unsteady.

'So it would seem, would it not, that the poison was intended, not for your wife, but for you?' persisted the coroner.

'Oh yes. I'm quite sure it was intended for me.'

The general stampede for the exit on the part of the gentlemen of the press – no doubt in search of telephones – which followed this sensational statement, meant it was a few moments before the next, and final, witness could be heard. This was Muriel Brierley who, as the late Miss La Mar's personal secretary, might have been supposed to have had particular knowledge of the deceased's movements on the last day of her life. But in this respect, she could add nothing to what had been said by the previous witnesses. She answered the coroner's preliminary questions in a voice dull with misery. Asked to describe her last meeting with her mistress, on the evening of the latter's death, she seemed momentarily taken aback. 'I . . . I saw her when I took her her letters to sign. That was at about a quarter past nine.'

'And you did not see her again after that?'

'No. At least . . .' She broke off.

A silence followed. 'You were going to add something, Miss Brierley?'

'I was going to say that I did not see her *alive* again after that,' was the reply. She blew her nose sharply. 'I'm sorry. I . . .'

'Thank you, Miss Brierley,' said the coroner. 'I realise how painful this must be for you. I have only one more question. You have been with your mistress for two years, you have told us, and so you knew her very well. Was there anything about her manner or behaviour on the last occasion you spoke to her which struck you as unusual?'

'I don't understand what you mean.'

'I mean, was she quite herself, or did she seem in any way different?'

'Oh no, she was just the same as usual.'

'Thank you, Miss Brierley. That will be all.'

'Why do you think he asked her that?' said Edith to her husband, as they were following the rest of the crowd out of the courtroom – now reverting to its quotidian function as village hall. 'Whether she was herself or not, I mean . . .' As ever with his wife's succinct way of expressing herself, Rowlands was equal to the task of sorting out the pronouns.

'I expect the coroner wanted to ascertain whether there might have been any grounds for supposing that Miss La Mar was in fear of her life,' he replied. 'Had she seemed frightened or upset – which, given that she had already received that poison pen letter, would not have been unreasonable – it would have suggested that she, and not Cunningham, was the intended victim.'

'Yes, it was very queer, what he said,' remarked Edith. 'Why do you suppose he should think anyone was trying to kill him?' Rowlands, who had not shared with his wife the information Iris Barnes has given him, concerning the death threats Cunningham had received, gave a non-committal grunt. The verdict – 'unlawful killing by person or persons unknown' – had been as expected, leaving matters open to further investigation by the police. For himself, he was glad that only another week remained of his holiday – the first time in all the years he'd been coming to Cornwall that he'd ever felt this. But there was no doubt that something had been irretrievably spoilt. That was always the way with murder, he knew. It destroyed more than just the life, or lives, it took. A quality of innocence, perhaps.

Chapter Ten

Back at the hotel, tea was being served – although a number of the guests seemed to have moved seamlessly into the cocktail hour. 'Whisky and soda for me,' Rowlands heard Hilary Carmody say. 'After that ordeal, I feel I need it.'

'It was rather tedious,' agreed Lydia Linden. 'I thought an inquest would be more like a real trial. More dramatic, I mean. Instead, it was terribly dull.'

'You're only saying that because you didn't have any lines,' put in Laurence Quayle, with his characteristic giggle. 'I thought it was perfectly thrilling. Horace's part, especially. When he said, in that wonderfully sepulchral voice, that the poison was intended for him, I thought I'd *die*. And let's not forget Muriel. Quite a promising little performance for a beginner, I thought.'

From which Rowlands assumed that neither

Cunningham nor Miss Brierley had yet joined the throng gathered around the tea table in the lounge, only to hear Miss Linden say in an undertone, 'Pipe down, Larry, they'll hear you!'

'Oh, I've no secrets from anyone,' said Quayle, in the slightly elevated tone which suggested to Rowlands that the young man was nursing some private amusement. 'Unlike some people I could think of.'

'How you do love making mysteries,' said the actress, in a bored tone.

'Not I,' said the young man innocently. 'Why, if something's on my mind, I just come right out and say it. Honesty's my middle name.' To which Miss Linden's reply was a snort of disbelief.

'You!' she said. 'You're about as honest as a rattlesnake.'

'Well, thanks very much – I *don't* think!'

A silence followed this little exchange which was broken by Eliot Dean. 'To think,' he sighed, 'that we've another week of this before we can pack up and go home . . . I call it quite inhuman of Carmody, I really do.'

'What? Being forced to spend another few days in these heavenly surroundings?' cried Lydia Linden. 'Sometimes I think you've been spoilt, ducky, I really do.'

'I was thinking of Dolores, as a matter of fact.' Dean sounded rather hurt. 'It really won't be the same without her.'

'You can say that again!' This was Laurence Quayle. 'I for one am delighted at the prospect . . . I mean of finishing the film,' he added. 'In case you thought I meant something else.'

'Oh, we all know what you meant,' said Dean sourly.

'As it happens,' replied Quayle, 'I'm probably the only one of all of us – film people, that is – who had no motive for killing her.'

'Larry, for heaven's sake! Dry up, won't you?'

'And then course there's the question of *opportunity*. I think that was brought out rather well at the inquest, don't you?'

'May I get you a sherry, Miss Brierley?' said Edith loudly, conveying by this means her disapproval of the actors' conversation.

'No thank you,' said the secretary. 'I . . . I think I'd rather have a glass of lemonade. It's so hot.' The Rowlandses agreed that it was hot; after which conversation lapsed, as so often with poor Miss Brierley.

'Really!' Edith said to her husband when the secretary, muttering something about going to sit down, had moved away. 'You'd think Mr Quayle and his friends might have the good taste not to joke about the poor woman's death on the very day of the inquest.'

Rowlands murmured an agreement although really he didn't see what difference it made whether it was the day of the inquest or not. There was something about all of this – an atmosphere – he didn't like one bit. He and Edith carried their teacups out onto the terrace where folding tables and chairs had been set out for the benefit of those who wanted to enjoy the last of the sunshine. But as they were about to sit down, they were hailed from another table. 'I say, do join me, won't you?' It was Iris Barnes. 'Such an interesting afternoon!' she remarked, as they did so. 'Cornwall is turning out to be a lot more eventful than I anticipated.'

'Yes, I imagine attending an inquest might be quite productive in your line of work,' said Edith, taking a sip of tea. There was a brief and – to Rowlands' ear – faintly startled silence.

'By my line of work I take it you mean writing detective stories?' said Miss Barnes. 'As a matter of fact, I did find it useful. It's given me a number of possible leads, as far as my story's concerned.'

'Oh, do give us an idea what it's about!' cried Edith. 'It's so exciting to meet a real author, isn't it, Fred?'

'Very exciting,' he said.

'I'm afraid I never reveal my plots until I'm absolutely sure how they're going to work out,' said Miss Barnes, with a little laugh. 'It might jinx the whole thing, you know.'

'Of course. I do see that.' Edith sounded a bit deflated. 'Do you have a title for this one, at least?'

'I thought of calling it *Crime in Cornwall*,' said the writer. 'Although I'm still not exactly sure yet what the crime is, or who's committed it.'

Dinner was a somewhat lacklustre occasion in spite of the efforts of Mrs Jago, whose lobster salad was the *pièce de résistance* of the meal. But conversation lacked the sparkle of previous evenings. Everyone was too depressed by the day's events to make much effort, thought Rowlands. It was only afterwards that he had cause to remember one particular exchange. It was that irritating woman, Daphne Simkins, who started it. The first course had been cleared away and a cold collation was being set out for those who wanted it. ('Funeral baked meats,' murmured Laurence Quayle.) 'I must say, it's been the most *extraordinary* holiday either of us can remember, hasn't it, John?' she said. The remark was addressed to her husband, but the silence in the room was such that everybody heard it.

'Hmph, yes, I . . .' her spouse began to reply, but she sailed on.

'I mean, not just all these unpleasant goings-on . . .' – it was thus she referred to the murder – 'but having a film company in our midst, to say nothing of a writer! It's all been rather exciting, hasn't it, dear?'

This time, John Simkins didn't even attempt a reply, perhaps guessing – correctly as it turned out – that his partner in life had more to say. 'I mean, I've been dying to ask: what's the film about? Not a murder mystery, I take it?' She gave a tinkling laugh. 'That would be too perfect, wouldn't it?'

'It's not a thriller, no,' said Hilary Carmody, evidently used to fielding questions of this sort from members of the public. 'More of a psychological drama.'

'Psychological fiddlesticks, if you want my opinion,' Colonel Rutherford was heard to mutter.

'But what is it *about*?' persisted Mrs Simkins, ignoring

this interruption. 'I gather there's a love story. I like a nice love story, don't I, dear?' Rowlands could well imagine the look on Simkins' face.

'Well, there's certainly a romantic element,' said Carmody. 'But I'd say it's more about mistaken identities. The way one doesn't always recognise who the person in front of one really is, until circumstances compel one to do so.'

'Oh phooey,' interjected Lydia Linden. 'It's a tale of star-crossed lovers, updated for the cocktail crowd.'

'Yes, but our version has a happy ending,' said Eliot Dean. 'Boy meets girl and gets girl – unlike the original.'

'Rather old to play Romeo, aren't we?' snickered Quayle. 'And if it resembles any Shakespeare play, it's *Richard III* – or the Scottish play. The ambitious upstart wins the day.'

'You are horrid,' laughed Miss Linden. 'It's a good thing we're friends, Larry, or I might take offence, even if I wasn't already offended by that lurid blazer. I mean, honestly! I know we're being casual this evening, but puce and lavender stripes . . .'

'I think it's a perfectly lovely combination,' was the reply. 'And it sets off that lilac frock of yours rather well, don't you think?'

'All right, you're forgiven for the blazer,' said the actress. 'But I still haven't forgiven you for calling me an upstart.'

'What makes you think I was referring to you?' said Quayle innocently. 'As a matter of fact, I think you'll be a great success as a leading lady, Liddy, darling. No, it wasn't you I was thinking of, at all.'

It was next morning that things took an unexpected turn. Rowlands and his wife were just sitting down to breakfast with those guests who still remained (the cast of *Forbidden Desires* having decamped to the village to continue with filming) when Anne burst into the dining room. She was followed by her cousin Billy, Danny Ashenhurst and Joan. 'Mummy!' she cried breathlessly. 'Dad! You've got to come. It's Walter.'

'What's the matter with him? Is he ill?'

It was Billy who replied. 'He's cleared out. I should know, because our rooms are next to each other, and his stuff was all over the place – clothes, papers. Now it's not there any more. His bed hasn't been slept in, either.'

'Do you think he's been kidnapped?' demanded Joan, with a certain relish.

'Be quiet, all of you.' This was Edith. 'I'm sure there's a perfectly reasonable explanation. I suppose,' she said to her husband, 'we'd better go and see for ourselves what's happened before alerting Jack and Dorothy.'

'Yes,' he said, getting to his feet.

'I'll come with you, if I may,' said Iris Barnes, from her table in the bay window. 'I'm quite good at tracking people down.'

But Walter's room proved as deserted as the children had said. The two drawers allocated to his things in the chest of drawers were empty; nor were there any of his clothes in the wardrobe. Books and personal belongings, too, had been cleared away with the exception of one heavy tome. '*The Oxford English Dictionary*,' said Edith, picking it up. 'Oh, look! There's a letter inside. It's addressed to you, Fred.'

'Read it, will you?'

She cleared her throat. '"*Dear Mr Rowlands, By the time you read this, I will have left Cornwall forever . . .*"'

Anne gave a cry of dismay.

'"*As a former soldier, you will know that I have no choice but to do what I believe to be my duty. If the Enemy is to be defeated, then it will be by those such as I who have vowed to take up arms against its evil force. I hope you will understand . . .*"'

'I'm beginning to,' said Rowlands grimly.

'"*And please do not try to stop me. I am doing what I know is right. Since my native land is already in the grip of the Enemy, I must go where the battle is still to be won . . .*"'

'He means Spain,' said Iris Barnes.

'Yes,' said Rowlands. 'I believe you're right. Is there any more, Edie?'

'Just this: "*I must ask you to forgive my bad English, and also to send my best wishes to Mr and Mrs Ashenhurst, who have been so kind to me. Tell them I will write as soon as I reach my destination. My heart is too full to write more. Your friend, Walter Metzner*".' Edith folded up the letter. 'It sounds as if he's made up his mind,' she said.

* * *

When he heard what had happened, Jack Ashenhurst was silent for a long moment. 'I was afraid of something like this,' he said at last. 'The boy's been awfully quiet lately – not that he's ever been the talkative sort. But he's seemed distracted, as if something were preying on his mind. I thought it was just the usual stuff that gets one down at his age. Girls, and so forth. It appears I was wrong.'

The two couples, with Miss Barnes and Anne in attendance, were in the small private sitting room the Ashenhursts used when not engaged with their guests. Billy and Danny had gone to continue the hunt for Walter in the places he'd been wont to frequent – along the beach, and clifftop. Soon, the men would join them before – if the search proved fruitless – recruiting some of the local constabulary for assistance. Although this, thought Rowlands, wasn't just a case of a young lad's going off for an early morning tramp. The letter proved that. 'Walter's always taken an interest in politics,' said Dorothy, who until that moment had said little, perhaps shaken by the news of what her charge had done. 'Why, only the other day I came upon him talking to Carlos about the situation in Catalonia.'

'Carlos?' said Iris Barnes sharply.

'Casals. Cunningham's chauffeur,' supplied Rowlands.

'Ah yes,' she said. 'It was Miss Casals who gave evidence at the inquest wasn't it?'

'It was.' A thought struck Rowlands. 'When was this, Dottie? That you saw Walter talking to Casals, I mean.'

'I'm not sure exactly. A couple of days ago, perhaps.'

'He was always going over to the stable block, to talk to Mr Casals,' put in Anne. 'He said it was the only way to find out what was really going on in Spain.'

'Then I think we should go and talk to Casals, and his sister, too,' said Rowlands, getting to his feet. 'It may be that they can cast some light on Walter's movements.'

'What's going on?' said Cecily Nicholls, coming in at that moment. She was swiftly put in the picture about Walter's disappearance. 'Oh dear, how very worrying!' she said. 'I'll come with you to talk to Mr Casals, Fred.'

But when they reached the stable block, there was no sign of the chauffeur or his sister. Repeated knocking on the door of the upstairs flat failed to raise either of them, and there was no one about in the stable yard, where Casals was usually to be found polishing the Rolls or carrying out other necessary maintenance. Nor was man or vehicle to be found in the garage. 'That's odd,' said Rowlands when this fact was confirmed by his companion. 'I'd have thought Casals would have put the car away when he drove Cunningham back from the inquest yesterday.'

'But Mr Cunningham took a taxi to the inquest,' said Mrs Nicholls. 'I know, because I called it for him. It was Bert Pengelly – our Mr Pengelly's brother, you know – who collected him and brought him back. Apparently, there was something the matter with the Rolls, and so . . .'

'Even odder, then,' said Rowlands, 'that it's no longer in the garage.'

'Perhaps whatever the problem was has been fixed?'

'Perhaps it has. It still doesn't explain where our man has got to – or his sister, if it comes to that.'

They were soon to find out, for just then, footsteps were heard crossing the cobbled yard, and a voice – Horace Cunningham's – said in an irritable tone, 'Casals! Drat the fellow! Why doesn't he answer?' Then, seeing the others, 'Ah, Mrs Nicholls . . . Rowlands. I wonder if you've seen my chauffeur about? He was supposed to report to me about some repairs he'd been doing to my car, but he hasn't appeared. Most inconvenient, because I'd been intending to take a drive along the coast this morning. Clear my head, after the, ah, unpleasantness of recent days.'

The feeling of unease which had started to afflict Rowlands ever since they'd discovered that the car was gone now prompted him to say, 'When did you last see Casals, Mr Cunningham?'

The other took a moment to reply. 'Hmph! It was just before dinner last night. I gave him the evening off, on the condition that he made sure the car was ready for me this morning.' Just the time when Walter Metzner was last seen, thought Rowlands, with a sinking heart.

'And Miss Casals – your late wife's maid – I don't suppose you've seen her in the past hour or so?'

'Caterina? No – why should I?'

Sensing from the older man's querulous tone that his patience was wearing thin, Mrs Nicholls hastened to tell him about Walter's disappearance. 'Since it would seem that he was in the habit of talking to Carlos Casals,' she concluded, 'we thought that he – Mr Casals – might have an idea of the boy's whereabouts.'

'Can't imagine why you should think anything of the kind,' was the reply. 'It's obvious to me what's happened. The boy's run off. Boys do, you know. He'll turn up before too long, when he's tired and wants feeding – you mark my words if he doesn't.'

'And Casals?' said Rowlands. 'Will he turn up too? You have to admit, it's rather a coincidence – the fact of their disappearing at the same time.'

'Coincidence?' echoed the entrepreneur. 'I suppose it is rather strange when you put it like that. The man promised me faithfully that he'd bring the car round for my drive once he'd seen to the problem with the engine.'

'Well, the car's not there now,' said Rowlands. 'Nor, it appears, is Casals – or his sister. And I'm willing to bet that if Walter's to be found anywhere, it'll be in the back of that car, on his way to Spain.'

When they got back to the hotel, Cunningham took himself off, muttering something about having to make a telephone call. It was a relief, thought Rowlands, not to have the man around while he himself broke the news of this latest development to his sister and brother-in-law. Quite apart from the fact that he wasn't family, Cunningham had made it clear that he took little interest in the welfare of the young German. Whereas, for Jack and Dorothy, Walter had become like another son, during these past four years. Certainly, Jack was all for telephoning the police. 'If you're right about this, Fred, then it's a case of abduction, surely? The boy's a minor.'

'He's sixteen,' said Dorothy. 'And grown-up for his age.'

'Even so.' Her husband sounded troubled. 'I don't like it one bit. Running away to Spain! Whatever next? If I'd had the faintest idea what he was contemplating, I'd have done everything in my power to stop him, as you would, too, Dottie, whatever you say.'

'I was only saying that Walter's old enough to make up his mind about things.'

'Not old enough to fight in a war, though,' said Rowlands, even though he had known plenty of lads Walter's age and younger who'd done just that in 1914.

'The question is,' put in Edith, 'what do we do now? I think Jack's right – we should call the police. There might still be a chance to stop him.'

'They've had at least twelve hours' start,' Rowlands pointed out. 'They could be in France already. And even if they haven't yet left England, we've still no idea which port they're heading to. It might be Plymouth, Poole, or even Portsmouth.'

'I'll ring up and find out the times of the sailings,' said Cecily Nicholls. 'If there's a chance that they haven't yet left, then . . .' Before she could finish speaking, there came a knock at the door of the Ashenhursts' sitting room, and Horace Cunningham put his head in.

'A word with you, Ashenhurst, if I may,' he said. 'Only I thought it best to inform you that I've decided to call in the police to deal with this latest development.'

'I see,' was the reply. It seemed to Rowlands that his brother-in-law sounded faintly put out at the other's having taken charge of matters without prior consultation. 'As a matter of fact, we were just about to do the very same thing. Has Inspector Trewin said what time he'll be here?'

'Oh, it wasn't the local man I telephoned,' said Cunningham with a certain hauteur. 'I think this is a case for Scotland Yard.'

'Scotland Yard?' echoed Ashenhurst. 'Well, I appreciate your taking Walter's disappearance so seriously, sir, but surely . . .'

'It's got nothing to do with the boy,' said the entrepreneur impatiently. 'I should have thought that was obvious.'

'Then I fail to see . . .'

'It's Casals the police will be after,' said Cunningham. 'And his sister, although whether she *is* his sister I'm inclined to doubt. Oh, yes,' he went on, 'I think you'll find that Scotland Yard will take a very close interest in those two.' He gave a grim little chuckle. 'As soon as I discovered they were missing, it all started to make sense. It must have been Casals who tried to kill me, and killed my wife by mistake. Or maybe it was the woman who was responsible. She'd certainly have had the opportunity. One thing's certain – they were in it together, you may be sure.'

* * *

After Cunningham had left the room, a brief conference ensued. Notwithstanding the entrepreneur's pre-emptive act of calling in Scotland Yard, it still made sense to inform the local police force about Walter's disappearance. Twenty minutes later, Constable Chegwin arrived, sounding somewhat out of breath from having pedalled up from the village on his bicycle. Rowlands took him into the drawing room, where – with occasional asides from the others – he brought the policeman up to date on the latest developments regarding Walter. Perhaps, thought Rowlands, he'd think the boy's disappearance a serious enough matter to involve his superiors.

But in this he was disappointed. Chegwin seemed to take much the same unconcerned attitude to what had happened as Cunningham had done. 'He'll turn up, never you fear,' he said cheerfully when Rowlands had finished speaking. 'I know what boys can be, having two of my own. Scamps, most of 'em. No doubt he meant to leave you a note, and forgot. He'll turn up for his dinner, you'll see.'

In vain did Dorothy argue that Walter wasn't the thoughtless type. In vain did Rowlands point out that the boy had in fact left a note. 'Running away to fight, you say?' chuckled the policeman. 'I'd say that was a bit of storytelling. Boys are like that – always fancying themselves as heroes of some adventure.'

'Even if you're right about Walter's having made the whole thing up and gone off somewhere nearby, mightn't he have fallen and hurt himself?' said Edith. 'These cliff paths can be very dangerous.'

'Well, if it'll set your mind at rest, Mrs Rowlands, I'll put the word out to see if anybody's spotted the lad in the neighbourhood,' said Chegwin magnanimously. 'Can't do any harm, can it?'

'Thank you, Constable,' said Rowlands. 'While you're about it, perhaps you could ask around to see if anyone saw a silver-grey Rolls-Royce heading in either the Plymouth or the Portsmouth direction yesterday night? It's an outside chance but it might make all the difference.'

'I can do that, sir,' was the reply. 'I take it that'd be Mr Cunningham's motor – the one that's missing?'

'That's right.'

'Can't be too many of those about,' laughed Chegwin. 'Leastways, not in Cornwall.' The constable was just taking his leave when Mrs Nicholls emerged from the study. Having spent the past half-hour telephoning the various ports from which the three fugitives might have departed, she had no very encouraging news to offer.

'There was a sailing from Plymouth at six o'clock this morning,' she said. It was now past ten, by Rowlands' watch. 'There's another at midday.'

'So the chances are, if they caught the earlier boat, that they'll already have reached France,' said Jack.

'It's much the same story with the Portsmouth sailings,' went on Mrs Nicholls. 'Although there are more of those. Sailings at seven, one o'clock and three, and then again at five and seven. Then there's Poole. One-thirty and four-thirty.'

'They might have caught any of them,' said Rowlands. 'The trouble is, we just don't know for certain. What time is the last sailing from Plymouth, did you say?'

'Five p.m.'

'Then that's the one I'll take,' he said.

'Fred . . .'

'Well, one of us has to go after him,' he said. 'Or two of us, rather, since I'm not so foolish as to think of going alone. Edie, it'll have to be you, I'm afraid. We can get a taxi to Truro, and the train from there. If we leave straight after lunch, we should be in Plymouth in time for the five o'clock sailing.'

'That's all very well, Fred, but I don't see how I can leave the girls and come with you. I mean, Margaret's very capable, but she's too young to manage the other two on her own, and with my mother still away in Scotland . . .'

'I hope I'm not interrupting anything?' said a voice. It was Iris Barnes. 'Only the door was ajar, and I couldn't help overhearing . . .' She came in, closing the door firmly behind her. 'And I wondered if I could be of help? You see, there's my car . . . I'd be very willing to drive you to Plymouth, Mr Rowlands. It is Plymouth you need to get to, isn't it?'

'Yes, but . . .' How the devil did she know that? wondered Rowlands. Even *he* wasn't sure which of the West Country ports Walter and the Casals pair had sailed from.

'You'll have to forgive my interfering like this,' went on Miss Barnes, as if she had heard the unspoken question. 'But I took the liberty of making a few telephone calls. I happen to have a contact who was able to verify that a silver-grey Rolls-Royce, with the registration GW 628, was seen in the vicinity of Plymouth Docks around two hours ago. My contact thinks they must have missed the earlier sailing, and will be taking the midday boat.'

There was a moment's startled pause before Jack Ashenhurst said, 'My goodness! I'd say that was a rather useful contact.'

'One collects them, as a writer,' was the demure reply. 'Research, you know. As it happens this particular contact is a retired policeman. So I think we can trust the accuracy of his observations.'

'I'm sure we can,' said Rowlands drily. 'And I'm grateful for your offer of help. But I'll still need someone to accompany me on the journey. Dottie, perhaps you . . .'

'Oh, I'll come,' said his sister. 'You needn't try and stop me, Jack. Walter's our responsibility, now.'

'I wouldn't dream of stopping you,' said her husband mildly. 'And I agree that we owe it to Walter's family to bring him back. Since there'd be no earthly use in having two blind men go in search of him, you'll have to go in my stead, Dottie. But I can't say I'm happy about it. Spain is a very dangerous place just now.' Miss Barnes gave a discreet cough.

'If I might make a suggestion?' she said. 'I think, with

all due respect to Mrs Ashenhurst, that it might be best if *I* were the one to accompany Mr Rowlands to Spain. Unlike the rest of you, I'm a free agent. I also happen to speak quite good Spanish.' Of course you do, thought Rowlands, amused in spite of himself at the deftness with which the secret agent had inveigled herself into their plans.

'But aren't you supposed to be writing your Cornish novel?' he asked, with an innocent air. 'Won't coming with me to Spain at such short notice disrupt all that?'

'Oh, I've reached a good stopping point in the story,' was the airy reply. 'So I can set it aside quite happily. And going to Barcelona – because I believe that's where your young friend and his companions are headed – will give me the opportunity to research a new book.'

'I think it's the best solution, Fred,' said Edith. 'Not that I'm at all happy about your going, but I see that it can't be helped.'

'It's very generous of you, Miss Barnes,' said Cecily Nicholls, who had listened to these various exchanges without comment until now. 'I'm sure I don't know how we can repay you for giving up so much of your valuable time . . . to say nothing of, well, the risk involved. As my brother says, Spain isn't the safest place.'

'It isn't too bad for foreigners,' said Iris Barnes briskly. 'At least, if one's careful to appear neutral when talking to Nationalists, and partisan, in the Republican camp.'

'You seem to know a lot about it,' said Ashenhurst.

'Yes, I try and keep myself informed,' said the novelist. 'In a previous life, I had to interview film stars for the women's magazines. Politics is infinitely less of a strain, believe me.'

Chapter Eleven

Lunch was a hasty affair, of soup and cold meat. Rowlands barely tasted what was put in front of him, so anxious was he to get on the road and, with luck, on the trail of the missing boy. But his newly elected travelling companion was adamant that they should have something to sustain them. 'In fact it might be a good idea to see if your Mrs Jago could let us have some sandwiches for the journey,' said Miss Barnes. Since Edith was busy packing a bag with clean shirts and other necessaries her husband might need for an absence of a few days, Rowlands took it upon himself to convey this request to the hotel's cook. In the kitchen, he found a somewhat hot and bothered Mrs Jago, presiding over the washing-up while taking every opportunity to find fault with Jenny Penhaligon.

'Now mind you give those knives and forks a good rub, to stop 'em going streaky.'

'Yes'm.'

'And you can give them kippers to the cat. Such a waste,' she mourned. 'Seems as our Mr Larry' – this was her name for Laurence Quayle, who had become a favourite – 'didn't fancy 'em this mornin'. Left his tray untouched outside his door . . . Not like him to skip his breakfast. "Mrs J," he says to me, "You poach the finest kippers this side of Inverary" . . . Afternoon, Mr Rowlands. What can I do for you?' Rowlands put his request. 'Sandwiches, you say? Think as how we might be able to do a bit better'n that! There's some cold chicken from yesterday, and some o' those pasties I was going to give the young folks for their tea. Baked 'em myself this mornin'. . . Think that'd do you?' Rowlands said it would. 'I can't think what's happened to young Sally,' the cook went on as she began to assemble the ingredients for this repast. 'She should've been here ten minutes ago. Unreliable, that's the trouble with these young girls, Mr Rowlands. Now, in my day . . .'

But they were never to hear what it had been like in Mrs Jago's day, because at that moment, Sally Trelawny came running in, flinging the kitchen door wide in her haste. 'Oh, Mum,' she gasped. 'Come quick! Something awful's happened. There's a man gone over the cliff. I think it's Mr Larry . . .' Having delivered herself of this shocking revelation, she burst into tears.

'Now, now, don't take on so,' said Mrs Jago. 'I'm sure nobody thinks you were to blame.' Which only made the girl cry harder.

'Where exactly was this?' asked Rowlands. It occurred to him that help should be summoned at once – if it were not already too late.

'On the c-cliff path,' stammered Sally. ''Bout half a mile back. I . . . I stopped to tie my shoelace an' I saw 'un. On the rocks sticking out jus' below the Point. He was lyin' there so still I didn't notice him at first. Then I s-saw his pink an' purple striped jacket an' I knew . . .' Her sobs grew louder.

'There, there,' said Mrs Jago. 'What you need is a nice cup of tea with lots of sugar. Well, if he's wearing that striped jacket of his, it's got to be Mr Larry,' she went on. 'Quite a fancy dresser, he is – or rather, was, poor soul.' At which Jenny, too, began to cry. 'Now don't you start, my girl,' said Mrs Jago. 'Or you'll have us all in tears.'

It sounded from what the girl had said as if Quayle must have been wearing a blazer, thought Rowlands. Now he came to think of it, there had been some remark about the man's garish taste in clothes at dinner last night. He hadn't been paying much attention. 'I'll get Mr Ashenhust to ring for a doctor,' he said. And the police, he added silently. Because if it turned out that Laurence Quayle was indeed beyond help, then there would be another suspicious death for that body of men to investigate. Mrs Jago blew her nose sharply.

'And to think I won't be seeing his cheery face ever again,' she said lugubriously. 'How troubles do rain down on us all, to be sure.'

In the hall, Rowlands almost ran into Iris Barnes, coming in through the front door. 'I've brought the car round,' she said. 'We can get going as soon as you like.'

'I'm afraid we won't be going anywhere for a while,' he said. Briefly, he explained what had happened. The Special Operations Agent let out a low whistle.

'Is it murder, do you think?'

'I couldn't possibly say,' replied Rowlands. 'We don't even know for certain if the man is dead. I was just going to call a doctor.'

'What's this?' Jack Ashenhurst had appeared at the top of the stairs. When Rowland had put him in the picture, he said, 'I'll handle this, Fred. Why don't you go and see if there's anything to be done for the poor fellow?'

'I'll come with you,' said Miss Barnes.

'I'd appreciate that,' said Rowlands, then, to Ashenhurst, 'When you've called Dr Finch, I think you should inform the police.'

Walking as swiftly as they could without actually breaking into a run, Rowlands and Iris Barnes crossed the lawn towards the gate that led to the cliff path. 'Do let me take your arm,' said the latter as they reached it. 'I realise that it's probably unnecessary, but . . .'

'I do know this path pretty well,' said Rowlands. 'But if it'll make you feel better, knowing that I'm not about to stumble over the edge to my doom, then please do.' She accordingly put her hand on the crook of his arm, and the two of them resumed their walk, at a slightly slower pace. After twenty years of living without sight – or at least with only a fraction of what he had once possessed – Rowlands had become adept at navigating his way through the world by using his other senses. Now, as they strode along, the sound of the sea to his right, combined with other, no less significant, sounds, such as the crunch of loose stones underfoot and the dry crackle of the grass on either side, kept him from straying too far from the path. The coconut scent of gorse flowers from the bushes that clustered thickly on the landward side of the path, and the smell of the wild thyme rising from beneath his feet, were other useful markers, letting him know, as plainly as if he could see, that he was (literally) on the right track. Nonetheless, he was grateful for Miss Barnes's solicitude. The path was broad and even here, but it grew narrower and steeper further on, perhaps at around the spot where Laurence Quayle (if it was indeed he) had gone over.

'What I don't understand . . .' began Rowlands, just as his companion said, 'The thing that puzzles me . . .'

'You first,' he said.

'All right. Just what did he – Quayle – think he was doing, going for a walk along the cliffs at night? Assuming it was at night, and not early this morning.'

'Exactly what I was wondering myself. By his own admission, he wasn't the fresh air type. Can you see him yet?' Because as they had now been walking for around ten minutes, at a moderately brisk pace, Rowlands estimated that they must be close to the place where Sally Trelawny had seen the body. *Half a mile back, hadn't she said?*

'I think so,' Miss Barnes replied. She let go of his arm for a moment and took a few paces towards the cliff edge, to take a closer look. 'Yes, it's Quayle all right. I'd recognise that blazer anywhere. What a horror!' Rowlands wasn't entirely sure if it was the blazer, or the fate which had befallen the unfortunate actor to which she was referring. 'He's lying on a rocky ledge, about thirty feet below where we're standing. Looks pretty dead to me. Although I suppose we ought to wait for an expert opinion.'

'This sounds like the doctor now,' said Rowlands. Because his sharp ears had caught the sound of Bill Finch's Morris Minor coming along the lane that ran beside the clifftop meadow in which they stood. It had been not far from here that he and Edith had overheard Cecily and Bill Finch talking so intimately. That had only been a few days ago, and yet it seemed an age, he thought. The car pulled up and, a moment or so later, Finch was hurrying across the field towards them.

'I came as soon as I heard,' he said as he drew near. 'Jack said there'd been an accident.'

'Yes,' said Rowlands. 'It's Laurence Quayle. He appears to have gone over the cliff just about here.'

'If it hadn't been for that narrow ledge jutting out from the cliff face, he'd have ended up in the sea,' put in Miss Barnes. 'Lucky for us he didn't.'

'But not so lucky for him,' said Rowlands grimly.

'No indeed, poor fellow.' Dr Finch paused for a moment, evidently contemplating the scene. He let out a breath. 'Hard to say from here, but it doesn't look good,' he said at last. 'Well, better take a closer look, I suppose. I'll just go and get my climbing equipment from the car.'

'You're well-prepared,' said Rowlands.

'Have to be, in a place like this,' was the reply. 'And I do a bit of climbing when I'm off duty. Helps to keep one fit, you know.' He returned in due course with ropes and a steel peg, which – to judge from the brisk sound of hammering that followed – he proceeded to drive into the ground at the cliff's edge. Then, having secured the end of one of the ropes to the peg, and looping the other end around his waist, he lowered himself over the cliff to where Quayle's body was lying, having first attached another rope to the handle of his medical bag. This Miss Barnes was entrusted with sending down to the doctor once he had reached solid ground.

Perhaps ten minutes elapsed while he made his examination; then a shout came from below, to signal that he was ready to come up. A few moments after this, Dr Finch, panting a little, stood once more beside the others on the clifftop. His verdict was succinct: 'Dead. Quite some time ago, I'd say. Rigor mortis has passed off, which would suggest at least six hours had passed. My guess would be that he's been there considerably longer than that. Since late last night, in all probability.'

'Can you give a time of death?' said Iris Barnes.

'As I said, sometime last night; my guess would be no earlier than midnight and no later than four o'clock this morning. One can never be as precise as one would like,' said Dr Finch.

'Was it the fall that killed him?' asked Rowlands.

'Most likely,' was the reply. 'Again, we'll have to wait until the PM to be certain. There is one odd thing, though . . .'

'Oh?' Miss Barnes could not conceal an interest that was more than merely casual. 'And what's that?'

'Well, he'd fallen onto rock, as you'll have observed,' said the doctor. 'But his face and shirt front are covered with sand, and there are grains of sand in his eyelashes, mouth and nostrils.' Before he could elaborate on what this interesting circumstance might mean, there came the sound of another vehicle – two, in fact – pulling up in the lane, followed by the slamming of car doors and the bass rumble of male voices. 'This'll be the police,' said Bill Finch.

'I believe you're right,' said Rowlands. And indeed within a matter of moments, they were joined by Inspector Trewin and his men.

'So what have we got here, then?' said the policeman after a curt greeting to Rowlands and the doctor. Miss Barnes he ignored. He took a few paces towards the cliff edge, the better to survey the scene. 'Hmph,' he went on after a moment. 'Doesn't look as if that gentleman will be going anywhere soon. Broken neck 'ud be my guess.' Something else now caught his attention. 'Who left this climbing gear here?'

'It's mine, Inspector,' admitted Finch. 'I've just been down to make an examination of the deceased.'

'Well, that'll save Dr Haggarty from a trip out here, which'll please him, no doubt. Let's get some photographs taken of the body.' He gave an instruction to one of his team – evidently the police photographer. 'When you've finished, Mr Angwin, we can get some men down there with ropes and haul the remains up. Any thoughts on time of death, Doctor?'

'My estimate would be no earlier than midnight, and no later than four a.m.,' was the reply.

'I'm obliged to you,' said Trewin as the team of policemen under his command began the laborious business of conveying the police photographer and his equipment onto the perilous ledge where Laurence Quayle's mortal remains now lay. 'I don't suppose you thought you'd be having to do with the police again quite so soon, did you, Doctor – or you, Mr Rowlands?'

'Well . . .' began Rowlands, but the inspector hadn't finished.

'If people will go wandering about these clifftops at night . . .' he said, in a ruminating tone. 'You can't be surprised if they have accidents.'

'Are you assuming it *was* an accident?' This was Iris Barnes.

'And you are, miss?' There was the slightest edge of condescension in the inspector's voice. 'Ah, you're the writer lady,' he said when introductions had been performed. The condescension was now even more obvious. 'Detective stories you write, don't you? Wonderful, the yarns that ladies like yourself come up with . . . And no, the police will be keeping an open mind about this . . . er . . . unfortunate occurrence. But it stands to reason that this most likely *was* an accidental death. These cliff paths can be treacherous.'

With the police once more taking statements at Cliff House, it had become all too apparent that the journey to Plymouth would have to be postponed until the following day. It was already two o'clock by the time Rowlands and his companion returned to the hotel. Even if they left now, they'd be lucky to make the five o'clock sailing. There was nothing for it but to wait until the next day, although that would give the Casals even more of a head start, thought Rowlands gloomily. News of the dreadful fate that had overtaken Laurence Quayle had got around the hotel by the time he and Miss Barnes had arrived back there – circulated, no doubt, by the kitchen staff – and it was a shocked and frightened cast of actors and other guests who met them at the door. Lydia Linden had become so distressed that Dr Finch had had to prescribe a sedative. Muriel Brierley, too, had retired to her room. Hilary Carmody, although less obviously upset than either of the women, had been withdrawn and silent.

Even Eliot Dean, whose feelings towards the deceased might have been supposed to be less than cordial, had expressed his dismay. 'I don't believe it,' he had said, helping himself to a restorative glass of whisky – a tonic he prescribed for anyone who came within earshot, even though no one else took him up on it. 'I just don't believe it. Only last night Quayle was sitting here, as large as life, and now . . .' Still an actor to his fingertips, he allowed a heavy pause to ensue. 'Gone!' he cried, knocking back the whisky. 'Snuffed out, in an instant.'

Rowlands wondered what Quayle himself might have said about such histrionics, but dismissed the thought at once. People often resorted to the hackneyed or orotund phase in times of crisis, he knew. Even so, 'snuffed out' was a bit much. It wasn't quite 'Out, out, brief candle,' but it was close enough. But then, people were true to type, for the most part, where matters of life and death were concerned. Colonel Rutherford had merely remarked that what had happened was a 'damned shame'. The fellow hadn't exactly been his cup of tea, of course, but it seemed a waste. Too many young men gone west in recent years, for his liking. Daphne Simkins had said she was sorry, but if people would go walking on the cliffs at night, then this kind of thing was all too likely to happen. She had said just the same to John only yesterday.

If Horace Cunningham made any remark concerning the young man's death, Rowlands wasn't aware of it. The entrepreneur (again, true to type, he thought) had seemed entirely preoccupied with his own affairs. 'If I might have a word, Mrs Ashenhurst?' he said, putting his head around the door of the private sitting room where the Rowlandses, the Ashenhursts and Mrs Nicholls had gathered to discuss this latest crisis. 'I'd . . . er . . . like to retain my room for a few days, if I may.'

'Of course,' said Dorothy. 'I think you've paid up to the end of the month in any case.'

'I won't actually be using the room for the next couple of days,' Cunningham went on. 'I've got to run up to London tomorrow – business, you know – so I'll be needing a taxi to take me to the station.'

'I'll see to it,' said Dorothy. 'What time will you want breakfast?'

'Oh . . . Ah . . . Eight o'clock, as usual. I don't have to leave terribly early. Although it's a dreadful nuisance being without my car. But I'm sure the Scotland Yard will track it down eventually. I believe their man will be arriving tomorrow. A pity I won't be here to meet him, but there it is.'

'I suppose he'll be wanting a room, too?' said Jack. 'Unless they can put him up in the village.'

'I imagine he'll have made arrangements,' said the entrepreneur. 'Well, good night. I'm going to turn in early. I hope you find that boy of yours,' he added, by way of a parting shot.

'Oh, I intend to,' said Rowlands.

'There is one thing, before you go . . .' This was Jack again.

'Yes?'

'Forgive me for asking, but I was wondering what arrangements you'd made about your wife?'

'My wife?' Cunningham seemed astounded at the question.

'I mean about the funeral. I expect it'll be in London, won't it? Only you might want to talk to Bert Pengelly about transporting the coffin to Truro.'

'Why should I want to do that? She'll be buried in the churchyard here. She had no family, and all her, ah, acquaintances, were film people. I've already spoken to the rector about it. He'll conduct the service on Friday. Now, if you're satisfied on that point, I'll say good night.'

'Well!' said Edith, in the thunderstruck silence that followed Cunningham's departure. 'I must say . . .'

'Don't, Edith,' said her husband. 'I'm sure whatever you say will only be what we're all thinking.'

As was his habit, Rowlands took a stroll in the grounds before turning in for the night. It would give him a chance to think things out, he thought. 'I won't be long,' he said to Edith. 'We've an early start tomorrow. Iris . . . Miss Barnes . . . reckons it should take us about four hours to reach Plymouth.'

'Does she?' His wife sounded unconcerned, but Rowlands knew her too well to believe that this was the case – a suspicion confirmed when she added, 'Fred?'

'Mm-hm?'

'Is there something you're not telling me about you and that woman?'

'What do you mean?' he said. Perhaps unwisely, he attempted a joke. 'You're surely not insinuating that there's anything improper in my relationship with the lady? Why, she's young enough to be my daughter.'

'That wouldn't stop some men,' said his wife drily.

'But I don't think you're that kind of fool. It's just . . .' She hesitated, then went on, 'I can't help getting the feeling that there's more to your "relationship", as you put it, than meets the eye.' Rowlands was annoyed to find he was blushing. How much had she guessed?

'I've told you, I met her once or twice in Berlin.'

'I thought she said you'd met in London?'

'We did,' he said reluctantly. 'The Berlin meetings came afterwards. Look, Edie, I can't tell you any more than that, I'm afraid. But I can promise you that if it weren't for this business with Walter, I wouldn't be going to Spain.' Edith sighed.

'It's a good thing I'm the trusting sort,' she said. 'All right. Go and have your smoke. I've already put some shirts and your shaving things in a bag for you. How many days do you think you'll be gone?'

'I don't know. Not more than a week, I hope.'

'So do I,' said his wife resignedly.

This conversation with his spouse left Rowlands feeling distinctly uncomfortable. There'd been times in the past when he'd keep things from Edith – in one particular case, it was to spare her feelings about his own, somewhat questionable, 'relationship' with another woman – but it didn't make him think very highly of himself. Not that he'd lied to Edith, exactly; he just hadn't told her the complete truth. Which was that the woman he was going to Spain with was a government agent. A spy, in other words.

He'd just lit a cigarette when he heard a light footstep

behind him. 'May I join you?' said Miss Barnes.

'Certainly.' But he rather wished she could have left him alone with his thoughts, troubled as these were. She accordingly fell into step beside him, resting her hand lightly on his arm as they descended the flight of shallow stone steps that led from the terrace to the lawn. When they reached the bottom, he remembered his manners. 'I'm sorry. Would you like a cigarette?'

'Very much.' She took it from the offered pack. 'I'll light it myself, thanks.' When she had done so, she took an appreciative drag. 'Nothing quite like the first one after dinner, is there?' He didn't think this needed a reply, and so merely smiled, waiting for whatever it was she wanted to say. 'I hope,' she went on after they had been ambling along in silence for a few minutes, 'that your wife isn't too worried about your going to Spain?'

'I think Edith's used to my ways by now,' he said. 'She knows I wouldn't be going if it wasn't important.'

'You're lucky she's so understanding.'

'Oh, yes. I'm very lucky.'

'If you think it would reassure her, do tell her that I'll be armed – and that I'm a very good shot,' said this surprising young woman.

'I'm not sure that it would reassure her, thanks all the same,' he replied gravely.

'Just as you like,' said Miss Barnes. 'I think,' she went on, 'that we'll say you're my cousin. Visiting Spain because of your interest in . . . mediaeval churches, shall we say? There are some wonderful churches in Spain.

Yes, I think that'll do very well. The rest you can leave to me.'

'I do have one question,' he said.

'Fire away.'

'It's just that . . . since you came all this way to, er, keep an eye on Horace Cunningham, for the reasons you've explained to me, I wondered why you seem so eager to set out for Spain? Given that Cunningham is going to be here, or rather, in London.'

'Just so,' said Miss Barnes. 'He'll be in London. And we've people in London who'll keep an eye on him, as you put it.'

'I see.'

'Yes, I expect you do,' she said. 'As for my wanting to go to Spain, that's easily accounted for. You see, the people you're trying to track down – Caterina Casals and her brother – are also of interest to my organisation. They've both been heavily involved in organising Republican resistance in the region.'

'And you say that Cunningham has connections to the Nationalists?'

'Precisely.'

'So you do think the Casals couple were responsible for Dolores La Mar's murder?' said Rowlands. 'I mean, if Cunningham was right about the poison having been intended for him, then it all makes sense. It was a political assassination that went wrong.'

'That's certainly one explanation,' Miss Barnes replied. 'And it can't have been a coincidence that

Caterina Casals was working as La Mar's personal maid, nor that her brother was Cunningham's chauffeur. Yes, I think there's a strong possibility that one or both of them carried out the murder.' Rowlands was silent a moment, remembering his encounter with the maid on the morning Dolores La Mar's body was discovered. *It is not I who have done this* . . . Why was it that he felt inclined to believe her, even though the evidence appeared so damning? 'So you see it makes sense for me to follow the suspects to Barcelona,' Miss Barnes was saying, 'and, at the same time, help you find the missing boy. Quite like old times, wouldn't you say?' she said, with a laugh.

'Oh, quite,' he said, remembering that time in Berlin. 'Do I take it you've some information about where Walter and the Casals couple are heading? I mean, you seem pretty confident that it *is* Barcelona.'

'I am,' was the reply. 'That's where the fighting's concentrated at present. And the Casals are Catalans, as I expect you know. Of course, they've had a head start, but we should be able to pick up their traces pretty quickly – at least, as long as they're driving that car.'

'The Rolls?' said Rowlands. 'I don't understand. Surely you don't think that Casals would risk driving such a conspicuous vehicle all the way to Spain? Why, it'd stand out like a sore thumb. To say nothing of the fact that it's stolen.'

'How else do you suppose he's going to transport his valuable cargo?' she replied.

'What cargo's that?' said Rowlands, although as he asked the question, an answer was already suggesting itself to him.

'Guns,' said Iris Barnes, confirming his suspicions. 'My contacts in London had a tip-off a few days ago about a consignment of twenty-four boxes of Lee-Enfield .303 rifles, intended for the Canadian Mounted Police. They were dispatched from the factory two days ago, bound for Plymouth Docks. Only it turns out that three of the boxes – each containing six rifles – were missing when the consignment was loaded onto the ship yesterday morning.'

'You think Casals has got hold of them somehow?'

'Let's just say it's a strong possibility,' said Miss Barnes. 'Only a car like the Rolls would be roomy enough – and strong enough – to carry such a weight. So I'm pretty certain we'll be able to follow it – and its cargo – all the way to Barcelona.' She let out a yawn. 'If you'll excuse me, I'm going to get some shut-eye. Tomorrow'll be a long day.'

Chapter Twelve

Having wished her good night, Rowlands lingered for a few moments to enjoy the peace and quiet, guessing that this would be his last chance to do so for a while. He hoped, wherever he was at that moment, that Walter was all right. For all his grand ideas about taking on the Fascist enemy, he was still only a kid. The sound of a footfall on the grass – so faint it would have been imperceptible to anyone without Rowlands' finely tuned sense of hearing – arrested his attention. 'It's me, Uncle Fred.'

'Hello, Billy. What do you mean by creeping around like this?'

'I wasn't creeping,' said the boy. 'Has she gone?'

'If you mean Miss Barnes – yes, she's gone. Why do you ask?'

'It is her, isn't it?' said Billy, ignoring the question. 'The woman from the train.'

'Yes.'

'Thought so. She's changed her hair, but I recognised her at once. Who is she, Uncle Fred?'

'I'm not sure. She works for the government, I think. Probably best not to say anything about it to anyone else, though.'

'I won't,' said Billy. 'I just wanted to know. Do you think Walter's in danger?'

'I hope not. With any luck we'll find him before he gets himself into any more sticky situations.'

'I want to come with you.'

'I don't think that would be a very good idea.'

'Why not? Walter's my friend. We've been through a lot together.' Which was no more than the truth, thought Rowlands, recalling that earlier Berlin adventure when the two boys, then aged eleven and twelve, had been on the run for almost two weeks in that dangerous city.

'You wouldn't do any good by coming along,' he said firmly. 'In fact, you might end up by making things worse for Walter.' They turned back towards the house, and mounted the steps to the terrace. 'If you want to help,' said Rowlands, 'the best thing you can do is to stay and look after your mother and the younger ones. Your stepfather'll need your support, too. What with all that's been going on these past few weeks, it hasn't been the easiest time for him, either.'

'I suppose not,' said Billy glumly. 'All right, I'll stick it out here.'

'Good lad.' They went in through the French windows,

which Rowlands shut and bolted. Any guests still walking about in the grounds could let themselves in by the front door. Before turning in, he went to look in on the girls. Margaret wasn't yet back from her walk with Jonathan – her 'curfew' had been getting later and later, Rowlands thought with a frown; still, if Edith thought it was all right, then he supposed it was all right with him. Anne was in bed reading, he noted with approval. Currently, it was *Sense and Sensibility*. So far she thought Elinor a bit of a prig, though Marianne was rather a fool.

As for Joan . . . 'What on earth's the matter, Joanie?' Because his youngest daughter lay curled up in a sobbing heap, with the sheet pulled over her head.

'My sea urchins,' was all he could get out of her.

'She's been like that all evening,' said her sister from the next bed. 'Apparently, somebody tipped out all the sea urchins from the bucket she'd collected them in, and made off with the bucket. Funny thing to pinch, if you ask me.' Which only made Joan sob louder, although whether this was for the loss of the bucket – a useful collecting tool for the aspiring naturalist – or that of the sea urchins, he didn't dare to ask. Only after he'd pressed two florins into her hand, with the instruction that she was to buy herself another bucket – and a spade too, if she wanted it – did her tears subside.

With the prospect of the journey in front of him, Rowlands slept badly, waking every couple of hours with a feeling of alarm, only to realise after consulting his watch, that it was not yet morning. This time, his dreams were (mercifully) not of the Western Front, but fragments of conversations and impressions from earlier in the day:

These cliff paths can be treacherous . . .

. . . think this is a case for Scotland Yard . . .

. . . valuable cargo . . .

When it was time to get up at last, he felt he'd been awake half the night. He supposed it was this, combined with anxiety about Walter, which had engendered the feeling of foreboding that now oppressed him. Having shaved and dressed, he said goodbye to a sleepy Edith, then took the bag she'd packed for him and went downstairs. Miss Barnes had already brought the car around, and so, after a hasty breakfast, they were ready to depart. 'I hope nothing else happens to stop us this time,' said Rowlands. The words were scarcely out of his mouth when there was the sound of a car turning into the hotel drive. The all too familiar sound of a Wolseley's engine. 'What now?' he groaned. Because the arrival of the police could only mean one thing – that there had been further developments. 'If Trewin tries to stop us leaving,' he began, 'I'll . . .'

'It looks as if he's brought reinforcements,' said Iris Barnes as car doors slammed and men got out. 'If I'm not mistaken, this is our man from Scotland Yard.' Because it was apparent as the group of men drew near, that one of them spoke with the accents of Midlothian.

'I tell you, Frank, the last thing I want is to get dragged into some dispute between what the AC thinks is the way to handle the case and an investigation by the local force. I'm here strictly as an observer . . .'

The speaker broke off abruptly. 'Well, I'll be . . . If it isn't the man himself! What are you doing here, Fred Rowlands? Or shouldn't I ask?'

'I'm here on holiday, Chief Inspector,' said Rowlands.

'Something of a busman's holiday, I'd say,' said the Scotland Yard man, then, to Inspector Trewin, who had been standing silently by, 'Mr Rowlands and I are old friends. He's been of considerable help to me in a number of my cases, haven't you, Fred?'

'Oh, I wouldn't go as far as to say that,' replied Rowlands, even though it was no more than the truth. He was conscious of the effect Douglas's encomium might have on the junior police officer, no doubt already resentful at having to surrender his case to the Yard. But Trewin, perhaps aware that any show of ill feeling might reflect badly, not only on himself, but on the Cornish force overall, merely remarked drily, 'I wish you'd said something earlier about your having had experience of police work, Mr Rowlands. I could've done with some help myself.' Which was handsome of him, thought Rowlands, remembering the man's earlier brusqueness.

'He really is a wily old fox,' said Iris Barnes, as the Jaguar sped along the coast road towards St Austell. She had to raise her voice to be heard above the noise of its powerful engine, combined with the wind – which, as the car's canvas top was down, threatened to blow her words away. 'He knew perfectly well why I'd come to Cornwall. "Looks as if your quarry's given you the slip", he said. He seemed to find it amusing.'

'I take it the Chief Inspector was referring to the Casals couple, and not Horace Cunningham?' said Rowlands, also having to shout to make himself heard. 'Although it does strike me as rather strange that he – and Inspector Trewin – seemed so relaxed about allowing Cunningham to go to London.' Because as they'd been exchanging pleasantries in front of the hotel, a third vehicle had drawn up in front. This was the local taxi, driven by Bert Pengelly, which had come to take the entrepreneur to catch his London train.

'Oh, the Chief Inspector's not worried about Mr Cunningham,' said Miss Barnes. 'You've told me yourself that he – Cunningham – will be back in Coverack for his wife's funeral on Friday. That's only two days away. And if he – the Chief Inspector – decides he does want to talk to Cunningham in the meantime, why, he knows where to lay his hand on him.' A suspicion that his companion knew more than she had so far admitted about the nature of Horace Cunningham's business in London now hardened into a certainty.

'You know where he's going, don't you?'

'I do. He'll be visiting his wife's lawyers in Doughty Street, to hear the reading of her last will and testament – and to find out exactly what he stands to gain.'

Rowlands was silent a moment. 'It's only four days since she died.'

'Rather soon to be thinking about the money, you think?' shouted Miss Barnes. 'But you see, a man in

Cunningham's situation can't afford to be sentimental.'

'I don't follow.'

'What's that? Can't hear a thing with this wind. Tell you what, I could do with a breather. There's a flask of coffee in the hamper. Let's stop for five minutes, shall we? We'll still be in plenty of time for the afternoon sailing.' With which she pulled over to the side of the road, and switched off the engine. When she had poured them both a beaker of coffee, she went on, 'The fact is, Horace Cunningham's in trouble – or his business is. Since the beginning of the war in Spain, his holdings in Spanish railway stock have suffered some severe reversals. That's why he's so keen for the Nationalists to win. If the other side prevails, they'll nationalise the railways and he'll lose everything.'

'I see. But surely a man like Cunningham must have other resources?'

'Fewer than you'd think. He's made some unwise speculations. He was lucky not to lose his shirt in '29. Some of these City types are little more than gamblers, if you ask me. No, it's his wife who had the money.'

'But she said he'd put money into the film . . . that he was its chief backer, in fact.'

'Did she?' Iris Barnes laughed. 'Well, she'd hardly admit to putting her own money into it. That really would have been a vanity project! But I do know that, of the two, she was the wealthy one. Partly because of her own successful career as an actress and partly as the result of some canny investments she made in other productions – Hollywood films, mainly. Yes, whatever her failings as a human being,

Dolores La Mar – or Mary-Ann Plunkett or whatever her name was – was a talented businesswoman.' Rowlands thought about this.

'So you're saying that, in a very real sense, Cunningham had a lot to gain from his wife's death?'

'That's right.'

'Then surely that gives him a motive for her murder?'

'Also right. And before you ask, "In that case, why are you haring off to Spain, instead of staying to keep an eye on him?" I'll remind you that we already have friend Cunningham under our eye, so to speak. If it was indeed he who arranged for Casals to murder his wife . . .'

'What?'

'Then this is the quickest way to find out. If he really is behind all this, then no doubt he paid the Casals pair handsomely to do the deed and vanish post-haste to Spain, which would point the finger of suspicion at them, and leave Cunningham himself in the clear.'

'It's diabolical,' said Rowlands. 'And he seemed so shocked by her death.'

'Murder often comes as a shock,' said Miss Barnes. 'Even to the murderer. Shall we get on?'

They set off once more, in a silence both seemed disinclined to break. Rowlands, not a little disturbed by what he had just learnt, found his thoughts returning to the scene they had left two hours before. Because as he had returned to the house to alert his brother-in-law to the arrival of the police, there had been an awkward conversation with Rowlands' sister. The two of them had been in the dining room when he had brought the news. 'Right-ho,' had been Ashenhurst's response when told that Chief Inspector Douglas wanted to speak to him on the matter of yesterday's accident. 'I'd better go and make myself known.'

Dorothy, however, had hung back. 'Fred!' she hissed. 'What am I going to do?' He hadn't understood her at first. 'He's here,' she went on, in an anguished whisper. 'That policeman . . .' At which Rowlands was reminded of what he'd forgotten in all the upset of Quayle's death – that there was something in Dorothy's past she was at pains to conceal, something of which only a few were aware, one of them being the Chief Inspector. 'Don't you see? After what happened, he's bound to suspect me of having something to do with that woman's murder.'

It had taken all his powers of persuasion to get her to calm down. 'You can't hide away all day. What would Jack think? And the Chief Inspector'll want to talk to everybody. You'll only make things worse for yourself if you try and stay out of his way.' They had run into Alasdair Douglas in the hall. To his credit, he had played a straight bat.

'Ah, Mr Rowlands, there you are! And this must be Mrs Ashenhurst. Your husband was just putting me in the picture about how things stand.'

'Was he?' said Dorothy. She was holding Rowlands' arm; he could feel her trembling.

'Yes. I gather the late Mr Quayle had been staying at your hotel for the past ten days or thereabouts?'

'Actually, it was nine days. The booking for the film company was from last Monday. The sixteenth.' Her voice was steadier now.

'Thank you,' said Douglas. 'That's very helpful. Well, I needn't keep you any longer. I'm sure you have a lot to do.'

When she had gone, Rowlands said to his friend, 'That was decent of you. You know she . . .'

'Och yes,' was the reply. 'I hadnae forgotten. Even though it's ten years since . . . well, what happened. But I hardly think your sister's got anything to do with Dolores La Mar's murder. Or indeed, with the death we're looking into just now. So she can set her mind at rest.'

Recalling the murder case to which the Chief Inspector had alluded – a case in which Rowlands himself had been involved – started a train of thought that led, by degrees, to someone else. Someone he found it impossible to stop thinking about once he had started doing so. Even though it had been five years – more – since he and Celia West had last met, she was as vividly present to him as if it were she, and not his present companion, who was beside him in the rapidly moving car. A memory of another journey by road – this time to Brighton – flitted across his mind, bringing with it a wealth of sensory impressions. The way the Hispano-Suiza had pulled away as she put her foot down, so that they'd seemed to be flying along the open road. The sound of her voice – warm, amused – and the delicious smell of her. Jasmine and roses and Turkish cigarettes.

Rowlands gave his head a brisk shake, as if to dislodge these dangerous thoughts. Wherever Celia West was now – or who she was with – was no concern of his, he told himself. The last he'd heard, she'd married again – to 'some Irish lord' as that unfortunate booby Quayle had put it; Rowlands hoped for her sake it had worked out.

He was roused from these reflections by an exclamation from Miss Barnes. 'Hell's bells! Get along, can't you? Oh, *do* get out of the way!' Because it was apparent, from the loud baa-ing of the startled animals – to say nothing of their distinctive odour – that the car had come upon a flock of sheep. These, it seemed, now filled the lane along which the Jaguar was attempting to proceed, forcing the vehicle to slow down to walking pace, a fact which evidently enraged the Secret Service agent. 'Stupid beasts! Why don't they move along? Hi there!' This to the shepherd, who presently ambled up. 'Can't you move these sheep? They're blocking my way.' The reply, delivered in a soft Devonshire accent, was unintelligible to Rowlands, but seemed to incite even greater fury in his companion, who now applied herself to the car's klaxon. The fearful blasts this emitted must have had the desired effect, for within a few moments the obstruction had cleared, and the Jaguar picked up speed again.

This encounter, and its successful conclusion, seemed to have a salutary effect on Iris Barnes's mood, for she began to whistle under her breath; Rowlands recognised

'The Ride of the Valkyries' theme from *Die Walküre*. 'You know, I've been thinking,' she said. 'There really *was* something very odd about that chap's death. I mean, apart from the question of what he was doing on the cliffs at midnight, there's the matter of the sand.'

'Yes,' said Rowlands. 'I wondered about that, too.'

'In fact, the more I think about it,' Miss Barnes went on, 'the more it seems to me that it wasn't an accidental death at all.'

'No,' he replied. 'I think it was murder.'

'Which begs the question, who was it that killed him? Since it couldn't have been Casals or his sister. I'd be interested to know,' said Miss Barnes, accelerating to overtake a slow-moving farm vehicle, 'whether Horace Cunningham has an alibi for the crucial period on Monday night.'

An hour later, they reached Plymouth, and drove straight to Millbay Docks. Miss Barnes went off to purchase their tickets for the ferry, leaving Rowlands with the car. Grateful for a chance to stretch his legs, he got out and lit a cigarette, breathing in, as he did so, the distinctive marine tang of the dockyards: a combination of salt water, tar and engine oil, and revelling in the rich tapestry of different languages – Dutch, French, Italian, Swedish, Hindustani, Malay – to be heard around him. Above all these, the mournful keening of seagulls told him, if he hadn't known it already, that he was within sight of the sea.

It had been ten years since he'd last set foot on a cross-channel steamer, during a pilgrimage to the war graves at Ypres with some of the men from his old regiment. Thinking about that occasion also brought back another, sharper memory – of a meeting with Celia West. It had been among the gravestones of the great cemetery at Tyne Cot, where so many of Rowlands' comrades had lain buried. It struck him that their relationship – love affair, friendship, or whatever it was – had somehow been mixed up, in one sense or another, with death. What might have been was always the saddest story; 'if only . . .' the saddest phrase. Once more he shook his head. Useless to think of such things, or to regret what one had never had.

Just then Miss Barnes came rushing up, in great excitement. 'The man in the ticket booth remembers seeing Cunningham's car – the silver Rolls-Royce. He remembers the Casals couple, too. Thought him a "nasty-looking cove". The woman was a "handsome piece, but sulky".'

'What about the boy?'

'He didn't see the boy.'

'Then I hope to God,' said Rowlands, 'that we – or rather, I – haven't come on a wild goose chase.'

'What do you mean? I've just told you we're on the right track.'

'But you said . . .'

'What I said was he hadn't actually *seen* the boy. But he certainly sold Casals three tickets. So I think we can safely assume that Walter's with them. The ticket chap said something else, too. It was when they were loading the Rolls onto the ferry. There was a bit of a kerfuffle because the car exceeded the weight limit by quite a lot.'

'That'd be the guns,' said Rowlands.

'Exactly,' was the reply. 'Anyway, Casals was ranting and raving about stupid English regulations, and how he'd never had this kind of trouble before. They had to call the Harbour Master to come and sort it out.'

'It sounds as if Casals made himself pretty conspicuous,' said Rowlands.

'Doesn't it just? Well,' she went on, 'I suppose we should retrieve the hamper with our lunch – and anything else we might need for the journey – before they winch my poor little motor into the hold. We've got six hours ahead of us before we reach the French coast. Do you play cards, by any chance?' Before he could reply, she gave an embarrassed laugh. 'I'm so sorry, I keep forgetting . . .'

Rowlands smiled. 'As a matter of fact, I do enjoy a game of cards – luckily I always travel with my Braille pack. As long as you don't think it'll give me an unfair advantage, I'll gladly give you a game of Gin Rummy.'

Over a substantial picnic lunch of cold chicken and potato salad, washed down with a nice Chablis, they discussed the murder of Dolores La Mar and the death which had followed it. 'All right. Supposing Quayle's death wasn't an accident . . . what was the motive?' asked Rowlands, his question somewhat muffled by the chicken leg he was gnawing.

'He must have found out something he shouldn't

have,' was the reply. 'Something that proved dangerous.'

'So he had to be silenced, you think?'

'Undoubtedly. I say, would you care for some of this Stilton?'

'Yes, please. Then what was it he found out?' said Rowlands.

'Presumably it had to do with Miss La Mar's murder.'

'I'd have thought so,' said Miss Barnes. 'Maybe he'd found some evidence that pointed to the killer.'

'He was certainly dropping some fairly heavy hints to that effect,' said Rowlands.

'Oh? What kind of hints?' Rowlands reconstructed for her, as far as he was able, the scene in the drawing room on the night before Quayle's death.

'He said something about its having been a "question of opportunity" – the murder, that is. I remember it particularly because I thought the remark was in rather poor taste.'

'Who was he talking to?' she said sharply.

'It was Miss Linden, I think. The two went about quite a bit together, as you'll have observed,' said Rowlands. 'But anybody could have overheard. We were all having drinks before dinner, if you recall, and so the room was pretty full. Dean was there, I think, and several others.'

'Was Cunningham there?'

'I think so. I don't always notice if someone's there or not,' he added drily. 'There's something else,' he went on. 'Something Quayle said at dinner, that struck me as strange. I only wish I could remember what it was.'

'Let's hope it comes back to you,' said his companion, starting to tidy away the remnants of their meal. When she had done this, she got to her feet. 'Shall we have a stroll around the deck? It's such a lovely afternoon. Then I'll take you up on that offer of a game of Rummy – or shall we make it Double Solitaire?'

Between the cards and brisk walks on deck, the journey passed pleasantly enough, and they disembarked just before eight p.m. at the little port of Roscoff. As Rowlands waited on the quayside (Miss Barnes having gone to supervise the unloading of her car), he found himself caught up in a group of men pushing bicycles, who were waiting to go on board. The ensuing awkwardness – 'O, pardon, m'sieur!' 'C'est rien . . .' – was soon dispelled once it emerged that several of the group had fought at Verdun and other places familiar to Rowlands from the war.

As cigarettes were shared, along with the memories of that terrible time, it emerged that the men were onion sellers – the famous 'Onion Johnnies' – setting off on the overnight boat to sell their wares across the Channel. The onions certainly smelt good; Rowlands hoped his new friends would find enough custom when they reached the other side. He knew that France had had its share of businesses going to the wall in the past few years. Since the crash of 1929, times had been hard, even for these cheerful entrepreneurs.

Since an hour or so of daylight still remained, they set off as soon as the Jaguar had been lowered onto the quayside, forgoing the pleasures of dinner at one of the harbourside restaurants, whose enticing culinary odours of garlic and moules pursued them onto the road leading out of the town. It was a fine evening, and there was little traffic on the Route Nationale. Miss Barnes was a fast, confident driver, and, for the second time that day, Rowlands surrendered to the onward motion of the car, enjoying the unaccustomed feeling of being abroad. Was it the smell of the place that was different? The feel of the warm breeze on his face? 'I've never been to this part of France before,' he said to his companion after they had been travelling for some time. 'Describe it to me, will you?'

'Well, it's not unlike Cornwall, as far as the landscape goes,' said Miss Barnes. 'Rocky coastline and fishing villages on the seaward side, gently rolling hills and small farms further inland. The farms are fairly few and far between. Stone-built, most of 'em, with slate roofs and shutters painted blue.'

'Ah,' he said. 'I can picture them.'

'The area's very popular with the art crowd, of course,' she went on. 'Go to any of the little towns along the coast – Quimper, Concarneau, or Carnac – and you'll find droves of them, with sketchbooks in hand, trying to capture some effect of sun on sea, or a picturesque view of fishing boats.'

'Very like Cornwall, in fact,' he said.

'Rather,' was the reply. 'The Bretons and the Cornish have a lot in common. The odd-sounding place names, for instance – all those *K*'s and *Z*'s.'

'Yes,' he said, remembering something his friend Percy Loveless, the painter, had once said, referring to his own youthful sojourn in Brittany. 'It's a wild country,' the latter had remarked, evidently approving of this fact. 'Like Corsica, or Sicily. Still pagan, beneath the surface . . .' Rowlands smiled to himself, thinking of the flamboyantly 'pagan' Loveless, swaggering around in his wide-brimmed hat and cloak. When last they'd met, the artist had, by his own account, 'turned respectable', in that he was painting portraits rather than the more avant-garde subjects he had favoured in the early days of his career.

'It's a pity we don't have time to take the coastal road,' Miss Barnes was saying. 'Although the N12 goes through some pretty country, too. Fields, for the most part, with woods dotted in between. Up ahead, just over the brow of that hill, I can see a gleam of water. A river or canal. On its far bank is a building that looks like a chateau . . . with turrets, you know, and pointed roofs. I think,' she concluded, 'we'll stop at Ploërmel. It's a walled town – mediaeval, I think. There's an auberge there which should have some rooms. We've a long drive ahead of us, so it makes sense to get a good dinner and a decent night's rest. I'd like to get at least as far as Bordeaux by lunchtime tomorrow.'

Chapter Thirteen

As they drove further south, it grew warmer, so that even though they had started out after an early breakfast, Rowlands was glad of the hat Edith had made him bring. With the Jaguar's canvas top down, and only the windscreen to shield driver and passenger from the remorseless sun (to say nothing of flies and dust), he had reason to bless his wife's forethought. He wondered how she and the girls were coping with the latest developments in the Cliff House affair. It had been bad enough to know that a murder had been committed once; a second suspicious death, raising the possibility that the killer was still on the scene, was even more disturbing.

Distracted by these thoughts, he hadn't been listening to what his companion was saying, even though, in other circumstances, her description of the landscape through which they were passing, with its rivers and vineyards, would have interested him. So he was startled when she said, apparently apropos of nothing, 'I wonder if our friend the Chief Inspector has pulled in Cunningham for questioning yet?'

Rowlands couldn't suppress a start – it was so close to the subject which had been on his own mind. 'So you do think Cunningham murdered Quayle?'

'I can't imagine who else could have done it. Cunningham's the only one with any sort of motive.'

'I suppose that is the logical supposition – if you believe that he murdered his wife.'

'Or arranged for someone else to murder her,' she said. 'Quayle must have seen, or overheard, something that convinced him Cunningham was the killer. You said yourself that Quayle was dropping hints that he knew more about what happened than he was letting on.'

'Yes, but . . .'

'Perhaps he tried to blackmail Cunningham? That would fit with what we know . . . Yes. He arranged to meet him on the cliff path that night, so that Cunningham could pay him off . . . or maybe Cunningham suggested the meeting place. That makes more sense. Then he – Cunningham – turns up and instead of handing over the money, he pushes Quayle over the cliff.'

'Quayle would have been on his guard,' said Rowlands. 'And he is – or rather was – a young man. Cunningham's forty years older. He couldn't have overpowered him on his own.'

'Which is where the sand comes in,' she said

triumphantly. 'A handful of sand flung in his face would have thrown Quayle off balance just long enough for Cunningham to seize the advantage, and tip him over the edge. He'd intended Quayle to fall into the sea, of course. If that had happened, we'd have been none the wiser. It was a stroke of luck that that ledge broke his fall.'

'And that Bill Finch called attention to the sand in his eyes and mouth,' said Rowlands.

'That, too,' agreed Miss Barnes. 'Not far to go, now. We'll be in Bordeaux soon. I must say, I'm looking forward to my lunch – and a nice carafe of the local wine.'

'I wonder how he got it there,' said Rowlands, still on the earlier subject. 'The sand, I mean.'

'In his pockets, I suppose,' was the reply.

'Then I just hope that Chief Inspector Douglas checks the pockets of whatever suit our man was wearing,' said Rowlands thoughtfully. 'And everybody else's pockets, too.'

Under different circumstances, Rowlands would have liked to have spent some time in Bordeaux: exploring the narrow, eighteenth-century streets of the cathedral quarter, or strolling along by the Garonne, which might be said to rival the Seine for sheer grandeur, his companion informed him. As it was, they were on the move again within two hours, having lunched at a little bistro Miss Barnes knew before refuelling the Jaguar at a garage on the outskirts of the city. It was here that they had their first stroke of luck. Because after that initial sighting of the silver Rolls-Royce by the ticket vendor at Plymouth Docks, there had been no further news of the fugitives until this moment. But when Miss Barnes returned from paying for the petrol, she was in high excitement. 'He – *le patron* – says that the Rolls passed through here about five o'clock in the afternoon, the day before yesterday. He remembers it particularly because they don't get many cars with English number plates. He even noted the number down – GW 628 – because he's interested in such things. Which means we're on their trail.'

'Did he see the boy?'

'What? Oh, I didn't think to ask . . .'

'Then I will,' said Rowlands. His – admittedly rusty – French proved to be up to the task of ascertaining whether the garage owner's sharpness of observation extended to human beings. '*Un garçon?*' he said, in answer to Rowlands' query. '*Oui. Vraiment. Il y avait un garçon dans la voiture, je crois. Un grand garçon, pas un petit enfant, vous comprenez . . .*' Rowlands thanked him. So it was indeed Walter, from the sound of it. He knew it was probably premature to feel hopeful, but this did seem as if it might not be long before they caught up with the boy and his ill-chosen companions. The thought of having to write to Walter's mother to say that her younger son had gone missing wasn't a happy one, always supposing that a letter would reach her, poor woman.

It was just past the hottest time of day when they

took to the road again, Miss Barnes insisting that she felt quite revived by *Gigot d'agneau* and a glass of the local wine. And so they continued on, passing through more vineyards and once, a field of lavender, whose heady scent brought back childhood memories for Rowlands of visiting a great-uncle's farm in Norfolk, where the plant also grew in abundance. After an hour or so, the road became increasingly steep and winding, and the terrain rockier and more precipitous. Here, great rivers – the Lot and the Aveyron – flowed between towering cliffs, and villages were perched on hilltops, seeming (so said Rowlands' obliging guide) to grow from the very rocks on which they sat.

Once more, Rowlands found himself wishing for a few hours to waste in idle meandering around just such a hilltop village, only to pull himself up short. The important thing – the only thing – was to find Walter, and bring him home. After all, he reminded himself, if it hadn't been for Walter, he wouldn't have set foot in this part of France in the first place. Still, it was hard not to feel touched by the romance of it all.

His companion, too, seemed inspired by a similar feeling as they drew within sight of Toulouse. 'A rose-red city half as old as time,' she murmured. 'Which city's that?'

'Petra, I believe.'

'I always think it should be Toulouse. It's a very pink city, you know, especially in this evening light. Do you want me to describe it?'

'You have,' he said. 'And I think you should be let off official guide duties until you've had a good rest.'

'I don't mind,' she said. 'It's been rather fun, having to 'see' things for someone else. It's made me look more closely at what I'd otherwise take for granted.'

'Yes,' he said. 'I've found the same applies to the other senses. One doesn't really appreciate something until one has had to do without it.'

They left Toulouse next morning as soon as it was light in order to get as far along the route as possible before it grew too hot. With the car's roof down, there was some breeze, it was true, but the cooling effects of this were offset by the searing heat of the sun; once more, Rowlands was glad of the protection offered by his hat. Along with the increasing temperature, came a vertiginous sensation as the road grew more precipitous; Rowlands could feel it in his stomach each time the car climbed an incline and dropped down again. It was like being on a roller coaster. Miss Barnes, concentrating on her driving, had fallen silent; nor did Rowlands, preoccupied with keeping his seat as the vehicle bounced over the potholes, remind her of her promise to describe the landscape to him. That it was mountainous he could work out for himself. Only as they drew into Perpignan, where they were to stop for lunch and to refuel the car, did he realise how keyed up the journey had made him. Here, in a little restaurant in the old quarter of the mediaeval town that was almost the last outpost of France before they reached the border, he and his companion sat over cassoulet and a bottle of red wine, considering what lay ahead of them. 'I think we'll go straight to the Hotel Continental,' said Miss Barnes after the two of them had sat for some time in an exhausted silence. 'We can have a bath and a change of clothes there . . . Speaking of which,' she added, 'you might want to remove your jacket and . . . I don't know . . . roll up your sleeves or something. I shall forgo frocks and hats for a blouse and cotton trousers. It doesn't do to look too smart in Barcelona, these days. They think it's bourgeois.'

'Who's they?'

'The militia. They're the ones in charge. Although whether it's the Anarchists, the Socialists or the Communists who're currently in the ascendant, I couldn't tell you.'

Less than an hour after leaving Perpignan, they were crossing the border into Spain – a procedure that necessitated showing their papers to a couple of bored Civil Guards, who seemed more interested in the car than its occupants, spending several minutes examining the contents of the boot (fortunately, it only contained the spare wheel, jack and the empty picnic hamper, said Miss Barnes, sotto voce, to Rowlands). They were satisfied at last, handing back the passports after a cursory glance (so she told him) and showing not the slightest interest in why these mad English were going to Barcelona. 'I suppose I must look much too old to be going to join the International Brigade,' joked Rowlands as they drove off.

'You're not so old,' was the reply. 'But you never know with the Guardia Civil. Most of them support the Republican cause – they've even renamed themselves the National Republican Guard – but some of them don't.'

'Rather confusing,' said Rowlands. 'If one doesn't know which side they're on.'

'Oh, it is,' she said. 'That's the trouble with this war. It's impossible to work out whether one's dealing with friend or foe, half the time.' Another three hours' drive along winding mountain roads, passing only the occasional farm vehicle, or donkey cart laden with firewood, brought them at last to the outskirts of the city. Here, the numbers of cars and lorries increased, since the road on which they were travelling was joined by another, ferrying traffic from the north-east, most of it military, said Miss Barnes. 'That's where the fighting is,' she added. 'Up in the mountains. Luckily, it shouldn't affect us.'

The Hotel Continental was situated in the heart of Barcelona, at the top of Las Ramblas, the broad pedestrian street bisecting the city from the Plaça de Catalunya, in the centre, to the Plaça de la Pau, down by the harbour. Along this thoroughfare, a few months before, said Miss Barnes, enormous crowds had paraded, brandishing the red flag of the Communist faction, or the red-and-black banners of the Anarchists, and singing revolutionary songs at the top of their voices. Now it was quiet. 'Things might get a bit livelier after dark,' said Rowlands' informant. 'You never do know, with Catalans.' She eased the Jaguar into a parking space outside the hotel, and, having bribed a gang of small boys to stand guard with the promise of cigarettes, led the way inside, leaving Rowlands to bring in the bags. Not that he minded in the least: since he was no use as a driver, he was only too glad to be able to make himself useful in other ways. 'Baths first,' said Miss Barnes briskly once she had signed the hotel register and collected the keys to their rooms. 'Then food. After we've had something to eat,' she went on, perhaps anticipating what Rowlands had been about to say, 'we'll have a scout around. See if anyone has seen anything of the Casals couple, and young Walter.'

Their rooms were on the third floor – 'I thought it'd be quieter,' said Miss Barnes – with balconies overlooking the street, or so she informed him, unlocking the door of her own room which was next to his. Impatient as he was to get on with the business which had brought them to Barcelona, Rowlands allowed himself a few moments to relax after the rigours of the journey. As his bath was running (and wouldn't he be glad of *that*), he made a brief reconnaissance of the room, which seemed comfortable in the extreme after the rustic inns where he and his companion had slept on the previous two nights. Here, the bed had a sprung mattress instead of horsehair, and there was a large wardrobe (not that he'd brought many clothes), a desk and chair – even an armchair. But how hot it was! Remembering what Miss Barnes had said, he went to open the glass doors onto the balcony. A breath of air was what he needed.

He stepped out. At once a shout came from the street below and a moment later, something whizzed past his cheek and struck the wall behind him, showering him with brick dust. Hastily, he stepped back inside. If shooting at passing strangers was what Iris Barnes had meant by things getting livelier, then he for one would be glad to get out of Barcelona as soon as possible.

But when he mentioned what had happened, as the two of them were having dinner in the the hotel restaurant, Miss Barnes only laughed. 'Oh dear! I thought things had quietened down a bit since May. That was when the city saw some real fighting. The Communists versus the Socialists – whom they (the Reds) accused of conspiring with the Fascists. It was all very noisy and ill-tempered.' She attacked her beefsteak with relish. 'Not often you get a steak as good as this in England.'

'No,' he agreed, a little nettled by her casual dismissal of the incident.

'I shouldn't take it to heart,' she went on, perhaps realising she'd made rather light of his being shot at. 'I expect he – whoever it was – mistook you for somebody else. There are a lot of hotheads about. As I said, it's all rather chaotic here . . . But here's a man who can give us a better idea of what's going on!' she exclaimed. A moment later, she was exchanging kisses with the newcomer. '*Hola Jordi! Cómo estás?*'

'*Bien, gracias, Iris. Y tú?*' It seemed for a moment

as if they had forgotten that they were not alone, and were going to rattle on in Spanish, but then Miss Barnes remembered Rowlands' presence.

'Jordi, allow me to introduce my cousin.'

'Fred,' supplied Rowlands, since the others appeared to be on first-name terms already.

'I am happy to meet you, Fred.' The two men shook hands. 'I did not know you had a cousin,' said the young man to Iris Barnes.

'Ah, there's a lot you don't know about me,' she replied archly. 'Sit down, why don't you? Another bottle,' she said to the waiter, who was hovering nearby. It struck Rowlands that a drinking session wasn't the best way to begin their quest, but no sooner had the thought crossed his mind than Miss Barnes said in a low, urgent tone, quite different from that of her earlier remarks, 'We need your help, Jordi. It's a serious matter.'

'Then you had better tell me all about it,' said the other. 'But wait until we are alone.' Because the waiter had returned with the wine and fresh glasses. Not until he had uncorked the bottle, poured a measure into each glass and left the three of them to themselves, did conversation resume. Rowlands was reminded of the time he'd been in Berlin in '33. There had been the same feeling of suspicion then – of not knowing who one could trust, and who might turn out to be an enemy.

'We're looking for Carlos Casals,' said Iris Barnes. 'And Caterina.'

'So those two are back, are they?' was the reply. 'I

have not seen them. You could try the Hotel Colón, or the Hotel Falcon, perhaps.'

'Isn't that a POUM hangout? The Casals are PSUC, surely?'

'Yes, but they – the Reds – cleared out all the POUM supporters in May. Those who weren't shot were thrown in gaol . . . a good thing, in my opinion. I do not not trust Trotskyists.'

'Jordi's with the CNT,' Miss Barnes explained, leaving Rowlands none the wiser. All these acronyms were making his head spin. Perhaps his expression gave away something of what he felt, for she added, 'That means he's an Anarchist. We – that is, my organisation – are in favour of the Anarchists as long as they behave themselves and don't throw too many bombs, eh, Jordi? We support the Socialists, too – up to a point. The Communists less so, because Stalin always wants to run things. What we won't put up with is the Fascists.'

'Glad to hear it,' said Rowlands, still not much the wiser. 'But about the Casals couple . . .'

'Yes, what about them?' interrupted the ebullient Jordi. 'What is it they have done that makes it so important for you to find them?'

'Murder, for one thing,' said Iris Barnes. 'A bit of gunrunning, too. But there's more to it than that. They've got a boy with them – a young German. Mad keen to join the fight against Franco, of course.'

'I've come to bring him home,' said Rowlands. 'I don't much care what the other two have, or haven't, done. It's the boy's safety that concerns me.'

Jordi let out a low whistle. 'You have got your work cut out for you, as you English say. What makes you think I can help you in this endeavour?'

'If you can't, then who can?' replied Iris Barnes, taking a swig of wine. 'You know everybody who's anybody in Barcelona. If the Casals pair are here – and we know they are – then you're the man to find them.'

'When was it that they arrived, did you say?'

'The day before yesterday, we think. They got a bit of a head start, for reasons we needn't go into. They were driving a silver Rolls-Royce. Hard to miss, I'd have thought.'

'Leave it with me,' said their friend. He finished what was in his glass, then got to his feet. 'It may be that I will have news for you in an hour or two. Shall I find you at the hotel if I call back?'

'I should think so,' Iris Barnes replied. 'Although we thought of going out for a while, just to see what we can pick up in the way of information.'

'Then be careful,' said the other. 'The Civil Guards are rather trigger-happy, these days. I will see what I can find out about the Casals pair – and the boy. He is German, you say? That will make him easy to spot, I hope. I will leave word for you with Pascual, at the desk, should you be out. Him you can trust. I do not know about the others who work at this hotel.'

He took his leave. Rowlands, feeling that they had made more progress in the past half-hour than in the preceding two days, went to get up, but Miss Barnes put a hand on his sleeve. 'Give Jordi a chance to get away, first,' she said quietly. 'It's better if we're seen together as little as possible. Jordi's a journalist, which is why he can come and go in most of the hotels without too many questions being asked. But he'll certainly have been followed here. Let's sit for another quarter of an hour and finish this excellent wine before we venture forth to see the sights.'

'Metaphorically, in my case,' said Rowlands. After his brush with death on the balcony, he couldn't help feeling a certain trepidation as they left the hotel and turned right along Las Ramblas; but the street was quiet, the only pedestrian traffic being couples like themselves (not that they were a couple in that sense, said Miss Barnes mischievously), out enjoying the evening air. His companion's remark made him think of Edith, and how much she, too, would have relished walking arm in arm along the tree-lined street, with its stalls selling fruit and flowers (it was surprising how fond revolutionaries were of flowers, said Iris Barnes), and its smells of roasting coffee beans, pungent cheeses and cured meats that drifted from the market of La Boqueria. One day, when all this was over, he'd bring her here, he decided. Poor girl, she'd had little enough foreign travel in her life, since she married him.

They'd been strolling for about ten minutes, his companion describing features of interest along the way, when she said, 'We'll go in here. The Café Moka. I fancy a cup of coffee, don't you?' He did, as it happened, although he suspected that the coffee, good as it smelt, wasn't the real reason why they were here; a suspicion confirmed a moment later as they sat down at a table on the terrace outside. 'Leave the talking to me,' murmured Miss Barnes, which Rowlands had little choice but to do, his Spanish being rudimentary. When their coffee arrived – brought by the patrón himself, it transpired – an exchange followed, of which he could make out only a few words: 'Casals' being one; 'Rolls-Royce' among the others.

'This used to be a meeting place for the POUM – the Socialists, that is,' said Miss Barnes as soon as the man to whom she had been speaking had gone back inside the building. 'Their HQ was next door. During the May disturbances, the Moka was seized by government Assault Guards, who made it their base during the fighting. But there's still a core of POUM sympathisers here. Guillem is one of them. He said he'll let me know if he hears anything of Casals. There's no love lost between the Socialist faction and the Stalinists.'

'So I've gathered,' said Rowlands. 'One wonders, amidst all the squabbling, how any of them find the energy to fight the Fascists.'

'Oh, they manage when push comes to shove,' was the reply. 'Once they're face to face with the enemy on the battlefield, petty rivalries tend to fall away.'

'Glad to hear it. So what are we going to do now?' Because, unreasonable as it might seem, considering that the woman to whom he'd addressed the question had just driven him halfway across France to get here, Rowlands had an overwhelming urge to get on with things. It felt all wrong to be sitting here, enjoying a cigarette and a cup of coffee while somewhere in the city Walter might be in danger.

'There's not much we can do, at present,' said Iris Barnes. 'Short of driving around Barcelona at night – which would be stupid for all sorts of reasons – we're far better waiting for some news from Jordi Morell. Guillem has his contacts in the city, too, as I've said. He's promised to leave word at the hotel if he hears anything about Casals – or the boy. So I'm afraid you'll just have to be patient a while longer.'

'I know,' said Rowlands. 'And I'm grateful for all that you've done. I could never have got this far without your help, Miss Barnes.'

'Call me Iris.'

'Thank you – Iris. It's just that I feel so useless.'

'Don't,' she said, reaching across the table to touch his hand for an instant. 'I'm not unknown in this city, as you may have gathered. Which isn't necessarily a good thing if one's trying to remain incognito. Having you here as my companion is proving very useful.'

'You mean I'm part of your disguise?'

'Something like that. As a woman on my own, I'm more conspicuous. As half of a couple, I can blend in with the crowd. So you see, you're providing me with some useful cover.'

'Well, that's something,' he said.

'Added to which,' Iris went on, 'I happen to know that you've got form when it comes to tracking down murderers. Alasdair Douglas speaks very highly of you.'

'I've had a few strokes of luck in the past, I suppose.'

'I don't think luck had anything to do with it,' she said.

'Perhaps not.' He hesitated a moment before putting his next question. 'What's your real reason for coming to Spain?' he said. 'I mean, I'm very grateful – we all are – that you've offered to lend a hand with finding Walter. But it's hard to believe that someone in your position should be able to spare the time for such an endeavour, with the political situation what it is.'

Iris Barnes laughed. 'You don't miss much, do you, Fred – I may call you Fred, mayn't I? In fact, I wonder if you don't "see" more than most . . . Yes, I've got another reason for coming to Spain, apart from tracking down your Walter. And no, I can't tell you what it is. You'll just have to trust me that it's of national importance, or I wouldn't be here.'

'That's rather what I thought. I suppose,' he added innocently, 'that whatever it is must involve the Casals, and Cunningham?'

'You can suppose what you like,' was the reply. 'Although I won't deny that the people you mention are persons of interest, as far as the British government is concerned. Cunningham, especially, because of his involvement with the Nationalist insurgency. Of course our position' – she meant the government's, Rowlands knew – 'is one of strict neutrality.'

'Of course.' He had the feeling that there was something she wasn't saying.

'It might have occurred to you, Fred, that what we're dealing with here is a proxy war – with the real combatants skulking in the shadows, supplying men, arms and equipment to the side they're backing, while their opponent does the same for the other side.'

'With Stalin supporting the Republicans and Hitler the Nationalists, in this instance?'

'Precisely. It's a stand-up fight between two of the great powers, with Mussolini cheering from the sidelines, and Britain and America holding the coats. As I said, we don't want to involve ourselves directly.' She finished her coffee, and set down the cup. Once more, he had the impression that there was more she could have said. 'Yes, it's a risky sort of game,' was her final comment. 'And Spain is where it's being played out.'

As they walked back to the hotel, she took his arm. 'What a nice, harmless looking couple we make,' she said. 'We might be tourists, just out to explore the city instead of . . . well, whatever we are.' A secret agent and a blind detective, supplied Rowlands silently.

'I suppose we make a good team,' he said.

'Just what I was thinking,' was the reply.

On their arrival back at the hotel, she went at once to the desk, to see if any message had been left, but Pascual (for this must be he) said that there was nothing as yet.

'He says he'll telephone my room as soon as he hears from Jordi,' she said to Rowlands. 'In the meantime, I'm going to get some rest. I suggest you do the same.' Even though it was only just past ten, Rowlands reluctantly agreed. It was frustrating to have to wait for news, but what else could they do? It was hardly practical to drive around the city, knocking on doors, in the hope of finding Walter. No, there was nothing for it but to have patience, and hope that the morning would bring results.

Chapter Fourteen

He had been asleep no more than an hour when he was awakened by the sound of knocking. Blearily, he stumbled out of bed and opened the door, to find Iris standing outside it. 'At last!' she said. 'I thought I'd never wake you. Well, come on, you'd better get dressed – I'll meet you downstairs in five minutes.'

'Wait,' said Rowlands. 'Won't you at least tell me what's going on?'

'They've found them – the Casals, and the boy,' was the reply. 'They're holed up in a house in La Ribera. Jordi'll take us there. If we hurry, we might still take them by surprise.' Rowlands didn't need telling twice. As swiftly as he could, he dressed and descended the stairs to where Iris was waiting. Outside, they found Jordi at the wheel of the Jaguar.

'It is best if I drive,' he said when the car's owner

objected to this. 'I know the quickest way to this place – it is in Passeig del Born, in the old part of the city. The streets are very narrow and hard to find for strangers. It is – how do you say? A labyrinth.'

This seemed to convince Iris, for she made no further protest, but got into the passenger seat, while Rowlands climbed in the back. Then they were off, racing through the midnight streets, which – once they had left the main thoroughfare – did indeed seem a kind of maze, full of twists and turns.

Rowlands felt his heart beating faster, with the excitement of the chase. 'How did you find them?' he asked. It was Walter he meant, even though he had posed the question in the plural. His fear had always been that, once he reached Barcelona, the lad would strike out for himself and go to where the fighting was. He hoped they wouldn't arrive too late to stop him. So he wasn't especially reassured by Jordi's reply.

'I myself have not seen them. It is someone else – a friend – who has told me where they are. Carlos Casals is well known here. His sister also. Both of them took an active part in the May events. It is said she shot more men than he did.'

'And the boy?' persisted Rowlands, averting his thoughts from the incongruity of this: the street fighter turned lady's maid. Perhaps, after all, Iris was right about who had killed Dolores La Mar.

'I do not know if the boy is with them,' replied Jordi. 'But he will not have gone far, I assure you. They – the

Casals – have been in Barcelona no more than twenty-four hours.' Which was quite long enough for an enterprising young man like Walter Metzner to get away, thought Rowlands grimly. Well, he would see what he would see.

The car hurtled around another corner, and another, and then jolted to an abrupt stop. 'We will get out here,' said Jordi. 'The street leading to Passeig del Born is too narrow for a car like this to pass. And the noise of the engine will alert them to the fact that we are here. Come, it is not far to walk.'

'Remind me never to let you drive any car of mine again,' grumbled Iris as she got out. 'I'll have the keys, if you don't mind. We might need to make a swift getaway, and I'd rather it didn't end in a smash, if it's all the same to you.'

'My driving is not as bad as that, surely?' laughed the young man. 'I have driven all kinds of vehicles. Motorbikes, army lorries . . .'

'Yes, that's all too obvious,' was the reply. 'All right. You'd better show us where we're going.' Once more, she took Rowlands' arm, although it seemed to him that she was as much – if not more – in need of guidance than he was. They began walking cautiously along the cobbled lane. And it really was very narrow indeed; Rowlands guessed that it must be an alley of some kind, leading between the backs of the houses. No wonder Jordi had eschewed bringing the car along here.

'Mind how you go,' murmured Iris in his ear. 'It's pitch-black. I can't see a thing.'

'I'm used to darkness,' he said quietly. Because to him it made no difference whether it was night or day. Sounds were his guide, as always. Footsteps – their own, and those of Jordi, a few paces ahead of them. A stifled cough – *that was Jordi, too, wasn't it?* But then came another sound – which, unless Rowlands was mistaken, was that of gun being cocked. 'There's somebody up ahead of us,' he whispered to his companion. 'It seems we're expected, after all.'

'Jordi! Look out!' But Iris's warning, conveyed in an urgent whisper, came too late. Before they could go another step, there came the sounds of a scuffle. 'Jordi?' She let go of Rowlands' arm. 'Jordi? Are you all right?' But before she, or Rowlands, could go another step, they found themselves surrounded. The cold touch of a metal barrel against his neck told Rowlands that at least one of their assailants was armed with a revolver. A voice barked a command in his ear, whose meaning was perfectly intelligible to him, even though the words themselves were unfamiliar.

'I think we'd better go with them,' he said – to which Iris muttered an agreement.

Jostled and prodded from behind by their captors, Rowlands and his companion stumbled along the narrow *calle* to the street at the far end. Here they found Jordi, guarded by two armed men. 'They took me by surprise,' he said. 'I did not see them until it was too late.'

'Yes, so we gathered,' said Iris tartly; then in a softer tone, 'Are you hurt? Let me look.'

'It is nothing.'

'*Calla*!' growled the man who'd prodded Rowlands with his gun.

'Shut up yourself,' was the reply. Things might have gone from bad to worse if they had not at that moment arrived at the house Rowlands guessed must be the one to which Jordi had been taking them. One of the gang members hammered on the door. After a brief interval, it swung open.

'Inside,' ordered the gunman, speaking for the first time in English.

'Not likely!' said Iris, then, as she was hustled in, 'I insist that you let us go immediately! Otherwise the British consul will hear about this.'

'I am afraid that will do you no good at all, *senyoreta*,' said a voice Rowlands knew. It was Carlos Casals, to whom he had spoken only a week ago when the man was still passing himself off as a chauffeur. He must have seen Rowlands in the same moment, for he added, with an unpleasant laugh, 'Ah, the blind Englishman, to whom I once gave a cigarette! You have come a long way in order to return the favour, *senyor*.'

Rowlands was in no mood for pleasantries. 'I believe you've got a boy called Walter Metzner with you,' he said. 'I'd like to see him at once, please.'

Again, Casals laughed. He seemed an altogether different character from the sullen, monosyllabic fellow of their earlier encounters, thought Rowlands. Now he exuded confidence and a scarcely veiled aggression. 'As to that,' he replied. 'I do not know exactly where the boy is at present. But if you are prepared to accept my hospitality for a while, I am sure I can tell you where to find him. You, too, *senyoreta*,' he added to Miss Barnes. 'As for you, Morell . . .' This was to Jordi. 'I have not yet decided whether to shoot you or to hand you over to the Guardia Civil. They would be pleased to get their hands on you, I have no doubt.'

He muttered an order to the men who had ambushed them, and they began to drag the young journalist away. 'Bastard!' he shouted (the word appeared to be the same in either language). '*Et mataré per això!*' – a phrase whose furious meaning ('I'll kill you for this!') was apparent, even to a non-native. He was abruptly told to hold his noise – or words to that effect – and marched upstairs, protesting loudly.

'If anything happens to him,' said Iris to their captor, 'I'll see you suffer for it, Casals.'

At which the other only laughed. Rowlands was starting to dislike that laugh. 'Fortunately for us both, Morell is more use to me alive – at present. Come.' Casals opened a door. 'Let us go in here. There is someone else who is impatient to see you.'

Because at that moment, there came another voice Rowlands knew. 'Why,' said Caterina Casals. 'It is the Englishman who was always so polite. To what do we owe the pleasure, *senyor*?'

'As I've already said to your brother, I'm looking for the boy, Walter. I believe you can tell me where he is.'

'And I have explained to the *senyor* that the boy is not here,' said Casals, ushering his captives into the room.

'Then I hope for both your sake's that he's safe and well,' interjected Iris.

'And why should he not be?' laughed Casals. 'He is with another of your countrymen, after all . . . But won't you sit down, *senyoreta*? I cannot offer you much in the way of refreshment, but there is some *Orujo* . . . Caterina, some glasses for our guests.'

'Not for me, thanks,' said Iris. 'That stuff'll knock your head off. Tell us where the boy is, and we'll be on our way . . . and I mean all of us, if you don't mind.'

'But my dear *senyoreta*,' laughed Casals. 'You do not think for a moment that we will allow you to leave? I am afraid you and your friends must remain here for the present.'

'Until you've delivered the guns, I suppose?'

This time Casals didn't laugh. 'How do you know about that?' he demanded.

'Oh, we have our ways of finding out,' said Iris. 'As it happens, I'm not the least bit interested in the guns, or how you got hold of them, or indeed who you're taking them to. But I do have some questions to ask you about something else. Something rather more important.'

'Oh?' The four of them had by now seated themselves at the rough pine table which, with its chairs, formed the principal furniture of the room as far as Rowlands could tell. The brandy bottle and glasses had been placed in the centre of this, but so far no one had touched a drop. 'And what is that?'

'I want to know,' said Iris calmly, 'who killed Dolores La Mar.'

The effect of this bombshell was immediate. Caterina Casals sprang to her feet with an exclamation, while her brother, who had just that moment uncorked the brandy in order to pour out a measure, banged the bottle down so hard that some of the spirit splashed onto the table, releasing its powerful aroma into the room. Even the two men Casals had stationed at the door started forward, with menacing growls, until ordered to stand back. 'I told you!' gasped the former lady's maid. 'They are still trying to put the blame for that woman's death on me . . . But I say to you what I said to the old man who interrogated me in the courtroom that day,' she went on, addressing the two English people. 'I did not kill her, and I do not know who did.'

'Are you sure about that?' said Iris, apparently unperturbed by this outburst. 'Won't you admit that you were offered money to go away when you did – by the person who actually committed the murder?'

'Who? Me? I was offered no money. Were you offered any money, brother?'

'No.' Casals, too, had recovered his poise. 'I would have been happy to accept if this had happened, but it did not. Nor do I know who is this person you mean – this man – for I suppose it to be a man – who has committed the murder.'

'I'm referring to your former employer, Mr Cunningham.'

'You think it was he who killed *l'actrui*? Yes, yes – I think it very possible.'

'It's also possible that she was killed by mistake – by someone who intended the poison that killed her for Cunningham himself,' added Iris slyly.

'Ah! So that is what you think?' Casals' tone was scornful. 'You are mistaken, however, *senyoreta*. If I had wanted to kill this man Cunningham – and it is true, I would like to see him dead, for what he has done to my country – then that is not the method I would have chosen. To use poison – that is the way of a coward, or a woman. If I wanted to kill Cunningham, there are other, better ways. A gun. A knife. One's bare hands.'

Rowlands decided that he had heard enough of this grisly bravado. 'Whether or not you killed Miss La Mar – or how you might have chosen to kill Mr Cunningham – doesn't interest me in the slightest,' he said. 'I want to know what you've done with the boy, and I want to know it now.'

'Have I not already said? He is with the Englishman – the so admired *Senyor* Orgreave. The *senyor* was driving a lorry full of his comrades to Huesca, and he found a place in it for the boy. It was lucky for him that we met when we did, was it not?'

'Very lucky,' said Rowlands grimly. 'Is that where the fighting is – Huesca?'

'There, or at Barbastro. I cannot say. The fighting is where the fighting is,' said Casals in a tone of indifference.

'I don't suppose it makes much difference to you,' interjected Iris. 'Since your battles are being fought in the streets of Barcelona. I imagine those guns you stole will find their way to Stalin's militias in the city.'

'What if they do?' was the reply. 'It is essential for the freedom of the Republic to put down the insurrection of the Falangist fellow travellers.'

'If you're referring to POUM and the CNT and all the other groups your lot disapprove of, then I'm surprised you let Walter go along with Geoffrey Orgreave and his cohorts. He's POUM, isn't he?'

'So they say.' Casals could not have sounded less interested. 'The boy wanted to go with him, and so I could not refuse him.'

'After all, he's only a foreigner,' said Iris sarcastically. 'Even if he is risking his life to fight for your cause.'

'The *Partido Obrero de Unificación Marxista* is not my cause,' retorted Casals. 'They are Trotskyist fifth columnists.'

'Traitors,' spat Caterina Casals. 'They will sell us out to the Francoists.'

'That's rich, coming from you,' said Iris. 'Seeing as you were working for one of the enemy for quite a while. Cunningham's a Nationalist supporter, isn't he? I'm surprised you could stick it for so long.'

'I did it because I had to,' said the other in an icy tone. 'Sometimes the Revolution requires such sacrifices.'

'No doubt. Although I fail to see why this particular sacrifice was required of you. Unless your reason for taking the job as his wife's maid was because you planned to assassinate Cunningham – was that it? Only the plan went wrong, so you had to scarper.'

'No, no, no! I have told you that I did not kill the woman!'

'Perhaps not. But I think you certainly meant to kill her husband. After all, it was you who sent those letters, threatening to kill him.'

A silence followed this allegation. 'What if I did?' said Casals at last. 'You cannot prove this. And, even if you could, you are in no position to do anything about it.'

'So you did send them?' put in Rowlands. It was something to get at least this puzzle cleared up.

'If I agree that it was I, you will only use it to say that I was the one who killed *l'actrui*,' said Casals. 'Whereas in truth I did not do this.'

'No, but you wanted to put the wind up Cunningham,' said Iris Barnes. 'Give him a taste of what it felt like, eh?'

'I do not understand you.'

'To frighten him,' she said. 'To make him feel under threat.'

'Perhaps so,' said Casals indifferently. 'It was nothing to what he and his kind have done to my people. Because of men like this Cunningham, bombs have rained from the sky – bombs purchased with money that he, Cunningham, has given to the Francoists. Women and children have been shot down in the street with guns

268

he has supplied. In return for this, he gets to build his factories and railways.'

'All this may be so,' said Miss Barnes coldly. 'But it doesn't justify cold-blooded murder.'

'And I have told you that I did not murder her! Nor can you prove that I sent those letters.'

'We'll see about that,' was the reply. 'But I don't have time to stand here arguing. I'd like you to release Jordi Morell at once, please. He's done nothing to deserve punishment at your hands, apart from bringing us here, which I asked him to do. Just out of interest,' she added, 'who was it who told you we were coming? Was it Guillem, from the hotel?'

'Not he,' said Casals, 'but another, whose name need not concern you. As for letting you go, my dear *senyoreta*, I am afraid that will not be possible. As you yourself have said, there is the matter of the guns to be delivered. And Morell must take his chances. My men have orders not to kill him, but I cannot promise that there will not be some "rough stuff", as you say. My people do not like Anarchists.'

'Well, I hope for your sake, Casals, that your men restrain themselves,' said Iris. 'And now,' she went on, 'I really must insist that you let us go.' Rowlands, who was sitting beside her, on one side of the table, facing Casals and his sister, heard her fumble in her bag. He guessed from the barely perceptible intake of breath that came from the other two that she must have pulled out the gun. She stood up, scraping back her chair on the tiled floor as she did so. The sound screened another, which was that of the door behind them opening. Rowlands heard this; she did not.

'Iris,' he said. 'Look out!' But it was too late.

Because a moment later, there was an exclamation from Miss Barnes as one of the men who had just come in grabbed hold of her from behind. The gun clattered to the floor. In the same instant, Rowlands – who had leapt to his feet at the sound of the girl's cry – felt himself seized and pinioned by another of Casals' crew. 'I am sorry that it has to be this way,' said Carlos Casals. 'But you leave me no choice.'

'Let the girl go, Casals,' said Rowlands. 'You've got me – and Morell – as hostages. That'll give you enough security until you've done whatever it is you've got to do.' His words fell on deaf ears. Casals barked an order to his henchmen, then turned once more to his prisoners. 'I regret that I cannot let you go, just yet,' he said. 'You have already delayed me long enough. And time is of the essence when one is fighting a war, as I am sure you know, *senyor*.'

Moments later, Rowlands and his companion found themselves bundled through a door and, saved from falling only by a timely warning from their gaoler, stumbling down a flight of stone steps into what turned out to be a cellar. 'You will remain here for the present,' said Casals, from the top of the steps. 'I wish it could be otherwise. But I am afraid I do not trust you not to alert my enemies to the fact that I have returned to Barcelona.

Secrecy, as well as speed, is vital to our plans.' He gave an order to one of his men, then addressed the English couple once more. 'I must leave you now, but you will not be harmed. You are to be given food and water. Only when I send word, will you be released.'

'If you think you can get away with this, Casals,' protested Iris furiously, 'you've got another thing coming.'

It was no use. The heavy door was closed, plunging the cellar into darkness, a fact which made little difference to Rowlands, but which his fellow captive bewailed at once. 'I can't see a thing! Have you any matches, Fred?' He said that he had not, his cigarettes and matches having been left behind at the hotel in the rush.

'But I can give you a general idea of the layout if you think it would help. I'd guess there's no exit this way.' He climbed the short flight of steps and put his shoulder to the door through which they had come. As he'd expected, it didn't budge.

Having retraced his steps, he took soundings. 'Well, it's a coal cellar, as I expect you can tell from the smell of it. About ten feet by fifteen,' he added, pacing it out. 'Low ceiling, although that's more of problem for me than for you. No windows, obviously . . . Hello! What's this?' His questing fingers had detected an irregularity in the surface of the far wall. The air smelt fresher here, too. 'There's some kind of opening. A coal chute, I think.'

'Where? You forget that I haven't your ability to see in the dark.'

'Just follow my voice. That's it. Can you feel that there's a change of air?'

'Yes.' She was suddenly hopeful. 'Do you think there's a way out?'

'I don't know. Perhaps.' But the aperture, which was closed off by an iron flap, proved too narrow even for the slender form of Iris Barnes.

'It's no use,' she said, after trying without success to get head and shoulders into the chute. 'I can't do it. All I've done is to get coal dust in my hair.' She was seized by a spasm of coughing, so that it was only Rowlands who heard the sounds from the street above, clearly discernible through the opening. Voices – one of which was Casals'.

'Listen,' he whispered to his companion. 'Can you make out what they're saying?' She put her ear close to the vent.

'He's telling them to hurry – there's no time to lose. It sounds as if they're heading for the Colón – that's the big hotel in Plaça Catalunya. It's the Reds' HQ.'

'So that's where . . .' Before Rowlands could finish what he'd been going to say, he felt the girl clutch his arm. Because there came another – loudly indignant – voice. '*Allunya't de mi*!' ('Let go of me!')

'It's Jordi,' whispered Iris. 'They must be taking him with them.'

This fact was confirmed by a brusque injunction to the prisoner to be silent, followed by the slamming of a car door. A moment later, there was the throaty purr of a Rolls-Royce engine starting up, then the vehicle moved off. 'Well,' said Rowlands after a moment. 'I suppose there's nothing for it but to make ourselves as comfortable as possible until we're let out of here.' He didn't voice the fear that was at the back of his mind, which was that it might be days before that happened. Was it his imagination, or was the atmosphere in here getting closer? He hoped Casals had meant it when he'd said they'd be provided with food and water. There seemed a dreadful ignominy in having come all this way, only to die in a stinking cellar. Iris seemed to pick up something of these thoughts, for she let out a groan.

'It's all my fault. If I hadn't pulled out that gun . . .'

'I'm sure the result would have been the same. Casals never meant to let us go.'

'I wonder how long they're going to leave us here?'

'We could try shouting,' he said. 'If we carry on for long enough, our guard – always supposing there's just one of them – might come and see what the matter is.'

This proved fruitless, however. Banging on the door only resulted in bruised knuckles, while shouting – even though it relieved the feelings – produced no result beyond a sore throat. 'Perhaps,' suggested Rowlands, after a prolonged session of this, 'we'd be better off trying to get some sleep.'

'Chance'd be a fine thing,' grumbled Iris, but she was already yawning, the long drive, followed by the night's excitements, having taken its toll. They made themselves as comfortable as they could on the floor, which was dusty, but fortunately, dry. Within a few minutes, Iris was asleep, her head lolling heavily against Rowlands' shoulder. Cautiously he shifted his position, to support her more fully, deciding that this would be best effected if he put his arm around her. That was better. He felt her soft weight against his chest. The smell of her hair – spicy and faintly animal – tickled his nostrils. Impossible not to find both smell and sensation arousing. He reminded himself sternly that even if he hadn't been a married man, the difference in their ages made such feelings indefensible. Still, there was no denying that, if one had to be stuck in a cellar with no certainty of getting out any time soon, there were worse people than the alluring Miss Barnes to be stuck with.

Hours passed, or what felt like hours; when Rowlands checked his watch, it was only just past two. He must have dropped off, too, because when he was next conscious of anything it was a quarter to four. Next to him, the warm bundle that was Iris Barnes muttered something, but did not wake. Rowlands' arm had gone to sleep; gently, he withdrew it from around the girl. 'Iris,' he murmured. 'Wake up. I've had an idea.'

Moments after this, piercing screams rang out from the cellar. 'Ajuda! Vine ràpidament!' Whatever her other skills as a secret agent, thought Rowlands admiringly, Iris Barnes was no mean actress. 'Help!' she cried again. 'Come quickly! Està mort!' ('He's dead!')

Footsteps sounded outside the door. 'Què ha passat?' said a voice. It sounded like the younger of the two men. Iris redoubled her screams.

'He's dead, I tell you! Open the door!' A silence followed. Rowlands heard his companion draw breath to give vent to another scream, when there was the sound of a bolt being drawn back. The door opened, and a nervous voice said, '*Què és tot el soroll?*' ('What's all the noise?')

'He's dead,' sobbed Iris. 'Come and look if you don't believe me.'

'But how?'

'How should I know? He won't wake up, although I've been shaking him and shaking him . . . Oh, don't just stand there! Help me!' This much Rowlands gleaned from the tone of these exchanges, if not their precise sense. He held his breath. Was the fellow going to take the bait? It appeared so. The door creaked open. Tentative steps could be heard descending.

'Where is he? I can't see a thing,' mumbled the young man, or words to that effect. Not that it mattered to Rowlands what exactly he said, because at that moment he sat up from where he had been lying – apparently dead, or unconscious – and seized hold of the Catalan's legs, pulling him off balance. There was a brief and undignified struggle.

'Don't move,' said Iris, sticking what must have felt very like a gun in the young man's ribs (it was in fact only a piece of lead piping, which Rowlands had found on the floor, during his recce of the cellar).

Swiftly, she relieved the Catalan of his gun. This she handed to Rowlands. 'If he makes any sudden move,

275

shoot him,' she said, speaking Catalan for the young man's benefit; then in English, 'The steps are a couple of paces behind you. Keep pointing the gun at him, won't you?' Thus saying, she edged backwards towards the cellar steps. Rowlands followed suit. Once they were on the right side of the door, Iris shot the bolt across. From within, came angry shouts, followed, a few seconds later, by furious hammering on the door. 'He won't get very far carrying on like that,' said the secret agent. She was silent a moment, listening. 'If I'm not mistaken, there's no one else in the house. Here – give me the gun, will you?'

'It's of little use to me,' said Rowlands as he did so. 'A good thing our young friend didn't realise quite how little use.'

'Hmph,' said Rowlands' companion, examining the weapon. 'I don't recognise this model. Looks as if it's of local manufacture. Probably an Eibar.32. Ugly-looking thing. Still, I suppose it's better than nothing.'

Since it was twenty years since Rowlands had last fired a gun, he had no opinion to offer on this. The only weapon he possessed – a standard issue Webley Mk IV, souvenir of his war service – now resided in a locked case on top of the wardrobe at home in Kingston. It had been ten years since he'd last handled it, and that had only been to reassure himself that it hadn't been recently fired. Suddenly, a wave of revulsion at the stupidity of all this playing at war swept over him. How he hated it, knowing all too well the price some would have to pay.

The shouting and banging had now ceased, the imprisoned man perhaps realising that his protests were futile. 'Come on,' said Iris. 'Let's get out of here before anybody comes back.'

Rowlands hesitated. 'Iris . . .'

'What's the matter?'

'I don't feel right about leaving him here. It may be hours, or even days before he's released.'

'He was prepared to do the same to us.'

'Yes, but we're armed and he isn't.'

'All right. If it makes you feel better.' Almost noiselessly (though the sound was audible to Rowlands) she slid back the bolt. Then they were out of the front door, and moving as fast as they could along the Passeig del Born and down the alley that led to the street where they'd left the Jaguar. It was four a.m. by Rowlands' Braille watch. To his surprise, he didn't feel in the least bit tired.

Chapter Fifteen

Mercifully, the car was still there. 'Let's see if I can remember the way back,' said Iris, putting the key into the ignition. 'What was it Jordi called this place? A labyrinth? He never said a truer word. I hope he's all right,' she added under her breath. 'It's my fault he's involved in all this.'

'I think he was involved already,' said Rowlands as the car pulled away. After a few wrong turns, and a few muttered curses from the driver, they found themselves back on the main road again. 'Where are we going now? The Hotel Colón?'

'Yes, but I want to stop off at the Continental first. It's only just across the square, and I need to change out of these filthy clothes.'

Rowlands made no demur, even though he was reluctant to delay any further. He took the opportunity to collect his jacket, and with it, his cigarettes and matches.

If he was going to be stuck in a cellar, or anywhere else, at least he'd have a decent smoke. And Iris was as good as her word when she said she'd only be five minutes. 'I'm used to getting changed in a hurry,' she said, reappearing at Rowlands' door well within the time specified. 'Unlike most women, I never bother with powder and lipstick unless the occasion calls for it.'

'Very sensible,' said Rowlands, recalling that he had heard Edith say much the same thing. Thinking about his wife gave him a pang. It had been no more than forty-eight hours since he'd left her, and yet it seemed like a lifetime.

'Although, on reflection,' went on his companion, 'I might need to resort to a bit of paint if I'm to get inside the hotel.' Thus saying, she fumbled in her bag – until recently the repository of her Baby Browning – and took out compact and lipstick, with which she effected some swift repairs. 'There!' she said. 'Now I look quite the thing.'

Having left the Jaguar in a side street, they walked to the Colón; it wasn't far, said Iris, and they'd be less conspicuous on foot. Rowlands could see the sense of this. He felt his companion slip her arm through his. 'Now just take your cue from me,' she murmured. 'We've the element of surprise on our side.'

'All right,' he said, wondering what damn fool scheme she had in mind now. He soon found out. As they drew near to their destination, their footsteps sounding loud in the silence, she let out a whistle.

'Well, well!' she said. 'What have we here? Parked right in front of the hotel, too. I believe this must be the famous Rolls-Royce. Silver-grey, isn't it?'

'That's right.'

'Registration number GW 628. This looks like the same car, all right.' Something else about it evidently caught her eye. 'Hello! What's this? I say, that *is* a stroke of luck.' But before Rowlands could ask what she meant, they were accosted by a tough-sounding individual.

'*No toques*!'

'We were just looking,' said Iris sweetly. 'Such a splendid vehicle. Ah, here's the hotel. Let's go in, shall we?' But when they tried to enter the building, they were met with a no less unfriendly response.

'*Sense intrada*!' shouted the man who'd warned them off looking at the car. To which Miss Barnes replied in English, 'Oh, but you *have* to let us pass!' She was speaking a little louder than usual, as if by raising her voice she could convince this ridiculous foreigner that she meant business. 'I absolutely *insist*. My husband and I need a room. I'm sure this hotel must have *some* vacancies.' Still talking, she marched into the lobby, dragging her 'husband' with her.

At the desk, she kept up the same stream of bright chatter. 'Yes, I know it's awfully late, but you're our last hope, you see. Our car's broken down, and we've been tramping about the city for hours looking for a hotel, and someone said yours still had some rooms and so . . .'

'You were misinformed, madam.' The man behind

the desk finally succeeded in getting a word in. 'We have no rooms available.'

'Oh, but you *must* have! As I said, my husband and I have been roaming the streets all night looking for a place to lay our heads. Come, come! Anything at all will do. What have you got on the first floor?'

'All the rooms on the first floor are taken, madam.' The manager hesitated a moment, as if unwilling to divulge any more. 'We have a large party in residence.'

'Well, what about the second floor?'

'All taken, madam.'

'The third floor, then? We're not fussy, are we, dear?' Rowlands agreed that they were not fussy.

'Perhaps there might be a room on the third floor,' the man agreed reluctantly.

'Splendid! Well, don't keep us waiting any longer, my good fellow,' said his tormentor. 'Hand over the key.' Which the manager, apparently torn between a desire to protect the interests of the large party occupying his establishment and a reluctance to lose further custom, accordingly did. 'Quick,' hissed Iris to Rowlands. 'Before he changes his mind. We'll take the lift. Just as I suspected,' she went on as they ascended to the third floor. 'The Reds have taken over the building. The first floor will have been commandeered by the bigwigs. Casals' lot will be on the second floor. I'll bet you anything you like that Jordi's locked up in one of those rooms.'

Rowlands couldn't fault this logic, but he did take issue with one minor detail. 'I thought I was supposed to be your cousin, not your husband,' he said as the two of them made their way along the corridor to the room Miss Barnes had secured.

'300, 301, 302,' she muttered. 'Ah, here's 304! I hope there's a decent bath . . . Oh, as to that,' she added carelessly. 'I thought it sounded better, saying we were a married couple. They might not have given us *two* rooms, you know.'

'I see that, but . . .'

'Don't worry,' she said. 'I don't imagine we'll actually be doing much *sleeping*. I'm going for a bath. Thank goodness they've given us some towels. I suggest you get forty winks while you can,' she added as she began to undress. 'You can take the chair. I'll have the bed, if you don't mind?'

'Of course not.' Having sat down, Rowlands composed himself for sleep. Not that sleep was a very likely prospect as long as his companion – now naked, except for a towel – remained in the room. What the sighted didn't realise was that there were other ways of perceiving a physical presence. The rustle of clothing being discarded. The smell of skin and hair.

'Do you know?' said the object of these reflections suddenly. 'It does feel rather as if we *were* married. I mean, there aren't many men I'd trust not to . . . well, forget themselves . . . in this situation.'

'Then it's as well that I can't see you,' said Rowlands evenly. 'Now go and have your bath.' For once, she sounded taken aback.

'I'm sorry. I didn't mean . . .'

'I know you didn't. Let's leave it at that, shall we?'

She said nothing more, and a moment later, he heard the door close behind her.

If he'd hoped to be asleep when she returned from the bathroom some twenty minutes later, it was not to be. His mind was racing, and not just because he was sharing a room with a rather alluring young woman. There was something about all this that he still didn't understand, and he couldn't settle until he knew what it was. Perhaps his companion – now busy towelling her hair dry, and smelling pleasantly of soap – had come to the same conclusion, for she said, 'I think you've a right to know my real reason for coming to Spain.'

He waited.

'As I've said, my organisation maintains a neutral position with regard to foreign wars . . . except where our own people are concerned.' Rowlands realised from what she said next that it was Service people she meant rather than the nation as a whole. 'We've a number of agents out here, keeping an eye on things,' she said. 'In the past few weeks, we've lost three – murdered by Nationalist thugs. We think they were betrayed – by someone working for both sides, in all probability.'

'I see,' said Rowlands. 'Is that why you're interested in Casals?'

'He's certainly top of our list of suspects. After all, he was working for Cunningham, who's been supplying the Francoists with money for arms.'

'Yes, but what about those threatening letters?'

'A blind,' said Iris. 'He'd want to make it look as if he and Cunningham were enemies, for the benefit of interested parties.'

'The Communists, you mean?'

'I do. And don't forget there was his sister to convince. We've no proof that she *was* involved in betraying our agents, whatever else she might have done.'

'Thank you for telling me,' said Rowlands. 'It makes more sense now.' Because of course her offer to help with finding Walter Metzner had always been merely another blind, he thought. 'You would have come to Spain even if I hadn't wanted to come.'

'Oh yes,' said Iris. 'But you were an added incentive. Now get some sleep. I'm going to. We've a long day ahead of us.'

It seemed as if only a few minutes had passed when a voice said softly in his ear. 'Fred! Wake up!' Instantly he was alert. It was five a.m. by his watch. 'It's starting to get light,' said Iris. 'Time we were moving.' In the bathroom along the corridor, Rowlands splashed cold water on his face, annoyed with himself for having slept so long. His companion, it emerged, had been busy, and not only with her ablutions. 'I've just been down to the second floor,' she said. 'I know where they're keeping Jordi.' There was only one man on guard outside the room, she explained. And this was the plan . . .

Rowlands wasn't all that keen on what she had in

mind, but agreed that he'd go through with his part in it. The two of them descended the stairs to the floor below. A few paces further brought them to a junction with the main corridor. 'You wait here,' whispered Iris. 'I'll engage him in conversation. When I say, "Here's my husband", that's the signal.'

'All right, but . . .'

'Shh! He'll hear us. Have you got the gun?'

Rowlands nodded. 'Good. Wish me luck.' Her heels clicked on the corridor's tiled floor. A moment later, he heard her say, with arch flirtatiousness, 'Not gone to bed yet?' ('*Encara no heu anat al llit*?') The guard muttered something in reply. 'Can't sleep, eh?' ('*No pots dormir, eh*?') 'Same as me . . .' A bit more bantering talk ensued, of which Rowlands could only surmise the content. But it was punctuated by girlish giggles on the part of the temptress. 'Bad boy!' she cried. ('*Noi dolent*!') Then in English, 'Oh, dear, here's my husband!'

It was Rowlands' cue. 'Now Freddie, there's no need to be jealous,' said Iris in a wheedling tone as he strode up, looking, he hoped, the very picture of an irate spouse. 'We were just talking, weren't we, Jaume?'

'*Sí, seynor*. Talking,' said the man in English.

'So there's no earthly reason to look so cross! Show him the gun,' she added, *sotto voce* to Rowlands. As soon as he did so the guard – Jaume, or whatever his name was – began protesting his innocence, or so Rowlands supposed from the way it sounded. 'Oh, Freddie,' exclaimed his 'wife'. 'You *are* silly to make such a fuss!

Jaume didn't mean any harm, did you, Jaume?' Then, as the man continued to protest, 'Stop that racket, do you hear? (*'Calla, m'escolta?'*) Now, do as I say and you won't get hurt. Open the door.' Another muttered outburst followed. 'Give me the gun,' said Iris, taking it from Rowlands, then, with all trace of sweetness gone from her voice, 'Open it, I tell you.'

Whatever he saw in her expression must have convinced the Catalan, for he did as he was told. 'Inside,' said Iris, in the same uncompromising tone. Then she and her prisoner, followed by Rowlands, were in the room. *'Hola*, Jordi,' she said, addressing its fourth occupant. 'I say, they have made a bit of a mess of your beauty, haven't they? Sorry we took our time getting here. Did you think we weren't coming?'

'I knew you would not be able to stay away from me for very long,' was the reply.

'You flatter yourself,' said Iris. 'Any more of your lip, and I'll leave you tied to this chair, black eye, or no black eye.'

'Do not do that, I implore you,' said Morell, then, in a tone of alarm, 'Look out! He has a gun!' Because the guard had seen his chance, while Miss Barnes was distracted, to go for his weapon. If it hadn't been for Rowlands' timely intervention – a strategically executed dead leg that rendered the Catalan momentarily *hors de combat* – things might have taken a turn for the worse.

'Oh, I say, well done!' cried Iris when their adversary had been disarmed. 'That was a neat trick.'

'One every schoolboy knows,' said Rowlands modestly. He held the guard at gunpoint while Iris finished releasing Morell from his bonds. He hoped his captive was unaware of how wildly inaccurate his aim was likely to be. Fortunately, it wasn't too long before Morell was free, and the other man tied up in his place.

'Better gag him,' said the girl. 'You can use his lovely red neckerchief. Can't have you shouting the place down, can we?' she said to the prisoner, whose furious response was thus safely muffled. 'Come on. Let's get out of here.'

Once the door had been locked behind them, the three made their way with all speed to the exit. It was not yet five o'clock; Iris had chosen her moment well, thought Rowlands. He supposed they would now go back to the Continental to collect the Jaguar, but as they emerged from the hotel entrance, it was to a further surprise. 'We'll take the Rolls,' said Iris. 'The key's in the ignition. Jordi, take care of that chap, will you?' This must be the man guarding the vehicle, whom they'd encountered earlier, Rowlands surmised.

'With pleasure,' said Morell grimly. There was the sound of a struggle, followed by the smack of fist against jaw, and then the dull thud of a falling body. 'When he wakes, he will have a bad headache,' said the journalist with some satisfaction. 'Which is no more than he and his friends gave to me.'

'Don't forget to take his rifle,' said Iris, already climbing into the driving seat. 'Fred, you get in the back. Jordi's going to navigate. And no, you can't drive,' she added as the young man got in beside her. 'I want to be in one piece when we get to Barbastro.'

At that early hour, the streets were empty of traffic, and the powerful Rolls soon conveyed them out of the city, and onto the road that would take them into the mountains. 'We're going to need some petrol before too long,' said Iris after they had been travelling for about an hour. 'This machine is a lot thirstier than the Jaguar – a lot heavier to drive, too.' The reason for this became apparent once they pulled over at the roadside inn which, Jordi informed them, also boasted a petrol pump. While he went in search of the proprietor of this establishment, Iris took the opportunity to stretch her legs. A moment later, Rowlands heard her call out excitedly, 'Fred, come and look at this!' He forbore from saying that, strictly speaking, this was beyond his capabilities, and got out of the car.

She was standing at the back of the vehicle, having just opened the boot, or so it became apparent. 'So what am I supposed to be looking at?'

'Guns,' she said. 'That's what's made the car so heavy.'

'How many cases are there?'

'Two. Casals must only have unloaded one case at the Colón. Presumably, he meant to distribute the rest around Barcelona. Well, he won't get the chance.'

Voices – Jordi's and the landlord's – were heard approaching. Hastily, Iris slammed the car boot shut. The next few minutes were taken up with refilling the car with petrol. Then Jordi announced that he was hungry.

The landlord, he said, had agreed to provide them with a hot meal – beds, too, if they wanted them. Jordi himself had had no sleep at all last night. A nap would be just the thing to set him up. But to these suggestions, Iris was resistant. 'See if he'll give us some bread and cheese for the road,' she said. 'We really ought to get going.'

'And I was looking forward to a nice plate of *Jamon y Huevos*,' grumbled Jordi. But he must have sensed her unease, for he made no further protest. Only when they were once more on their way did he ask, 'So tell me, Iris, what is the reason for this hurry?'

She laughed. 'When I decided to pinch the Rolls, it was only to stop Casals from pursuing us,' she said. 'I didn't realise we'd have a cargo on board.'

'I do not understand,' said Jordi. 'What is this cargo of which you speak?'

'Two crates of Lee-Enfield rifles,' was the reply. 'How does it feel to be a gunrunner?'

As they began to climb into the foothills of the Pyrenees, the road grew steeper and the air thinner. Even with its load of guns, the Rolls managed the gradient with ease, and with little traffic on the road apart from the by now familiar donkey carts and the occasional military vehicle, they made good time, and were pulling into Barbastro by late morning. They found the town swarming with militiamen of various nationalities – Rowlands heard French, Polish, Italian and Dutch voices mingling with those of the Aragonese – as, having parked the car in a side street near the cathedral, the three of them went looking for a place to eat. In a little restaurant off the main square, a table was just being vacated by a cheerfully noisy group. They were speaking Spanish, but it wasn't an accent Rowlands had heard before. 'Mexicans,' muttered Jordi. 'Quite a number of them have joined our movement. Quick! Let us take these seats before anybody else does.'

When he and his companions had sated their appetites with a spicy bean soup filled with chunks of garlic sausage, and washed down with rough red wine, Rowlands returned to the matter in hand. 'Where can we find this man Orgreave?' he said. 'If he was on his way to Barbastro yesterday, then he must still be here, surely? We'll have to ask around.'

'Your department, Jordi, I think,' said Iris, scraping the last vestiges of soup from her bowl.

'All right, all right,' grumbled the journalist, through a mouthful of bread. 'I will do what I can. But this is not my town, you understand. I have no contacts here.'

'Well, do your best,' was Miss Barnes's brisk reply. 'Orgreave's quite a well-known figure in these parts, I'd guess. Somebody must know where he is.'

But the search proved fruitless. Jordi asked at bar after bar, but the answer was always the same: '*No sé.*' Nobody knew where Geoffrey Orgreave or his young protégé was to be found. Or perhaps it was just the native suspicion of the Aragonese for the Catalan accent that kept people silent. Rowlands decided to take the initiative. His Spanish was rudimentary, but his French, though rusty, was certainly up to the job of making enquiries. And Barbastro was full of Frenchmen, from the sound of it.

'*Excusez-moi. Où peux-je trouver Monsieur Orgreave, s'il vous plaît?*' he demanded of a group of militiamen encountered in the street, whose heated discussion of a recent game of football played against a team from a rival platoon betrayed their nationality. A bit of head-scratching followed before one of them piped up, '*Il est dans les montages. À Alcubierre, je crois.*'

'That is where the fighting is,' said Jordi when this was relayed to him.

'Then that's where we'll go,' said Rowlands.

It was past two o'clock by the time they set off again, and the heat was intense. Even with the windows rolled down, the car was like an oven. Nor was the road smooth going. More than once during that two-hour journey, Rowlands found himself jolted out of his seat by the bucketing of the vehicle over the potholes. Some of these, much larger than others, resembled the craters left by shellfire. As they drew nearer to the battle zone, other signs of the conflict – buildings pockmarked with bullet holes, or, in some cases, reduced to rubble – were remarked upon by Rowlands' companions. 'It's not far now,' said Iris, who was map-reading, Jordi having taken over the driving. 'If we follow the track for another five miles, beyond that ruined barn, it should bring us within sight of the Front.' As she spoke, there came a distant – but, to Rowlands, all too familiar –

sound: the *crump* of a big gun, loosing off a shell.

At the same moment, a lorry came labouring up the slope behind them, almost forcing them off the road as it overtook. 'Bloody peasants!' muttered Jordi angrily. 'Stick to your own side of the road, imbecile!' Falling in behind the vehicle, which threw up copious amounts of dust as it went, brought them at last to the hamlet of Alcubierre, and beyond it, the front line. As they entered the village, Jordi slowed the car to a crawl in order to enquire of a passer-by where Senyor Orgreave was to be found. The answer to this query appeared to be satisfactory, for he set off again at speed, along a track which grew rapidly stonier and more uneven. After another half a mile or so, he brought the Rolls to a lurching halt. 'This is as far as we can go, if we don't want to break the axel,' he said.

And indeed they were quite close to the front line here as Rowlands was instantly aware when he got out of the car. A distinctive smell, compounded of human excrement, rotting food, rough tobacco, and cordite took him back twenty years, to the time he'd spent in the trenches. A visceral feeling of revulsion overcame him at the memory. It was that foul smell, which was the stench of war, that had brought it back. For an instant, an image from the past – of a trench filled with the bodies of German soldiers, bloated with corpse gas in their field-grey uniforms – flashed across his inner eye. One of the ironies of his life was that such horrors were among the last things he ever saw. 'Are you all right?' said a voice. Iris Barnes. 'You look a bit sick. Stinks a bit, doesn't it?'

'It does.' He couldn't trust himself to say more. Jordi, meanwhile, had got into an argument with a couple of militiamen – mere boys, from the sound of them – who were loudly disputing his right to leave the car there. This contretemps was complicated by the fact that one of the youths was speaking Italian, the other a language Rowlands didn't recognise – Czech or Polish. Iris now joined in the row, switching between the two languages in her eagerness to get her point across. For a few moments, pandemonium reigned. Then, 'What's all the row?' said an English voice. 'Can't a fellow have a bit of a snooze without you lads shouting the place down?' He broke off, evidently having caught sight of Iris. 'May I be of assistance, ma'am? You seem to have got yourself lost.'

'Oh no,' said Iris. 'We're not lost at all. You must be Mr Orgreave.'

'Yes, that's me. But I don't believe I've had the pleasure.'

'Iris Barnes. And these are friends of mine. We've driven up from Barcelona to find you.'

'Well, you've found me,' said the Englishman, with a laugh. 'Only I'm afraid I still don't see . . .'

'We've brought you some guns,' said the girl. 'A dozen Lee-Enfield rifles, to be precise. I take it you won't refuse them, when we've come so far?'

'I should say not. Where are they, these rifles?'

'In the back of the Rolls,' was the reply. 'Perhaps you

could get some of your men to unload them?'

'With pleasure,' said Orgreave. 'Lee-Enfields, did you say? That'll make a nice change from the broken-down old Mausers we've been issued with – some of 'em forty years old and hardly fit for use. I must say, this is awfully good of you, Miss Barnes. Lorenzo, Pavel – give me a hand with these crates, would you?' But before he and his acolytes could carry out the task of unloading the weapons from the car, Rowlands stepped forward.

'I believe you know the whereabouts of Walter Metzner,' he said. Orgreave stopped in his tracks, nonplussed.

'I'm sorry, I didn't catch your name, sir.'

'Frederick Rowlands. I'm a friend of the boy's family. I gather he's joined your outfit. Where can I find him?'

'What did you say the lad's name was? Walter . . .'

'Metzner,' said Rowlands. 'He's from Berlin, originally. I understand he travelled up from Barcelona with you yesterday.'

'I do remember the chap now. Serious type, with glasses. Told me he was eighteen, though he looked younger. They all lie about their ages. Don't think his name was Walter, though.'

'It sounds like him all right,' said Rowlands. 'Where is he, do you know?'

'The fact is, I'm not entirely sure,' was the reply. 'He joined a patrol that was heading to one of our positions in the hills, early this morning. He seemed keen to get a taste of what life on the front line is like.' He laughed.

'He'll find that it's far less exciting than he's imagined. Just a lot of waiting around in the blazing sun for the chance of taking a potshot at the Fascists.'

'Yes, I remember the waiting around,' said Rowlands drily, at which remark the other must have taken a closer look at him, for he said, 'Of course, you'll remember the last show, sir. I was just too young for that one.'

'Can't say you missed much,' said Rowlands. 'Now, about young Metzner . . .'

'I can take you to him,' said Orgreave. 'But it might make sense to wait until dusk when things quieten down.' As if to underline his remark, there came the sound they had heard before, only this time a lot closer: the earth-shattering blast of shellfire.

'That was close,' said Rowlands when they could hear themselves speak again.

'Yes. They're about two miles off, encamped on that ridge. We can't seem to dislodge them, however hard we try . . . Although these beauties should help,' he added as the two militiamen unloaded the boxes of guns from the car boot, at Miss Barnes's direction, and levered open the first of them. 'Ammunition, too – what luck!'

'They wouldn't be much use without it,' said the girl.

'No indeed,' was the reply. 'We're desperately short of ammo.'

'Where are your field guns?' asked Rowlands, who took a professional interest in such weapons, having operated an eighteen-pounder gun during the Great War. Orgreave laughed.

'Where indeed? I'm afraid we don't run to such refinements. Even our two machine guns were captured from the Fascists. They're much better equipped than we are, of course.' He took a rifle from the box. 'This one's for me, I think. A nice change from the museum piece I've been stuck with. Who knows? I might actually kill somebody with this. You can bring those along to my quarters,' he said to the two militiamen. 'We'll see about distributing them later.' He turned once more to his guests. 'Can I offer you a cup of coffee? It seems the least I can do after you've brought us such riches.'

Chapter Sixteen

'Which newspapers did you say you wrote for, Morell?'
said Geoffrey Orgreave as the four of them, having
squeezed themselves into his cramped living quarters, sat
drinking mugs of what turned out to be quite palatable
coffee. 'My wife sends it up from Barcelona,' said their
host. 'Although stocks are running low, even in the city.'

'I write for a number of papers. *Solidaridad. Tierra y
Libertad . . .*'

'Ah! So you're a member of the black flag gang?'

'A supporter, not a member. I also write for *La
Batalla*. But it is true to say that I support the *Federación
Anarchista Ibérica* against the Stalinists.'

'Good man,' said Orgreave. 'I don't think much of
Stalin's crowd, myself. More coffee, Miss Barnes? I'm
afraid I haven't anything to eat. Dinner's not until seven
when we can offer you some of the local mutton stew,

although you'll be hard pressed to find any mutton in it. Yes, what is it?' ('*Si, que es eso?*') he said in an altered tone as another of the militiamen – this one a mere boy, from the sound of him – stuck his head in at the entrance to the dugout. A rapid-fire exchange in Spanish followed, from which Rowlands picked up only that something untoward had happened. 'Confound it!' said Orgreave, confirming this impression. 'Those stupid lads have got themselves into a pickle, and your young German's among them. It appears that some bright spark had the idea of sneaking across enemy lines – in broad daylight, mind – to try and capture one of their machine guns. Walter volunteered to go with him. Whose idea was it?' he demanded of the boy who'd brought the news.

'The English one ('*El inglés*') – Peter.'

'That hothead! I might have known it.' He picked up the Lee-Enfield and loaded it. 'I'd better go and see what's to be done.'

'I'll go with you,' said Rowlands.

The others, too, were on their feet. 'I will come, too,' said Jordi. 'My readers will want to know the latest news from the battlefield.'

'And you needn't think you're leaving me behind,' said Iris Barnes.

A communication trench, with walls about six feet high, led from Orgreave's dugout to the ridge, zigzagging as it went for a distance of several hundred yards. As Rowlands felt his way along it, he discovered that its walls were built of heavy stone slabs, topped with sandbags: a sturdy construction, by the standards of some he had seen. 'Yes, it's not too bad along here,' said Orgreave when the other remarked upon this. 'Trouble is, it runs out after a couple of miles. The ground's just too rocky for digging, and the Fascist lines are rather too close to ours to allow much deviation either way. But I agree they're quite solid, as fortifications go.'

'When you've fought, as I have, in torrential rain, you come to appreciate a well-built trench,' said Rowlands.

'I don't doubt it,' was the reply. 'You were in France, I suppose?'

'Yes, and Flanders. That was the worst. Seas of mud. Still, those days are long gone, thank heaven,' Rowlands added quickly – in case Orgreave took him for the kind of man who was given to boring people with his war stories. 'How much further is it, do you think?'

'About half a mile. You can wait here, if you like. No need for us all to carry on.' Because, as they'd been going along, they'd collected a couple more men, at Orgreave's behest, so that their party numbered eight, including Rowlands himself. 'Perhaps you could persuade Miss Barnes to stay with you?' added Orgreave. 'This isn't really women's work.'

'I'm surprised at you, Mr Orgreave!' said Iris, overhearing this. 'Given how many brave women have joined the Republican cause. And I'm quite capable of looking after myself, as it happens.'

'I don't doubt it. But watch out from now on. We're

only about three hundred yards from the enemy lines here. They usually have a sniper or two in position.'

'I'll come too, if it's all the same to you,' said Rowlands apologetically. 'Only if anything's happened to Walter, I ought to be there.'

'Well, I can't stop you,' said Orgreave, with a sigh. 'No doubt our journalist friend here will want to have a close-up view of the action, too. I just hope when you write the piece, you'll make us sound like heroes.'

'You may trust me for that,' said Jordi. 'I will tell my readers how bravely our fighters are striving to . . .' But whatever he'd been going to say was cut short by a hail of bullets. Fortunately, these whistled harmlessly overhead.

'See what I mean?' said Orgreave grimly. 'Keep your heads down, everybody.' From then on, the group maintained a cautious silence as it edged its way along the trench towards the stretch of open ground that would form the next – and most difficult – obstacle.

Here, the fortifications petered out into what seemed to Rowlands to be no more than a shallow ditch. Beyond this, a barbed wire fence marked the edge of No Man's Land. 'We're making for the pillbox at the top of that hill,' said Orgreave, to Rowlands. 'I'll go first, with Pavel and the rest. You and Morell and Miss Barnes wait here. When it's safe to follow, I'll give the signal.' Then there was no sound but the distant thump of the big guns from somewhere across the ridge, and – nearer at hand – the clatter of loose stones being dislodged as Orgreave's patrol scrambled up the hillside. Rowlands held his breath, expecting any moment that there would be another outbreak of enemy fire, but it seemed that Orgreave and his men had got through without mishap, for there came the sound of a low whistle.

'Take my hand,' whispered Iris. 'We'll go together. Jordi, you can give us cover.'

Then it was their turn to run, slipping and sliding on the sandy terrain, until they, too, gained the safety of the hilltop and its stone-built redoubt. Just as they did so, there came a fresh burst of gunfire, so that they were forced to fling themselves flat while around them the bullets threw up clouds of dust and grit. 'Are you all right?' said Rowlands to his companion.

'Think so,' she muttered, then, betraying alarm for the first time, 'Where's Jordi?'

'Here,' gasped the journalist, stumbling into the hut after them. 'That was a close thing, was it not?'

'It'll be closer still before we're done,' said Orgreave. 'We may as well sit tight until it's dark. From what I can gather, the two lads must have crossed enemy lines not far from here. I don't suppose,' he added, 'that anybody's got a cigarette?' Rowlands produced his, and the group settled down to wait until nightfall when, said Orgreave, he and one of the others (there was some dispute as to who this should be) would go over into enemy territory, by the route the boys had taken earlier. 'There's a spot about fifty yards from here where the wire's been cut. We've used it on previous raids,' he said. 'Only I wish the young fools hadn't tried to go it alone – getting themselves killed in the process, in all probability.'

Rowlands couldn't help but agree, but he said nothing, not wanting to make things worse for Walter. Recalling a conversation a few weeks before, he wondered what Dorothy would have said if she could see them now – huddled together in this cramped shelter as they waited to rescue a couple of schoolboys from a botched adventure. Would she think it all quite so heroic as she had then? Knowing his sister, he rather supposed she would.

As darkness fell, the temperature dropped, and Rowlands was glad of his jacket, which had seemed an encumbrance before. He became aware that whispered preparations were being made, by Orgreave and the Polish lad, Pavel. The remaining militiamen were charged with the task of providing cover. 'All right,' said Orgreave. 'Let's go.' Then they slipped out into the night. Rowlands held his breath, half-expecting a renewal of the firing which had plagued them earlier. But there was nothing. A heavy stillness lay over the battleground. He checked his watch: just gone seven. Hadn't Orgreave said that was when the fighters stopped for dinner? Perhaps it was also dinnertime for the other side – even Nationalists had to eat, he supposed. Time – perhaps a quarter of an hour – passed.

'Can you see anything?' said Rowlands to Iris Barnes.

'Nothing yet,' was the reply. 'It's very dark. Luckily there's not a full moon.'

Another fifteen minutes went by, then, 'I think I see something,' she whispered. 'Yes . . . it's definitely them.'

'How many are there?'

'I can't make it out. Two . . . no, three . . . They're carrying somebody between them.' Rowlands' heart sank. It was as he had feared: there had been shooting, and one of the boys was wounded – perhaps dead. He didn't permit himself to wonder who it might be. After what seemed another age, but was in fact only two or three minutes, there came the low whistle he had heard before – Orgreave's signal to the men inside the pillbox that those approaching were friend, not foe. A few seconds more, and they were safe inside the hut. Orgreave and Pavel, supporting someone between them, someone who groaned softly, as he was set down.

'Walter?' said Rowlands, hardly daring to hope. 'Is that you?'

'*Ja* . . . It is I, Herr Rowlands.' The words emerged as a sob. 'I did not expect . . .' He gave a gasp of pain, and couldn't go on.

'What's the matter?' said Rowlands. 'Are you hurt?'

'It is nothing.'

'Broken ankle,' said Orgreave tersely. Having divested himself of his burden, he sat down on the floor of the hut, breathing heavily. 'Give him some water, will you? He's had a nasty shock. We found him at the foot of the enemy's parapet – must have slipped and fallen. He'd been lying there for hours. The other chap wasn't so lucky. Shot through the head as he climbed over, poor little devil. Still, it would have been quick, which is some consolation.' When all three of the returning party had rested for a few minutes, he went on, 'All right. Let's get going. With any luck, they won't have changed the guard yet, so we should make it through without too much difficulty. If you take his other arm, Mr Rowlands, I think we'll be able to get down the hill all right. Pavel, you and the others give us some cover, will you?'

'OK, boss.'

The three of them set off down the sandy slope, with both men doing their best to support the injured youth, so that he put as little weight as possible upon his ankle. But if he felt the shocks and jarring which were inevitable in spite of their efforts, he gave no sign of it, although it must have been agony at times, thought Rowlands. Only when they reached the relative safety of the trench, did he allow a groan to escape him. 'All right,' said Orgreave. 'We're through the worst of it, now. If you can hobble another couple of hundred yards, young feller, we'll see about getting a splint put on that ankle.'

'Thank you,' said Walter, then, before they set off once more, 'Mr Orgreave. I must say something, please.'

'Spit it out, then,' said the other, not unkindly. The boy drew a breath.

'I want to say that I am sorry . . . for what happened. I should not have agreed to go with . . . with Peter. If it were not for that, he would be alive still.'

'I shouldn't blame yourself,' said Orgreave. 'From what I know of that lad, it was his idea. I suppose I'll have to write to his parents,' he added gloomily. 'And we'll have to see about retrieving his body. But that can wait. Come on. Let's get you back to quarters. Tell you one thing, though, young Walter – you're lucky you've got people looking out for you, that's all.'

The mood in the Republican camp that night was sombre as Rowlands, his companions, and the men who'd accompanied them on the rescue mission, ate their pans of greasy mutton stew and talked of what the next few hours would bring. There was speculation about a big attack that was rumoured to be about to take place. Some said it would be tomorrow; some the day after that. Rowlands wasn't really paying attention. Tired as he was, after the rigours of the day, his mind was still racing, and when dinner was over and the time came to settle down to sleep, he found it impossible.

Venturing out of the dugout where the others were sleeping, or trying to (not including Iris, who had taken herself off to sleep in the car), he fumbled for his cigarettes. A couple remained in the pack; he lit one, taking care to shield the match flame with his hand as he did so, to prevent its offering a target to an enemy sniper. It was an old trick from his army days – not the only thing he recalled of that far-off time. The filthy food was another, as was the sweaty fug of men (and women, too, these days) living in too-close proximity.

A slight sound, as of a loose stone being dislodged, alerted him to the fact that he wasn't the only one to be wakeful at this hour. *A sentry, no doubt?* But then a voice he knew said, in an anxious whisper, 'Herr Rowlands?'

'Hello, Walter. Can't sleep, either?'

'No.'

'Well, let's find a place to talk where we won't disturb the others.' A few paces further on, an embrasure in the wall of the trench – intended, no doubt, for riflemen – provided such a place. 'Cigarette?' said Rowlands when they were seated on the low stone shelf provided for the purpose.

'Thank you, but I do not smoke.'

'Sensible chap.'

'Please give me a cigarette,' said the young man suddenly.

Rowlands did so, waiting until Walter had lit the thing and coughed a bit as he got used to it, before he said, 'It wasn't your fault, you know – what happened to that other lad.'

'If I had not agreed to go with him to capture the machine gun, he would not now be dead,' was the reply. 'That is the truth, Herr Rowlands.'

'Maybe so. And it's something you'll have to live with. But don't forget it was his decision as much as yours.'

'I do not forget.' There was a long pause, during which both smoked their cigarettes. Poor little blighter, thought Rowlands. He'll carry this with him for the rest of his days.

'I suppose,' said Walter, after a moment. 'You have come to take me back to England with you?'

Rowlands, too, paused before replying, 'That's up to

you, of course. But with your ankle crocked, you won't be much use, as far as any fighting goes, for at least a week.'

'I am not much use in any case,' said Walter. 'My eyes are bad, so I cannot see well to shoot. I am not big and strong, like some.'

'There are other kinds of strength,' said Rowlands. 'In a year or two, if you keep on with your studies, you can apply to Oxford or Cambridge – or perhaps Edinburgh, since you want to study medicine.'

'Yes, but . . .'

'Don't you think your mother's going to be just as proud of you when you qualify as a doctor as she'd be if you got mentioned in dispatches?'

'I do not know where my mother is,' said the boy in a small voice. 'Or if she is still alive.'

'All the more reason to do what would make her proud.'

'*You* were a soldier,' said Walter. 'You fought for your country.'

'Yes. And I lost my sight in so doing.' Mentioning his blindness – the result of a wartime injury – wasn't something of which Rowlands made a habit, but if it meant the lad saw sense then it was worth the momentary sacrifice of his own dignity.

Another silence ensued. Then Walter sighed. 'You must think me a great fool,' he said.

'Not at all,' said Rowlands. 'You're a brave young man. You volunteered to fight, for a noble cause.

Whatever happens, no one can take that away from you. Now let's go and get some sleep, or neither of us will be fit for anything in the morning.'

But there was not much sleep for any of them that night: by the time it got light, the guns were already booming, and the atmosphere in the camp charged with apprehension. 'There's something afoot,' said Geoffrey Orgreave when Rowlands joined him for a hasty breakfast of coffee and rolls. 'They've been bringing up reinforcements from the north all week.' 'They' being the Falangists, Rowlands supposed.

'What will you do?' he asked. Orgreave gave a dry laugh.

'Sit tight until our own reinforcements get here,' he replied. 'There's a train-load of POUM militia due into Huesca today. Thanks to you, we've some nice new rifles with which to equip them.'

'A dozen rifles won't get you very far,' said Rowlands.

'It's better than nothing, I assure you.' Orgreave hesitated a moment, then said, 'I've another favour to ask you, actually.'

'Ask away.'

'Could you deliver this letter to my wife?'

'With pleasure.'

'She's staying at the Continental, as it happens. Miss Barnes tells me you've got rooms there, too.' Rowlands acknowledged this fact. 'It's just that getting news through is tricky, with all this going on.' He spoke as if the war were a mere inconvenience – on a par with a spell of bad weather, or a run of cancelled trains.

It was not yet six when they said their farewells, and set off down the mountain. Iris was driving, since (as she said) she was less inclined to take the treacherous corners at speed than her co-driver, while Rowlands and the boy sat in the back of the Rolls. Just before they set off she said to Walter, 'Know how to use one of these things?' It was the gun she'd confiscated from the guard at the hotel, or so Rowlands gathered. Walter took it from her.

'I . . . I think so,' he said.

'Good. Because I can't drive and shoot. I'll need someone to keep a sharp lookout for snipers as we're going along. Jordi – Mr Morell – can take the right-hand side, and you can take the left, OK?'

'OK,' said Walter. And Rowlands guessed that, in that moment, the intrepid Miss Barnes had gained yet another admirer.

The journey back to Barcelona proved uneventful, as Rowlands had anticipated, since they were, after all, in friendly territory. The only activity they saw was on the Republican side: truckloads of militia being ferried up from the town, to join Orgreave and his cohorts on the front line. As the lumbering military vehicles went past, throwing up clouds of dust, snatches of revolutionary songs drifted back – a favourite being '¡Ay, Carmela!' whose unmistakeable refrain was everywhere that summer:

Solo es nuestro deseo,
rumba la rumba la rumba la.
Solo es nuestro deseo,
rumba la rumba la rumba la
acabar con el fascismo,
¡Ay Carmela! ¡Ay Carmela!
acabar con el fascismo,
¡Ay Carmela! ¡Ay Carmela!

Rowlands could not but admire the bravery of these men and women, knowing, as he did, the likelihood that their ill-equipped and inadequately trained numbers would be no match for the Nationalist forces, whose troops were supplemented by those from Mussolini's Italy, and whose weaponry and war machines were supplied by Hitler's Germany. He knew that was why Walter had wanted to join the Republican side, seeing in its struggle, no doubt, a chance to hit back at the regime which threatened to destroy his family, if it had not already done so.

And it was this, in turn, which had prompted Rowlands' own mission to rescue the boy. Because if it were the case that Walter's mother and siblings were already dead, then Rowlands saw it as his duty to protect the family's only survivor – not that he could say this to Walter himself.

They made good time and, having stopped for a hasty lunch in Barbastro, were driving into Barcelona by early afternoon. Another few minutes would bring them to the hotel. It was then that Walter, who had been silent for much of the journey, said, 'That car is following us.'

'The black one, do you mean?' said Iris.

'*Ja*, the Armstrong-Siddeley. I noticed it, because you do not see many English cars here. It has been on our tail since we turned off the coast road.'

'How many people in it?'

'Two. Both men. They are wearing hats, so I cannot see their faces.'

To her credit, Miss Barnes didn't question what Walter had said, but only murmured, 'Let's give them a run for their money, shall we?' She put her foot down, so that the Rolls, which had been going at a steady forty miles per hour, suddenly accelerated. Moments later, they took a sharp left-hand turn into what Rowlands surmised, from the twists and turns that followed, must be one of the networks of side streets for which the city was famous. 'I'm going to drop the Rolls back where we found it,' she said. 'But we'll take a roundabout route to the Colón. Don't want to make it too easy for our friends in the Armstrong-Siddeley, do we?' Rowlands wondered who these 'friends' might be. The fact that it was an English car suggested they weren't Casals' people. Then who could they be? Unless Walter had been imagining things. But this he didn't believe. The boy had grown up in Nazi-controlled Berlin. He knew all too well what living under surveillance was like.

Having dropped off her three passengers at the Continental, Iris went to carry out her plan of returning the Rolls to where it had been parked when she had 'borrowed' it, two days before. She refused Morell's offer of accompanying her on this mission. 'It's too dangerous for you, Jordi. What if you're seen? Casals is already out for your blood.'

'What makes you think he isn't out for yours?' he retorted. 'You have stolen the guns he intended for his people. He will not be very amused by that, I think.' She paid no attention to his protests. 'I wish . . .' began Morell as the car drove off, with a jaunty toot of the horn. He broke off, with an exasperated sigh.

'No sense in wishing,' said Rowlands. 'She knows what she's doing.' But he spoke with more conviction than he felt.

Morell took his leave, saying that he'd return to the hotel that evening. It was left to Rowlands to secure a room for the night for his young charge before taking himself off to his own room, and the luxury of a long soak in a hot bath. Feeling a new man after this, he was getting dressed when he remembered that he was still in possession of Orgreave's letter. He checked his watch: it was coming up to half past five. There'd be time to deliver the letter before dinner.

At the desk, he was told that Senyora Orgreave had not yet returned to the hotel. It was her custom to dine here, however, and so (said the desk clerk) she must soon appear. Resolving to wait until that eventuality, Rowlands remembered that he hadn't yet telephoned

Edith with the news about Walter. He accordingly booked a call to England – it would be an hour earlier there, of course – and sat down to wait. As he did so, there came a commotion at the door. Booted feet stamped into the lobby. Loud voices demanded answers to questions. One angrily repeated phrase leapt out at Rowlands: where was 'the traitor ('*el traïdor*') Morell'?

'I don't know ('*no lo sé*'),' was the desk clerk's reply. The men – Assault Guards, Rowlands learnt afterwards – seemed disinclined to believe him. Rowlands thanked his stars that Morell had made himself scarce when he had; obviously, Barcelona was becoming too hot for the journalist and his fellow Anarchists.

Just then, Rowlands' call came through; as he rose to go and take it in the telephone booth behind the desk, he found his way barred by the man who had asked for Morell. '*Passaport,*' snapped this individual, which Rowlands had no difficulty in translating. Resisting an urge to tell the other to go to hell, he produced the document, and waited while the Assault Guard flicked through it.

'Tell him,' he said to the desk clerk, 'that if I miss my telephone call because of him, I'll make a formal complaint to his superiors.' Perhaps, fortunately, before this message could be relayed, the Guard handed back the passport, muttering something, no doubt uncomplimentary, about the English.

'I say, you *were* a long time!' Jack Ashenhurst's voice came loud and clear down the receiver. 'Everything all right there?'

'As much as you'd expect,' said Rowlands guardedly. One couldn't be sure who might or might not be listening in. 'The main thing is, Walter's safe and well.'

'Thank God for that.'

'Yes. We set off for home tomorrow. How are things there?'

'Much the same as they were when you left. Film people cluttering up the place. Still, they leave at the end of the week. If you hurry back, you might just catch them.' Jack gave a hollow laugh. Edith, it transpired, hadn't yet returned from taking the girls shopping. 'She *will* be pleased to hear your news. Any message for her?'

'Just send my love.'

'Three minutes, Caller,' said the Operator.

'Cheerio then, old man. Back in a couple of days.' That brief contact with the world he'd left a few short days before filled Rowlands with sharp feelings of longing. To be home once more, with his girls about him. Having replaced the receiver, he emerged into the lobby (from which the Assault Guards had now departed), and heard himself addressed.

'I gather you're looking for me?' It was a woman's voice – rather an agreeable one, he thought. 'I'm Eileen Orgreave.'

Chapter Seventeen

'How do you do, Mrs Orgreave? My name's Frederick Rowlands. I've a letter for you from your husband.'

He handed it over, then started to move away, to give her the chance to read it in private. But she must have decided to defer the pleasure, for she said at once, 'I say, must you go? I usually have a drink when I get back from work – perhaps you'll join me?'

Rowlands said that he'd like that, then, as they took their seats in the hotel bar, 'So you're actually working in Barcelona? I hadn't realised.'

'You thought I'd merely come to keep my husband company in his great endeavour?' she said, with some acerbity. 'Not an unreasonable assumption, I suppose. But I do in fact have a job – working for the Independent Labour Party. We've an office here. Two beers,' she added, to the waiter.

'Let me get them.'

'No, no. I invited you. And you've been kind enough to act as Geoffrey's messenger – and to put up with my appalling rudeness. Oh, don't deny it! I bit your head off just now. It's only that I get so tired of people thinking I'm the little woman.'

'I'm sure nobody who met you would make that mistake,' said Rowlands. At which Eileen Orgreave laughed.

'Touché. I do like a man who isn't afraid to stand up to me.'

'As the only man in a household of five women, I'm used to having my opinions robustly criticised,' said Rowlands drily.

'I begin to like you more and more, Mr Rowlands,' said his vis-à-vis, taking an appreciative sip of her Estrella. 'Tell me, how was my husband when you saw him last?'

'He seemed in remarkably good spirits for a man existing on very little sleep, rotten food and the likelihood of being under attack within days,' he replied, guessing that she wouldn't thank him for making things out to be better than they were.

'Ah! It's like that, is it?' she said. 'Geoffrey always *did* like taking on heavy odds. Although,' she added, 'I'm not sure he'd be much safer if he were here in Barcelona, what with all these Communist gangs roaming about – yes, I saw our friends just now. Little better than uniformed thugs, if you ask me. They've already arrested some of our comrades in the POUM. Shot a few of 'em, and flung the rest in gaol. God knows what would happen to Geoffrey if he were to return from the Front. No doubt he'd be denounced as a Trotskyist stooge, like all the others.'

'Worrying for you,' said Rowlands, thinking that if he were in Orgreave's shoes, he'd cut his losses and go back to England. No sense in ending up in gaol – or worse – just to prove a point. Which was why he himself would never be hero material, he supposed.

'What's really galling about this whole affair,' Eileen Orgreave was saying, 'is that these people are meant to be on our side. How we'll ever win this war, if we keep fighting amongst ourselves, beats me. But you haven't told me how you came to meet my husband,' she went on. 'You're not a journalist, by any chance?'

'Certainly not,' laughed Rowlands. 'And my soldiering day are very much over, as you can probably tell from looking at me. No, my reason for going to the Aragon Front was a personal one.' Briefly, he outlined Walter's story. Eileen Orgreave listened in silence until he had finished, then she sighed.

'Poor boy! He must have been terrified. So many of these young chaps have rushed to join the Cause without the faintest idea of what they're letting themselves in for.'

'Yes,' said Rowlands, thinking of the boy – Peter – who'd died.

'I think that woman's looking for you,' said Mrs Orgreave. 'Red hair. Very attractive. Your wife, perhaps?' Rowlands opened his mouth to refute this assumption, then shut it again, not knowing which of her cover stories Miss Barnes might choose to employ on this occasion. But when, having spotted them, she came and sat down at their table, it became clear that she'd reverted to an earlier persona – one Rowlands had encountered during their Berlin escapade.

'Sorry to barge in like this – but aren't you Eileen Orgreave?'

'That's me.'

'Iris Barnes. I'm doing a series of articles for *Woman's Own* on 'Women in the News'. Wonder if you'd let me have a few words on 'Life on the Front Line' – from a woman's angle? Just the sort of thing to interest our readers.'

'I'm hardly on the front line here. As I was saying to your husband . . .'

'Cousin,' said Iris quickly. 'We're travelling together. So what about it, Mrs Orgreave? I take it you were in Barcelona during the May disturbances?'

'Yes, but . . .'

'Witnessed some of the fighting? Saw the crowds marching along Las Ramblas, singing '¡Ay, Carmela!' at the tops of their voices?'

'Yes.'

'Men in khaki uniforms and red kerchiefs clambering onto armoured cars. Pretty girls with guns. All that.'

'You seem to have written it already,' said Eileen Orgreave drily. 'I don't see what more I can add.'

'Oh, the personal touch is what our readers like.

Dodging the bullets on the way to buy bread. 101 Ways With Canned Beans. That kind of thing.'

'Well,' began Mrs Orgreave doubtfully. 'I'm not sure I . . .' But just then they were joined by the other member of their party. Rowlands performed the introductions.

'Walter, this is Mrs Orgreave.'

'Hello, Walter,' she said. 'I gather you saw some action at the Front yesterday?'

'I . . . Yes, that is so,' he stammered.

'Then I think you deserve a beer,' she said, clicking her fingers to summon the waiter. 'Same for you, Miss Barnes?'

Conversation grew general – the progress of the war being the main topic. If Madrid were to fall . . . But so far the capital was holding out against the incursions of the Francoists. If the British government would only throw its weight behind the Republican cause . . . Eden was playing safe, of course. Although his policy of so-called non-intervention was decidedly one-sided, in Eileen Orgreave's opinion. 'No doubt he feels he must keep in with the capitalists who've invested in Nationalist-held industries. Men like Horace Cunningham, with holdings in Spanish railways and iron ore, are major donors to the Conservative Party.'

'Yes, I'd heard something of the sort,' said Rowlands guardedly.

'Cunningham,' interjected Iris. 'Isn't he the one who married that actress – Dolores La Mar? I did a piece on her for the magazine a while back. Rather a shock to hear she'd handed in her chips.'

'Has she?' said Eileen Orgreave. 'I hadn't heard. I'm afraid we don't get the British papers here – or only infrequently. And then it's likely to be the *Daily Worker* rather than the *Daily Mail*.'

They went into dinner – Mrs Orgreave having agreed to join their little party – and the rest of the evening passed pleasantly enough, in talk of other things. Eileen Orgreave was avid to hear news of home, in particular, what was current on the London stage. 'I used to love going to the theatre, as a girl,' she said. Miss Barnes obliged with tales of actor and actresses she'd interviewed: Sybil Thorndike was marvellous, of course; Vivien Leigh very pretty – 'with rather your Irish colouring, Mrs Orgreave' – but difficult to draw out; Noël Coward was charming, and had signed Iris's programme for *Tonight at 8.30.*

Rowlands became increasingly aware of Walter's silence, which had persisted throughout the meal. Of course the lad was shy, but . . . 'Fancy a breath of air before turning in?' he said to the young German.

'I would,' was the reply. Leaving the women to their conversation, which had now turned to the proposed interview, the two of them went out. Since it would have been inadvisable to venture into the street, with so many armed men roaming about, they contented themselves with a turn along the terrace at the back of the hotel, which was deserted at that hour.

'Anything the matter?' said Rowlands. 'Only you

seem a bit quiet. Ankle hurting you, I expect.'

'It is not that.' The boy sounded agitated. 'I hate it – all this talk of . . . of actresses . . . when men are dying.' Rowlands forbore from saying that women were dying, too. Instead he lit a cigarette, and handed the pack to Walter.

'Help yourself.'

'Thank you.' Walter was silent a moment, then he burst out, 'It's all so horrible.' It seemed to Rowlands that the boy was referring to something beyond his recent experiences at the Front, unpleasant as these had been.

'What is it you mean?'

Another silence, then he said, 'I saw her, that night – the night the actress was killed. I did not realise what it meant at first, but later, after she was dead, I remembered that it was she whom I had seen going into the actress's room.'

'Who are you talking about?' asked Rowlands, disentangling with some difficulty this multiplicity of pronouns.

'The Spanish woman. Miss Casals.'

So that was it! thought Rowlands. The boy had got himself into a stew about nothing. 'Let me get this straight,' he said. 'You saw her – Miss Casals – going into Miss La Mar's room that evening. She's already admitted as much, you know. She went to turn down the bed, and settle her mistress for the night. All part of her job, as Miss La Mar's maid.'

'Yes, yes,' said Walter impatiently. 'But this was much

later. In the middle of the night. I could not sleep, and so I got up to go for a walk. It was midnight, because I happened to look at my watch. It was then that I saw her coming out of the actress's room.'

Rowlands considered the implications of this. 'Have you said anything to anyone else about this?'

'No.'

'Good. I shouldn't, if I were you.' Rowlands shuddered to think of the consequences, if Caterina Casals got to hear that the boy she'd helped to run off to Spain had seen her at the murder scene around the time the murder was committed. One thing puzzled him. 'If you knew Miss Casals had been in her mistress's room around the time of the latter's death, why on earth didn't you speak up before? It might have saved a lot of trouble.'

'I . . . I didn't realise it was important until afterwards,' said Walter. 'The policeman who interviewed me asked merely when I had last seen her – the actress – alive. I said it was at dinner, the night before she died. He did not ask me about Miss Casals.'

'But you must have realised there was something strange, to say the least, about the fact that she was in Miss La Mar's room at such a late hour?'

'I had other things on my mind,' said Walter. 'I wanted to get to Spain. Carlos Casals said he would take me. That was all I cared about,' he added, suddenly sounding like the schoolboy he was.

'Well, I'm glad you've told me,' said Rowlands. 'I should put it out of your mind until we get home. It's a job for the police from now on.'

Troubled by what Walter had told him, Rowlands found that sleep did not come easily, and it wasn't until the small hours that exhaustion overcame him at last. He'd been asleep no more than an hour or so when something – the sound of a footfall in the corridor outside, perhaps – brought him instantly awake. Knowing, from past experience of insomnia, that he would be unable to get back to sleep, he got up and, having put on his dressing gown, cautiously opened the door. As he did so, there came the creak of another door closing, along the corridor. Iris Barnes's room, he thought. Perhaps she had got up to visit the bathroom? Perhaps not. It might be a good idea to check that all was well.

He hesitated no more, but made his way cautiously in that direction. Reaching the room, which was three doors down from his, he tapped on the door. 'Everything all right?' There was no reply, but an indistinct sound – as of somebody trying to call out, and being silenced – came from within. He tried the door, which was unlocked. 'Iris?' he called softly. He took a step inside.

'Come any closer, blind man, and I will blow her brains out,' said a voice. It belonged to Caterina Casals.

'I'm rather afraid she means it,' said Iris Barnes.

Rowlands held up his hands, to show he was unarmed. 'Is this about the guns?' he said. 'Because I can assure you that it was entirely my idea to make off with them. Miss Barnes had nothing to do with it.'

'Do you think I will believe that?' said the Catalan

woman furiously. 'I know it was she who planned it all, and who has also caused Carlos to be taken away by the men put on his trail by the Fascist Cunningham.'

'I don't know anything about that,' protested Iris. 'And do stop pointing that thing at me. Since it's my gun, I happen to know that it's likely to go off very easily, if you're not careful.'

'Maybe that is what I want,' was the reply. 'Because of you, my brother is in the hands of his enemies. They came for him last night. I do not know where he is, or if he is alive or dead .'

'I still don't see what that's got to do with me,' said Iris. 'I tell you, I haven't laid eyes on Cunningham since I left England.'

'By returning the Rolls-Royce that was Cunningham's to the Colón Hotel, you led Cunningham's men to Carlos,' the other woman replied. 'They would not have found him otherwise. Therefore it is you who must pay the penalty.'

'Wait,' said Rowlands. 'What proof have you that they were Cunningham's men? A man like your brother must have many enemies.'

'They spoke English,' was the reply. 'And they recognised the car – I heard them say so.' This seemed pretty conclusive. Rowlands thought of the black Armstrong-Siddeley which had been on their tail when they had entered the city. Presumably those had been Cunningham's men, on the lookout for the boss's distinctive silver-grey Rolls-Royce. The fact that it led them to the Hotel Colón, and not to the Continental, had been due to Iris's cunning. So, in a way, she had been responsible for Carlos Casals' abduction.

'Be that as it may,' said Rowlands, 'it's hardly Miss Barnes's fault that they were after your brother.'

'So you say,' replied Miss Casals. 'But I tell you, if they kill Carlos, it will be because she led them to him. And for that,' she added coldly, 'she must pay the price.' There came the sound of a gun being cocked.

'Then you'll have to kill me first.' With this, Rowlands threw himself forward, so that he was between the two women.

'It is your choice,' said Caterina Casals. 'You are as much to blame as she.'

But as Rowlands prepared himself for the shot that now seemed certain to follow, there came another voice.

'Drop the gun.' It was Walter. He must have crept into the room under cover of the others' voices.

He was evidently armed, too, for the Catalan woman said, 'So you would shoot me, would you, ungrateful boy? Are you forgetting that it was I and my brother who brought you to Spain?'

'You would have come anyway,' the lad replied coolly. 'Drop the gun, I said. Now kick it over here.' She must have done so, for a moment later, Iris said, 'I'll have that, if you don't mind. Nice to have my own gun back.'

'I suppose you are going to kill me?' The other woman sounded as if it didn't much matter to her, either way.

'What would be the good of that?' said Iris. 'I've nothing against you. Besides, it might have escaped your notice, but we're on the same side. I don't like Franco and his gang of bully boys any more than you do. Nor am I a fan of his supporters, of which our Mr Cunningham is one.'

'Yet you came all the way to Spain to accuse me of trying to murder the old man,' said Caterina scornfully.

'I came to Spain for quite another reason, as you well know,' replied Iris. 'But since we're on the subject, did you mean to kill Cunningham?'

'I have already told you that my brother and I did not get the chance. Whoever killed my late mistress, the actress, made sure of that.'

'So what were you doing in Miss La Mar's bedroom at midnight on the night she was killed?' said Rowlands. There was a moment's started silence, then, 'Who told you that I was?'

'Never mind. Just answer the question.'

'Very well. It does not matter, since you cannot prove that I was there. I thought I heard a noise . . . somebody coming out of her room . . . at about that time. I am a light sleeper, and my room was next to hers. A cupboard,' she added haughtily. 'But then, I was only her maid.'

'You can cut all that,' said Rowlands. 'Go on.'

'There is not much more to say,' said Caterina. 'I thought I heard somebody, as I have said. I went to see who it was, but there was nobody there. Only my mistress – and she was dead,' she added, with a queer little laugh.

'What was it you heard exactly?' persisted Rowlands. 'Footsteps? A door closing?'

'Both of these,' was the reply. 'Now,' she went on, 'if you do not wish to kill me, then you must let me go, since we have nothing more to say to one another.' No one spoke, and she went out, closing the door behind her with a sharp click.

'Do you believe her?' said Iris when the Catalan woman had gone.

'I don't know,' replied Rowlands. 'I suppose I'm rather inclined to. As she said herself, there's no proof that she was there, and so it would have made no difference if she had admitted to murder.'

'I am not making it up,' interjected Walter hotly. 'I did see her go into the actress's room.'

'I don't doubt it,' said Rowlands. 'And it's plain that she knew of her mistress's death several hours before Cunningham gave the alarm. But that doesn't make her a murderess.'

'It puts her at the scene soon after the murder was committed,' said Iris.

'True, but it still doesn't mean she did it. What motive did she have, after all? She as good as admitted that she and Casals were after Cunningham, not his wife.'

'And now Cunningham's thugs have got Casals,' said Iris. 'I don't imagine it will end well for him. Which is perhaps no more than he deserves.'

After a scratch breakfast of coffee and rolls in the hotel dining room, the three of them separated – the two men to collect the bags, and Iris to settle the bill at reception.

When Rowlands and Walter joined her a few minutes later, she seemed perturbed at the fact that there had been no message from Jordi Morell to explain why he hadn't returned to the hotel the previous night. 'I'm afraid something's happened to him.' she said as they made their way to where she'd parked the Jaguar. 'If Caterina Casals has decided to revenge herself on those she considers to blame for her brother's abduction, then Jordi's the next obvious candidate.' Rowlands, who had been thinking much the same thing, said nothing, but Walter burst out, 'It is all my fault. If you had not come here, you – and Mr Morell – would not have been exposed to such danger.'

'Nonsense,' said Iris. 'Danger's rather a part of my job, you know. And Mr Rowlands is no stranger to it, either. As for Mr Morell, he's been risking his life for months, writing the kinds of articles he writes. None of it anything to do with you, young man, although I hope you don't make a habit of running off to war. His Majesty's Government can't afford to spare me on a regular basis.'

'I . . . no . . . of course not,' stammered Walter as they turned into the side street which ran behind the hotel, and which served as a car park for the establishment. 'I . . . I am very grateful to you for . . .'

But he never finished his sentence, because Rowlands, who had heard the footsteps before the others did, cried, 'I say – look out!' He whirled round to face the assailant – if that was what he was – but it was Walter who managed to collar the youth.

'What do you want?' he demanded, perhaps forgetting that the other lad spoke no English – a fact evident from the flood of Catalan invective which ensued. 'Let me go, you fool! (*'Deixa'm anar, tonto!'*) I have a message for the lady.' (*'Tinc un missatge per a la dama.'*)

'Hand it over, then,' (*'Entregueu-lo,'*) said Iris; then, having scrutinised it, 'It's from Jordi. Looks genuine enough. That's for your trouble,' she said to the lad who'd brought it, handing him some coins. When he had taken himself off, she read aloud: '"*Meet me at eight-thirty a.m. at Parc Guell, under the viaduct. Come alone. I have urgent information for your eyes only . . .*" Hm,' she said. 'I wonder why he wants me to go all the way out there? It's out beyond Gracia. Well, he'll have his reasons, no doubt.'

'I don't think you should go alone, whatever he says,' put in Rowlands. 'After all, there may be some of Casals' people lurking about.'

'True.' She thought for a moment. 'All right. You'd better get in the car. You too, Walter. You can come with me to the park and wait for me at the entrance while I find Jordi. It's still only eight o'clock, so we should be in plenty of time.'

The Jaguar was soon racing through streets still mercifully free of traffic towards the park, which was located on the north-eastern side of the city. 'It's a kind of grand folly,' Iris explained. 'Built by an eccentric genius called Antoni Gaudí at the end of the last century. He's the one responsible for that extraordinary edifice,

La Sagrada Familia – their cathedral, you know. It's a pity you can't see it, Fred, because it's really quite a sight, with four towering spires – it was originally meant to have twelve – and the most bizarre decorations. Gargoyles, dragons. Like something out of one's wildest dreams . . . or nightmares. Anyway, Guell Park is more of the same. A sort of demented fairytale, with pavilions and colonnades straight out of the Arabian Nights.'

'It sounds a fascinating place,' said Rowlands. 'Perhaps, while you're having your talk with Morell, Walter could describe some of the more outlandish features to me?' Walter said that he'd be happy to, and the rest of the twenty-minute journey passed in silence. It seemed to Rowlands that, despite her show of unconcern, Iris was worried about something – the 'urgent information' Morell was to impart, perhaps? They reached the park at last.

'Well, here we are,' said Iris. 'It's certainly deserted, at this time of day. I can see why he chose it now.' She switched off the engine. 'I shouldn't be more than ten minutes,' she said. 'The viaduct's over that way,' – this was to Walter – 'so keep away from there, if you do decide to go for a walk. You can't miss it,' she added. 'It's a weird construction that looks as if it was built out of dried mud. All the pillars supporting the structure slant at a crazy angle. Quite unsettling if, like me, you prefer your architecture with nice straight lines and sharp corners.' Then, with a brisk tapping of heels on the stone pavement, she was gone.

After a minute or two, Rowlands and Walter got out of the car, and walked the short distance to the main entrance of the park. This was reached by a double flight of stone steps, leading up to a colonnade of Doric columns, and was guarded by a giant salamander, said Walter, whose scales were made of coloured mosaic. They climbed the steps to the echoing hall, whose marble floor and broad stone columns offered a pleasant coolness, in contrast to the increasing heat outside. Rowlands could happily have stayed there, but he sensed that his young companion was eager to see more of the place, and its whimsical features. And so they climbed another staircase that led onto the roof of the pavilion. This commanded a panoramic view of the city, as well of the buildings of the park. 'Those houses are very charming,' said Walter. 'They remind me a little of some we have in the Grunewald forest, in Berlin. Like those from the story of Hansel and Gretel. Quaint – is that the word? But also a little frightening.'

'Can you see Miss Barnes yet?' asked Rowlands, who had sat down on the curving stone bench that ran the length of the terrace. It was lavishly decorated (so his fingers told him) with yet more mosaic. 'She's been gone quite a while. I wonder if we ought to go and find this viaduct with the slanting pillars?'

'I think I see her,' said Walter after a moment. 'The red blouse she is wearing is conspicuous, *ja*?'

'Is she alone?'

'*Nein* . . . Herr Morell is with her, I think . . . That is

331

strange . . .' A note of uncertainty had entered Walter's voice. 'It looks as if . . . I cannot be sure, because it is too far for me to see clearly . . . But it may be that he has a gun.'

'Come on,' said Rowlands, getting to his feet. 'I don't like the sound of this.'

They descended the steps from the terrace rather faster than they had come up them, and hastened in the direction in which Walter had seen the others disappear. Below the viaduct of which Iris had spoken, was a colonnade of sorts, whose pillars – so Rowlands discovered when he touched them – were made out of sun-warmed clay bricks, uneven but not unpleasant to the touch. 'Can you see them?' he said in a low voice to Walter, who was just ahead of him.

'*Nein*. I cannot. But I am certain that I saw them go in here. She went in first and he . . . he followed her. He had a gun in his hand, I am almost sure of it.'

Rowlands touched the boy's arm, to caution him to silence. Because from up ahead came the sound of voices. 'My dear Iris . . .' This was Morell, but a Morell very different from the one Rowlands had encountered before. This man was a virtual stranger. 'You surely don't think that I will allow you to leave now? I regret to say that you have become too dangerous to our cause.'

'It was you all along, wasn't it?' said Iris, ignoring this. 'You who betrayed our agents to the Francoists, and who alerted Cunningham's thugs to the whereabouts of Carlos Casals.'

He made no attempt to deny it. 'Such a pity, little Iris, that it has to be this way. You and I could have been such friends . . . more than friends, perhaps, had your blind Englishman not come between us. Oh, I have seen the way you look at him! You women are strange creatures. To prefer a man like that – a man who can never appreciate your beauty – to one capable of enjoying it to the full.'

'You betrayed your own side,' said Iris, again paying no attention to this last remark. 'I don't know how you could bring yourself to do it.'

'Very easily,' was the reply. 'They will be the losing side, after all. That must be apparent, even to you. Why else is your government holding its hand? When General Franco is victorious, we will see how quickly the British will rush to support him.'

'Perhaps,' said Iris. 'There are certainly some elements in the government who are in favour of the Nationalists. One thing we're not in favour of, though, is people killing our agents – or selling them out to the Nazis.'

'All this is of no account,' said Jordi Morell coldly. 'You have left me no choice but to bring our beautiful friendship to an end. In the service of the Cause . . .' – here his voice hardened into one Rowlands recognised as that of a true fanatic – 'such things are of little importance. It is a pity, as I say, that you will not live to see the triumph of the New Order.' There was the sound of a gun being cocked.

'You'll regret this, Morell,' said Iris. For a woman facing death, she sounded remarkably calm. 'The British

Secret Service doesn't take kindly to having its agents murdered. If you kill me, there will be another sent in my place to deal with you.'

Morell laughed. 'Poor little Iris! Always so brave. But it is I who will have the last word.'

At that precise moment, Rowlands stepped out from behind the pillar where he and Walter had concealed themselves. 'I wouldn't speak too soon, if I were you, Morell,' he said.

'*You*!' Morell must have whirled round at this unexpected interruption, or so Rowlands surmised, because a moment later, a shot rang out. There was a cry, then the sound of a falling body. 'Iris,' gasped the traitor. 'You . . . you . . .'

'Save it, Jordi,' snapped the girl. 'You were going to do the same to me. Get his gun, Walter.'

'I . . .' The dying man's breathing was becoming laboured. 'I would have . . . killed you . . . yes . . . but for . . . the Cause.'

'What makes you think you're the only one with a cause?' she said. Then, after another moment, 'He's gone. Let's get out of here.'

Chapter Eighteen

The three of them said little on the drive to the Spanish border. Rowlands could only guess at the thoughts that occupied his companions during those few hours, but for himself, he was sick at heart. The episode with Jordi Morell had left a bad taste; that was the thing about treachery – it poisoned everything. After what he had witnessed – two violent deaths and as many attempted murders in two days – Walter seemed numb with shock, replying only in monosyllables to Rowlands' enquiries as to whether he was hungry or thirsty, and seeming indifferent to the splendours of the landscape through which they were passing. Nor did Iris Barnes have anything more to say on what had passed between her and Morell during that last encounter. Perhaps this was merely the caution of the trained operative, reluctant to say anything which might compromise her mission;

Rowlands thought it was more than that, however. During the few times he had been with Iris in Morell's company, he'd had the distinct impression that there had been a rapport between them. Whatever Morell himself had thought (and Rowlands recalled the young man's jealous words concerning Iris's supposed feelings for 'the blind Englishman'), it had seemed to him that the attraction had not been all one way. He supposed that, as with a good deal else in her complicated life, Miss Barnes would have to find a way to bury such feelings.

Over a late lunch in the walled mediaeval town of Carcassonne, she shook off the mood of melancholia which seemed to have possessed her since their hasty departure from Barcelona, to the extent of describing some of the former's more striking features for Rowlands' benefit: 'It was built as a fortress, commanding the river valley. Most of it – the castle, for instance – dates from the thirteenth century, although some parts are much older. The history's pretty bloody, of course.'

'Most history is,' said Rowlands.

The rest of the journey passed like something in a dream, with towns and villages flashing past, at breakneck speed. Toulouse, Montauban, Bordeaux. When at last they stopped to rest for the night at a roadside inn on the approach to La Rochelle, all three travellers were exhausted, or so Rowlands surmised from the alacrity with which his companions said their good-nights, and made for their respective rooms. He himself, thankful to stretch his legs after hours cramped up in a hot car, took a turn in the little orchard behind the inn, to smoke a cigarette.

The night air was pleasantly cool, and he breathed it in, its fresh taste mingling with that of the smoke. What a hellish few days it had been . . . and yet there had been moments of exhilaration, of feeling intensely alive. He supposed war was like that. The most unimaginable horrors got mixed up with glimpses of unforgettable beauty, so that it was hard to separate them when you came to look back.

The sound of a footfall on the dry grass alerted him to the fact that he was not alone. 'I saw you from my window,' said Iris. 'Give me a cigarette, will you?' He handed her the pack, and she lit one. 'There's something I have to say,' she said after a moment or two. 'You can't mention what happened to anyone . . . not even your wife.' He supposed it was the killing of Jordi Morell to which she was referring, although it wasn't entirely clear.

'I wasn't going to,' he replied.

'Good.' She exhaled a mouthful of smoke. 'I knew I could trust you.'

'Oh, you can certainly do that – under all kinds of circumstances,' he couldn't resist saying. 'Your secret is safe with me.'

'Is it?' It may be that she picked up the ambiguity in what he said, for suddenly he felt her lips brush his cheek. 'Thank you.' He wasn't sure how to react to this, and so he merely smiled. 'You know,' she went on hesitantly. 'If things had been different . . .'

'But they're not,' he said. 'Which is probably as well – for my peace of mind, if not for yours. Let's get some sleep, shall we?'

They reached Cornwall very early on the morning of the thirty-first of August. A period of rest and recuperation from the rigours of the journey followed, but it wasn't long after this, and after a suitable interval for celebration of the safe return of Walter, that Miss Barnes announced that she would have to return to London on the following day. 'Other fish to fry,' she said mysteriously. Rowlands knew better than to enquire what it was she meant. To the Ashenhursts she expressed herself less cryptically. She was sorry to leave them after so short a time, but her editor was kicking up a fuss about her latest set of page proofs, and wouldn't be fobbed off. 'The trials of an author's life,' she sighed as the company congregated in the lounge for preprandial drinks. This group consisted of the three couples, and their respective offspring, as well as the Colonel and his lady, and the dwindling band of film people. Horace Cunningham had already returned to London, having come back to Cornwall three days before for his wife's funeral. It had been a sparsely attended affair, Edith said to her husband. Just the film crowd – Carmody, Dean, Miss Linden, Miss Brierley, and a few of the technical people, as well as a handful of locals, drawn as much by curiosity (she surmised) as by the wish to pay their respects to the deceased.

Laurence Quayle had yet to be buried. His body was

still at the mortuary, awaiting collection by his next of kin, whoever that might be. There was an elderly aunt, said Miss Linden (who had perhaps known the dead man best). Larry's parents had died when he was a baby, during the influenza epidemic. Otherwise he had been quite alone in the world.

But all such melancholy talk was banished on that last evening, which was dedicated to welcoming the heroes home. 'Well, I'm jolly glad you weren't killed, old man,' said Billy to his cousin – handsomely, thought Rowlands, considering the lad had missed out on what must have seemed to him like a ripping adventure. To which Walter muttered something unintelligible. 'What's that?' demanded the irrepressible Billy. 'I do hope, old man, that you're not going to give me some boring pi-jaw about "noble sacrifice". It must have been the most tremendous fun, joining the Brigade, and getting to shoot with real guns.' He spoke with some regret. The only gun which had ever come into his possession now lay at the bottom of the sea. In the face of this challenge, Walter reminded stubbornly silent.

'Don't tease him, Billy,' said Jack Ashenhurst.

'I wasn't. It's just he's being so beastly oysterish about it.'

'I think,' said Miss Barnes, 'that chaps who've done something really brave don't generally like to talk about it.' And there the matter was allowed to rest – or almost.

'Such a pity you have to leave before you've written your Cornish mystery,' opined Daphne Simkins to the authoress. 'I was so looking forward to reading it, wasn't I, John?'

'Oh, don't worry,' was the breezy reply. 'I've got all the material I need. This time next year *Crime in Cornwall* should be joining the others on the bookshop shelves.'

Nor was Miss Barnes the only one to be quitting Cliff House in the immediate future, it transpired. The cast and crew of *Forbidden Desires* – sadly depleted as it was – would also be returning to London, within the next couple of days. 'We've got all the footage we need to finish the picture,' said Hilary Carmody. 'It won't be the film we set out to make, but it'll still pack them in at the local Odeons and Kinemas.'

'Let's hope so,' said Lydia Linden, with a tremulous laugh. 'Or we might all be out of a job soon.'

'Oh, I think you'll find that the public will come in droves,' said Eliot Dean. 'If only to see Dolores's last picture.' The silence which followed this remark was broken by Mrs Nicholls' announcing that dinner was served.

'From the sound of it, there won't be many more evenings like this,' said Daphne Simkins as the company trooped into the dining room, and dispersed to its respective tables. 'I mean, with everybody leaving, it'll soon be just the regulars, like ourselves. It's been a most *interesting* summer, though, hasn't it, dear?' she added to her spouse. 'What with all these films being made and novels being written, and . . . er . . .'

'Murders being committed,' muttered Dorothy to her

brother, who frowned and shook his head at her.

And it did seem as if the shocking events of ten days before were no more than just another piece of fiction, of no more substance than the fanciful creations of a detective story writer, or those designed for the cinema screen. The police, it appeared, had finished with the hotel residents – at least for now – and taken their investigations elsewhere. Only Chief Inspector Douglas of the Metropolitan Police remained in the locality; he had a few days' leave, he said to Rowlands, and might as well take it here as anywhere else. The Blue Anchor had provided him with a comfortable berth, and if he felt like stretching his legs, a walk along the clifftops was just what the doctor ordered.

Which was in fact where he and Rowlands found themselves, a couple of mornings after the latter's return from Spain. 'I understand you caught up with the woman and her brother?' he said as the two friends strolled along. Rowlands guessed it was the Casals to whom he was referring, and that it was from Iris Barnes he had learnt this.

'Yes,' he replied. Invited to expand upon this, he did so while the Chief Inspector listened in silence.

'Well,' said the policeman at last, pausing to fill his pipe and light it. 'You *do* seem to have turned up a pretty story! So you reckon it was the Spanish woman who did for her – seeing as she was the last person to enter the room?'

'She says she only went into the room because she

heard somebody else coming out of it,' said Rowlands. 'And I'm inclined to believe her.'

'You always did have a soft spot for the ladies,' said Alasdair Douglas. 'I suppose you don't believe her capable of putting the poison in her mistress's glass.'

'If you'd met her, you'd believe her capable of anything,' was the reply. 'It's the question of motive I can't get over.'

'Yes, indeed. Motive is the key,' said Alasdair Douglas. 'Although it doesn't take us much further. Given that all of 'em – Dean, the Linden girl, Carmody and the lady's husband – had good reason to want to put her away, it comes down to a matter of "you pays your money and you takes your choice".'

'And,' said Rowlands, 'of opportunity.'

'And of opportunity, as you say. Let's take 'em in order. Could it have been Dean you heard talking to her that night?'

'Do you mean when I was in the garden, or later the same night?'

'Either time – but let's start with the garden.'

'It couldn't have been Dean – or Carmody, for that matter. They'd both left the hotel by then, as had Miss Linden.'

'So they had. Filming, or some such.'

'That's right.'

'All right. Leave them out of it for now. Who else is there? Quayle? Perhaps he was blackmailing her? He sounds the type.'

'It certainly could have been him.'

'Trouble is,' said the Chief Inspector, meditatively sucking on his pipe, 'we can't ask him. But put him down for now. Who else?'

'Well, if you're excluding the Simkinses, who'd gone to bed (and can vouch for one another), and Colonel and Mrs Rutherford, who'd gone back to their cottage . . .'

'We'll leave them out for the minute. Although I don't see what business any of those respectable people could have had in the lady's bedroom.'

'Then that just leaves Miss Brierley.'

'The secretary, you mean? Mousy little thing, isn't she? Looks as if she's frightened of her own shadow. As a matter of fact, she says she did visit Madam's room that evening. Puts it an hour earlier than the time you mention – nine to nine-fifteen at the latest. Wanted Madam to sign some letters. Denies there was a shouting match, but then she probably took all that sort of thing as her deserts.'

'I think it was common knowledge that Miss La Mar bullied her,' said Rowlands.

'Well, whether or not Madam had a go at her that night is neither here nor there,' was the reply. 'She'd left the woman's room by nine twenty-five at the latest. Asking for a mug of hot milk in the kitchen at nine-thirty. Witness – a certain Mrs Jago – corroborates her story. If, as you say, Dolores La Mar was alive at eleven-thirty when you heard her talking to person or persons unknown in her bedroom, then Miss B can't have been the one to slip her the poison. Hubby says he called good night to her at around eleven-forty when he went to bed. So one can assume she was still alive then. No, I'm afraid the most likely candidate for First Murderer is your Spanish popsy. If your young friend Mr Metzner is right about seeing her come out of her mistress's room around midnight, then she was the last person to see Miss La Mar alive. Probably popped the poison in her glass then and there. Next thing you know, Madam's woken up, taken a swig, and . . . Bob's your uncle,' said Douglas.

'But surely whoever was in Miss La Mar's room around half past eleven also had the opportunity to poison the water in the glass. By the way, I assume that the water in the carafe was tested for poison, too?'

'Indeed it was,' said the Chief Inspector. 'In point of fact, we think it's there that the arsenic was introduced. There were no traces of arsenic in the empty wrapper for the sleeping powder.'

'Ah!' said Rowlands. 'So if it wasn't the sleeping powders, then it must have been the poison in the ring that did for her. And there's no reason why that couldn't have been dropped in the carafe at any time during the evening.'

'None whatsoever,' was the reply. 'And from what I can gather, everybody who was seated around the dinner table that night – and no doubt some that weren't – knew about the poison in that infernal ring. Which is why,' Alasdair Douglas went on, 'the question of motive is important. Who wanted her dead – and why? Eliot Dean is certainly a possibility. He had eyes for the Linden girl, which had put Madam's nose out of joint, from what you've told me.'

'Yes, but it's hardly a motive for murder.'

'Don't be too sure. Dean and the La Mar woman had a bit of history, as we know, being what the yellow press likes to call "intimate friends" at one time. Supposing Madam threatened to cut up rough? It could've spoilt his chances with the girl.'

'Perhaps,' said Rowlands, not entirely convinced by this.

'Then there's the girl herself,' went on the other.

'Surely you don't think she could have been responsible?' objected Rowlands.

'Like I said, I'm ruling nobody out at this stage,' was the reply. 'And she had a motive, too. Dolores La Mar was threatening to have her thrown off the picture, which, if you think about it, gives our Mr Dean another motive too, since he was in love with the lassie.'

'Hmm,' said Rowlands.

'Then there's Carmody,' Douglas went on remorselessly. 'He had perhaps the strongest motive of the three, since he'd stand to lose the most if the picture was cancelled, in terms of professional reputation, and so forth. It seems to me he was our likeliest candidate for the man you heard quarrelling with her that night around half past eleven. He'd have had the opportunity to slip the poison in her glass then.'

'What about Horace Cunningham?' said Rowlands.

'He'd have had the best opportunity of all, since he shared a bathroom with his wife. Nothing easier than for him to enter her room on some pretext, and drop the poison into the carafe. And if we're talking about motive, he had the best one of all. Money.'

The Chief Inspector laughed. 'You'd put it above those other tried and tested reasons for killing – love and professional pride?' he asked. 'I'd say you were right, Fred. And don't think we haven't been keeping an eye on Horace Cunningham. While you were off gallivanting around Spain, we set a watch on him that was every bit as close as if he'd been holed up in the Cliff House Hotel with all the others. We know all about his visits to the solicitors, ye ken. The will was read on Thursday, at his insistence. Wanted to make sure he was the chief beneficiary.'

'And was he?'

'Och, aye. It all goes to the husband. Apart from a few small legacies to servants.'

'Including Muriel Brierley, by any chance?'

'As it happens, yes. She gets £50. Not much for two years' servitude.'

'Is that how long she's worked for Miss La Mar?'

'So it appears. She'll have to find another job now, won't she? Let's hope for her sake it's with somebody who treats her like a human being.'

Rowlands murmured his agreement. For a few moments, the two strolled along in a silence that was broken only by the keening of seagulls, and the soft swish of the waves, far below.

'So when does he get it?' said Rowlands at last. 'The money, I mean.'

'Och, it'll be a few months, yet. But o'course, as sole legatee, our Mr Cunningham'll be able to get a lot on credit.'

'Only I gather he'd been in financial difficulties lately,' said Rowlands. Again, the Chief Inspector laughed.

'Who told you that, I wonder?' he said. 'No, let me guess. The redoubtable Miss Barnes, I reckon.'

Rowlands admitted that this was the case. 'That's what put the idea of Cunningham as chief suspect into your head, I'll warrant,' chuckled the Chief Inspector. 'Well, I'll not say it's the worst idea you've had.'

'He could have killed Quayle,' said Rowlands. 'Whereas Caterina Casals and her brother were already off the premises by the time of his murder.'

'True,' was the reply. 'But what makes you think he had a motive for pushing the fellow off a cliff? We still haven't settled that it *was* murder.'

'Oh, it was murder all right. I'm convinced of it,' said Rowlands. 'I mean, how do you explain the sand that was in his mouth and nostrils and down the front of his clothes?'

'There are other ways it could have got there,' said Douglas. 'For instance, he could have fallen while he was on his way to the cliff path. If he'd cut across the beach, that is.'

'I suppose that's possible,' Rowlands allowed. 'Although it doesn't answer the question of why he went to the cliff path at all. He wasn't the type who was given to such forms of exercise, especially not at night.'

'It's suspicious, I grant you,' was the reply. 'And maybe somebody did throw sand in his face before shoving him over the edge. But I can tell you, it wasn't Cunningham.'

'But . . .'

'There wasn't a trace of sand in the pockets of any of his suits,' said Douglas. 'Including the one he was wearing when he left for London the morning after. Don't think I didn't have a thorough search made of his wardrobe and effects. No sand to be found. I'm sorry, Fred, but you'll have to look elsewhere for Quayle's murderer, if indeed he was murdered. As for who it was that killed Cunningham's wife, I think it's clear that he didn't give her the poison himself. A man like that is accustomed to paying others to do his dirty work. No, I still think the most likely candidate for the murder of Dolores La Mar – or Mary-Ann Plunkett, or whatever she called herself – is the lady's personal maid, your dark-eyed señorita.'

With the departure, early the following week, not only of the Chief Inspector – 'Duty calls,' he said regretfully – but of the film company, life at the Cliff House Hotel resumed its former tranquillity, with nothing to disturb the even tenor of its ways. An occasional dispute over whether a shot was in or out during one of the tennis matches being played once more on the court outside the rooms previously occupied by the dead actress was the only disturbance to this uneventful routine; a difference of opinion as to the advantages of a game of Bridge over those of listening to a concert on the wireless, the only other source of controversy.

It was on one such evening that the Rowlandses, eschewing both the pleasures of music and of cards, set off for a walk along the beach. The tide was out, and the damp sand at the water's edge made a firm surface for walking. Rowlands drew in a deep breath of the mild, salt-tasting air, feeling it to be a cleansing agent, sweeping away the hideous events of the past two weeks. His wife was talking of something – the letter she'd received from Frances in Poole, confirming their arrangements for next week – he wasn't really paying attention. The sound of her voice washed over him, blending with the gentle shushing of the waves. Suddenly, he felt her give a start (she was holding his arm); a moment later, she stooped to examine something – a piece of flotsam, Rowlands supposed. 'I say, that looks awfully like the one Joan was looking for,' she said. 'In fact, I'm almost certain it's the same one.'

'What are we talking about?' he asked patiently. Even after almost twenty years of being married to a blind man, Edith still occasionally forgot to be specific when describing things.

'A bucket. Or rather, the bucket – the one Joan was so upset about losing.'

'Don't touch it!' he said. 'Although I don't suppose it'll make much difference – now.'

'What on earth do you mean, Fred? It's just a child's

bucket. A little rusty, from having been in the sea, but still quite serviceable.'

'It's unlikely that there'll be any fingerprints by this time,' said Rowlands. 'But we'd better not take any chances.' He took a handkerchief from his pocket and, taking care to wrap the clean cotton around the handle, gingerly picked up the bucket. 'If I'm not mistaken,' he said grimly, 'we've just found the murder weapon that did for Laurence Quayle.'

Arriving back at the hotel as the other guests were assembling for pre-dinner drinks, the Rowlandses quickly separated – Edith to change her shoes and powder her nose, and Rowlands to put his find in a safe place until such time as he could notify the police. The bottom of an empty trunk provided just such a place and, having hastily washed his hands and combed his hair (for dinner was informal tonight, as it had been most nights since the company had departed), he went downstairs. It was now as clear to him as if he had witnessed it himself how the murder of Laurence Quayle had been accomplished.

An assignation had been arranged, verbally or in writing, and the doomed man had gone to meet his murderer, thinking, no doubt, that he was the one with the upper hand. Blackmailers seldom understood the danger in which they placed themselves, he thought. It was not the first instance he'd come across of someone trying to use information of a dangerous nature for financial gain, only to find himself hoist with his own petard. And so Quayle had gone to that fatal meeting on the clifftop, to find someone waiting there for him – someone who'd come prepared, carrying a child's tin bucket full of sand. This, flung in the young man's face, had caused him to stagger, and – blinded and choking – he'd needed only a good, hard shove to tip him over the edge. Yes, Rowlands could just see it. 'I must say, you're looking awfully grim, old man,' said Jack Ashenhurst as his brother-in-law joined those assembled on the terrace where the former was dispensing drinks. 'Not bad news, I hope?'

'Not exactly,' was the reply. 'I'll tell you about it later. Hello! Is that Dr Finch I hear?'

'Call me Bill, do,' said Finch, in a tone of great affability. 'Yes, I'm dining here tonight, as Cecily's guest.'

'Naturally, he couldn't turn down the chance of a decent meal,' put in Mrs Nicholls. 'What that landlady of yours considers proper fare for a hardworking GP doesn't bear thinking about.'

'I'll have you know she does a very good sausage and mash,' said Bill Finch. 'I won't have Mrs Bolitho maligned. Besides which,' he went on, with mock severity, 'I resent the implication that I'm only here for the food.'

'I apologise unreservedly,' said Cecily. It seemed to Rowlands that the two were in on some private joke. 'Actually,' she went on, 'Bill does have another reason for coming here this evening.' Rowlands felt his wife give him a nudge.

'I suppose I'd better come clean,' said the doctor. 'The fact is that this lady . . . Cecily, that is . . . has done me the honour of agreeing to be my wife.'

'Told you,' murmured Edith in Rowlands' ear.

'So if you'll all raise your glasses, I'd like to propose a toast.'

'Hold hard,' said Ashenhurst. 'We can do better than sherry. Don't we have a few bottles of that champagne left, Dottie?'

'We do indeed. I'll fetch them,' she said.

'Then drink up, everybody, and we'll have a proper toast. It isn't every day,' said Ashenhurst, 'that my favourite sister gets engaged.'

Inspector Trewin was less than enthusiastic about Rowlands' find. When, after the latter's telephone call, the policeman had stopped by the hotel, it seemed only in response to the fact that Rowlands was a friend of the Chief Inspector. Nor did Trewin's sceptical tone alter after Rowlands had produced 'Exhibit A' (as Ashenhurst had called it). And there was undoubtedly something ridiculous about the suggestion that a red-and-blue striped tin bucket might have been employed to bring about a man's death. 'Where was it that you found this . . . er . . . object?' was the inspector's first question after Rowlands had explained his theory.

'On the beach, you say?' Rather, his aloof manner seemed to imply, where one might expect a toy bucket to fetch up.

Even after Rowlands had qualified his reply by saying that the bucket had been found directly below the cliff where Laurence Quayle had fallen to his death, Trewin seemed unconvinced. 'You're suggesting that whoever was responsible for Mr Quayle's murder – and mind, we're not yet sure it was murder – went along to meet him carrying this bucket?' Put like that, it did sound rather unlikely.

Trewin agreed, however, to take charge of the alleged murder weapon, pending further evidence pointing to the identity of the perpetrator. 'Find a piece of newspaper and wrap that up, Sergeant,' he said to his subordinate as he took his leave of Rowlands and Ashenhurst. 'Might as well run it over to the lab for the fingerprint boys to take a dekko. Not that I expect them to find anything,' he added.

So that was that. The following day, Rowlands and his daughters went back to London; the girls would be starting school the week after next, and preparations had to be made. Edith was to spend a few days in Poole with her old schoolfriend, as planned. But Helen, Rowlands' mother-in-law, would be on hand to make sure uniforms were pressed and school books collected up. It seemed a rather tame ending to a rather too exciting affair.

Rowlands himself was back at work – his role as Secretary to St Dunstan's, the institute for the war-blinded, requiring his expertise on all manner of things, from processing orders for the home-based workers subsidised by the organisation in the manufacture of tea trays, plant stands and magazine racks, to assisting Sir Ian Fraser, the Head of St Dunstan's, in the seemingly endless planning meetings that would lead up to the opening next year of the new purpose-built accommodation near Brighton.

The second week of September arrived and the girls went back to school. Edith returned from her holiday. The news from Spain continued to be bad. Looking back on that episode in his life, Rowlands thought it seemed like a strange dream. He could hardly believe that barely a month had passed since he and Iris Barnes had been dodging the snipers on the Aragon Front.

Of that lady he had heard not a single word since her departure from Cornwall at the end of August. In his more idle moments, he wondered if the two of them would ever meet again. Nor was there any news of the investigation into the murder of Dolores La Mar. After the excitement surrounding her death had died down in the popular press, the whole affair seemed to have gone quiet. With other things to think about, Rowlands pushed it to the back of his mind.

Then one day, he returned from work with the evening paper he always bought on his way home. The newspaper vendor at Waterloo knew him by sight, and kept a copy ready for him. He got in, and went upstairs to change into his gardening clothes, it being a fine evening. With luck, he'd get the grass mown and rolled before dinner time. But when he came downstairs, in the expectation of a cup of tea before beginning his labours, he found Edith in an agitated state. 'Fred! You'll never guess what's happened!'

'I don't suppose I will unless you tell me.'

'It's that man. Horace Cunningham. He's only gone and shot himself. Listen to this . . .' She found the piece in the paper she'd been reading: "'*Police were called to the Eaton Square home of Mr Horace Cunningham, the entrepreneur, where the body of a man in his sixties was discovered to have died from a gunshot wound. Police are not treating the death as suspicious.*" That means it was suicide.'

'I expect you're right.'

'It doesn't say that he left a note.'

'That'll come out at the inquest.'

'So it will. It's tantamount to a confession of guilt, wouldn't you say? I mean, he must have known the police were after him for his wife's murder.'

'I think we should wait and see what the police think,' said Rowlands. 'But yes, it does seem to point in that direction.'

Chapter Nineteen

'Shot through the right temple,' said Chief Inspector Douglas. 'A neat enough job. Gun held in the right hand, o'course. He'd have been dead almost before his head hit the desk in front of him.'

'Suicide,' said Rowlands. It was not quite a question, but the other must have heard it as such, for he said, 'No doubt about it. He left a note.'

'What did it say?'

Alasdair Douglas laughed – a dry, mirthless sound. 'You are a stickler for the facts, aren't you? It said, in as far as I can recall, that he was sorry for what he'd done, and that he couldn't live with himself until he'd made amends.'

'He said that, did he?'

'As near as makes no difference. Why? What's wrong with it?'

'Only that it seems rather an odd choice of words for a suicide note.'

Again, the Chief Inspector let out a chuckle. 'Particular, aren't you, Fred? What should it have said, in your opinion?'

'I don't know. It might have been more specific.'

'Meaning you'd have liked him to put his hand up to his wife's murder in so many words?'

'I suppose so,' said Rowlands. A thought occurred to him. 'What'll happen to the money?' Because, as Iris Barnes had intimated, Dolores La Mar had been a wealthy woman. Douglas took a moment to fill his pipe.

'No idea. For all I know, it'll go to the local cats' home. Does it matter?'

'Probably not.' The two men were in Alasdair Douglas's office at Scotland Yard. Since the visit was an informal one, there had been no need for their conversation to be recorded by one of the Chief Inspector's subordinate officers, and so – to Rowlands' relief – they were able to speak quite freely.

'I should've thought,' said the Scotsman, 'that you'd have been glad to have the matter cleared up. Given that you suspected Cunningham all along.'

'That's true.' A further pause ensued as the Chief Inspector lit his pipe, and got it drawing to his satisfaction. From outside, came the sounds of traffic along the Embankment, interspersed with the hooting of a siren from a passing barge as it moved slowly along that stretch of the river.

'But you're still not convinced that he did for himself, eh?' said Douglas. 'Like I said, you're a hard man to please. We in the police force can't afford to be so pernickety. When we've got a suspect with as strong a motive for murdering his wife as Cunningham, who then puts an end to himself because he can't live with the guilt of doing so, and is considerate enough to leave a note, we consider it Case Closed. Take a tip from me, Fred,' he added, dropping the jocular tone for one of greater seriousness. 'Don't go looking for complications where they don't exist.'

Which would have been the end of what Rowlands had come to think of (taking a leaf out of Miss Barnes's book) as the Cornish Mystery. Whatever the truth of the matter, the facts were certain: somebody had murdered Dolores La Mar (née Mary-Ann Plunkett) and, in all probability, Laurence Quayle, too. That somebody – assuming it to have been Horace Cunningham – had taken his own life. Case Closed, as the Chief Inspector said. And so, in spite of certain unanswered questions that persisted in nagging at him – chief of which was the question of what made a man who had killed cold-bloodedly for financial gain decide to throw money and life away in a fit of remorse – Rowlands put the whole affair out of his mind. Other things – work, family life – took precedence. Then, quite by chance, the whole thing flared up again.

Six months had passed since Rowlands had returned to London; five since he'd heard the news of Cunningham's death. Nothing could have been further from his thoughts than that grisly event, or the events in Cornwall which had led up to it. If he thought about last summer's Cornish holiday at all, it was in connection with another and much happier event, which would require his and Edith's presence within the next fortnight. This – the wedding of Bill and Cecily – was to be a quiet affair. Edith had decided against buying a new outfit since the bride herself would be wearing a coat and skirt rather than the more traditional white satin, it being a second marriage for her; 'and because neither Bill nor I want any fuss.' Edith had elected, instead, to have her pearls restrung, making a double row out of what had been a single rope (a style now as out of fashion as short skirts and cloche hats). With her 'new' necklace, and her best hat, she said she thought she'd pass muster.

The jewellers where she'd taken the pearls was in Bond Street; they caught the 53 bus from Waterloo to Oxford Circus, and walked from there. It was a fine spring morning, and Rowlands was enjoying the all too rare pleasure of strolling along in the sunshine with his wife while she window-shopped, and commented upon what she saw – as much, he suspected, for her own enjoyment, as for his information: 'What a ridiculous little hat! There's hardly anything to it – just a bit of ribbon and some net, for which they'll charge ten guineas . . . I see waists are coming back. I'll have to cut out sugar in my tea.'

'You've got a perfectly good waist.'

'And I do think the new spring colours are nice. Pale

yellow and mint green and a rather pretty sort of old rose shade. I wonder if Cecily would like to borrow my sapphire brooch,' she added inconsequentially. 'Only blue's her colour and it'd be Something Borrowed, you know . . .' To which Rowlands, who wasn't really listening, merely nodded and smiled. 'I thought we might get a bite of lunch at Selfridges' restaurant after we've collected my necklace from Boodles,' his wife was saying as they turned off the busy thoroughfare, with its rumbling traffic of buses and taxis and its slowly moving crowds, and began walking towards the emporium in question. As they did so, a car – a Rolls-Royce, thought Rowlands – came purring along the street and pulled up in front of the shop. Someone – the chauffeur no doubt – got out and opened the door for his passenger. This was a woman, to judge from the waft of expensive perfume that came Rowlands' way ('Shocking,' said Edith afterwards, which turned out to be, not a comment on the wearer, but the name of the scent). '*Do* come along,' said a lazily imperious voice, to whoever it was that now followed her out of the car – some minion, thought Rowlands. 'I haven't got all day.' The voice was oddly familiar, but try as he might, he couldn't place it.

'N-no, madam,' stammered the minion – maid or companion. 'Sorry, madam.' Then the two of them entered the shop, a little ahead of the Rowlandses, to be greeted by the manager with an effusiveness no doubt proportionate to the unknown woman's perceived value as a customer.

'I want to see what you've got in the way of diamond bracelets,' she announced.

'Diamond bracelets? Certainly, miss. Come this way please,' said the manager, leaving a junior member of staff to deal with the Rowlandses.

It wasn't until they'd collected the pearls and were walking back along Bond Street once more, that Edith said, 'I don't suppose you realised who that was, did you? It took me a while, too, given the way she was dressed. I'm sure her frock was a model, and that fur stole was a mink, or I'm a Dutchman.'

'If it's the lady with the taste for diamond bracelets you're talking about,' said Rowlands, 'she did sound awfully familiar. But I can't think where we'd have run into her sort, in the usual run of things.'

'Oh, but we did,' said Edith. 'In Cornwall, not six months ago. I'll give you three guesses which of our fellow guests at the hotel it was.'

'Not Miss Linden?' For some reason, this idea that it might have been filled Rowlands with dismay.

'No, you silly man. The other one. The secretary. Muriel Brierley. Funny. She was such a quiet, dowdy little thing. I hardly recognised her just now, dressed to the nines in expensive clothes, and reeking of scent. If I hadn't heard her speak, I'd never have known it was the same girl. I suppose she must have come into money. She'd never have been able to afford diamond bracelets on a secretary's wages.'

They had by now reached Oxford Street, and were

turning in the direction of Selfridges when Rowlands came to a standstill. 'Edith,' he said. 'Would you mind very much if we skipped our lunch? Only there's something rather urgent I need to do.' Knowing her husband as she did, Edith didn't waste time in arguing, but, at his insistence, hailed a taxi. Soon they were speeding along Oxford Street and down Whitehall, towards the Strand.

'What's all this about, Fred?' said his wife as, having paid off the taxi, the two of them went in through the imposing gateway of Somerset House. He told her. For once, she was lost for words. 'But . . . but Fred,' she managed at last, as they entered the building and made for the Requests desk. 'If you're right about this, it means . . .'

'It needn't mean anything,' he said grimly. 'Although I'm rather afraid it does.'

When they asked to see the document in question, the young woman behind the desk said brightly, 'That's funny. It looks as if this one's been requested quite recently – only last year, in fact. Yes, here we are . . .' She consulted the register in front of her. 'May eleventh, 1937. The day before the Coronation – fancy!'

'Does it say who it was who requested it?' Rowlands was conscious of holding his breath while she checked again. 'No, there's no name. Just the initials of my colleague, who'd have signed the document out.'

'Might it be possible to speak to her? She might remember.'

'She might, but you won't be able to speak to her, I'm afraid.'

The young woman gave a slight, faintly disapproving sniff. 'She left to get married at the end of last year.'

'No matter,' said Rowlands. 'Perhaps my wife could take a look at the document now?'

'Certainly,' was the reply. The librarian placed the heavy volume on the desk in front of Edith, open at the relevant page. 'Family, are you?'

'Yes,' said Edith.

'No,' said Rowlands at the same time. 'Not exactly,' he amended. 'It's to do with a will.'

'It usually is,' said the girl. 'Well, I'll leave you to it.'

The house was in Holland Park – one of those tall white stucco-fronted ones that always made Edith think of the ones along the seafront at Brighton, she said; although these would doubtless be a lot more expensive. They'd got the address by the simple expedient of ringing the jewellers, claiming to have found a glove belonging to the 'lady in the mink stole' who'd been in the shop before them, and wanting to return it to her. As Rowlands prepared to mount the steps to the front door, his wife clutched his arm. 'I don't like it, Fred. Telling fibs to get her address is bad enough, but if you're right about what this woman's done, then you could be in danger. Why won't you let me come with you?'

'She won't talk to me if there's a witness,' he said, gently freeing himself from her agitated clasp. 'Don't worry. I'm not afraid that she'll try anything – she's got too much to lose. Now, I want you to do what we've agreed. Take the taxi back to Waterloo and wait for me in the station buffet. If I'm not there in an hour, call Alasdair Douglas at Scotland Yard. You know the number.'

'Yes. But Fred . . .'

'Go on.' He kissed her, then gave her a little push. 'The taxi's waiting.' He waited until he heard her get into the cab and shut the door. Then, as it pulled away from the kerb, he climbed the steps, of which there were four, and rang the bell. So long an interval ensued before anyone came to answer it that he began to wonder if he was going to be disappointed, after all. Perhaps there was nobody in? He was about to reach for the bell pull once more when the door opened. He stated his name and business and the man – it would be a butler, of course – replied that he'd see if madam was in. Which meant she was. 'Tell your mistress,' said Rowlands as the servant started to walk away, 'that it's a friend from Cornwall.'

'Oh, it's you,' said Muriel Brierley as, a few minutes later, he was shown into the room where she awaited him – a large room, to judge from the distance from which her voice came. He crossed an acreage of soft carpet, which muffled his footsteps so that it felt as if he were walking on a cloud. He took care to avoid knocking into the furniture that lay between the door and the fireplace next to which she sat, and from which a pleasant heat was issuing (the day being sunny but chilly). Fortunately, the only object he encountered was the back of another chair, facing hers, on the opposite side of this. 'I wondered who it might be. I don't remember many "friends" at that place.' She meant the hotel, he supposed. 'But you weren't the worst, by a long chalk. Although,' she added, as if speaking the thought aloud, 'I do wonder how it was you found me.'

Rowlands explained. 'So it *was* you in that shop! I thought you looked awfully familiar. Your wife was with you, wasn't she? What have you done with her?'

'She's waiting for me, Miss Brierley.'

'Oh, don't just stand there – sit down, won't you?' He did so, although it felt far from being a social call. 'And then perhaps,' she went on, 'you'll tell me why you've come? I don't imagine it's just to reminisce about our delightful hols on the Cornish coast. Unless, perhaps, it is,' she added sharply.

Rowlands took a deep breath. 'You're Mary-Ann Plunkett's daughter. Or Dolores La Mar's, if you prefer.'

'*She* preferred it,' said Muriel Brierley. 'So you've found that out, have you? I'd like to know how.'

'The same way that you did, I suppose,' said Rowlands. 'I assume it was you who asked to see your mother's marriage lines at Somerset House a year ago?'

'You *do* know a lot.' It was said in a tone of grudging admiration. Unless it was sarcasm. 'Although one might ask what it's got to do with you? I suppose you're after money.'

'Your father's name was Daniel O'Leary,' went on Rowlands, ignoring this last remark. 'An infantryman in the Irish Guards. He was posted to the Western Front in 1914. I assume he met your mother when he was home on leave, in the spring of 1915. You were born the following January.'

'I suppose you looked up my birth certificate, too?' said the girl, all amusement gone from her voice. 'I must say, you've got a nerve.'

'Your parents were married in July 1918, after your father was invalided out of the army. He had been gassed, and so his health was poor, but he wanted to make it right with your mother before he died, which happened when you were still an infant.'

'I was four,' said Muriel Brierley.

'At which time,' Rowlands went on, 'your mother had you adopted – so that she could pursue her acting career, one assumes.'

'One assumes correctly,' said the young woman coolly. 'She couldn't wait to get rid of me.'

'The couple who adopted you were called Brierley. You took their surname.'

'Not only that,' said Miss Brierley. 'She . . . my mother . . . had me christened Theresa. Shortened to Tessie. My adoptive mother disliked the name and chose Muriel instead. I've always loathed the name, but what can you do?'

'Around two years ago, you discovered that Dolores La Mar was your real mother . . .'

'It was she – Mrs Brierley – who told me,' the girl interrupted. 'She saw her picture in the paper – my mother's, that is. "Why, that's the lady who brought you to live with your dad and me,"' she said, adopting an accent several notches down the social scale from the one she now affected. '"Funny, she's changed a bit. She didn't wear all that lip rouge and eye paint when she came knocking on our door. But it's the same one, I'd swear to it. Looks like she's made a name for herself in the pictures . . ." Mrs Brierley was very fond of the pictures,' added her adopted daughter, with faint contempt.

'So you applied for the job of secretary to Miss La Mar,' went on Rowlands. 'Although you didn't know at the time whether your parents were ever married. You said nothing to your employer of your belief that you and she were related.'

'How nicely you put it,' said Muriel Brierley, and this time there was no mistaking the sarcasm in her voice. 'No, I didn't think it'd go down awfully well, somehow, if I told her I was her little by-blow.' She laughed. 'It's not the sort of news many women – least of all a woman like her – would be likely to welcome.'

'Yet you carried on working for her, even when you knew what kind of woman she was.'

'Yes,' she admitted. Then with an attempt at bravado he found more touching than a more direct appeal to his sympathy, 'She was my mother wasn't she? I felt I owed it to myself to stick it out. Even if it meant finding out that she didn't give that' – clicking her fingers – 'for anybody but herself.'

'A year ago you discovered the truth,' said Rowlands. 'Your parents had actually been married – albeit a year or two after your birth – and so, according to the legislation introduced ten years ago, you would stand to inherit your mother's estate, in the event of her death.'

A silence followed this statement, which was broken at length by Miss Brierley. 'I say, how remiss of me! Would you care for some tea?' She touched the bell before Rowlands could refuse the offer of hospitality. A parlour maid duly appeared. Her mistress gave the order, in the same imperious tone Rowlands had heard her use to her maid outside the jewellers. No wonder he hadn't recognised her voice at first – it was so unlike the meek tones in which she'd been wont to express herself during their sojourn in Cornwall.

When the servant had gone, he said, 'Why didn't you reveal what you'd learnt to your mother straight away?'

Another silence. When she spoke again, it was with a sullenness that made her sound much younger than her twenty-two years. 'It was difficult,' she said. 'She was always surrounded by people. Film types. Nattering away.' She momentarily assumed another accent: '"Darling, you were *wonderful* . . ."' It seemed to Rowlands that she'd inherited something of her mother's thespian gift, if not her charm. 'And even when they weren't around, *he* was there.' By which she meant Horace Cunningham, Rowlands supposed. 'Anyway,' she added quickly. 'Who says I *did* reveal it to her?'

'I heard you,' said Rowlands. 'Or rather, I heard Miss La Mar replying to what you'd said. It was you who was in her room, on the evening she died, wasn't it?'

'I've never denied I was there,' said the girl defiantly. 'There were letters to sign. But I'd left her room by nine twenty-five. There are witnesses. Ask the police. And that was at least two hours before she died.'

'You had ample opportunity to drop the poison into the carafe,' he retorted. 'She didn't pour the water from the carafe into her glass until she was ready to take the sleeping powder, which we know couldn't have been until after eleven-thirty, because I overheard her talking to someone in her room.'

'Who's to say *they* didn't poison her?' demanded Muriel Brierley. 'People were in and out of her room all evening, from the sound of it. Any one of them could have put the poison in her glass – or in the carafe, if you will.'

'Yes, but you were the only one who returned at midnight to check that she'd drunk it.'

'Who says I did?' she said in a low voice. 'You can't have seen . . .' They were interrupted at the moment by the servant with the tea tray. 'Put it down there, and leave us,' said Miss Brierley curtly. When they were alone once more, she said, 'You're bluffing. How could you have seen anything, being blind?'

'You're right. I couldn't. But I never said it was I who was there. Someone else was, though.'

'You're lying.'

'I assure you, I'm not.' Then, as she set out cups and saucers and began to pour out.

'No, I won't have any tea, thanks.'

'Afraid I'll drop some poison in it?' laughed the girl. 'It would certainly be one way of getting rid of you.'

'But not of an inconvenient corpse,' he replied. 'To continue. Someone else had seen you going into your mother's room at around midnight. It was Laurence Quayle, wasn't it?'

'I don't know what you're talking about. This is all a complete fantasy. You can't prove a word of it.'

'Perhaps not,' said Rowlands. 'But just indulge me for a moment, will you? I think this is what happened that night, as far as I've been able to piece it together. You went, as you say, to Miss La Mar's room at around nine o'clock, or five past. While you were there, you decided to confront her with the fact that she was your mother. Perhaps you thought she'd welcome the news even though, as you've remarked, she was hardly likely to do so. Perhaps you thought you'd give her a chance to redeem herself. She didn't choose to take it, unfortunately. Instead, she became very angry. She threatened you with the sack if you told anyone else what you'd told her. You realised from what she said that, far from wanting to embrace you as her long-lost daughter, she had every intention of casting you off. In short, she rejected you.'

'She said that if I tried to use the . . . the fact of our

connection to make a claim of . . . of any sort upon her, she'd put her lawyers onto me,' said Muriel Brierley in a stifled voice. 'She . . . she made it plain that she wanted nothing more to do with me.'

'It must have been devastating for you,' said Rowlands gently. 'She wasn't a kind woman. But there was no need to have killed her.'

'Who says I killed her?' The girl's voice was cold. 'You can't prove a thing.'

'No more can I. Nevertheless, I believe you did kill her. You did it almost on impulse. The ring with the poison was on her dressing table. You seized your moment, perhaps when she'd turned her back for an instant to open the French windows onto the balcony. You dropped the poison into the carafe and let fate take its course, returning two hours later to check that she was dead. Only somebody saw you, or rather, two people did. One of them was Laurence Quayle – unluckily for him.'

'I don't know what you mean.'

'You thought you'd got away with it, at first,' said Rowlands, ignoring this intervention. 'Dolores La Mar's death would be treated as a suicide. If that failed, then suspicion would most likely fall on the person who would benefit financially from her death – her husband. Then Quayle started up with his blackmailing threats – I was there when he made one of them, you know – and you realised he couldn't be allowed to live.'

'What a wonderful storyteller you are!' said Miss

Brierley. 'I don't know why you don't set up shop like that lady you're so friendly with – Iris Barnes, isn't it? Your tales are as good as hers, any day!'

'You arranged to meet Quayle on the clifftop on the night of his death, to discuss terms. You're only a slight young girl, and so he thought he'd nothing to fear from you. But you took along a tin bucket filled with sand you'd scooped up from the beach. After you'd thrown it in his face, he was blinded and off balance. You found it quite easy to push him over the edge of the cliff to his death.'

'Marvellous,' chuckled the girl. 'I hope you've got a good title for this one!'

'You allowed suspicion for both deaths to fall on Horace Cunningham,' said Rowlands, paying no attention to her last quip. 'Perhaps you drove Cunningham to kill himself; it's hard to say for certain. Whatever the truth of it, his death has been a lucky break for you since it's left you as your mother's sole heir. And she of course was a very wealthy woman.' All the while he had been talking, Rowlands had been conscious of the sounds of tea-drinking going on: the stirring of a spoon round and round; the nervous rattle of a cup in its saucer. Now Miss Brierley set down her cup.

'D'you know,' she said, making a not very convincing attempt at a light laugh, 'I'm getting rather fed up with your stories, Mr Rowlands. I think I'd like you to leave now. Don't call again.'

'If you turn yourself in,' said Rowlands, 'I'd be willing

to support you in a plea of extreme provocation. I heard the way she spoke to you that night. It was cruel, what she said to you. And you'd had months of her bullying. Perhaps something snapped.'

'They'd still hang me,' said the girl. 'Or lock me away for life. I'm not prepared to give up all I've got, just because it suits your particular brand of morality. Do you make a habit of this sort of thing, Mr Rowlands? I wonder it hasn't made you a lot of enemies. A blind man like you has to be careful whom he upsets, I'd say. All too easy for accidents to happen to someone like you, who can't easily defend himself – wouldn't you agree?'

'I wouldn't advise it,' said Rowlands. He got to his feet and moved towards the door, keeping his face turned towards her. 'If anything happens to me, I've got friends at Scotland Yard who'll want to know why.'

He felt behind him for the door handle. At that precise moment, the door opened and someone put his – or, as it turned out, her – head in. There was an astonished silence, then, '*Deu meu!*' said a voice. 'What is he doing here?'

And then, at last, the final piece of the puzzle fell into place. 'I thought I told you I wasn't to be disturbed!' snapped Muriel Brierley.

'You were so long a time that I felt I must see to whom you are talking,' was the reply. 'And I find that it is this man.'

'Hello, Miss Casals,' said Rowlands. 'I can't say I'm entirely surprised to see you again.'

'I didn't realise that you two knew one other,' said Miss Brierley. It seemed to Rowlands that there was a tremor of fear in her voice. 'Quite a coincidence, I must say.'

'Oh, there's nothing coincidental about it,' he said.

Chapter Twenty

'It was Caterina Casals who shot Cunningham, of course,' said Rowlands. 'In revenge for what happened to her brother. She made him – Cunningham – write that letter, too. It wasn't a suicide note, but a confession that he'd been the one behind Carlos Casals' arrest and detention. We don't know if he was personally responsible for the man's death in prison, but given that he was hand in glove with the Nationalists, we can assume . . .'

'Aren't we assuming rather a lot here?' interrupted the Chief Inspector. Rowlands was once more sitting opposite him in his office at Scotland Yard. 'All this is supposition. We haven't a shred of proof.'

'The circumstances point to it,' said Rowlands. 'Caterina Casals returned to England, bent on confronting the man she held responsible for Carlos's death – confronting him and punishing him, as it turned out. She was an expert shot, as we know, and it was easy enough for her to make the thing look like suicide, especially after she'd forced Cunningham – presumably at gunpoint – to write that note.'

'The only prints we found were Cunningham's.'

'Child's play for a professional assassin, such as she is, to contrive.'

'And you're suggesting that, having got Cunningham out of the way, she then went to Muriel Brierley, asking for her share of the winnings?' said Alasdair Douglas dubiously. 'You haven't explained how it was she knew that Brierley was a beneficiary under Dolores La Mar's will.'

'I think she overheard Miss La Mar's row with the Brierley girl that night,' said Rowlands. 'She admitted entering the room not long after Miss Brierley had left it – to turn down the bed, she said. I think she was listening at the door. She heard Muriel Brierley confront Miss La Mar with the fact that she was her daughter. So she kept a close watch on her after that. Saw her coming out of La Mar's room later that night and put two and two together. Her first thought, after she'd killed Horace Cunningham, was to break the good news to the heiress.'

'And to demand her cut.'

'Yes.'

'Hmm,' said Douglas. 'It all fits, I suppose. But why would Brierley agree to give her anything?'

'Because, as I've said, Casals had seen Miss Brierley coming out of the room at midnight, and knew the girl had a cast-iron motive for murder.'

'I see that, but . . .'

'You're going to say, why didn't Brierley just deny it? My answer is because it was too dangerous,' said Rowlands. 'Caterina Casals had something on her, and, unlike Laurence Quayle, she was a formidable opponent. After all, she'd already committed one murder. Besides which,' he added, 'Miss Brierley owed her new-found fortune to Caterina's actions. She could hardly accuse her of having murdered Cunningham without revealing her own part in the affair.'

'Two murderesses, each with an unbreakable hold over one another,' said Douglas. 'Well, it's certainly one way of looking at this. A pity we won't be able to act on the information.'

'Why not?' said Rowlands, although he had a fair idea. He hadn't waited almost a week before going to Scotland Yard with his suspicions for no reason. He'd never yet been instrumental in getting a woman hanged.

'Because in all likelihood,' was the reply, 'they'll have flown the coop. If they'd any sense at all, they'd have been packing their bags the minute you were out the door. When,' he added sternly, 'you should have come straight to us, instead of waiting five days. I could have you on a charge for obstructing the due process of the law.'

'I needed to be sure,' said Rowlands. 'Accusing somebody of murder isn't something one does lightly.'

The Chief Inspector emitted a sound expressive of

disbelief. 'I suppose I'd better send a car round there,' he said. 'Although I've no doubt that the ladies in question will have made themselves scarce.' Which indeed proved to be the case. When the police arrived, the house in Holland Park betrayed no sign of the occupancy of its recent tenants. Wardrobes had been emptied of all but their hangers; chests of drawers stripped of everything but their lining paper. Nor did there remain a scrap of food or drink in the larder, although the old woman who'd been engaged to clean the place before it was shut up admitted that she'd taken home what stores there were. When questioned, the house agent said that the ladies had left only a poste restante to which mail was to be forwarded; this was found to be a newsagent's in Whitechapel, whose proprietor denied any knowledge of Miss Brierley and her companion. It appeared that they had vanished off the face of the earth.

Weeks went by. The news from Spain continued to worsen. After the Nationalists had broken through to the Mediterranean during the Aragon Offensive in April, the government had tried to sue for peace, but Franco was demanding unconditional surrender. Things were looking bleak for the Republicans. As for Geoffrey Orgreave, he had barely escaped with his life, after returning to Barcelona to recuperate from wounds received on the Aragon Front. The newspapers said he was now back in London, staying at his wife's family home in Greenwich. Recalling his memorable encounters with Orgreave, and his formidable wife,

Rowlands wished them both well, wherever they were.

In other news, *Forbidden Desires* was released to favourable reviews which made no mention of the turbulent events surrounding the film's creation. Its young star, Miss Lydia Linden, was reported to be going to Hollywood for her next picture – 'a frothy, light comedy', said the writer, one Iris Barnes, in *Film Weekly*.

Then, one Saturday afternoon in June, Edith Rowlands came home from a visit to the hairdresser's in Kingston, bringing with her a smell of setting lotion, and a copy of *Woman's Own*. 'Fred!' she cried, rushing into the garden, where her husband was enjoying a quiet glass of beer after raking up the grass cuttings. 'You'll never believe this!' She flapped the magazine she was holding under his nose. 'I found it at the hairdressers. It's definitely her in the photograph, although she's using a different name.'

'You'd better read it to me,' he said, knowing that this would be the quickest way of finding out who it was she meant.

'I was just going to.' She cleared her throat. '"*The cream of Buenos Aires' high society turned out last Saturday for the Ambassador's Ball,*"' she read aloud. '"*A distinguished array of guests included . . .*"' There followed a string of names which meant nothing to Rowlands, then, '"*Miss Theresa O'Leary, the heiress, with her companion, Miss Casals . . .*" Wasn't that the name of the maid at the hotel?' demanded Edith. 'The Spanish one?'

'Yes, that's her. Is she in the photograph, too?'

'You can't really see her face, because she's hidden by the ridiculously tall egret headdress of the woman in front. But I think it must be her. And Miss Brierley – or Miss O'Leary, as she's now calling herself – looks just as she did when we saw her that day in Boodles. If anything she's even grander. Floor-length ivory satin, according to this . . . and that *has* to be a diamond necklace.'

'Buenos Aires, eh?' said Rowlands. 'She said she liked Argentina. Well, if she's got any sense, she'll stay there.' As he had reason to know, the resources of the Metropolitan Police were unlikely to stretch to extraditing a suspected murderess from a South American country without an extradition treaty with Britain, on what was largely circumstantial evidence. Edith flipped the magazine shut, and sat down with a sigh of relief on one of the wicker garden chairs.

'I see you've started on the beer,' she said.

'Yes,' he said. 'Would you like one?'

'I'll stick to tea, thanks. It does seem rather shocking,' she went on, 'that she and that other woman shouldn't have to pay for their crimes.'

'Oh, I've no doubt they'll pay,' said Rowlands. 'One way or another.' As he sipped his beer, he thought of what it must be like, with each watching to see which way the other would jump – like a pair of wary cats. High society parties aside, it wouldn't be a comfortable life. Never to be able to relax one's vigilance in case one's enemy – who was also one's dearest friend – decided she'd had enough of the arrangement. He wondered how long it had taken Caterina Casals to persuade Miss Brierley to name her as sole beneficiary in her will. Really, there was a certain poetic justice to the thing. 'The biter bit,' he murmured.

'What's that?' said his wife.

'Nothing.'

He thought back over the whole affair, whose disastrous events had been set in motion just over a year ago, and which had culminated in so much unhappiness and death. 'I don't think it was the money which made her do it – Miss Brierley, I mean. That was secondary,' he said. 'What she wanted was to be accepted by the woman she knew to be her mother – the woman who'd abandoned her as a child. When that acceptance wasn't forthcoming, her feelings of frustrated love turned to hate. Dropping the poison in the carafe was an act of impulse, not calculation. A throw of the dice, if you like.'

Edith gave a disbelieving sniff. 'Perhaps so. But she certainly did her utmost to cover things up afterwards. If that wasn't calculation, I don't know what is.'

'True. But I think by then she was in a panic. When Quayle threatened to reveal what she'd done – and thereby expose her secret – she struck out blindly. Again, I think it was the rejection she couldn't bear – that anyone else should know about it, I mean.'

'Oh, you always make excuses for them!' Women, she meant. He didn't deny it. But in spite of the things she'd done, he couldn't find it in himself to condemn Muriel Brierley. The murderous rage to which she'd given vent had been the expression of a terrible pain. All she'd wanted was the things most people wanted: a family, a secure home, someone to love.

'Do you know,' he said, and it wasn't quite the non-sequitur it seemed. 'I think I've been very lucky, on the whole.' To which Edith replied only with another faint sniff.

'I'll make that tea,' she said.

CHRISTINA KONING has worked as a journalist, reviewing fiction for *The Times*, and has taught Creative Writing at the University of Oxford and Birkbeck, University of London. From 2013 to 2015, she was Royal Literary Fund Fellow at Newnham College, Cambridge. She won the Encore Prize in 1999 and was long-listed for the Orange Prize in the same year.

christinakoning.com